THE
GREAT
DIVIDE

ALSO BY CRISTINA HENRÍQUEZ

Come Together, Fall Apart

The World in Half

The Book of Unknown Americans

THE
GREAT
DIVIDE

A NOVEL

CRISTINA HENRÍQUEZ

ecco

An Imprint of HarperCollins*Publishers*

THE GREAT DIVIDE. Copyright © 2024 by Cristina Henríquez. All rights reserved. Printed in the United States of America. No part of this book may be used or reproduced in any manner whatsoever without written permission except in the case of brief quotations embodied in critical articles and reviews. For information, address HarperCollins Publishers, 195 Broadway, New York, NY 10007.

HarperCollins books may be purchased for educational, business, or sales promotional use. For information, please email the Special Markets Department at SPsales@harpercollins.com.

Ecco® and HarperCollins® are trademarks of HarperCollins Publishers.

FIRST EDITION

Designed by Alison Bloomer
Map illustration by Mike Hall

Library of Congress Cataloging-in-Publication Data has been applied for.

ISBN: 978-0-06-329132-4

23 24 25 26 27 LBC 5 4 3 2 1

WANTED!

BY THE ISTHMIAN CANAL COMMISSION

4,000 ABLE-BODIED LABOURERS FOR PANAMA.

2-YEAR CONTRACT.

FREE PASSAGE TO THE CANAL ZONE AND BACK.

FREE LODGING AND MEDICAL CARE.

WORK IN PARADISE!

RATES OF 10¢–20¢ PER HOUR.

WAGES PAID EVERY FORTNIGHT.

APPLY TO RECRUITING STATION
IN TRAFALGAR SQUARE.

ALL APPLICANTS WILL BE SUBJECT
TO MEDICAL EXAMINATION AND
VACCINATION REQUIREMENTS.

J. M. GRASSLEY
Agent, I.C.C.
1907

1

SOMEWHERE OFF THE PACIFIC COAST OF PANAMÁ, IN THE CALM BLUE WATER OF THE
bay, Francisco Aquino sat alone in his boat. He had built the boat
himself from the trunk of a cedar tree that he had stripped and
carved with nothing but a stone adze and a crooked knife, whittling
it and smoothing it, running his hand over every surface and curve,
whittling and smoothing again, until he had fashioned that single
tree trunk into what he believed was the most magnificent boat on
the whole of the sea.

Francisco sat holding his paddle across his lap. His knees were
bent and his bare feet were flat on the floor of the hull next to his reel
and a wooden bucket that he used to bail water out of the boat when
too much got in. His net hung off the side.

Every day but Sunday, Francisco rose before dawn and walked
to the shore and untied his boat from its post. He rowed through the
waves and, when he was out far enough, he secured the knots on his
net and let the net drop. Then he rowed again, slowly, listening to the
water hiccup each time he pulled the paddle up through the surface
and slipped it back in. He had to advance at just the right speed
to create drag for the net. Too slow and the fish were not fooled.
Too fast and they fled. It was a delicate balance, but Francisco had
trawled in these waters for most of his life, and he knew what to do.

A breeze came from the east and ruffled the brim of his hat.
Gently, the boat rocked side to side. He waited for the best moment
to start. The water would tell him when. Francisco nudged the
bucket with his foot, then nudged it back. Birds swooped overhead.
He opened his hands and studied his rough, calloused skin. Once,
a long time ago on a rainy afternoon speckled with sun, Esme had
taken his hands in hers and turned his palms up. There is a map,

she had told him, in the lines of your hands. A map of what? he had asked. And what had she said? He always tried to remember, but he never could.

Francisco folded his fingers into fists and sighed. The ocean spread endlessly around him, glittering in the early sun. In the quiet, his boat listed and swayed.

His eyesight unfortunately was not what it used to be. Francisco squinted out at the horizon to the place where, supposedly, ships one hundred times bigger than his little boat would someday line up, waiting their turn to sail across Panamá. He sputtered a laugh. It was a ludicrous idea, impossible to believe. Every sailor and explorer who had ever landed on these shores had dreamed that ships would one day travel from ocean to ocean by way of Panamá, although exactly how they expected to get from one side to the other was anyone's guess. The spine of the great Cordillera Mountains, running straight through the isthmus, stood in the way after all, and of the many miraculous things Francisco had heard in his life, he had never heard of a ship that could sail through a mountain. So they would cut the mountains, they said, break the spine, and once that was done, the water from both oceans would gush forth from each end and join to create a way through. A delusional dream. Putting not one but two oceans in a place where for millions of years there had only been land. Who could believe such a thing?

Francisco lifted the brim of his hat and squinted harder, trying to see the phantom shapes of steamers and schooners and battleships and boats, all the vessels that they swore would come through. He looked, but instead of ships, all he could see sitting on top of the water was the brilliant blue sky. Perhaps the problem, he thought, was that a person needed faith to be able to see things that did not exist, to imagine a world not yet made. In addition to so many other things, Francisco had lost his faith a long time ago.

2

ON THE ATLANTIC SIDE OF PANAMA, AROUND THE MIDWAY POINT OF THE SIDEWINDING coast, a ship eased into port at Colón. It was a Royal Mail paddle wheel steamer with tall white masts that had sailed from Barbados carrying some twenty-three thousand letters down belowdecks and some eight hundred passengers up above. The passengers were men mostly, hailing from St. Lucy and St. John and Christ Church and every parish in between. They were dressed in their finest suits, standing shoulder to shoulder on the deck, packed in tight, clutching tin trunks and suitcases and feverish hope.

Among them, sixteen-year-old Ada Bunting sat on the deck with her arms round her knees. It was the first time she had ever been on a ship, and for all the six days of the voyage she had sat huddled behind two chicken crates stacked on top of a black steamer trunk, praying she would not be found. The morning she had left home, she had written a note on her old school tablet and propped it on the kitchen table where her mother would be sure to see it when she woke up. That she was going to Panama was nearly all the note said. Then, in the early dawn, Ada had put on her gardening clothes—tattered trousers and a button-up blouse—carried the canvas sack she had packed all the way to the wharf, and managed, amid the commotion and the crowds, to slip on board the ship without being seen.

For every waking hour, the chickens in the crates had clucked and bawked and screeched, and Ada found that if she shushed them, they only clucked more. She thought they must be hungry, so on the second day she crumbled a few of the crackers she had brought and dropped the crumbs in between slats of the crates and watched as the chickens picked them up with their beaks. That settled them somewhat. On the third day, Ada fed them crackers again and listened as they made contented warbling sounds. On the fourth day, she shared some of the sugar apple she had packed, being careful to pick out the seeds first. On the fifth, she peeled back the lid on a can of sardines, and after eating most of them herself, licking the saltiness off her fingertips when she was done, she fed the chickens the rest. By the sixth day, all the food she had brought with her was gone, and the only thing she had to give the chickens was the same reassurance her mother always gave her: The Lord will take care. She had to believe that was true.

As soon as the ship came to a stop, everyone rushed to get off. Ada waited till some of the swarm had cleared, but even when she stood up no one, thank goodness, paid the least bit of attention to her. People were too busy gathering their things and straining to see, past the sailboats and palm trees lining the shore, just what Panama looked like now that they were here. To Ada, the part of town she could make out past the end of the wharf looked a lot like Bridgetown, a row of two- and three-story wood-frame buildings facing a main street, shops with awnings and buildings with signs, and the fact that it looked so familiar was both a disappointment and a relief.

Cradling her sack in her arms, Ada shoved her way portside together with everyone else. The seat of her trousers was damp, but the trousers, which her mother had sewn, had served their purpose of helping her blend into the crowd of what was primarily men. She had seen only a few other women this whole time, and all of them were older than she was. Ada had worn boots for the trip, too, black leather boots that had been a gift from a man named Willoughby Dalton, who had been courting her mother for the past year or so. Every so often, usually on Sunday when he knew they would be at home, Willoughby limped slowly up to their door with a new offering in his hands—wildflowers or breadfruit or a small clay bowl. A few months earlier he had come with a pair of black boots. The boots were worn in the heels and the laces were frayed, but when Willoughby held them out, Ada's mother had taken them and said,

"Thank you," as she did each time Willoughby arrived with a gift. And as he did each time, Willoughby said, "You quite welcome," and remained on the porch as though he were waiting to be invited in. It was always the same unfortunate dance. Her mother nodded and edged the door closed, and only when it shut all the way did Willoughby turn round again and walk home.

The ropes running up the masts snapped in the wind, and people jostled and shoved. When Ada came to the gangplank, she angled herself behind a man who had brought his own folding chair, hoping that the chair would shield her from the two white officers who were down on the wharf. At the base of the gangplank, they were shouting, "Labor train! Labor train that a'way!" and pointing toward town. People streamed off the ship headed in the direction the officers said, and it seemed to Ada that her best chance of going unnoticed was just to keep up with the flow. She had made it this far, but there was still a chance that one of the officers would think it suspicious, a young woman traveling on her own, and if they pulled her aside and learned that she had not paid, they would almost certainly put her back on the ship and send her home. Ada squeezed her sack to her chest as she stepped down onto the pier and walked past the officers. Even from behind the folding chair she could hear them talking. One of them said to the other, "Send word to the captain that the cargo has arrived." She was sixteen years old, but she knew enough to understand that they were not talking about the mail.

||||||

WHEN ADA STEPPED aboard the train, which was really nothing more than a chain of open-air wood-framed cattle cars, it was stuffed with passengers from the ship, people carrying suitcases and baskets and plants and crates. She pushed through to the back corner of the car and held on to a post with one arm. With the other she held on to her sack. Besides the sardines and the crackers and the sugar apples, she had packed two sets of underclothes, a dress, a vial of almond oil for smoothing her hair, a pieced cotton quilt she had taken from her bed, and three gold crowns. She wished she had thought to bring more food, but she hadn't. She had a mind that outpaced her good sense, her mother always said, and there on the train, Ada smiled, hearing her mother scolding her in her head, hearing that particular tone. Her mother had no doubt seen her note by now, and Ada could almost hear her tone—much more severe—about that, too, about going off to Panama on her own like she had, even though it was with good reason.

Her sister, Millicent, was sick, in need of a surgery that they could not afford. As a seamstress, her mother did not earn much, and Ada would have gotten a job herself except that in Barbados these days, work was hard to come by. But in Panama, everyone said, finding work was as easy as plucking apples from trees. If everyone else could go and pluck them, Ada had thought, then why shouldn't she? She would stay just long enough to earn the money for Millicent's surgery, then she would go back.

As the train started off, Ada peered at the faces around her, so many young men dressed in suits, all of them looking just as tense and expectant as she herself felt. Past the city, the train clanked over a low bridge and through leafy trees before emerging into a field wide enough to see the dark green mountains in the distance. When it rattled to a stop near a small town, a handful of people hopped down and walked toward a cluster of wood-frame buildings raised up on stilts. A man whose suit sleeves stopped short of his wrists looked out and, to no one in particular, said, "This where we to stay?"

A man wearing muddied khaki trousers and a blue work shirt laughed. "What you expect? A grand hotel?"

The man in the too-small suit pointed to the houses on the opposite side of the tracks, a row of neat buildings painted white with gray trim, and asked if they couldn't stay there instead.

The man dressed in work clothes chuckled again. "Them the gold houses." He pointed toward the camps. "The silver housing for us."

When the man in the too-small suit looked puzzled, the other man said didn't he know? Everything in the Canal Zone—the commissaries, the train cars, the dining halls, the housing, the hospitals, the post offices, and the pay—was divided on the basis of silver and gold. Gold meant the Americans, and silver meant them.

At each new village or town, more men hopped off. The train emptied out. Ada had no idea where she was meant to go. At some point, a man standing near her inched closer and said, "What about you? You have someplace to sleep? Only white women allowed in the camps, you know."

Ada clutched her sack tight.

"I got a place you can lay your head, though." The man patted his thigh.

Ada turned to face him. "I would sooner lie down in hell." She let go of the post and walked to the other side of the car, and at the next stop, as soon as she could, she jumped off—at a place called Empire, according to the trainmaster who shouted it aloud.

|||||

THE OTHER MEN who had gotten off, too, walked out past Ada toward the camps. If it was true that she was not allowed there, as she'd been told, then she would have to make a camp of her own out in the trees. Tomorrow she would try to find work, but for now she was so exhausted that all she wanted was to lay her head down and rest. At home, she and Millicent and their mother all shared the one bedroom at the back of the house, and they each had a husk-stuffed mattress propped up on frames that their mother had built. It would feel so good, she kept thinking, to lie in that bed now, to stretch her body all the way straight, locking her arms over her head and pointing her toes. She would have to settle, though, for spreading her quilt out on the ground if she could find a clearing big enough to spread it upon.

A few steps into the forest, the air grew cooler, and it smelled of things alive. Ada heard slithers and crunches and whistles and taps. Everywhere she walked, the soft ground was covered by twigs and moss, flowering bushes and logs. She pushed aside fronds to find puddles and mud. There was no dry clearing anywhere she could see. The day darkened as she carried on, and she was so tired that she had a mind just to drop down in the brush when she spotted what looked like a boxcar among the trees. It was rusting and rotting, half hidden by vines and a veil of thick brush, its back wheels sunk in the mud, the whole thing askew. She stood staring at it for a time to see if anyone else was near, but she heard only the sound of animals rustling in the trees. She walked up closer and called out, "Hello?" When no one answered, she stepped all the way up to the open doorway, which was level with her head, and said it again. She reached up and knocked three times on the floor. Nothing still. *Well, the Lord will take care*, she thought, and she hoisted herself up inside and lay down.

||||||

IN THE MORNING, the hiss and tick of insects filled Ada's ears. She sat up slowly and looked around, remembering where she was. Sunlight leaked through the seams of the wood boards, giving her enough light to see the whole inside of the boxcar now. There was not much to see except for cobwebs and clumps of stray leaves.

Ada had slept in the clothes she had worn on the ship, and now, in the soggy, thick air, they were so damp that they stuck to her skin. From her sack, which was next to her on the floor, Ada pulled out the dress she had brought, a patchwork dress of brown and yellow squares, made by her mother, and changed into it instead. She stood up, tugged the sleeves down at her wrists, smoothed out the pleats over her hips. She stepped into her boots and spit on her palm, leaning down to rub the mud off the toes. Then she picked up her sack. A dry dress and clean boots were a start. Now she had to find food and she had to find work.

||||||

IT WAS RAINING lightly in the forest. A low mist clung to the air. *Somewhere out here*, Ada thought, *there ought to be food*. In the light of the day, she saw things she had not been able to see the night before: vines and creepers hanging from branches, leaves shaped like swords that were tangled with ferns. Everything everywhere was dazzlingly green. Olive green, jade green, emerald green, lime green, green lost in shadows, green lit by the sun. She walked through green curtains and over green carpets, hoping to find something she recognized— jackfruit or sea grape or pawpaw—and knew she could eat. Panama, she had heard, had bananas aplenty, and she peered up into the trees in case she saw any now. At home, it would have been easier. At home, Ada knew which trees bore fruit and which bushes yielded berries so ripe she could pop them with her teeth. In the garden plot behind their house they grew corn and arrowroot and cassava and herbs, and they ate what they grew or else they traded it with the neighbors sometimes, the best trade being when their mother gave away ears of corn for cherries that Mrs. Callender grew from a tree in her yard—the sweetest, juiciest cherries in all of Barbados, Mrs. Callender claimed—and when Ada ate them, she was certain Mrs. Callender was telling the truth. Ada's mouth watered now thinking of those cherries. There had to be things to eat out here in the forest, and she could probably find them if she looked for long enough, but her stomach was clawing, and her dress, which had felt so good when it was dry, was now wet from the rain, and her boots were once again covered with mud, and she was impatient, which was one of her worst traits according to her mother, who said that Ada never waited long enough to let things come to her.

|||||||

THE TOWN WAS busy. Ada crossed over the far side of the railroad tracks that split Empire in two and walked down the paved streets of the American side, thinking she was more likely to see signs for work on that side at the same time that she was looking for food. The flags hanging from balconies and flying in the breeze told her whose side it was. She had never seen the United States flag in person before, although she had seen an image of it in an atlas once, in the girls' school where both she and Millicent had gone. It was in that same atlas, an oversized pamphlet whose pages were held together by thread, that Ada had first seen a map of Barbados, too. Whereas the map of United States had spanned two full pages, Barbados in its entirety took up only the lower half of a left-facing page. Before that, it had not occurred to her that Barbados was any smaller than any other place in the world. But once she saw it, she could not help but wonder what it would be like to go somewhere else. As far back as she knew, everyone in her family had been born in Barbados and had stayed there since. Not long after Ada was born, her mother had walked away from the sugar plantation where she had lived all her days, and the story of that parting was one she had told Ada and Millicent numerous times—always with pride. Every time Ada heard it, she had the same thought: Her mother could have gone anywhere. When she left the plantation, she could have walked clear to the other side of Barbados or sailed to the other side of the world. But at the moment of all possibility, the moment when anything might have occurred, her mother had walked until she was just outside the official boundary of Bridgetown and plopped down again. She had crossed the line, but only by a toe. She had kept her world small, and now all these years later her mother did not have anything beyond that world, not even a dream as far as Ada knew.

The street, lined with two-story buildings and shops, was filled with carriages and mule carts and people walking briskly in the drizzling rain. The women carried parasols, and the men had their hats. Ada had neither, and though her hair was pinned back into a bun as usual, she had not bothered to fix it when she woke up, and that, combined with the drizzle, probably meant, she thought with a smile, that she looked a fright. Growing up, she was always the one who had dirt on her dress and scabs on her elbows and hair she refused to comb unless it was Sunday and she was going to church, and even then she did it not because she imagined God cared but because her mother did.

By the time Ada had passed a printing shop and a barbershop and a blacksmith shop, all in a row, the rain had stopped. Her stomach growled. There had to be a market somewhere, maybe on the other side of the tracks. With her sack in her arms, she stopped in the street, wondering whether she should cross back over and look for one, when a man standing at the entrance to an alley whistled to her. She would have turned away had he not pointed to a wooden wheelbarrow next to him piled with fruit. "Papaya, mango, piña, mamey!" the man sang as she walked toward him. He picked up a mango and held it aloft.

Ada was hungry enough that she could have eaten everything in that wheelbarrow, and even in the shadow of the alley, she could see so much bright, bursting fruit that she started working her tongue.

"You say mammee?" she asked. "Mammee apple?"

The man swapped the mango for a fruit that was tapered at one end with a pitted brown skin. "Mamey," he said.

It certainly looked like mammee apple. They were not yet ripe in Barbados, but each year come April, Ada looked forward to them. Her mother would soak the flesh in saltwater to cut the bitterness and she and Millicent would either eat them plain or else her mother would use them to make apple jam.

"How much for one?" Ada asked.

"¿Quieres?"

"How much money?"

But the man only smiled at her.

Ada set her sack on the ground and felt for the coins she had brought. Three crown pieces that her mother kept tucked away. Ada had discovered them once when she was poking around, and every time afterwards when she had looked, they were untouched. Her mother was saving that money, maybe, but Ada had brought it along with the faith that soon enough, she would make it all back and then some. Now, Ada drew out one coin and held it up for the man to see. A crown was far too much for a single piece of fruit, but at that moment she did not care. She needed something to eat. She could almost taste that mammee apple, could almost feel the juice of it running all down her gums.

The man took the coin and, holding it between two fingers, turned it back to front and front to back, examining it. He nodded appreciatively, slipped the coin into his pocket, and handed Ada the fruit.

With her fingernail, Ada immediately peeled away the thick skin and bit into the flesh. It was so tender that she thought she might cry. She pulled out the fruit with her teeth, all while she stood at the entrance to the alley with her sack at her feet and the man looking on. She ate every bit of the meat down to the pit, and that she sucked till the flavor was gone. Then she tossed it onto the ground and wiped her mouth with the back of her hand.

The man standing next to the wheelbarrow was staring at her wide-eyed, in awe.

Ada grinned. "Thank you," she said as she reached down and picked up her sack.

She felt better now that she had a little food in her stomach. As soon as she could, she would find a way to write a letter and send it home. If her mother was worried, which Ada imagined she was, then a letter might help ease her mind. If her mother was angry, which Ada also imagined she was, there was not much she could do about that.

3

EIGHT MONTHS BEFORE ADA BUNTING BOARDED A MAIL SHIP THAT TOOK HER AWAY from the only home she had ever known, Marian Oswald, with her husband, John Oswald, eagerly stepped aboard a United Fruit Company steamer departing from New Orleans and heading to Panama. Prior to the steamer, Marian and John had traveled by passenger train from Bryson City, Tennessee, near where they lived, a trip of nearly a full day during which Marian sat with her hands in her lap, gazing happily at the world rushing by, while next to her John read. The train was outfitted with a dining car that had crisp white tablecloths and also with a drink car staffed by two attendants who kept urging John, who did not drink, to have a whiskey sour and who were baffled when he ordered only a club soda instead. In still another train car, John had taken the opportunity to have his shoes shined by a Negro porter whom Marian had urged him to tip, although John said, "He is doing his job. A man should not be rewarded for doing what he ought." Marian was carrying no money with her, but if she had been, she told herself, she would have found a way to slip the porter a coin or two.

The accommodations on the ship were similarly luxurious. The steamer, one vessel in what would come to be known as the Great White Fleet, carried thirty-five thousand bunches of bananas in its hold and fifty-three passengers in staterooms above. The Oswalds stayed in a stateroom spacious enough for two twin beds with a dressing table in between and two windows that would have offered a view of the sprawling ocean had John not closed the small curtains over them on the grounds that seeing the waves constantly rise and fall would surely make them feel ill. The closed curtains did not help. Or, they helped John but not Marian. Marian had never been at sea, and she spent the majority of the five days of the voyage vomiting into a tin pail that the ship's doctor, who attended to her, poured out over the side of the ship each time it was full. The doctor brought water, but Marian could not keep it down. Water, she wanted to tell him, was precisely the problem. She was desperate for land. When the signal went up that they were approaching the Panamanian shore, Marian had never been more grateful in her life.

To everyone else on the ship, the sight of the port town of Colón was evidently reason to grouse. Marian herself had not known what to expect, but as she watched from the deck, she saw in the distance a row of brown wooden buildings and, on the street in front of them, people walking about, men carrying beams of lumber on their shoulders and women carrying baskets of fruit on their heads. Half-clothed children crouched on the ground. There were donkeys and mule carts, wandering chickens and stray dogs. The water by the pier was as brown as everything else. Marian overheard one woman call it "a dispiriting hodgepodge." That seemed unfair. Marian was curious more than anything else, and the only thing that bothered her as they anchored was the foul smell of the tremendously humid air. As soon as she caught a whiff of it, she threw up again over the side of the ship. John, standing beside her, glanced at her and frowned. She wished he would offer her his handkerchief, but he did not, and she wiped her mouth with her own hand instead.

A ginger-haired Marine from Louisiana who had become friendly with John over the course of the voyage—they had played, according to John, a mean game of checkers while Marian was ill in the room—was standing with them at the rails of the ship. He said, "Why, we sailed to a swamp!"

John nodded. "That's right. And we shall clean it all up."

‖‖‖

THE OSWALDS TOOK a carriage to the house. In time they would learn that to get anywhere along the canal line, it was far easier to travel

by train, but that day, the day of their arrival, they traveled by carriage. The two gray horses that led them were emaciated and weak,
and the driver, a Panamanian boy, slapped them repeatedly with a
switch as though it were punishment, not better care, that would
make them walk faster. Marian cringed each time the switch struck.
The Oswalds had horses back in Tennessee, two magisterial stallions
that they kept stabled on their property. The horses had been a wedding gift from John's father, who believed that every man should
know how to ride. At the wedding, his father had laughingly told
a crowd of people how, as a boy, John had shown little interest in
learning how to mount, how to canter, how to gallop at full speed.
"That is a deficiency I intend to amend." But even once the horses
were his, John never enjoyed them. Instead, it was Marian who every
day went out to the stables to groom them with a curry comb and
feed them apples as treats. She had named them Horace and Charles,
after writers she loved, and unless it was pouring rain, she saddled
one or the other and rode every day over the lush green acreage the
Oswalds owned, which was framed by the Great Smoky Mountains.
When she was riding, Marian felt free, even though she never went
beyond their plot of land.

Not long after they acquired the horses, Marian had persuaded
John to ride with her—once. It was early morning, and the sun lit
the underside of the clouds. As soon as the horses broke out of their
trot, John lost his balance and fell onto the ground, flat on his back.
Charles, the horse he had been riding, galloped ahead a few more
strides, then stopped.

Marian circled back and dismounted Horace, holding his reins
in one hand. John's glasses were on the ground and she picked them
up. She knelt next to him and asked if he was okay. She worried that
something might be broken, and later that worry was confirmed by
a doctor who told them John had broken two ribs. When she asked,
however, John merely said, "My glasses, please," and then looked
away, as though embarrassed, after she gave them to him.

Marian got him back to the house. He walked slowly beside her while she guided Horace and Charles by the reins. Neither John nor she spoke. After Marian hitched the horses in the stable, she went to the bedroom where John had gone to lie down.

"Where does it hurt?" Marian asked.

He pointed to his chest.

They had been married for six months by then.

"May I?" Marian said, reaching for one of the buttons on his shirt.

John nodded.

Standing over him, Marian undid all the buttons and looked. She was not used to seeing his bare chest, especially in the daylight. Usually John slept in his underclothes, covered from his neck to his ankles, and because he slept clothed, she did, too. Every night after John put out the lamp and they lay next to each other in the dark, Marian waited for his hands to find her, to unbutton her nightgown and do the things a husband should do with his wife, all the things Marian desperately wanted him to do, but John never so much as rolled on his side and draped his arm over her, never nibbled her earlobe or trailed his fingertips down her neck. Night after night she waited. Weeks passed. Months. And when she grew tired of waiting, Marian turned to him instead, tugging her fingers beneath the collar of his shirt, feeling the soft, thin skin at his throat. That became their pattern, and if she reached between his legs as she did sometimes, then she could get him interested enough that he would take her in a kind of blind rush, all brusque action and speed, as if he were charging toward some finish line, and suddenly he had a roughness about him, a roughness that thrilled her. They were a storm in the night, tempest-tossed and blustering, though in an instant it was done, and as soon as it was, John went back to his side of the bed.

The day John fell off the horse, there was no immediate bruising Marian could see. Still, she went to the washroom for a roll of cotton gauze and returned to the bedroom with it. She slid her hand under the small of John's back, threading the cotton through and bringing it up around his torso.

He flinched.

"Does it hurt?" she asked.

John gazed up, but not at her. In all the time she would know him, there would always be something inscrutable about him, something she could not quite unlock.

"No," he said at last. Then: "I'm sorry."

Silently and with care, Marian tied off the cotton wrapping just tight enough that she hoped it would heal what might be broken underneath.

||||||

THE CARRIAGE STOPPED at the base of a hill. There was no way the horses could make it up the incline, so in the broiling heat of the day, John and Marian had to get out and walk. Someone else would bring their bags later that afternoon.

They followed the footpaths worn into the grass, making their way past banana trees and lime trees with small, spoked blossoms. In between the trees, scattered all over the hillside, were crude shacks, planks of unpainted wood holding up thatched roofs. Some had water barrels out front and some had clothing hanging from sticks that had been staked in the ground. A Black man in overalls who was standing outside watched the couple walk past.

"Hurry," John told Marian. "The house is just up there."

He pointed to the top of the hill, where a large white house stood alone, graced by the sun. It was two stories tall with a broad, screened veranda that swept across the front and wrapped around to the sides.

"It's too much," Marian said.

John said, "It's our own house on the hill." Theodore Roosevelt, whom John admired, had a house in Oyster Bay that he referred to as such. "It is our bit of paradise above everything else."

||||||

THE EVENING AFTER John had received the cable requesting his presence in Panama, Marian caught him outside, behind the house, gazing at the blue-gray mountains creased with shadows. She walked out to join him. The crickets were twisting their legs and raising a song, and the air was lovely, cool and dry.

"They want me in Panama," John said. He did not turn toward her.

It was a summons John had wished for. Marian had expected it was only a matter of time before it arrived.

She looked out at the mountains as well. She had spent all her life in Tennessee, the only one of four children born to her parents to survive past the age of five. Her mother had been a prim woman who kept a tidy house and whose single indulgence was an occasional piece of licorice root that she chewed in the evenings until it was feathered and soft. Her father, with whom Marian got along best, had been a lumberman who used to take her on walks along the banks of the river and point out the trees: hickory, oak, poplar, spruce, fir. In the evenings, when she should have been practicing the needlework she had learned in school, she instead spent hours by candlelight reading the almanac, the only book besides the Bible that her parents kept in the house. Her parents had both passed years ago, but still Marian loved that land, the mountain laurel that blossomed in June and the rhododendron that crowded along roadsides and the elk that roamed and the hemlock that spread.

"Officially, I would oversee the laboratories of the Board of Health, but I would be given free rein to go after malaria, to eradicate it at last. As they were able to do with yellow fever, of course." John paused. "You're familiar with the science, Marian. What do you think? Can it be done?"

John, she knew, had watched from the sidelines with envy these last few years as other men had brought yellow fever under control in Panama. And he was right—she was familiar with the studies and the reports.

She faced him. "I don't see why not."

John nodded, though he kept staring out at the trees. The contours of his silhouette were familiar to her—the slope of his nose, the sharpness of his chin.

They had been married for ten years by then. They had met in Knoxville, where Marian had gone to study botany at the Female Institute. To help pay the tuition, she had gotten a job on the side. At the time, there was a timber boom in Tennessee. All through the Appalachians, trees were coming down, and the sound they made when they fell, that terrific boom, was a word recast by humans to mean something good. There was so much burgeoning industry, so many mills and manufacturers, that demand was high not only for lumbermen but for administrative personnel to keep the companies afloat. A job at Oswald Lumber had been easy to get. The Oswalds also owned a farming company and a machinery company. They owned half of Knoxville, some people said. Of those three business ventures, each of the three Oswald children had chosen one, walking into a future that was ready-made. Marian worked as a stenographer at the lumber company for three years, drafting bills of lading and purchase orders, before she caught a glimpse of John Oswald, who was the youngest of the three Oswald boys as well as the outcast, the only one of them rumored to have the ambition to make his own way. She admired that about him before she knew anything else. John had come into the office one day for a word with his father and had taken a look at her instead. A long look that made her skin tingle. She was seated behind an unvarnished oak desk, and she knew how she appeared—distinctly unglamorous and plain. Yet he stared at her from across the room and then strode over to her and, almost before he had planted his feet, said, "If you are free, may I take you out tonight?"

It was the first time that a man had shown the least bit of interest in her. For the rest of her life, she would wonder what John had seen in her that day. She asked him once, but he looked at her with such blank incomprehension that it crushed her soul. She just happened to be sitting there, she supposed, and if it had been another girl in her place, perhaps he would have asked her out instead. That girl might have said yes or she might have said no, and Marian's life, operating in some parallel sphere, would have gone on untouched. But no, it had happened to *her*, and she knew there must have been some reason for it.

He took her to an elegant ice-cream saloon in Market Square, and that night Marian learned that John was conversant in all sorts of far-ranging topics. He spoke of Oscar Hammerstein preparing to open a theater in New York City and the work of Louis Sullivan in the Midwest. He had opinions about President Cleveland and about the Wilson-Gorman Tariff that had just been passed. When he asked Marian if she had heard of a man named Nansen who was attempting to sail to the Arctic, she said, "Of course. And did you know that his ship, which he calls *Fram*, means 'forward' in Norwegian?" John had looked at her as though he were both surprised and impressed.

Within a year they were married. Marian graduated from school. There had been some thought in her mind that she could get a job in her field, as a scientific assistant perhaps, but when she brought it up John said, "Why? What would come of it? And there's no need, Marian. Not anymore." He meant to be reassuring, but she resented the notion that it was difficult for a woman to matter much outside of marriage, and she had found it suffocating instead.

They bought a large house in a small town in Sevier County, Tennessee, about thirty miles from Knoxville. John, whose career aspirations lay beyond the lumber company, wanted distance from his family and their influence. The town, with its general store and blacksmith shop and school and church, reminded Marian of the way she had grown up. She spent the days alone, teaching herself how to cook and bake, strolling by rivers and creeks, breathing in the fresh mountain air, wandering through carpets of wildflowers and over the needled forest floor, soft as a sponge after rain. Many afternoons, she read outside in the sun. Gray's *Lessons in Botany and Vegetable Physiology*, *Principles of Scientific Botany* by Schleiden, Mendel's

Experiments on Plant Hybridization. When she tired of reading, she took Horace and Charles for rides, and when she spoke to them it was often the only time all day that she heard her own voice. John had begun work at a small laboratory, researching the theory that mosquitoes were responsible for spreading disease. It was a discovery that had been made seventeen years earlier by a Cuban doctor named Carlos Juan Finlay and then put to the test by an American doctor named Walter Reed. But by the turn of the century, many people still found it hard to believe. How could this frail little insect, no heavier than a cobweb, propagate diseases that could take down men? The skepticism only made John persevere. "It is indisputable fact," he told her once. "And we will prove it to them." John often worked into the night, and Marian's evenings were as solitary as her days. She had entered marriage with few expectations. She had been grateful, mostly, that anyone had wanted to marry her at all. But she had grown up an only child, without many friends, and she'd hoped that marriage, at the very least, would be an end to loneliness. It was not. Even when John was home, his mind was still on his work. He was perpetually distracted, lost in thought, physically present sitting in his armchair but mentally somewhere else. If Marian hoped to have a conversation with him, she had to ask him about work. Only then did he light up. In time she learned that if she brought up the books she was reading, then John would talk about those, too. He was interested in the science even if he was not interested in her.

When he told her about the job in Panama that evening behind the house, he had seemed relieved to hear her express her confidence in the likelihood of his success. "You're right," he had said. "Panama may well be the last malarial frontier. And anyone responsible for eradication . . . well, those are the men that will go down in history, you know." His eyes had been fixed on the horizon when, suddenly, he had reached for her hand. Marian had startled but let him take it. That was his entreaty. She recognized it for what it was. He so rarely touched her. That he did it then signaled the depth of his determination. Perhaps, she had thought, they would be happier there. Perhaps the change would rouse something in him.

"I do know," Marian had said, staring out at the land. "And there is no one better suited than you to lead those men."

John had turned and looked at her with such gratitude that for an instant she mistook it for love.

||||||

TWO WEEKS AFTER arriving in Panama, at one of the many evening affairs that, Marian had quickly discovered, she and John were obligated to attend, Marian learned that while their "house on the hill" seemed excessive to her, there was at least one residence on the isthmus even larger. It was a house in Ancón that had been built at a cost of $100,000 for a French engineer named Jules Dingler. In the autumn of 1883, two years after the French had begun their attempt at digging a canal, Dingler had arrived with his wife, his son, his daughter, and his daughter's fiancé.

"And do you know what he said just before he left France?" the man telling the story had asked.

Tonight's affair was a formal mingling in a ballroom, the sort of thing neither Marian nor John enjoyed. They had somehow gotten swept up into a small group of six other people, all of whom were listening in thrall as the man told the tale.

"He said, 'Only drunkards and the dissipated take yellow fever and die there.'"

"But that was common wisdom at the time," one of the other men said.

"How far we have come! Isn't that right, Oswald?"

Standing next to Marian, John nodded and said, "Quite so."

"Poor Dingler could have used the benefit of expertise like yours."

"Do you mean—did he . . . perish?" a woman wearing long satin gloves asked.

"No, no, he did not, my dear. But mere months after the Dingler family arrived, his daughter contracted yellow fever and—"

The woman gasped.

"Exactly," the man said. "Then in short order his son. Then his daughter's fiancé. Then his wife."

"Every one of them from yellow fever?" someone asked.

"Yes."

"And what about Dingler?"

"He eventually sailed back to France, heartbroken I'm sure."

Everyone stood in a stupor until one of the men said, "You sure know how to liven a party, Badgley."

"I thought it courtesy that our new guests should know."

"Know what?" someone else said. "That the whole place is cursed?"

Badgley smiled. "Well, now, it may have been once, but not anymore. Yellow fever is gone, and Oswald here is going to do the same for malaria." He clapped John on the shoulder. "Isn't that so?"

Marian saw John redden slightly. He was more comfortable shining a light on mosquitoes than having a light shined on him. "That is the idea, yes," he said.

With his hand still on John's shoulder, Badgley said, "Don't be so modest. Your reputation precedes you. We all hear you're the man for the job. What do you say? Do you really believe it's possible to rid this pesthole of malaria once and for all?"

John forced a tight-lipped smile, and after a moment, finally Marian spoke up to save him. "It's entirely possible. And you're right—he's the man for the job."

||||||

THERE WERE TWO seasons in Panama: the wet and the dry. They had arrived in the dry, at the start of the year when the evening breezes were cool, but by May, when rain started streaming from the sky, John cautioned Marian not to spend too much time outdoors. "The mosquitos are rampant when it's wet. They thrive in such conditions."

"But what will I do?" she asked.

He did not answer that. "The weather will improve in January," he said.

In all her life, Marian had never seen so much rain drop out of the sky. In Tennessee when she was a girl, she used to plunge her hands in the mud puddles that yawned across her family's property and grab for frogs after a storm had passed. Whether it sprinkled or poured, her father always looked out the window and said the same thing: "The trees will be happy, at least." She wondered what her father would think of the rain here. It often came in a surge. The wind picked up and sent the tops of the trees nodding about, and the rain slashed through the air. And then, abruptly, it would stop, as if the sky had snapped shut, and the sun shone again. But the intermission, she had learned, was usually brief, just long enough for the clouds to gather more rain before unleashing it again.

For several weeks after the wet season began, Marian sat on the veranda and looked out at the rain. Through the copper screens, she could see a bit of the town down below, a few buildings as well as the train station where all day long black locomotives pulled in and out. Everywhere she looked, people came and went, even in the worst downpours, and she watched them with resentment. How could John honestly expect her to stay indoors all the time? The books they had brought were covered in mold. There were no horses to ride. And she had not come all this way merely to sit on a porch.

The first time she went out, Marian simply walked down the hill and back up again, just for the pleasure of leaving the house. She slipped in the mud on her way down and landed flat on her rear, and she laughed at herself, and laughing felt nearly as good as walking itself had. When she returned to the house, she rinsed her clothes in the washtub and cleaned off her boots, and by the time John came home from work, he was none the wiser.

Eventually she ventured farther, past the foot of the hill into town. Even in the rain, life carried on. Men walked down the street with their hats soaked to the point that the brims hung straight down. Women clutched parasols and sidestepped puddles. And Marian walked, just happy to see all of it.

The town of Empire was at the highest point of the canal route, roughly midway between the Pacific Ocean and the Atlantic. It was perched on a ledge that overlooked the immense Culebra Cut, the nine-mile-long segment of the canal impeded by the mountains, which had to be dug through. Sometimes Marian walked out to look at that, too, peering down over the steep descent, and each time she was dizzied by the scale, which was so colossal that it almost seemed inhuman. Three million years earlier, Marian had read, underwater volcanoes had erupted and sent great reservoirs of sediment up through the surface, connecting two continents and forming the bridge of land upon which they all stood. Now, evidently, the task was to divide it again, to open the land from sea to sea. What nature had accomplished, men wanted to undo.

|||||||

MONTHS HAD PASSED, and the rain was still falling.

Inside the house, Marian took a commissary booklet from the cupboard in the kitchen and pulled on a rain cape. The cape covered most of her dress but stopped at her knees. Past that, she would just have to get wet.

The cook, Antoinette, was standing at the stove, lifting the lid off a large iron pot of fish stew. When Marian said she was going out, Antoinette arched an eyebrow and asked if she thought that was wise, with so much rain coming down.

"I think it's just fine," Marian said, pinching a fold of the cape. "That's why I have this."

Antoinette had come recommended by another couple on the isthmus who hailed from Georgia and whom the Oswalds had met early on at a welcome supper that had been organized on the Oswalds' behalf. Marian had worn a silk voile dress with repoussé lace and had done her hair in a softly coiled pompadour, neither effort which John recognized, and on the ride over, he had wanted, as ever, only to talk about work. He sought her opinion on a statistical anomaly that had been brought to his attention that day, and though she urged him simply to gather more data, the problem distracted him through six courses of food. Quietly, he had eaten his turtle soup and roast turkey and everything else they had been served while all around the other guests reveled and laughed. At one point when he reached for his glass, he knocked over a lit candlestick and set the tablecloth on fire for a brief moment until one of the other men at the table jumped up and doused it with water from his drinking glass. John shrank in his seat, and the host made a joke to smooth over the moment, and no one spoke of it after that. But Marian knew it was the sort of thing for which John would chastise himself. The only good that came out of the whole evening was when the woman seated next to Marian, the one from Georgia, asked whether Marian had managed to find any help yet. "Help?" Marian said. "The options here are dreadful," the woman said. "The Negroes here are not like the Negroes back home. They will not do what you say, and it seems no amount of scolding can make them work any faster than they do." She did know of a good cook, though, a woman from Antigua, and she gave Marian the name. Marian had never had a cook or a maid or any help in that way—not when she was young and not in her married life, either—but John, who had grown up with such people, convinced her to give it a try. "It was one thing in Tennessee, but it is all different here. Don't tell me you would know what to do with a coconut. And I quite like to eat."

Now Antoinette lowered the lid of the pot and wiped her hands on her apron. She was forty-seven years old and still as shapely as she had been as a younger woman, though her hair was graying at the temples and the veins on the backs of her hands were more prominent than they used to be. She looked at those veins in displeasure sometimes, wishing for the days when she had been more supple, more ripe. In Antigua she had made a living cooking stewed saltfish and goat water with yams and callaloo, the last of which was her specialty, and people in the neighborhood were willing to pay because her food was so good. But as good as it was, she still did not make much. A few years back, her husband, whom she had loved for twenty-three years, had gone and plucked some young flower that was half his age. She had not suspected him capable of such a thing, but he had done it, and the reason, Antoinette assumed, was because a flower newly in bloom smelled sweeter than one fading fast. She had borne four children for him. Not long after her husband ran off, her brother fell on hard times, so he and his two children moved in with her, too, and that was three extra bellies to fill. Though she was a cook, a total of eight people to feed, including herself, in addition to all the other paying customers in the neighborhood who numbered about a dozen or so, was far too much cooking for such little reward. In Panama, someone told her, she could cook half as much and earn twice the amount. As it turned out, that person's calculation had been off by a bit. In Panama, Antoinette learned, she could cook less than a fifth of what she had been cooking before and earn three times as much.

The stew needed to simmer for another few hours. She would serve it for supper that night. After she served it she would go back to the room she rented in a crowded tenement in Panama City, and think about her four children whom she had left behind under her brother's care, and wonder whether the money she sent back every two weeks meant they were eating well, especially her youngest, Arthur, who was eight and who had always been undersized.

"I expect I'll be back in an hour," Mrs. Oswald said now, and before Antoinette could ask another question, she left.

||||||

THERE WAS A commissary store at nearly every town along the canal line. The Commissary Department also oversaw an ice factory, laundry services, a bakery that baked over twenty thousand loaves of bread a day, a printing plant, and a train that went out each morning to deliver orders directly to people's houses. But the stores themselves were the principal draw. They were stocked to the brim with canned vegetables, biscuits, matches, shoes, baseball gloves, camphor balls, cornmeal, corned beef, hair pomade, soap, nail buffers, towels, handkerchiefs, satin ribbons, taffeta ribbons, Vaseline, parasols, fabric, lace, fingerbowls, ice-cream dishes, butter dishes, hangers, clocks, codfish, sugar, Welch's grape juice, cigars, sponges, grass rugs, furniture oil, rattraps, eggs, sausage, lamb, pork, livers, steak, cream cheese, Neufchâtel cheese, Roquefort cheese, Swiss cheese, Gouda cheese, Edam cheese, Camembert cheese, Pinxter cheese, MacLaren's cheese, St. Charles evaporated milk, Nestlé condensed milk, Quaker oatmeal, Quaker corn cakes, grapefruit, cranberries, beets, tomatoes, celery, spinach, sauerkraut, turnips, parsnips, squash, eggplant, silverware, ladles, graters, sifters, tongs, whisks, coats, stockings, buttons, hats, pipes, every luxury and convenience imaginable.

Marian needed none of it. Going to the commissary was just an excuse to get out of the house.

By the time Marian arrived and stepped inside, her rain cape was heavy with water and her kid-leather boots were wet all the way through. She slipped back the hood and stomped her feet a few times. Molly, the young cashier, glanced up and, upon seeing Marian, smiled and waved. Marian had always found the girl, who had come to Panama with her parents, to be unfailingly friendly. She had long straight blond hair that, against the custom, she wore down. Perhaps it was nothing, but Marian interpreted it as a small act of rebellion, and she felt a fondness for Molly because of it.

"Good afternoon, ma'am. It's still raining, I see?"

"It will be raining until January, I'm afraid."

Molly smiled. Before Panama, she had lived in Hawaii, where it rained, of course, but not as much as it did here. With her parents she had also lived in Cuba and the Philippines, but so far, despite the rain, she liked Panama the best. She had a camera, a 4x5 field camera about the size of a loaf of bread, that she had lugged with her to every place she had gone, but unfortunately in Panama she hadn't had many opportunities to use it yet. She thought she might like to be a journalist one day, even a female news photographer traveling the world with her camera, but she had not told anyone that. In any case, it was only a hobby for now.

When Mrs. Oswald did not move from where she had stopped just inside the door, Molly called, "Is there anything I can help you find today, ma'am?"

Marian stayed by the door because the rain cape was dripping, and she did not want to trail water all through the store. At Molly's question, she glanced around. The things she longed for in life—companionship, knowledge—were not to be found in any store on this earth.

"I don't know," Marian said. "Is there anything new?"

"Well, we did get a shipment of papaya just this morning. It's from Florida, I believe."

"Papaya?"

"Yes, ma'am. I stacked it up there."

Molly pointed, and Marian turned to see, up on a table, large yellow papayas—the largest she had ever seen—stacked in tiers like a cake. She looked back at Molly. "But papaya grows here."

"Here?"

"In Panama."

Molly, unsure of the point, thought it best just to agree. "Yes, ma'am, it does."

"Then why has it been imported from Florida?"

"I . . . I don't know, ma'am. But I do know that the papaya we have in the store is quite fresh. It just arrived."

"From Florida."

"Yes, ma'am."

Molly wrung her hands, and Marian saw with regret that she had made the young woman flustered.

"In that case," Marian said, still standing by the door, "I will take one. Or two, actually. I will take two."

Molly's eyes brightened. She left the register, walked over to the tiered display, and took two papayas off the top. She liked papaya, but of all the fruits in the tropics she liked the bright-sour taste of passion fruit the best. Molly returned to the register and set the papayas on the counter while she rang them up. "Forty cents, ma'am."

Marian tore the appropriate coupon out of her commissary booklet and paid.

The rain was still falling when Marian left, and it drummed against her rain cape as she walked. She was carrying one papaya in the crook of each arm. Like babies, she thought, and immediately, she stopped. She did not know where that thought had come from. Like babies. In the middle of a muddy street in Panama, she started to cry.

At Marian's insistence, a year into their marriage, John and she had tried to have children. At the right time of the month, Marian would unbutton her dressing gown in bed, and John would climb on top of her, and when he rolled off afterwards, Marian lay on her back with her knees bent upright as she had heard that she should to increase the odds. She lay perfectly still and waited, her dressing gown splayed, while John drifted right off to sleep. They tried for a year without any success. Once, Marian's cycle was late and for two whole weeks she had lived on a raft of hope, but then the blood trickled in, brown blood that left a small stain.

She went to three different doctors during that time, men who poked and prodded her only to conclude that there was nothing wrong. No one prodded John to find out the same. It was presumed that a man could not be to blame. Keep trying, was the advice.

When Marian told John, he said, "Is that what you want?"

It had stung her a little, a question like that. "Yes," she had said.

For several months they tried. And then the following spring Marian found she was pregnant. Her cycle was four weeks late, and her breasts were wonderfully tender to the touch. She was so happy then, keeping track of each passing week on a calendar that she hid in a drawer. Two days after Marian marked the passage of the eighth week, two days after a full eight weeks during which she had held something inside her, a baby becoming, Marian found in her knickers pindots of blood so small that she had to look closely before she realized what they were. Without telling John, she balled up the knickers and threw them away. She told herself that she was far enough along now that it was not what she feared it might be. But that night Marian awoke with cramps so vicious that John immediately hitched a carriage and rode into town to bring the doctor back to the house. By morning, the bleeding was done. The baby was gone.

It was all different after that. They could try again, John said, but Marian said no, and she did not unbutton her dressing gown again, not for that reason or any other. Their nearest intimacy after that would be lying side by side in bed, and neither of them would reach for the other—never again. John did his work, and they were cordial with each other, and Marian looked at him sometimes and felt an exquisite pain. She wanted to love him, and she wanted so badly for him to love her, but neither of them, it seemed, could understand how.

By the time Marian walked back through the front door, she had been out in the rain for hours.

Antoinette was setting the table in the dining room, and at the sound of the door, she looked up, relieved to see that Mrs. Oswald had returned—though she was wet as a fish, carrying two papayas in her arms, and her cheeks were flushed to an almost scarlet red. Her rain cape dripped a ring on the floor.

"Is he here?" Marian asked, panting.

"Mr. Oswald? No, ma'am."

Marian felt her chest unlatch with relief. She breathed, then she coughed.

"Ma'am?" Antoinette stepped toward her.

"I'm fine," Marian said. "I imagine I need to get out of these clothes, that's all. Will you take these?" She gave Antoinette the papayas. "Take them and do something with them if you like, but I don't want to see them again."

Antoinette nodded. She had never known anyone to have bad

feelings toward a papaya before.

She watched as Mrs. Oswald peeled off the rain cape. "I need to get dry."

Antoinette took the cape from her, too, and though she said nothing more, she saw Mrs. Oswald shiver as she walked up the stairs to the bedroom to change.

4

DOWN THE HILL FROM WHERE THE OSWALDS LIVED, PAST THE TRAIN STATION, past the town of Empire with its machine shops and clubhouse and commissary and post office and stores, down a steep terrace of 154 steps, down, down, down into the Cordillera Mountains, into the base of a man-made canal that was presently 40 feet deep and 420 feet wide and growing by the day, thousands of men worked in the rain, shoveling mud, wrapping dynamite, laying railroad track, and swinging pickaxes at the sheared rock walls.

Every morning these men, who had come from all over the world—from places like Holland, Spain, Puerto Rico, France, Germany, Cuba, China, India, Turkey, England, Argentina, Peru, Jamaica, St. Lucia, Martinique, Antigua, Trinidad, Grenada, St. Kitts, Nevis, Bermuda, Nassau, and Barbados most of all—converged in one place: the Culebra Cut. They poured in on labor trains and scrambled down the mountainside, and when the whistle blew, they worked. From sunrise to sundown, they opened the earth. They stood in mud that came up to their knees. They breathed in coal smoke from the locomotives that ceaselessly shuttled past. Their ears pounded with the hammer of rock drills that echoed against the carved mountainsides. Their hands blistered and bled from squeezing the handles of their picks and their shovels for hours on end. Their legs ached, their shoulders burned, their backs felt as though they were breaking, about to snap in two. They were wet all the time. They could never get dry. They were covered with mud. They could never get clean. Their boots fell apart. They shivered with fever. They sang songs in the rain. They swung their arms and they shoveled again and again.

|||||

OMAR AQUINO, SEVENTEEN years old, stood in the Cut and wiped his arm across his brow. It was near the end of September, and rain poured off the brim of his hat. He felt a wave roll through his head from the front to the back, and he stood still, waiting for it to pass. The waves had been coming all day, making him dizzy for a second or two.

"You okay?" the man working next to him asked.

"Yes," Omar said.

"You need rest?"

The man's name was Berisford. Twenty years old, wearing a red handkerchief tied around his neck, he had arrived from Barbados only a few days ago.

Behind them, a locomotive pulling a chain of empty one-sided flatcars rattled on the track, then came to a stop. Steam shovels lowered their necks to scoop up the rock and clay that the men had picked loose, then rotated until their jaws hovered over the idling flatcar beds and, with a crash, dumped it all down. When the flatcars were full, the yardmaster would give the signal and the locomotive would drag the cars off, hauling the spoil away. Seamlessly and without pause, a new chain of empty flatcars would roll in, ready for more. All day long this was the rhythm. The men swung, the steam shovels scooped, the trains rolled in, the trains rolled out.

A strange sort of music, Omar sometimes thought, but one that he liked. Six months ago he had walked to the administrative offices of the canal and asked for a job. All the way there, he had practiced what he intended to say. "I want to help build your canal." Omar had taught himself English well enough to read it in books, but he rarely spoke it aloud. The man at the administrative office had asked where he was from and when Omar said, "Panamá," the man had looked stunned. "We don't get many Panamanians walking in here." Omar did not know whether he was supposed to respond to that, so he said again what he had rehearsed. "I want to help build your canal." The man had crossed his arms and leaned back in his chair, making an appraisal.

Omar was slender and not terribly strong, but he was willing, and if the man had asked why Omar wanted the job, he was prepared to say that it was because he believed the canal would be the future of Panamá, that by having such an important waterway here his country would forever be connected to the rest of the world. But the real reason Omar wanted the job—the reason he never would have said out loud to the man—was that his life so far had been small and lonely. Every day he woke up without anywhere to go or anyone to see. He wanted to give purpose to his purposeless days, wanted to be around people and stop feeling lonely so much of the time. What better way to do that than to join the biggest undertaking known to man, to which thousands of people had come, and which happened to be occurring in the very place where he lived?

In the end, however, the man had not asked. He had merely shrugged and said, "What the hell, we'll give it a try."

That night, when Omar told his father what he had done, his father had laughed as though Omar had told him a joke. When Omar held up the brass identification tag that had been given to him, stamped number 14721, his father turned serious and said, "It is true?" Instantly, his expression went from serious to panic-stricken. He kept staring as Omar silently tucked the tag back into his pocket. "You are one of them now?" his father asked, furrowing his brows. "No, no, no!" He paced back and forth as he repeatedly clapped his hands in fury. Through the clapping and the shouting, Omar had tried to explain. He just wanted to see what it was like, this project that no one could stop talking about. He wanted to meet other people. He wanted something meaningful to do every day. The way his father had fishing, he would have this. But his father would not listen to him. He kept clapping and squawking like a deranged parrot, saying, "No, absolutely not. No, no, no," until finally Omar understood that nothing he said would be of any use. He stopped trying to explain and stood quietly while his father continued clapping for another half-minute. Then his father struck his hands together one last time and declared, "¡Ya! ¡Basta! No more!" Those were the last words his father had said to him. No more. Now nearly six months had passed, and neither Omar nor his father had spoken to each other since.

Omar set his pickax in the mud and leaned on the handle. He took a deep breath. Along with the waves in his head, he kept having chills.

Berisford asked him again if he needed to rest. Before Omar could answer, Clement, who was alongside them, said, "No such thing as rest. Not here anyway. Only men resting is them that dead."

Clement, who was from Jamaica, had always been surly, but something about Berisford made him quarrelsome, too.

Ignoring him, Berisford looked at Omar and said, "You need my kerchief? Wipe your face?"

"I am okay," Omar said, forcing a smile. He had his own handkerchief in the back pocket of his trousers, but he appreciated Berisford's concern. In his few days on the job, Berisford had been friendlier to Omar than anyone else.

Omar took one more deep breath and wrapped his hands around his pick. As he swung, he watched their foreman, Miller, walk down the line through the mud in his tall rubber boots. All day long he paced and shouted at them in American English as he puffed on Havana cigars.

"One million cubic yards this month, boys," Miller yelled over the grind of the shovels and the patter of rain. "That is the goal!"

Next to Omar, Berisford widened his eyes. "One million, he say?"

Clement said, "Too much for you, eh?"

"No."

Clement tsked. "This work not for the weak."

Berisford gave a mighty swing. Then he straightened up, looked directly at Clement, and said, "How come them let you do it, then?"

Prince, a Trinidadian who worked with them, too, laughed. Clement just glowered before he swung again.

Unsteadily, Omar raised his pick over his head and cast it back.

He felt the weight of the iron head tug down over his shoulder. It was heavier today, or else he lacked the strength he had other days.

He wished his father would speak to him again. There was no one else in the house, after all, for Omar to speak to. His mother had died when he was only a few months old. Of an illness, his father had told him once when he asked—an illness that could not be cured. Omar had never known her, although at times he told himself that he had. He had swum between her bones, after all. He had known her from the inside out. It was true he did not remember her, though. Instead, all his memories of childhood involved his father: his father sanding the wood from a tree, his father sprinkling the rooster feed out back, his father trimming Omar's hair over the basin, his father licking his fingers after a meal—and his father fishing, of course. That was the principal thing. Fishing was so much a part of his father that without it, Omar hardly knew who his father would be.

Every day at dawn his father walked out of their house at the edge of the bay and untied his boat and paddled out and cast nets into the sea. When his father was gone, to keep himself busy and because he wanted to help, Omar swept the floors and hung the wash and cut the weeds and cleaned the tools. He picked limes from the trees and squeezed them till they were pulpy and dry.

He would have liked to go to school, but the nearest primary school was too far away, and even if one had been closer his father did not see the use. "Schools do not teach fishing," his father said. Every once in a while when Omar was young, his father made a point to show him how to wrap a handline, how to sharpen a hook, how to sliver bait. These were the lessons worth learning. And they were all preparation for the day his father finally took Omar out on the boat.

Omar had risen early that morning, eager for something new, something different to do with his time—and he had thought he was ready. But from the moment he stepped into the boat, Omar had found himself stricken with fear, an unnameable fear that only grew stronger the farther they went. Having grown up by the bay, he knew how to swim, but he was strangely petrified of the water, it seemed. Eventually his hands were shaking so much that he had trouble getting them to do what he wanted. There was the way he tangled the net, the way he was suddenly incapable of tying a knot, the way his stomach turned each time the boat swayed. The fear had a hold on him until he and his father returned to the shore. And the way his father looked at him then—with pity—was something that Omar would not forget. He knew he had failed. His father had never taken him fishing again.

When Omar was not doing chores, he spent much of his time wandering outside by himself. He talked to the frogs that squatted beneath the spiny aloe plants or to the butterflies that flitted among the tall grass alongside the dirt road. The frogs stayed in one place when he spoke, so Omar crouched down next to them but did not pick them up. The butterflies, however, were fitful, so Omar caught them and cupped them between his palms, feeling their fluttering wings while he whispered his secrets or sorrows before letting them go.

Once in a while, Omar climbed down to the shore and listened to the scrabble of the crabs and the shush of the waves. He stood on the sand and stared into the distance, trying to catch a glimpse his father somewhere on the water, straining to see any flash of the boat in the sun. Sometimes he thought he saw something, but it was always too far away for him to be sure.

In the evenings when his father returned to the house from a day spent at sea, one of them cooked the fish he had caught, and together they ate at the same table, and if his father was not too exhausted, they talked. The conversation tended toward ordinary things—his father's physical pains, how many fish he had caught, whether or not Omar had brought in the wash. Occasionally his father would grumble about someone he had encountered in the market, someone who had done something in a way his father believed it should not be done. "What is this world coming to?" his father would ask, and Omar would say, "I don't know, Papi."

Now, though, when they were both in the house at night, they avoided each other. His father still brought home fish and cooked it for dinner, but he left Omar's food on the table and took his outside where he sat on a barrel and ate with the hens and roosters behind the house. Omar sat at the table by himself, and when he finished eating he silently walked to his bedroom and lay down on his palm-stuffed mattress and stared at the ceiling, achingly listening to the sounds of his father shuffling through the house, until he fell asleep.

By the time Omar woke in the morning, his father was gone again, out on the sea.

||||||

"FASTER NOW!" MILLER yelled from the berm.

Down the line, someone in the gang—Miller could not tell who—started to sing. It might have been a different song from the one they'd been singing before or it might have been the same. Miller did not know, nor did he care. He was willing to tolerate the singing if it made the men work faster. There had been a change of command not long ago, and the new fellow in charge of everything here was an Army man, so there could be no mucking around.

Miller threw down the stub of his cigar and drew another from the pocket of his overalls, cupping his hand as he lit it. The rain had worked its way down into his boots, and his toes were slick when he wiggled them. He took a few quick puffs of the cigar before yelling again.

"There's a week to go before the end of this month. Now is the time to push, you hear? The boys at Culebra are closing in, but we can best them if we try."

Each week Miller made it a point to look at *The Canal Record*, where the excavation totals for various segments of the line were printed for all to see. No single division had yet managed one million cubic yards in a month, but it was a goal within reach, and Miller wanted to be the one responsible for reaching it. He imagined the sorts of accolades and recognition that would come his way if he did.

It was possible *The Canal Record* would write a profile of him, even run his photograph alongside it.

"They say," he went on, "that this will be the deepest cut to the earth ever made by man. Consider that, now! You'll be part of history, see?"

Maybe that would inspire them to work faster, Miller thought. It *was* history in the making, wasn't it? The president himself had said as much. It was the destiny of the United States to build the canal. The dream that had begun four hundred years earlier was theirs to fulfill. And if they could do it, they would be a major power—indeed the major power—on the world's stage. With this one single water-way, the United States would be able to control the shipping routes, and thus the trade, and thus damn near everything across the whole of the globe.

Miller looked again at the men under his watch—island men by and large. He'd heard many a reason why they had been recruited here. They were accustomed to the climate, they spoke English, they could better withstand disease. In the end, he didn't care so long as they got the work done.

Miller promenaded along the berm and watched the men swing their picks as they sang. Their job was to feed the steam shovels that rumbled behind them, hungry for dirt. Only Americans were allowed to handle the shovels, and each had an engineer high up in its cab as well as a craneman balanced out on the arm. Either was a job Miller might have liked to try himself—they carried a certain prestige—but as it was, he was stuck down here on the ground.

Before coming to Panama, Miller had been a railroad man. His father had died when Miller was thirteen, leaving his mother and him in a pinch as far as money was concerned. It was his mother who raised him, a broomstick of a woman who made the meanest sweet potato pie known across three counties. Miller was a handful, and he was the first to acknowledge that she had done her best, but after a certain point, there was nothing more she could do. Miller was fighting at school, roughing up anyone who looked at him sideways. After school, he kept fighting in the streets. He was foam-mouthed angry, and for the longest, stupidest time he didn't know why. Perfectly obvious, of course. The absence of his father was a force, a ripping gale of wind that nearly tore him in two. When he dropped out of school, his mother pleaded with him to go back, but schooling, Miller had come to believe, was not made for a boy like him. From what he had seen, it was just a means of getting people to behave in agreed-upon ways while fooling them into thinking it was for their own good. Miller was certain his life had other things in store.

He fell in with the railway when he was all of sixteen. He was aimless, and the railroad gave him a direction to follow, somewhere to go. It took him first to Charleston, where, in the employ of the newly formed East Shore Terminal Company, he helped build a waterfront spur. Two years later, he helped open an artery so that trains carrying cotton could get where they needed to go. He saw firsthand how important that artery was. Without the artery, there could be no running blood. Movement was key. Transportation was all. Those were lessons that Miller would never forget.

In 1893, sensing it was time to move on, Miller ventured west-ward, sucking freedom into his lungs. As his chest expanded, so did the country. The railroads offered hazardous work. He'd seen men killed trying to couple together cars with a link and pin, men sand-wiched and crushed, skulls and bones broken like twigs. But if you had luck on your side, then the pay was worth the risk.

The railroad took Miller out through the Corn Belt with its acres of long prairie grass. Most of the folks there were farmers, working the land, making good use of it, which was the same thing he felt he was doing when he laid railroad track. What was the land for if not to support the men who walked upon it?

Those were the days when the great wheel of innovation was turning with speed. Telephones could suddenly carry a person's voice across space. Electricity somehow bolted through wires and lit up people's homes. And horseless carriages were coming, from what Miller heard. American ingenuity was on the advance.

Miller landed in South Dakota, where he spent a few years among the Black Hills and slept at night beneath a basin of stars. Other railroad men came and went. There was Riley from Georgia, who cooked black-eyed peas most nights over an open flame; Lee from Kansas, who carried a Winchester rifle engraved with his initials; a man who introduced himself as Bill Jones, though everyone knew this was just a name cowboys went by when they did not want to give their own. Most of the men were bachelors, either by their own design or by God's, and after a long day of work there were always a few, including him, who would tromp into the nearest town to find a saloon and spend their earnings on a much-needed drink. Miller pushed farther westward, but railroad opportunities were dwindling by then, the bulk of the track in the United States already having been laid. By the time he reached California, he had the feeling he had come to the end of the world.

That's when Panama beckoned. All the men Miller knew were talking about it. The U.S. government was hiring railroad men by the hundreds, having them lay the track that was essential for moving dirt and machinery through the growing canal. To be associated with the enterprise was to be granted a certain cachet. Plus, the money was good and the housing was free.

Miller started off doing railroad work, but when the majority of that work was done, he took a job as a foreman instead. The pay was fair, but he had thought there would be more to it than keeping men in line all day long, sunrise to sundown. That was what it amounted to, though, his great contribution to the great Panama Canal. What's more, it was hotter than Hades and wetter than the world during Noah's big flood. Hell's Gorge, the men called it, and between the black smoke and the heat and the slime and the rocks and the constant deafening clamor, the name was certainly apt. No one had warned him about all of that. Instead, what he'd heard about the canal was all the trumped-up huzzah: The greatest feat of engineering the world has ever seen! The future of civilization! The salvation of the tropics! He had bought into it all, and now it was what he was trying to sell.

||||||

HIGH ABOVE WHERE Miller stood and where the men toiled, a group of tourists were walking along the ridge overlooking the Cut. The women, in cream-colored dresses, held parasols over their heads to protect themselves from the rain.

"You see them?" Berisford asked Omar.

"Yes," Omar said as he tried to shake off yet another chill. They were coming more frequently now.

"Don't seem they seeing us, though," Berisford said, gazing up.

A man named Joseph, who Omar knew had been a preacher in Jamaica before joining their gang, said, "We part of the scenery, like so much else."

From the berm, Miller took note of the one man on the line who was standing still, looking up, and he turned to see what had captured the man's attention. At the top of the ridge, he saw some pretty American ladies walking in the rain. Well, he should have known. Miller took a minute to admire them, too, before walking down the berm. His boots squelched in the mud and reminded him of that unpleasant slickness between his toes. When he had planted himself right in front of the man, Miller pinched the cigar out of his mouth and said, "You see something you like?"

Berisford, still squinting up at the tourists, was so startled that he nearly dropped his pick.

"Pretty, ain't they?" Miller went on.

Omar swung his pick while he watched out of the corner of his eye. Clement and Joseph and every other man on the line kept swinging without pause, back and down, back and down, keeping the rhythm. Prince whistled along.

"You hear me talking to you?" Miller said.

"Yes, sir," Berisford said.

"Well, I asked you a question."

"I don't know, sir."

"Don't know what? Whether they're pretty or not? Wasn't that you who was just looking up there?"

"I can't recall, sir."

"Can't recall?" Miller shook his head. "Listen here. Their pretty ain't made for you, boy. Keep your eyes off them and down here on your work."

"Yes, sir."

Omar was still watching, and he saw Clement turn his head just enough to catch a glimpse, too. In the rain, with his pick on his shoulder and his sopping-wet hat on his head and his red handkerchief tied around his neck, Berisford stood.

"Well, get to it, then. There's one million cubic yards of dirt to be dug this month—if you recall." Miller grinned.

Slowly, without looking at Miller or anyone else, Berisford raised his pick off his shoulder and swung.

‖‖‖

MIDMORNING, AS HE did every day, the Quinine Man tramped through the Cut. Omar had never been happier to see him approach. He hoped a cupful of quinine would help stop the feverish chills he had been feeling.

"Quinine!" the man called.

Berisford groaned. "Lordie! Again?"

Prince stopped whistling and said, "He come every day."

"But I don't like what he bring. Such a nasty-nasty taste."

"What you care how it taste?" Clement said. "Quinine keep malaria away. Just drink it down like a man."

"You saying I not a man?"

"No. I saying drink the quinine so you don't get sick."

"No pay if you sick," Prince said. Then he corrected himself. "Unless you American."

Clement nodded. "Americans fall sick, they still earning money in the hospital bed."

"But not us?" Berisford asked.

Prince shrugged. "Such is life in the canal."

The Quinine Man stopped in front of Omar and poured the bitter liquid from a canteen into a small paper cup. Omar, shivering in the rain, took it and drank it as fast as he could. The Quinine Man poured more and gave Berisford and Clement one cup each. Clement took his and drank it all in one gulp. He made a show of smacking his lips and smiling at Berisford when he was through.

Berisford held the cup between his fingers and peered at it with disgust.

"For your health!" the Quinine Man encouraged.

"You can do it," Omar said.

Berisford sighed. "I rather it be rum."

"We all rather that," Prince said, chuckling.

Joseph nodded his assent.

Berisford kept staring down at the cup, and Omar watched with dread as Miller ambled over.

"There a problem?" Miller asked, after he took the stump of a cigar out of his mouth.

"He don't wanna drink," the Quinine Man said.

"That so?"

Miller pinned his gaze on the man before him and sighed. "You again. Why you always causing trouble for me?"

Berisford stayed quiet.

"Drink the quinine," Miller said.

"I drink it yesterday, sir."

"Well, hallelujah, but it comes every day. Now, I know God might have shorted you brains, but that means today you have to drink it again."

Berisford did not move.

"Goddamn it, hurry up now, you're wasting precious time."

In the drizzling rain Berisford looked down at the cup in his hand. In the parish of St. Andrew, where he was from, there was a pond he used to visit sometimes on Sunday afternoons after church. As long as no one was watching, he would take off his clothes and step into the water and swim. The water, dappled with shadows and sun, had as many cool spots as warm, and the sensation of his bare skin moving through them both was one he enjoyed. It was a different kind of wet than standing out in the rain, and he wondered if it was different because one was a wet he chose and one was a wet that fell down upon him whether he liked it or not.

"I got to move on," the Quinine Man piped up.

Inwardly, Omar pled with Berisford to drink. He imagined Prince and Clement and Joseph were all thinking the very same thing.

"Drink the damn stuff now," Miller said, emphasizing each word.

Finally, Berisford raised the cup to his lips and sipped.

Miller smiled. "That's the way. We're taking care of you, see?"

Omar saw Clement shake his head as the Quinine Man filled another cup and moved on down the line.

"Back to work now," Miller said before he walked away, too.

5

AS HER ELDEST CHILD LAY SICK IN THE BEDROOM AT THE BACK OF THE HOUSE AND her youngest was across the ocean on her own, Lucille Bunting sat at the kitchen table with a carved pencil in her hand and tried to write. The pencil had been a gift from Willoughby Dalton, a man who periodically walked the three miles from Carrington Village, where he lived, to her house on Aster Lane to give her gifts of his own making or things he had acquired somehow. The first time Willoughby had come to their house, a good year ago now, he had arrived carrying some cassia flowers in his arms. He had stood at the edge of their property and stared at the house like he was unsure, now that he was there, what to do next. Lucille had watched him through the window. She recognized him from church—he wore the same unfashionable gray felt hat, one that curled at the brim, and he had a bit of a limp—and he stood outside for so long without moving that finally she walked away from the window and went to do other things. A full hour later, when the sun went down, Lucille had circled back to the window and saw Willoughby walking away with the flowers still in his arms.

He returned the next day with different flowers—plumeria this time—and when he came to the edge of the property, again he paused, and at the window Lucille crossed her arms, prepared to watch the same strange show. But then Willoughby hobbled past the edge, all the way up the dirt walk to the house. She craned her neck to see the slow way he stooped in front of the door, the way he laid the flowers down, and the even slower way he stood back up. He walked off again.

Then one afternoon Willoughby knocked on the door. Lucille answered it and found him standing next to the heap of flowers, the ones at the bottom soggy and browned. She had not moved the flowers because she had wanted to see how long this could possibly go on.

Willoughby smiled and slid his felt hat off his head.

"Good afternoon," he said. His voice was nice, buttery and soft.

Lucille did not speak.

"I bring you some flowers," he said. He shifted his weight and tried again. "I've seen you. Been seeing you for some time. Can't seem to stop, and my mind tell me that might mean something."

He waited.

Lucille had never heard anyone talk that way, so open and pleading it was almost like he had come to show her a wound, an aching spot in himself that he was hoping she would tend. She could have if she wanted to—aside from the outmoded hat, he looked decent enough—but she did not know why she should. She said, "Seems people always look for meaning in things that don't mean much at all."

Willoughby, with all the flowers at his feet, slowly placed his hat back on his head. He nodded once before he turned, and then he stepped down into the dirt and walked back out to the road with nothing in his hands, nothing whatsoever to hold on to—neither flowers nor the person for whom he had come. For a minute Lucille felt sorry for him—he looked so sad—but Willoughby, and every other man for that matter, held little interest for her. Each time he came back after that, Lucille simply accepted the gifts and then sent him on his way, like tossing a fish back into a creek. The miracle was that that old fish just kept swimming up to the same spot.

Still, the things Willoughby brought were frequently useful, and the pencil, which he said he had whittled himself until it was smooth with a nice fine point, was an example of that. Lucille's main use for it had been to mark bolts of fabric and to trace pattern pieces to make sewing a little easier than it had been in the past when she simply trusted her eye to measure lengths and envision shapes. Now, though, it had another use: writing letters, if she could remember how to write them. Lucille held the pencil over a smooth sheet of writing paper and considered just what it was she wanted to say.

||||||

LUCILLE HAD GROWN up on a medium-sized sugar plantation in Bridgetown, a plantation owned for 180 years by the Camby family and upon which her own family had worked for nearly half as long—first her great-grandparents, then her grandparents, then her parents, then her. That continuity of lineage among one family in one place was unusual, and it was among the reasons that her parents, who had been born full free, chose to stay on the property even when they might have made a life somewhere else. They had roots there. Generations of the Bunting family were buried on those grounds. They lived their life there because to them that was simply where life was lived.

In the story that had been passed down to Lucille, when the Queen of England decreed in 1834 that all slaves in British territories be freed, Lucille's grandparents, knowing no other life, had rented a plot of land on the Camby estate and built a house on a patch of rocky land by a copse of mango trees. It was a small wooden house with one room at the front and one room at the back, raised up on lumps of limestone to keep it off the soggy ground and to keep the centipedes away. Her grandfather, her mother liked to recall with a chuckle, had an unnatural fear of centipedes, and Lucille, who knew hardly anything else about him, always imagined her grandfather yelping and jumping up on a chair at the sight of one, an image that made her chuckle, too.

Upon emancipation many other people on the plantation, friends who had worked alongside Lucille's parents and her grandparents for years and years, left the grounds of the estate and went out into the world. Some only went elsewhere on Barbados, which at 166 square miles was hardly enough world to contain everyone now that people were free to go where they wanted and to live where they pleased. Lucille's mother had told her the story of a woman named

Becky and her husband, Abraham, who had packed their few belongings and kissed everyone on the plantation farewell before setting off down the long gravel road that led out to the wider world, only to walk back up that road nine days later telling everyone that they might as well stay where they were because there was nowhere to go. All the land was used up. What they meant, Lucille's mother explained, was that almost all of the arable land on the island was already owned by the white planters who had once owned them. After their return, Becky and Abraham arranged to rent a small plot on the Camby estate, enough space to build a small house and grow a few crops for themselves. During the day, they worked the same land they had worked before they were free, only now they earned a wage. It was the best they could do. And it was what many other people did, too. "Officially unchained," her mother said at the end of the story, "but tethered just the same."

By the time Lucille was five, she worked weeding the fields in the morning under the early sun. By the time she was ten, she was feeding the livestock, and though she had been instructed in the art of efficiency, she lingered sometimes with a cow she had named Helena, listening to it as it lowed, and she took extra care to comb an ox that she called James. When Lucille was twelve, her mother, who did not want her only daughter to have a life in the fields, saw to it that Lucille went to the school that the Cambys ran on their grounds. There were free schools in Bridgetown by then, but the closest one was at least a forty-five-minute walk there and back, time when tenants could have been working instead, and rather than lose that time the Cambys operated a school of their own. On Monday through Friday, Madam Camby, who had no qualification other than that she herself had been educated, sat at the front of a shed outfitted with benches that several of the tenants had built and taught children their letters and numbers as well as some of her personal observations about the natural world and matters of history. She brought books over from the great house sometimes, and she held them up for all to see, though if any student leaned forward to look at the pages up close, she always jerked the book back lest it be touched. So much held up as a promise was kept just out of reach.

In the evenings, after school and supper, Lucille's mother would sit with her daughter and teach Lucille how to sew, a skill that would serve her the rest of her days. Every year each tenant on the plantation was given a single long piece of linen from which they made clothes. But that linen was precious, so Lucille's mother used a piece of scrap fabric to demonstrate how to sew a whip stitch and a ladder stitch and a basting stitch and the difference between them. By the light of the hearth, she showed Lucille how to finger fold a pleat and how to tack down a dart and how to properly fell a seam so that even from the inside, a garment would not appear undone. When that piece of fabric was filled up with thread, they would pull out the stitches and reflatten it with a warmed block of wood, then they would use it again. Lucille had a gift, and before long, when that piece of fabric was falling apart, her mother gave her the linen, and she made all her family's clothes. She loved to sew, the feel of working the fabric with her own two hands, the satisfaction of the thread slipping through. After the linen was gone, she used a bedsheet to sew. The worst whipping she ever got in her life was delivered by her father after she took the front facing of her bedquilt apart from the back and used it to make herself a new dress. That dress, though, was so striking, with its colorful squares all down the bodice and the skirt, that Madam Camby, upon seeing young Lucille wearing it into the school shed one day, asked her where she had gotten it from. When Lucille replied, with some trepidation, that she had made it herself, Madam Camby had frowned and told her to run home and change. "And leave the one you are wearing up at the house. Put it on the back steps." Lucille did as she was told. She thought it was only a matter of time before her parents would hear about it and that once they did, she was in for an even worse whipping than the one her father had recently delivered. But instead of punishment, what came to Lucille the next day was the dress, folded and delivered by one of the house servants out to the Buntings' small home, and on top of the dress was a note in Madam Camby's good writing-hand: an order for two more dresses, "not made of quilts, but made with the same fine workmanship" to be worn by the house-maids. That was how Lucille became responsible for making all the house servants' garments thereafter, an effort for which she was not paid beyond the bolts of fine woven poplin that Madam Camby sup-plied and from which Lucille was permitted to keep any yardage that she did not use.

That was also how, a few years later when Lucille was nineteen, she met the eldest Camby son, the one who had gone to university in England and returned with his wife, Gertrude, to run his family's estate. Lucille had walked up to the great house one morning with a stack of newly finished dresses in her arms. She went around to the back door, prepared to hand the dresses to the housemaid Jen-net as she always did, but instead she saw a handsome, well-dressed white man whom she did not recognize jiggling the knob. Lucille stopped about ten feet off and watched. The man mumbled under his breath. And then, as though he sensed someone was looking at him, he glanced over his shoulder and met her eye. Lucille saw him blush. He let go of the doorknob and took several steps back. "This always used to stick when I was a boy, too. It's a wonder no one has ever managed to repair it," he said. Lucille said nothing, and the man stared at her until Jennet flew through the door and took the dresses from Lucille and then, noticing the man, froze and said, "Sir." He smiled amiably—he had an endearing smile—and said, "Evidently it can only be opened from the inside." Jennet, confused, said, "Sir?" and the man looked past Jennet to once again meet Lucille's eye, this time as though they shared a private joke between them.

That was Henry Camby, Lucille was to learn, and that moment would be the beginning of many more private moments between them to come.

A little more than two years after that day, Lucille would leave the Camby estate. When she did, her first child, Millicent, was one year old, and her second, Ada, was only a few weeks in the world.

Just as her mother had not wanted her to know a life confined to the fields, Lucille did not want her daughters to know a life confined to the estate. That time had come to an end. She wanted to give them more. She would take the house, the one that had served the Bunting family for so many decades, with her when she went. Henry Camby would declare that the house belonged to Lucille by virtue of heritage, a rationale that no one on the Camby estate had ever heard invoked—and one that would never be invoked again. For a time, it had been the talk among all the tenants, Henry Camby giving Lucille Bunting the house like he had. That gesture, combined with the Bunting girls' appearance, confirmed what most people already knew. It was an occurrence so common that beyond the estate grounds, on the island at large, no one remarked on it at all.

On a Sunday morning in 1891, Lucille and a few other tenants she had known for a long time took apart the house piece by piece. They pried back boards and removed the door from its hinges. They loosened the windows and popped them out of their frames, like eyes from sockets. They unstacked the stones from the hearth. Then they piled everything into carts and wagons and paraded down the gravel path that led to and from the estate, the white pebbles in the path blowing up a chalky dust as the wheels crunched overtop. It was the first time in her twenty-one years on the earth that Lucille had ever walked all the way down that path. With Ada tied to her front and Millicent tied to her back, she walked. She kept her eyes straight ahead. Because she did not know what was out there, she had no destination in mind, and the procession carried on in a general northeastern direction until the sun went down and Lucille told them to stop. "Here," she said. She believed the darkening sun was a sign from God, an indication that she was where she should be. They had come to a dusty road that Lucille would later learn was called Aster Lane. It had only a few other houses on it. By lantern light her friends, tenants who needed to be back at the Camby grounds by morning to work, started to build. First a foundation with uprights in each of the four corners. A floor that was eighteen feet long by ten feet wide. Then walls up from there. Windows inset. They knew how to do it. Their houses were so often taken from them, by man or by God, that they had to know how to rebuild. It took the greater part of the dark hours, but by the time the sun rose, it was done. The same small house in a brand-new place. The same small house in a brand-new life. Lucille, more exhausted than she had ever been in her life, had stood back in the glorious morning sun and, bursting with pride, looked at the house and thought how far she had come. It was no more than three miles from where she had been born and had spent all her life, three short miles, but to her it was a whole world away.

||||||

THERE WAS NO turning back. Lucille had been the first of the Buntings to go somewhere new, and once she was gone, with two babies to care for all on her own, she had to figure her way. She had brought with her all the bolts of fabric she had accumulated over the years, all the leftovers and scraps she had kept sorted by color and print, and she used them to sew clothes while the children slept, sewing even though her eyes were heavy and she pricked herself with the needle many a time. It was in a new place, but she sat by the light of the same hearth where her mother had taught her and listened for her mother's voice guiding her through how to ease a sleeve or gather a skirt. For eight years since her mother had passed, Lucille could count on hearing that voice from time to time when she was sewing, as though her mother were with her. But now, as hard as she listened, Lucille could not hear it. She would never hear it again. She would have no help, no one to depend on besides herself. To be independent was what circumstance required of her. It would be up to her to make sure that her girls never went to bed hungry, not for food or for love or for any of the necessary things of this life.

It cost one shilling a week taken out from what little she earned, but when they were old enough Lucille insisted on sending the girls to school. They had both come out light, and Lucille understood that the lightness meant that they had the chance to become things that Lucille never could. In the evenings, between stitches, Lucille watched her daughters drawing letters on their slate tablets with chalk. She recognized the letters, recalled them from her afternoons in the shed, and as the girls drew them out, the letters appeared like old friends. She smiled at them sometimes as though they might smile in return. But mostly she watched and tried to fill in the gaps for the things that she did not know, the things she could not remember, the things she had not been taught. Millicent was careful—the chalk would screech as she deliberately dragged it over the slate—and Ada wrote faster, more interested in getting the work done than in doing it right. No matter how many times Lucille scolded her, Ada always finished first and set the tablet aside to go back out on the porch and listen to the crickets or hunt for them in the long grass. Both things were a privilege—the schooling as well as putting it aside.

Beyond schooling, just like her mother before her, Lucille aimed to teach Millicent and Ada certain practical things: how to sew a hem or mend a tear, how to cook barley in the pot, how to hammer a nail and file a board, how to reckon money, how to chop wood. At home, Lucille put the girls to work in the small garden she had planted out back, teaching them how to harvest cassava, pumpkin, arrowroot, eddo, and yam. She taught them about herbs and plants, what they could do with things like milkweed and pigeon pea and crab's-eye vine. And all the while she sewed clothes that earned them enough to get by. In an average week, she could make one fine garment. She was forever pulling bits of thread off herself. She rolled them between her fingers sometimes until they formed little balls, and she lined them up across the hearth until there were so many that she cleared them away. She was talented enough that she could have made clothing to order for white women in Bridgetown who had their wardrobes imported from England or from ateliers in France, but she did not have access to the fabrics that white women preferred—velvets and chiffons and silk lace. Everything she made was of either cotton or muslin, common fabrics that she worked to elevate by how brightly she dyed them with things like beetroot and yarrow or how she mixed prints. The garments she made were distinctive that way, sought out in the market by Black women and colored women who wanted to look their best. She did not, as a rule, make clothing for men.

|||||

THAT MORNING THERE had been a storm setting up to the south, and the smell of rain had roused her. Not rain falling, but rain coming. The air was fuzzy with that particular smell. Lucille had lain still in bed for a few minutes upon waking, breathing it in and listening for thunder, but all she heard was the sound of the birds, who seemed so blithely unconcerned by any change in the weather that it made her wonder whether she was wrong. Maybe there was no gathering storm. Maybe she only wanted there to be. She was not the only one who would have welcomed rain. The drought had been going on for so long that hardly anyone on the island could get any crops to grow. Work was scarce. People were hungry. A good rain might help ease the struggle, she thought.

She lay for a full five minutes before she rolled over and saw that Ada was not in her bed. Millicent was there, sleeping soundly, thank God, but Ada was not. Quickly, Lucille sat up and looked around. The room was sparse. Three beds crowded in did not leave space for much else. Ada's bedsheet was turned back. Her quilt was gone. Lucille got out of bed and hurried to the front room, but all she found there, on the table by the hearth, was Ada's school tablet, propped up against a canister as though it wanted to be seen. Lucille walked closer and read.

> *I am going to Panama to earn money for us. I will send word*
> *when I arrive.*

Lucille spun around, surveying the room. She had the thought that Ada, even at her age, was playing a hiding game and would step out from behind the cupboard or the door, grinning brightly, the longer Lucille looked. But when some ten seconds passed and Ada did not appear, Lucille, with a sinking feeling, walked to the front door, opened it, and stepped out onto the porch in her nightgown. She looked down, but the parched earth was too dry to register footprints. Across the street, the view was the same as it ever was: the Penningtons' house with the same three-legged pot on the porch, the Callenders' house with its row of cherry trees. Everything the same. The sinking feeling slipped down into dread. It was not until Lucille stepped back into the house, her mind racing, the dread whipping up into panic, that she noticed that the pair of black boots in the corner was missing. Months earlier, Willoughby had brought those boots as yet another one of his gifts and Lucille had set them on the floor and not touched them since. But as soon as she saw that the boots were not there, Lucille knew it was true. Ada, her impetuous, strong-willed daughter, really had gone off to Panama all on her own.

।।।।।।

NOW LUCILLE HELD the pencil poised over the paper. What was she to say? That she was cross? That she was full of terrible worry? That in a way, an odd way, she did understand? Lucille held the pencil in midair. As soon as Ada sent word, *if* she did, Lucille wanted to have something ready to send in reply. When she had left the Camby grounds, her mother's voice had not come to her anymore. No matter how cross or worried Lucille might have been, she wanted Ada to know she was with her somehow.

There was so much to say and nowhere to start. Lucille sat by the lamplight and tried, but she had never been good at forming letters, and so far nothing was coming out right.

6

WITH MORE FOOD IN HER BELLY AND LESS MONEY IN HER SACH, ADA WALKED ALONG
the main street in Empire. One mammee apple was not so much,
but it was something, and it had tasted as good as anything Ada had
ever eaten, except maybe for her mother's black cake, a treat that
her mother made once a year for Christmas and that Ada spent all
the 364 days in between looking forward to. A ripe mammee apple,
when she was as hungry as she had been, was second only to that.

As Ada walked, she wished she had not thrown out the pit and
instead had thought to save it in her pocket so she could suck it
again. Maybe there would have been some flavor left, some little
trace she had missed. Maybe she should go back and look for the pit,
or maybe buy a second mammee apple, she thought, but she didn't.
Her stomach was quiet for the moment at least, so she kept walking
ahead.

Judging by the sun, it was just about noon. The heat in Panama,
it seemed to Ada, was equal to the heat in Barbados, but the air was
more humid, so thick that if she had reached out and closed her
hand, she would not have been at all surprised to be able to grab
ahold of it like a clump of mud. But even in the sluggish air, the
street was bustling just the same as in Bridgetown. Carriages led by
horses clapped down the road, and carts led by mules in turn led by
men rattled and clanked. Women walked about carrying baskets on
their backs or their heads or in the crooks of their arms. Well-attired
people stood on street corners and talked. Every building looked
clean and brand new.

Even before leaving home, Ada had heard that the most common
job for a woman in Panama was doing the wash. She disliked doing
the wash, but she would not be choosy, she told herself. If work as

a washerwoman was the only work she could get, she would take it. On washday at home, her mother sent Ada and Millicent to the basin behind the house, where they were supposed to scrub their dresses clean. Millicent was dutiful in this, scrubbing all around the hem and the collar, coaxing out the grime of the days, but Ada usually just dunked her dress in the water, watching the fabric balloon up where the air got trapped underneath, swishing it around the whole basin once before drawing it out and declaring she was done. Millicent would sometimes shake her head and tell Ada to drop the dress back down. Then she would let go of her own dress and work on Ada's instead. She would soak it again, rubbing her thumb in the spaces between each button, biting her lip as she worked. She did it with love, and Ada let her. She always let Millicent take care. Now Ada wanted to take care of her sister the way her sister had always taken care of her.

||||||

WHEN MILLICENT HAD first fallen ill, no one had been alarmed. A bit of congestion required tea and a good night's rest, that was all. But little by little, Millicent kept getting worse. After a few days, she developed a cough, wet-sounding and loose, and she no longer had the energy to even get out of bed. Mrs. Pennington and Mrs. Callender, both of whom lived across the street, and even Mrs. Wimple, who lived farther west down the road, all came to the house to see if they could help. They brought teas they had brewed, but none of them— not the sage tea, not the lemongrass tea, not the bay leaf tea—made any difference as far as anyone could tell. Mrs. Wimple suggested an Obeah man she knew, but Ada's mother did not believe in such things and she told Mrs. Wimple so. Mrs. Wimple had shaken her head and said that Ada's mother was not "saltwater true," a charge Ada had often heard levied against her mother, who did not always behave or dress or live in the way other people expected her to. It was a charge that boiled down to one thing, Ada thought, and it was her favorite thing about her mother: She was independent of mind. Mrs.

Callender, whose own children were grown, had gone into the bedroom to see Millicent, and when she came out she had laid her hand gently on Ada's mother's shoulder and said, "You need a doctor just now." And Ada had watched her mother nod once, as though Mrs. Callender had simply said out loud something she already knew.

It was not until a week later that a doctor finally arrived at the house. He was a white doctor from town who charged 10 shillings for an in-house examination in addition to the cost for mileage to get there. He was smartly dressed in a suit and necktie, and he strode into the bedroom with an air of authority and briskly did his exam. The year before, there had been an outbreak of typhoid fever that touched more than five hundred souls. Four years earlier, a scourge of smallpox swept through the island. There was always something, it seemed. Ada and her mother had sat in the bedroom, her mother twisting her fingers and Ada's stomach in knots, waiting to see what was wrong. Millicent was weak, lying on her side in the bed, her body bent like a sickle.

When the exam was complete, the doctor turned toward them and asked, "How long the cough?"

"Two weeks," Ada's mother had said.

The doctor nodded as though he had expected as much. "She developed pneumonia. I cannot say how."

"Pneumonia?"

"The good news is that she survived it. The worst of the pneumatic infection itself has passed. The bad news, I am afraid, is that she has residual fluid in her chest. It cannot remain there. The mortality rate is quite high in that case." Ada's mother had gasped, but the doctor went on. "She needs surgery. A rib resection it is called, to remove the excess fluid."

"Surgery? When?"

"She will likely be stable for a few weeks. But the longer the fluid is allowed to pool, the worse it will get. Eventually it will entrap the lung, which will almost certainly lead to collapse." He had stood up then as if he had said all there was to say.

"You can't do it now?" Ada's mother had asked, jumping up when he stood.

"The surgery?"

"Yes. I can pay you directly."

"The fee for that particular surgery is fifteen pounds."

At the sound of the number, Ada watched her mother's face drop.

"You could take her to the General Hospital, of course. As she is no longer infectious, they may well admit her."

"But you can do it yourself?"

"Yes, but—"

"I rather you do it here, then."

"They have made many improvements in the hospital in the last years. It is perfectly safe."

But Ada knew that her mother did not trust the hospital, just as she did not trust the bank or any institution aside from school and the church. To her, the hospital, overcrowded with the infirm, was simply the place where people went to die.

"Fifteen pounds?" her mother asked again.

"Yes. And the cost for mileage, naturally."

After the physician had gone, Ada knelt next to Millicent's bed and stroked her hand lightly along Millicent's back. She had thought her sister had fallen asleep, but after a few minutes Millicent whispered, "I'm scared."

Ada slowed her hand. "Don't be," she said.

"It's coming for me."

Even without asking, Ada knew what she meant. She reached down and squeezed Millicent's hand. "It's far away yet." Ada swallowed hard. Softly she said, "It won't be coming for a well long time."

Millicent said nothing, and because she was kneeling anyway, in her mind Ada started saying a prayer. But in the middle of the prayer, through the open window, Ada heard a strange, muffled sound. Her mother had not come back inside after seeing the doctor out to his carriage, and now, Ada realized, standing in the garden behind the house where she thought no one could hear her, her mother was crying. In all Ada's sixteen years, she had never heard her mother cry, but she was sure, as she knelt there, that that was what the sound was.

It was the very next day that Ada packed her things and boarded the ship.

||||||

SHE WAS STILL walking, still looking for signs in shop windows advertising employment within when, up ahead in the middle of the road, Ada saw a swarm of people bunched like bees on a scrap of honeycomb, shouting and gesturing down at the ground. If Millicent had been with her, she would have tugged Ada's elbow and urged her to keep walking, to steer clear of a scene that had nothing whatsoever to do with them, but Millicent was always trying to stay out of trouble and Ada, according to her mother, was the opposite. Forever running toward something, her mother often said.

Ada walked up to the edge of the crowd and stood on her toes, straining to see. There were maybe a dozen people standing around, talking over each other and pointing, and in the center of everyone, Ada saw a young man lying still on the ground, his eyes closed, his hat halfway off his head.

"What happened?" she asked.

No one answered her.

Besides the hat, the young man was wearing a dirty blue work shirt and khaki trousers crusted with mud.

"He dead?" Ada asked, but again no one answered her. Then she saw the man twitch. She glanced around at all the people standing over him, men and women alike, dark faces and light, all of them shouting and waving but doing nothing to help. Without thinking twice, Ada shoved her way through the crowd and knelt down next to the man.

Somebody gasped. A man yelled, "Don't touch him! He's sick as a dog!"

Up close, Ada could see his chest rise and fall. His hands were clenched at his side. His olive skin was slick with either rainwater or sweat.

Ada leaned over the sack on top of her thighs and said to him, "It's all right."

Around her, the people in the crowd kept clamoring—"Leave him be!" "You're a fool!"—but Ada ignored them. She stayed bent forward and watched the man's face. Then, softly, she started to sing a hymn she knew. Her mother often cautioned Ada and Millicent not to sing in front of other people anywhere but in church. "God is the only one who can forgive voices like ours," she said laughingly. But hearing the songs in church always made Ada feel better, and as this man was suffering, Ada thought maybe the smallest bit of a song would bring him some peace. When the man unclenched his hands, she was pleased to see she was right. She glanced at his chest. Still breathing, it seemed.

Ada sat back on her heels and peered up at the faces around her. "He needs a doctor," she said.

Several people nodded, but nobody moved.

"We need to get him to a hospital," she said.

"There's a field hospital near," someone shouted.

"No, if he sick with Chagres fever, he need the hospital at Ancón," another voice said.

From the ground, Ada asked, "How far is Ancón?"

A man wearing suspenders at the front edge of the crowd said, "Too far to walk. He got to go on a hospital train. They come regular, but I don't know myself when the next one arrives." He blinked with each word that he spoke.

Ada said, "The hospital train . . . it comes to the station here?"

"Yes."

The station was only two blocks away. "Okay, then, let's go."

The man stopped his blinking and opened his eyes wide as two moons. "I'm not touching him, no."

"But you said it yourself. We have to get him onto the hospital train."

The man shook his head. "He got the fever from what I can see."

Frustrated, still kneeling, Ada scanned the crowd, and when she spotted two of the strongest-looking men in it, she pointed to each of them and said, "Come and help me lift him now."

The two men were Albert Laurence from Port-au-Prince and Wesley Barbier from Fort-Liberté. Though they had both come from Haiti, they were strangers to each other before that day—Albert worked at one of the machine shops in Empire and Wesley was stationed at Culebra setting off dynamite—but after that day they would become lifelong friends, and years on they would still reminisce about the time a young girl with the determination of the apostle Paul and the courage of Ruth plucked the two of them out of a crowd and enlisted them do something that both of them were terrified to do.

The pair stepped forward and lifted the sick man up. One held his armpits and the other his feet, and together they started down the street toward the station house. Ada hurried next to them. They had to stop twice to adjust their grip. Neither of them spoke, but Ada saw them exchange wordless glances every now and again. Numerous people from the crowd followed behind.

Soon they were at the railroad station, a small wooden depot where a locomotive idled. Two passenger cars were coupled to the engine and behind those, two empty flatcars. The men hoisted the young man up onto the bed of one of the flatcars, and Albert, who knew English well enough to get by, asked the engineer, who was seated in the cab up front, to take the man to the hospital at Ancón.

"This is not a hospital train!" the engineer shouted down.

With her heart beating fast, Ada strode up to the engine herself. "There's a man on this train who needs the hospital now."

"But I have told you already, this is not a hospital train."

"He needs a doctor."

"I am sorry, but that is not me."

"Please!"

"He will have to arrive there some other way. This is not a hospital train. This is a passenger train, I'm afraid."

Ada gritted her teeth. "You have your passenger."

The engineer shrugged.

Ada huffed and glanced back at the flatcar. Everyone from the street who had walked to the station was huddled around.

Then someone shouted, "His lips gone blue!"

Ada turned to the engineer again, sitting high in his cab. "He's dying!" she said.

The engineer poked his head out the window and looked back to see, but he gave no indication that he was willing to move.

Indignation spiraled up within Ada. She had half a mind to yank open the door of the engine and drive the train herself. Instead, she opened her sack and dug her hand deep inside and pulled out one of the two crowns she had left. She took a deep breath and held it up. "If I give you this, you will take him?"

The engineer looked down. He leaned out of the cab far enough to snatch the coin from Ada's hand. For an instant, she had the sinking thought that he had taken her money and even so would not do what she had asked, but then she heard the blast of the whistle. Suddenly, the train lurched ahead.

It was still in her sight when Albert, whose name Ada would never know, walked up to her, smiling, and shook her hand. She smiled in return before watching him walk away.

She hadn't realized how hard her heart had been beating until the crowd fully dispersed. The sun was high in the sky. In less than one day, she had spent more than half of her money—one coin to save herself from starving and another to hopefully save a young man's life. The skirt of her dress was filthy where she had knelt down, and her boots were caked to the ankles with mud.

Carrying her sack, Ada stepped down off the train platform.

Directly across the street was a white man in a crisp white linen suit staring at her. He had one hand in his breast pocket beneath his lapel. He slid it out and started walking toward her. Ada tightened her jaw, bracing herself for something, though she was not sure what. Notice from the ship captain that she had not paid her passage? Something else she had already done wrong?

When the man crossed the street and came to where Ada stood, he stopped. "You weren't frightened?" he asked.

Through brass-rimmed spectacles that glinted beneath the brim of his pristine white hat, he peered at her with cool blue eyes. He was somebody important. That much was clear. "He was sick, you know. With malaria, no doubt."

Ada nodded.

"But you were not frightened of catching it yourself?"

"No."

"Why not?"

"I believe the Lord will take care."

The man pushed up his spectacles, though they had not slid down and thus had nowhere to go. "Where are you from?"

"Bridgetown, Barbados."

"And what is your name?"

"Ada Bunting."

"You are here for the purposes of the canal, I presume?"

"I am here for the purposes of finding a job. I heard there is plenty of work in Panama."

"And do you have a job? Currently?"

"Currently no, but I am looking for one."

The man arched an eyebrow and beneath his clipped mustache gave away the barest hint of a smile. "I believe you can stop looking," he said. "Come with me."

7

FRANCISCO'S SON OMAR HAD NOT BEEN HOME IN DAYS. THAT WAS UNUSUAL.

Francisco stood on the dirt road that led up to the house and waited that first night, crossing his arms and uncrossing them and crossing them again, impatient, listening for footsteps in the dark. He heard crickets singing in the weeds and the rustle of the ocean, but there were no sounds to indicate the boy's approach. The moon was behind the clouds. After a while, so tired he could hardly stand, Francisco went back inside and burned a candle and waited in a stiff wooden chair. He fell asleep there with his head bent back over one of the slats, and when he woke to the crowing roosters in the morning he had a pain that reached from the top of his scalp all the way down between his shoulder blades. Trying to stretch it out only made the pain worse. He rubbed his neck with his fingers to no avail. Slowly he stood up and shuffled to Omar's bedroom at the back of the house. His son was not there. Francisco went back outside, this time into the bright blaring sun, and stood again on the road, peering down the length of it. It was bordered by tall grass and small fruit trees, and the roadbed was muddied at this time of year—muddied but today untouched. Theirs was the only house this far out at the edge of the bay. No one else came this way. If the mud showed no footprints, then it meant that Omar had not come home.

Francisco trudged inside. He could have stood outside all day, but what would that accomplish? He had work to do, fish to catch and to sell. He could go looking for the boy, too, he supposed, but how? Aimlessly walking through fields and city streets, calling Omar's name? Going to La Boca and hoping to find a single errant boy among thousands of men? Both would be pointless, and, as for the latter, he refused to step foot there. La Boca was Francisco's name for the canal, how he thought of it in his mind: a mouth, a gaping hole, ravenously consuming everything in its path. It was as his hero, the great Belisario Porras, had said: Panamá was being swallowed up by the United States. Francisco refused to be swallowed, too. He refused to wade into enemy territory among that army of invaders. That his son decided to do it day after day was a grave disappointment, a humiliation that he found nearly intolerable.

The next morning, Francisco went out to sea and did what he had done his entire life: fish. It was the same thing his father before him had done, one of the truly honorable professions, Francisco believed. For as long as people had inhabited this land, they had fished from its waters, its rivers and seas. The very name Panamá meant "abundance of fish."

Francisco unfastened his boat, which was tied to a post that stood between two large rocks on the shore, and climbed inside. He shoved himself off and battled against the choppy, brusque waves until he was out far enough to cast his net into the water, then slowly he paddled. The boat wobbled. The sky was pink with morning light. As he paddled, he stared at his hands, at his fingers that would not work the way they used to. They were stiff and stubborn. Like him, he supposed. They hurt when he held the paddle these days. Where was Omar? Why had he not come home? Had something happened to him? Francisco tried to put that last thought out of his mind. Maybe it was nothing. After all, Omar was old enough now that he made his own choices, as he had made abundantly clear. Maybe he had found a new place to stay, a place all to himself, and had not told him about it. And of course Omar would *not* tell him since they were not speaking and had not been speaking for all of six months. So maybe that was it—a new place—that was all. And yet, Francisco felt the frantic pulse of a hummingbird inside his chest. He sighed and peered over the side of the boat at the deep, murky water rippling past. Every day out here by himself, he tried to see through it, down to the bottom, to the things that were lost. But he never saw what he wanted to see.

||||||

THE CITY FISH market was attached to another, larger market that sold poultry and fruit. Every day after netting his catch, Francisco paddled over, tied his boat at the pier, and hauled his bag up onto land. He carried it through the stench and noise of the other market until he got to the fish market, where he set the bag down and dragged it across the slick, bloody floor straight to the stall of the only buyer he ever used, a man named Joaquín who lived in the city and who, Francisco had found, paid the best prices of anyone there.

Joaquín was a bear of a man, with broad, rounded shoulders and a neck as wide as his head, but his distinguishing feature was the grin he commonly had on his face. Francisco had been doing business with him for nearly twenty years by then, and although the grin went away at times, it always came back.

"My friend! How are you?" Joaquín said when Francisco walked up.

Francisco did not answer, and Joaquín bent down to get a good look at his face. "You look terrible," Joaquín said.

"I did not sleep well."

Joaquín patted the table next to him. "Dump them out here. Hopefully the fish today look better than you."

The catch that morning had been chiefly cod and corvina, with one lone lobster somehow mixed in. Everything was still stiff-alive, in the liminal state between life and death, and when Francisco poured the fish out onto the table, they twitched.

With his bare hands, Joaquín began to sort through. "Why didn't you sleep well?" he asked. "You had bad dreams?"

"No."

"No? That is like me. I never have a bad dream. I never have a good dream, either. When I sleep, I sleep. Valentina, however, is a different story. My wife has the sorts of dreams that wake her up in the middle of the night. But the worst part is that she proceeds to wake *me* up to tell me about them, as if there is a rule that we should share the same dream. I love my wife as you know, and we share many things, but I do not believe we need to share that. 'Let me sleep, woman!' I want to say."

Francisco nodded. He knew Joaquín loved to talk.

"One time she had a dream about a horse whose four legs were cut off at the knees and yet it was trying to run, and she woke up sobbing. 'Isn't it sad?' she kept asking me. 'But it is not a real horse,' I pointed out. A mistake. I should not have said that. She went from being sad about an imaginary horse to being mad at me for not being sad about the imaginary horse. We were up for an hour in a fight over it!" Joaquín shook his head. "Lately she has been having bad dreams about the house. The house disappears in a puff of smoke, the house is devoured by cockroaches. I told you, didn't I, about the rumor circulating that everyone in her hometown will have to move? Everyone! Even her sister, who still lives in their childhood home."

Francisco nodded again. Joaquín had told him numerous times that the North Americans wanted to build a dam in Gatún, causing everyone in that town to move.

"Yes, well, I try not to judge. Why is it that her sister still lives in that house in the first place? And she lives there alone! Why is she not married by now? Don't answer that. I know the answer, and if you saw her, you would know the answer, too. But there must be some man somewhere who does not mind her looks." Joaquín grinned. "As I said, I try not to judge. And of course I do understand that she would have an attachment to the house where she grew up. Myself? I have been to that house, and between you and me, I prefer my apartment in the city. Even so, I do understand. The house is important—to both her sister and Valentina. They have memories there. The thought of having to desert it, of it being destroyed . . ." Joaquín shook his head. All this time he had been sorting the fish, and now he stopped. "I'm sorry. Let's talk about happier things. How is your boy? I do not hear much about him anymore."

Francisco grimaced. The last thing he wanted was to talk about Omar.

"Oye, did you hear me? I asked how is your boy? What is he doing these days?"

Francisco scanned the market, searching for a way he might change the subject, but all he saw was vendors doing business with clients, everyone around him carrying on. The sound of voices mingled in the air amid the brackish odor of fish.

"Have you taught him how to fish yet?" Joaquín asked.

"No."

"No? How old is he now?"

"Seventeen."

"Well, what are you waiting for?"

Years ago, Francisco had taken the boy fishing. He did not always know how to be a good father, the ways to guide a young boy, but he knew how to fish, and that, if nothing else, was something he could pass along to his son. The outing, however, had not gone as planned. Omar had seemed terrified from the moment they pushed off from the shore, gripping the sides of the boat, and by the time Francisco asked him to open the net on the floor by his feet, somehow, in unrolling it, Omar managed to tangle the whole thing. It had taken Francisco a full ten minutes to unravel it, and when at last that was done, he showed Omar how to tie it to the side of the boat. A basic knot, but even at that, Omar had struggled. "Calm yourself," Francisco had said with some concern. Maybe the boy was not cut out for fishing. But it was not until the poorly knotted net slipped into the ocean that Francisco suspected the true source of Omar's fear. The water was powerful, and Omar had a connection to it beyond what he knew. Yet it seemed that the boy could sense it somehow. Quickly, Francisco had snatched the net from the water before it sank, and when he sat back on his heels, holding it up, he had said, "You see? Everything is okay." But Omar sat rigidly, looking as though he might cry. He did not relax until they stepped back onto land. By then, Francisco knew with certainty what he had seen. Not wanting to subject Omar to a torment that was beyond his comprehension, he did not ask his son to go fishing again.

"Eh, maybe it makes no difference," Joaquín said, brushing past Francisco's silence.

"What?"

Joaquín began weighing the fish as he went on. "Do you know the number of times I have offered to take my son Horacio around the market, to teach him about my profession? But each time I bring it up he tells me no. 'The world is changing,' he says. 'The world is bigger than fish.' Of course he is right in a way. The world is changing before our eyes, is it not? But that has always been so, and still people need fish." Joaquín frowned at the cod he had just set on the scale. "This one is not good. I can keep it to feed to the dogs, but I cannot pay you for this one."

Francisco looked. "What is wrong with it?"

"The color is not good."

Joaquín grabbed the fish by the tail and flung it across the room. It skidded across the floor and stopped when it hit the wall. Immediately, three dogs crowded around and began fighting for it.

Joaquín grinned. "Now they have a treat." He laid the next fish on the scale and carried on. "The problem with young people is that they will not listen to us. They think that after spending half the amount of time on this earth, they somehow know twice as much as we do."

Joaquín was almost done weighing. So far there were seventeen fish today by Francisco's count, not including the one that had gone to the dogs. Seventeen fish should come out to 35¢, give or take, enough to buy another day of existence. Of course, Omar was earning money now, too, but Francisco considered it blood money, and even if Omar had offered to help pay for their expenses—things like coffee and bread—Francisco would have refused.

Joaquín slapped the last fish down on the scale. Satisfied, he tossed it onto the glossy heap with the others. On the floor beneath the table was a pink puddle of blood.

"Eighteen today, friend, plus the lobster," Joaquín said. He counted out the coins and handed them to Francisco.

"So what will he do?" Francisco asked.

"Who?"

"Horacio."

Joaquín rolled his eyes. "I do not know. He earns money here and there, but he does not have the sort of job he can rely on. Nothing steady, you understand? Valentina tells me that just because he has no interest in the fish market does not mean all is lost. He could still find a respectable job. As long as he does not work for the Yankees and their canal, I guess." Joaquín snorted.

Francisco's face burned. He stayed quiet.

"Children," Joaquín said. "What can you do?"

Slowly, Francisco nodded. But standing there, he felt exposed, as if Joaquín knew something dark and shameful about him, or anyway about Omar, which by extension implicated him, and suddenly he just wanted to leave, to get out from under the glare.

He turned to go. As he walked away, he heard Joaquín yell, "Until tomorrow, paisa!" But Francisco, in his searing humiliation, said nothing in return. And when one of the dogs, a dog with speckled black-and-white fur, came over sniffing at his feet, Francisco shoved it aside so hard that it whimpered, and he would feel bad about that for the rest of the day.

||||||

TWENTY YEARS AGO, the first time Francisco saw Esme, she was standing in the square in front of the Catedral Metropolitana. She was wearing a bright purple dress with a ruffled top and a skirt that hung to the ground. Her raven-dark hair was parted in the center and pulled into a tight bun at the nape of her neck. At the time Francisco was twenty-two years old. He had seen many striking women before, but not a woman like Esme, who, even from a distance, Francisco could tell had the darkest eyes he had ever encountered, deep-set and rimmed by the darkest lashes, like the wings of a bat. She had a mole beneath the outer corner of her left eye, like a drop of ink, as though the darkness had overflowed and left a mark.

Francisco was mesmerized. He could not stop looking at her. Esme was talking to a friend in the square, and when she sensed Francisco staring, she turned her head to meet his gaze. Francisco felt himself shiver. Now the darkness was trained upon him. Her friend turned, too, but Francisco took no notice of her. Everything other than Esme dissolved. He could see only her, etched out in relief from the rest of the world.

The day was overcast, and clouds roiled in the sky, promising rain. Francisco walked across the square as if drawn. He could barely feel his feet touching the ground. When he came to Esme he said, "I beg your pardon. My name is Francisco. I would be pleased to meet you." He held out his hand. She did not give him hers— neither her hand nor her name. She smelled like a flower. He repeated himself. "I beg your pardon. My name is Francisco. I would be pleased to meet you." She kept her dark eyes pinned on him and he felt oddly entranced. There was some kind of magic in the depth of those eyes. Her friend giggled. At that, Francisco realized he still had his hand out in midair. He tried to lower his arm but found that he couldn't. His arm simply would not move. It was as if it had been turned into stone. Could that be? Panicked, Francisco broke Esme's gaze and looked down. As soon as he did, his arm fell to his side. He wiggled his fingers to make sure they still worked. He shook his arm and then shook his head, wondering what had happened to him.

Afraid to look up again, Francisco backed away, then turned and hurried across the square. He ducked into an alley and flattened himself against a cool wall. After a minute, he peeked around the corner, but when he looked, both the girl and her friend were gone.

||||||

IT WAS ONLY a dream. It must have been. That is what Francisco kept telling himself in the days after. Lunacy to think that a woman's gaze could render him, or even part of him, immobile. He was a man who dealt in the physical world. If he could hold something in his

hand, then he knew it existed. If he could smell something or taste
it or hear it or see it, then he believed it was real. Everything else—
mystery, faith, magic most of all—held little meaning for him.

Down the road from his house, nearly a half mile away, there
was a woman, Doña Ruiz, who claimed she could see the future,
that one's fate could be mapped out in the lines around one's mouth,
and that she could communicate with the dead. People came from
all over the city to see her, and once, after the fire of 1894, a fire that
left five thousand people without homes, the line for her services
was so long that it stretched all the way down the long dirt road
to Francisco's small house. Francisco had gone out to the line of
unfortunate beings and studied them one by one—a woman with
a gold hoop through her nose, a man who stood biting his nails to
the quick, a woman holding the hands of two children who were
only as tall as her knees. The line went on and on. He looked at the
people with pity, and when they looked back at him and asked him,
as some of them did, what he was doing, he laughed. What was *he*
doing? What were *they* doing but wasting their time? Even after Doña
Ruiz walked partway down the road and shouted at him to leave her
paying customers alone, Francisco laughed. Even after Doña Ruiz
crossed her eyes and spit on the grass and said, "You will see," and
even after five dead frogs appeared belly-up on his property and his
best hen stopped squawking and died, Francisco merely shrugged.
Others might have thought there was something magical about these
occurrences, but he knew better. There had been so much rain that
week that the frogs had simply drowned, and the hen—well, she was
just old.

But the girl made Francisco rethink all of that.

He went back to the square, hoping to see her again. He stood
in the exact same spot and looked in the exact same direction at the
exact same time of day, but she did not appear.

And then one day when he was out in his boat, he saw another
boat in the distance, not too far away. That in itself was typical. Other
men fished those waters, of course. What was strange, what caught

Francisco's breath in his throat, was that the boat was sailing toward him, and when it was thirty or so feet away, he saw that the person inside the boat was the girl. She was wearing a simple white dress this time, but her raven hair was pulled back in a bun at the nape of her neck just like before, so glossy that it shone like glass in the sun. Francisco waved, but she did not wave back. Quickly, Francisco dragged in his nets and paddled out to where she was, his heart beating hard. The morning was bright and perfectly clear. He paddled closer and closer . . . and then he seemed to sail right through her. He looked back over his shoulder, but now there was only the open empty surface of the water. He turned in every direction, and she was not there. But she had been there only a moment earlier! Francisco peered over the side of his boat and gazed into the water. Had she capsized? Or sunk? That seemed impossible, but how many other explanations could there be? Francisco sat back on his heels, mystified. She had been there and now she was not. Was he losing his mind? He had been a perfectly rational man until now. It was as though this woman, whoever she was, had cast a spell over him, as though one instance of looking straight into her eyes had been enough to make him completely possessed.

Francisco smelled her before he saw her again. He was at the fish market, selling off his catch, and Joaquín was standing in front of him with his hands in the pockets of his stained apron, waiting to see what Francisco had brought. They were new acquaintances then, two young men who had done only a few transactions with each other. As Francisco opened the bag that day, it released not the briny, coarse odor of fish but a powdery, delicate fragrance.

"Do you smell that?" he asked.

"Smell what?" Joaquín said. "The fish?"

"No."

"Because if the fish smells rotten already, then I do not want to buy it."

"Not the fish." Francisco inhaled the sweetness again. "Something . . . like flowers."

"Flowers?" Joaquín said. "We are in a fish market, not a field, my friend!"

Francisco, still holding the top of the bag open so that Joaquín could inspect the fish for their fleshiness and sheen, turned to look back over his shoulder. The powdery aroma grew stronger. The market was crowded. Raw fish lay on pallets and tables, dripping seawater and blood onto the floor. Sellers wandered about. Francisco kept turning his head, trying to identify the source of the sweet smell, when across the market he saw the dark-eyed girl who had been haunting his dreams. Instantly, he dropped the bag. Joaquín yelled, "Hey! Where are you going? We are not done here!" Francisco walked quickly, afraid that, as had happened on the water, as soon as he got to her, she would disappear again, but when he was within several feet of her, she was still there, and as he barreled closer, she looked at him in alarm. He stopped when he was right in front of her. The powder-like scent was overpowering now. Francisco reached out his hand to touch her arm, just to make sure she was real. She creased her dark brows and yanked her arm away.

"I am sorry," he said. "I wanted to see . . ." He had the good sense to stop himself and clear his throat. "I beg your pardon. My name is Francisco. I would be pleased to meet you."

As she had in the square, the girl stood still, expressionless. As he had not in the square, Francisco also stood still. By now, he had ascribed so much power to her—though in actuality she had done nothing at all—that he was almost afraid of her. Almost. This time, though, he refused to run.

"If you would allow me," he said, "I would be honored to take you for a walk."

He waited, looking into her eyes, awash in the smell of flowers, his heart beating with the wildness of the wind-whipped sea.

Esme looked him in the eye and was impressed to find that for as long as she looked, he held her gaze. She had not recognized him at first as he charged across the market toward her, but now—yes, she remembered his face. He was handsome. He had a strong chin and dark, hooded eyes. As she looked at him, she thought about how all her life men had been scared of her, like skittish field mice. Men looked at her and stared, and she had learned to let them because usually it went no further than that. They stared for a while and then they tore themselves away, shaking their heads as if there was a ringing in their ears or a cobweb in their brain that they were trying to work loose. The bolder men would, after staring, say something banal, and Esme had found that if she did nothing at all, it rattled them so much that they scurried away. Bemused and disappointed, she watched them go. Men were cowards. Every once in a while, she looked at herself in a pane of glass held at an angle to the sun to see what they saw. But when she looked, she saw merely a girl with dark eyes and a long aquiline nose. She saw no reason why a man should run from her in fear. And yet they did. And that was the last she saw of those men. None had the nerve to find her again and not one, in all her eighteen years, had had the balls to ask her out properly. Not one, until then.

||||||

THE COURTSHIP WAS easy, all things considered. Esme's family, Francisco learned, came from the mountains in the region of Veraguas. Tumultuous people, Francisco took this to mean. Ascent and descent was in their blood, a jagged up-and-down life. And it turned out he was right. Esme was a woman of many moods, mercurial until the end. One day Francisco would see her standing at the stove, stirring a pot of sancocho, smiling sweetly and humming a tune, and the next day she would lock herself in the bathroom and weep or sit in a chair and stare at the floor, and nothing Francisco could say or do seemed to pull her out of the morass. He pressed his ear to the bathroom door and listened to her cry, but when he knocked, she would not answer, not even to tell him to go away. When she stared at the floor, he dragged a chair over and sat next to her, hoping she would glance up at him, but she did not.

Those were periods of darkness. A small pool in her soul flooded her, and Esme would sink, and though Francisco would offer his hand, she was either unable or unwilling to take it. It was best those days just to let her be. Eventually, after a few hours or, at the extreme end, a few days, she would resurface and come back to him. In that way, being with Esme was an exercise in patience. Francisco learned that if he waited, she would always return.

And when she did, away from the darkness, Esme exuded incredible light. No one he knew laughed like she did, a full-body laugh that sometimes caused her to snort, and she was not embarrassed by that. No one else made him feel like she did—more aware of everything, infinitely more alive. He experienced with her the kind of happiness that felt so out of proportion to everything he knew that he had to stop and ask himself sometimes, *Is this happiness? Is this what it feels like?*, just to be sure. He was, simply put, taken with her, and to Francisco's surprise, she seemed equally taken with him.

One night as they lay in the bed, which smelled thoroughly of violets now, and Francisco kissed her shoulder across to her neck, Esme murmured, "The only one . . ."

"The only one what?" Francisco asked.

"Mmmmm?"

"The only one, you said."

"Ah." She ran her hand through his hair. "You were the only one with the courage to come after me."

But it was not courage, he knew. Something else drew him to her, like a wave to the shore. It was, he had started to believe, akin to divine fate. He almost laughed at himself for thinking it. Divinity! Fate! Ideas he would have scoffed at in the past. But Esme had changed something elemental in him. Because of her, he believed in things that he had not believed in before. Why, earlier that same week he had walked to the house of Doña Ruiz and found her sitting on her front patio, stroking the back of an iguana she held in her lap. "Congratulations," she had said as Francisco approached. "I hear you have been married." Francisco stopped in the road. It was untrue. He had felt himself lean toward laughter, his old response to the nonsense of Doña Ruiz, and he chided himself for coming to her. He had come to get her advice, to see how to handle Esme's erratic disposition, not for a confused message about something she had heard—and heard from where? Doña Ruiz went on. "I am sorry. I said that too soon. I have heard it, but you have not yet. Leave now and come back in a few months' time so I can say it again. It will make more sense to you then." She shrugged. "Sometimes I get ahead of myself." Francisco had been flummoxed. He had stood in the dirt road under the furious sun and looked at this woman petting an iguana in the shade of her patio. What was she talking about? And had she really just told him to leave? He had been on the verge of leaving of his own volition, but once she had suggested it, he almost wanted to stay out of spite. But also—he did want to go. He wanted to go and never come back. Francisco stood in the road, paralyzed by indecision. The maddening thing was that Doña Ruiz seemed to recognize all that was going through his mind at that moment, for she smiled at him. Patronizingly, Francisco thought. If he left now, she would believe it was because of her influence. If he stayed, she would pat herself on the back for that, too. Occasionally when he was fishing, a school of fish swam beneath his boat from one side to the other. He watched them dart back and forth, but he lost sight of them sometimes. When that happened, he had learned, it was because the fish had gathered directly under the boat and hovered there in the shadow, but to him up above they had effectively disappeared. Francisco walked over to a large boulder along the road and sat down behind it. He circled his arms around his knees and made himself small enough that Doña Ruiz could not see him. He sat still. He stayed there until dark when he heard Doña Ruiz get up off the patio and walk inside. Only then did he stand up, too, and return home.

He had told Esme none of that, of course. But he mulled it over himself. What could explain such behavior? It was so unlike him. Hours huddled against a boulder, that day in the square, what had happened to his arm, the afternoon on the boat, the fragrance of violets in the fish market. What could explain all of that besides the belief that some greater force was at work, something deific that had impelled him toward her? Francisco had not thought that a woman like Esme could exist, but even after he accepted that she was in fact very real, it diminished none of her mystery. She was always to him, from the first moment back in the square, the most magical being ever to walk the earth.

||||||

THEY WERE MARRIED in the Catholic Church by a Catholic priest who delivered the entire Mass in Latin, so Francisco had no idea what he was saying. The priest's words and incantations were either a blessing or a curse, but Esme smiled so beatifically throughout the ceremony that Francisco had to believe it was the former. Only later, after everything happened, would he wonder if he had been right.

What Doña Ruiz had said that strange day now made perfect sense, as she had predicted it would, but Francisco did not go back to her house as she had instructed. There was no need. Later he would wonder about that, too—whether by not going back, he had made a costly mistake, whether he had angered Doña Ruiz perhaps, enough that she cast a spell that determined his fate.

After the wedding, Esme moved into the small house overlooking the bay. The earthen floors darkened when it rained and the thatched roof leaked sometimes during the worst downpours, but that was of little concern, especially in those early days when Francisco and Esme were both so fortified by love that it seemed that nothing could go wrong. When they left the front door open, as they often did, the smell of the sea stepped right inside, mixing with the smell of violets, and when they made love, Francisco licked Esme's skin till his tongue stung with salt.

They lived too far from the city to walk there often with ease, especially in the heat, so while Francisco went fishing during the day, Esme stayed home. She was used to the vitality of the city, used to strolling with her girlfriends and buying food on the street. In her new life she was happy but bored. She picked limes from the trees and squeezed them till they were pulpy and dry. She drank all the juice. She saved the seeds and when she had collected enough, she pierced each one with a needle and, using a long strand of her hair, threaded them together into a necklace that she wore. She walked down to the water where the sea stretched like a blue velvet field to the edges of the world in three directions and plopped down in the sand, listening to the faint sigh of the water as it skidded up and dragged back out. It came again and again, and as long as she listened, she could never decide whether the sigh was from sadness or surrender, or whether they were one and the same. When the sun was too hot, she sat in the shade of the banana trees and watched processions of ants. She chewed her nails and spit them out. She cooked patacones, frying them once, then smashing them between two flat rocks and frying them again before sprinkling them with salt. She ate them, and then she made more. She lit candles and prayed. She touched herself not because her new husband failed to satisfy her desires but because there was nothing else to do and because it felt good. In the evenings after he had gone to the market to sell off the day's catch, Francisco came home. Esme stood on the shore and watched as he tied up the boat and climbed over the rocks to where, in the frail evening light, she was waiting for him.

||||||

QUICKLY, ESME BECAME pregnant, and for the next nine months after that, from the roof to the floor, the small house was bursting with joy. And from her head to her toes, Esme was bursting with life. Her dark eyes glowed, her skin seemed to shimmer even at night. She asked for octopus to eat and coconut water to drink. She lay in the bed with her feet in Francisco's lap while he counted her toes and she laughed. Her hair, already thick and dark, grew six inches in a month and before long was down to her knees.

In the middle of his sleep, Francisco heard Esme sometimes,

awake, talking to the baby, narrating the recipe for arroz con pollo or explaining how to judge when a papaya was ripe or, most often, singing him songs.

It was possible, Francisco would think later, that every human being only gets a certain allotment of joy and theirs had come in a windfall, the entirety of it used up across those nine glorious months. For after the baby was born, at what should have been the most jubilant time in their lives, Esme turned suddenly morose. For the first few weeks, she did not get out of bed. Staying in bed was one thing. Francisco understood that her body, after creating a new life, needed time to recover. But her spirit as she lay in the bed was melancholy. She did nothing but stare at the wall. She was naked under a thin bedsheet that was stained with brown spots of dried blood and yellow crust, and though Francisco offered to wash the sheets and pull a nightdress over her head, when he said these things, Esme did not move, much less answer. When he brought her food, she did not eat. A few times Francisco asked if she had any ideas for names for their son, but she maintained her silence. Finally, tired of saying "el bebé" all the time, Francisco proposed Omar because "mar" meant sea. Esme did not object.

During those weeks Francisco did not fish. From the very first day, when Omar cried, Francisco brought him to Esme and nestled him up to her swollen breast. Esme lay still on her side, staring at the sun-streaked wall. Omar whimpered and cried.

"He is hungry," Francisco pleaded. "He needs to eat."

Finally Francisco reached down himself and cupped Esme's heavy breast in his hand and lifted it up just an inch to meet Omar's small mouth. The baby rooted around. Then, miraculously, he began to suck. The entire time Esme hardly batted an eye.

When Omar ate and slept were the sole times Francisco had any reprieve. And then he was so exhausted that all he could manage to do was wash his armpits and between his legs, or take a shit, or eat fried fish or a cup of rice, the only two things he knew how to cook, and sit by himself and worry about Esme, about the way things had turned, and in the next second try not to worry. He kept telling himself it would all be okay. He prayed to God to make it so.

And then one day when Francisco woke in the morning, Esme was not there. Ecstatic, thinking she had emerged from her melancholy at last, Francisco got out of bed. Omar, not even two months old, was asleep at the foot of the bed, swaddled in a blanket so meticulously wrapped that it amplified Francisco's hope. He rushed out of the bedroom expecting to find Esme at the stove, making something to eat, or bathing herself finally, dabbing on the violet water that he loved so much, but everywhere he looked, there was no trace of her. On a hunch, Francisco went outside. Before he even walked down to the shore, he could see that the boat was gone. His stomach dropped. He ran down to the water and screamed, "Esme!" into the white morning sun. "Esme! Esme! Esme!" Francisco flung himself into the ocean and started to swim. He swam like mad until he reached the boat, bobbing listlessly on the water. He held on to the side and looked all around. But unlike the instance more than a year earlier when he had paddled out to meet her, Esme had not only vanished—she was gone.

|||||

FRANCISCO THOUGHT OF all this again now that Omar had not come home. Omar had inherited certain traits from his mother—her dark, brooding eyes, her sensitive nature, her slender frame. And of course the one time that Francisco had taken the boy out on the water he had witnessed Omar's reaction to it—but Francisco hoped against hope that his son was not like her in that way. If he had believed in a benevolent God, he would have prayed, but he didn't—not anymore—so he merely hoped and he waited for Omar to return.

8

WITH HIS EYES CLOSED, OMAR LAY ON HIS BACK, SHIVERING. HIS HEAD THROBBED.
When he clenched his fingers he could feel the smoothness of a bedsheet under him, and he knew that he was still in the hospital, though as hard as he tried he could not recall how he had gotten here.

Among the last things he remembered, he had gone for a walk after lunch, which was something he did every day while the other men in his gang dozed in the shade. He could have rested, too, he supposed, but since he was young, he had been in the habit of taking walks by himself, and he liked seeing places and people that took him outside of his otherwise insular life. Once, when he was eight years old, walking down the road that led away from his house, Doña Ruiz had called to him and said, "Why are you always out here, boy?"

Omar's father had warned him to avoid Doña Ruiz. "She can make people do very strange things," his father had claimed. "Like what?" Omar had asked. But his father had declined to elaborate and had merely said, "Keep your distance from her."

So when she called out to him that day, Omar did not immediately answer.

"Don't you speak?" Doña Ruiz asked. She was sitting on her front patio, wearing a long skirt that hung low in the space between her spread knees. "Come closer."

Omar did not move.

"I see," Doña Ruiz said. "Your father has filled your head with lies, is that it? Well, I have known your father for a long time, and few men more stubborn have ever walked on this earth." She smiled as if they were on the same side, and the smile made Omar feel less afraid. "Come, joven," she said.

It would be the first time in his life that Omar defied his father. Omar walked toward the house, through the yard that was scabbed with dirt and weeds.

"You are always out here by yourself," Doña Ruiz said when he was all the way up at the patio. "You don't go to school?"

Omar shook his head.

"I did not think so." She turned her head so that she was peering at him sideways, as though she were studying him, then she held up a finger and said, "Wait here." She got up slowly and waddled into the house, and when she returned she had a book in her hand. She came out to the edge of the patio. "Do you know how to read?"

Again Omar shook his head.

"I did not think so about that, either. Well, then, sit down, joven, sit."

Omar sat in the dirt, and Doña Ruiz shuffled back to her chair. She spread her knees wide again and opened the book on her lap. Then she started to read.

Omar did not know what she was reading, but he liked the sound of her voice. The rhythms of what she read were almost like a song. It was poetry, she told him, written by a Panamanian named Anselmo López, who was from the highlands of Chiriquí. López was known for writing about the splendor of nature, about the sun and the trees. One poem Doña Ruiz read was about a grasshopper, its nimble grace captured so perfectly in words that Omar was spellbound.

Every day for a week Omar went back and Doña Ruiz read a little bit more. He sat on the ground and she sat in her chair, and one day when it was so windy that the pages of the book flapped no matter how much Doña Ruiz held them down, she stopped in frustration and said, "What if you did it yourself?"

"What?"

"I could teach you to read."

"But I like listening to you."

"Ah, no. You will like this better. Look."

Doña Ruiz turned the book face out and ran her crooked finger beneath the words as she said them aloud. "You see, all the letters make their own sounds." Little by little, she taught him each letter's particular shape. She showed him how to connect those shapes to their sounds. Then how to set the sounds next to each other, like a string of pebbles, and let them clink together to make new sounds, sounds that filled up a word, and words that filled up a sentence, and sentences that filled up a page, and pages upon pages that filled up his mind.

And after he could do that, Doña Ruiz brought out a new book.

"The Bible," she announced. She explained how in this edition, for every page written in Spanish, there was a facing page in English. "Do not concern yourself with the English yet. For now, take it with you and read the Spanish when you can."

Omar hesitated.

Doña Ruiz said, "It will save you from feeling so lonely."

Still Omar did not take the book.

"I won't tell your father," Doña Ruiz said.

"No one has given me a gift before," Omar said.

Doña Ruiz smiled knowingly. "Take it. And once you have read every word, come and find me again."

Omar kept the book close. During the day, he sat on the rocks warmed by the sun and read. The book had a pebbled black leather cover and pages as thin as the membrane beneath the shell of a hard-boiled egg. He turned them one by one and used a blade of grass to mark his place. He did not understand everything that he read, nor did he always believe even what he did understand. But he kept going. Sometimes he compared the facing pages, one word at a time, to see which of the Spanish words he had come to recognize matched the English words on the other side. Certain words repeated often enough that he was able to learn the English for them this way. Eventually, he tried speaking the words in English out loud, but there was no way to know if he was pronouncing them right.

Months later, when he had read every word at least once through, Omar walked back up the road with the book under his arm. Doña Ruiz was there on her patio as though she were waiting for him.

"I finished," he said.

Doña Ruiz crossed herself and whispered, "En el nombre del Padre, y del Hijo y del Espíritu Santo."

Less fearful now, he walked up to the patio and gave her the book.

She smiled at him. "You need something else now, yes?"

"Yes."

He thought she meant he needed another book, but instead she said, "Bueno. I am getting older, you see. The things that were easy for me in my youth are not so anymore. I have items to pick up in the city sometimes. I used to walk to get them, but it takes me far too long now. Perhaps you could run into the city from time to time and bring my items to me."

That was how Omar, every so often, started making trips into the city on his own. It took him an hour and a half to walk there and back. Doña Ruiz would send him with slips of paper that he was to hand the person she had told him to find. She taught him a few phrases in English in case anything went awry. Things went awry more often than he expected—he lost the paper, or the person reading it could not decipher Doña Ruiz's handwriting, or he took a wrong turn—and when he had to speak English, the white men he was speaking to always looked shocked. Eventually Omar was walking to the city even when Doña Ruiz did not ask. He did not go to the market or to the bullfights. He went to the areas where the American immigrants gathered—the train station and the hotels—and he listened to them speak and wrote down what they said. He learned English this way, bit by bit. At home he practiced pronouncing the words out loud, saying them to the frogs and the butterflies, and even at night, he whispered sentences to himself, quiet enough that his father, who he knew would not approve, could not hear. Then he went back and learned more. When the Americans saw him, they often gave him odd, scornful looks, but Omar found that if he was quiet and kept his hands in his pockets, no one bothered him much.

That was the way he had walked ever since. Quietly, with his hands in his pockets. It was the way he had been walking after lunch through Empire, where not only Americans but people from every nation on earth, it seemed to Omar, were walking, too. Here no one looked at him with scorn, for in his work clothes and boots, he was one of them. His father had reservations about all of these people who had descended upon Panamá, but Omar felt proud to share his country with them, and every once in a while, when he gathered the nerve, he smiled at them or lifted his hat, hoping to make them feel welcome in this place that he called his home.

Lying in the hospital now, he remembered that he had been walking and then had passed a small bakery, and while usually he would have gazed longingly at the sugared desserts in the window, his lunch had not been sitting well in his stomach, and he had felt too nauseous for that. Suddenly he had felt dizzy, too. Across the street, he had seen an old woman sitting in a rocking chair, sewing with a needle and thread, and then the woman and her chair had both tilted sideways.

After that the only thing Omar could recall was something so peculiar that he wondered if he had imagined it. He remembered the voice of a girl singing to him.

||||||

THE DOCTOR ON rotation, Dr. Pierre Renaud, who had come from France to Panama against the advice of nearly everyone he knew, made his rounds. He had a smooth amethyst-colored stone that he kept in his right trouser pocket, and he rubbed it as he walked. He had found the stone once during a stroll along the Indrois River and had believed ever since that it was good luck. In all the years he had practiced medicine and carried it, the stone had not once let him down.

Pierre had been in Panama for just over a year, attending to patients in Ancón Hospital. There was another hospital at the Atlantic terminus in Colón, but the hospital at Ancón was the primary one. It was a sprawling campus of wards, kitchens, lavatories, nurse dormitories, and physicians' cottages, all connected by walkways. The wards themselves were designated by some combination of ailment, gender, and race, or by all three. Somewhat inexplicably, Pierre felt, he had been stationed in the colored men's ward.

Countless Frenchmen before him had been to Panama, of course. Some twenty-seven years earlier, they had come here to build their own canal. Pierre, who had been an adolescent at the time, had scarcely paid attention to the details, but he knew—as everyone did—that the effort had ended in spectacular collapse. The failure of the French. That was the sum of the story as it had been told. Pierre wanted, in his own small way, to rectify that, to prove that a Frenchman in Panama—and certainly a gifted Frenchman like himself—could succeed. But since the day he arrived, he had been stuck in the colored ward, and he was still puzzling over why that should be. Of course, a life was a life, a patient was a patient, of course of course, and he would do what was right, but still, it was a demoralizing assignment, and it bruised Pierre's pride.

In the American wards, which were situated in the finest locations, one could walk out onto large, screened verandas encircled by bright bougainvillea and fragrant rosebushes and take in a view that reached to Panama City. Or so he had heard. According to his colleagues, it was breathtaking. The best vista in all the tropics, they said.

In the ward where Pierre worked, Ward 13, there was neither a screened veranda nor a view. The space inside was long and narrow with metal beds lining the walls, every bed occupied by a man. Miserable men. One after the next. Men curled on their sides, men panting with thirst, men coughing up blood.

A year ago, when Pierre had first arrived, yellow fever was the chief concern. Every person with even the slightest chill feared that they had contracted it and would certainly die. Thousands did. Thankfully, yellow fever in Panama was now a thing of the past, due in large measure to Colonel William Crawford Gorgas, the white-haired Army doctor whom everyone, it seemed—even Pierre—liked.

Pierre had dined with Gorgas once, among a group of twenty or so other men and their wives. They had been served a wonderful rack of lamb, Pierre recalled, though the accompanying wine had left much to be desired. Pierre had been disappointed at that dinner not to have had the chance to speak with Gorgas himself, but even from afar he found Gorgas genial and charming.

Years earlier, as everyone knew, Gorgas had managed to rout yellow fever in disease-ridden Havana, and he had arrived at the start of the Panama project determined to do the same thing. His first directive had been that every open container with water be emptied at once, open containers being the places where *Stegomyia fasciata*, the species of mosquito that transmitted yellow fever, preferred to lay her eggs. Throughout the zone every saucer, barrel, can, and cistern was drained. In churches, the holy water in the fingerbowls was replaced each day. Any water that could not be poured out—puddles or rainwater held in the fold of leaves—was doused on the surface with oil to smother the larvae that might be wriggling below. Before long it was common to see fumigation brigades roaming about, gluing strips of newspaper over windows and doors, placing pans of sulfur inside houses and shops, setting them aflame, letting the resulting smoke suffocate every mosquito it touched. Other brigade men spent their days tacking up screens in every American building, which itself, from what Pierre understood, was a bureaucratic battle. But Gorgas succeeded. By the end of 1906, yellow fever was effectively gone.

The challenge before Gorgas now was malaria, and it was proving harder to tame.

Malaria was spread by a different mosquito species, the *Anopheles*, whose habits were harder to predict. Instead of congregating near dwellings, it liked to fly—and breed—farther afield. Its bite caused such minimal swelling and itch that often people did not know they had been pierced—and therefore could not report it—until they were already ill, making outbreaks harder to track. And its larvae could survive for hours, even under a layer of oil, which meant that no matter how diligently the fumigation brigades roved, malaria carried on.

The great hope for solving the malaria problem was a man named John Oswald, whom, rumor had it, Gorgas himself had asked to come down. Pierre knew little about Oswald except that apparently no one on earth understood *Anopheles* like he did. He was here, it was said, to enact new initiatives that would lead to eradication at last. If he could do it, Pierre knew, if he was as good as everyone said he was, then his name would forever appear alongside Gorgas's in the history books.

As a physician, Pierre sincerely hoped it could be done. What he had seen up close of malaria was truly appalling. Fever and chills so violent that at times the legs of patients' beds vibrated audibly against the hospital floor. The only known remedy for malaria was quinine, a liquid so bitter that the nurses mixed it with whiskey to mask the taste, but the cover of alcohol made it only slightly more palatable. And for many, the quinine had little effect. Death came for them in the end.

It was part of the profession, of course, to be acquainted with death and disease, but before coming to Panama, Pierre had never seen quite so much. Men crushed by rocks; men maimed by the swinging arms of steam shovels; men whose legs had been severed from their torsos by barreling trains; men burned by a live wire; men who had fallen off cliffs; men who had fallen off bridges; men who had fallen off cranes. Once, a man had walked into the ward with his ankle swollen to the size of a coconut, claiming that a ten-foot-long snake had clamped its jaws around him as he tramped through the brush. Pierre had been the only doctor in the room, and as he stood weighing what to do, a nurse hurried forward and tied a tourniquet around the man's calf. C'est dommage. Two hours later, the man was dead.

Pierre's responsibility was to treat every man who arrived, to get them back on the job as soon as possible. Of course, despite his best efforts, not every man could be saved. For those cases, the hospital kept a stack of coffins at the ready out back. Sixty years earlier, Pierre knew, when the Americans built a railroad across Panama, there were so many deaths among the laborers—men from China and the Indies—that the railroad company, without space to bury them all, pickled the bodies and shipped the cadavers to medical schools to use for research. These days, however, the bodies were placed in plain pine coffins and loaded on trains. If the bodies inside the coffins were white, the trains took them to the grassy cemetery at Ancón. If they were colored, they were taken instead to a place called Monkey Hill.

Now Dr. Pierre Renaud peered down at the young boy who lay before him—a native Panamanian, he noted with surprise—who had arrived that morning via passenger train. The boy was sick with malaria. Pierre rubbed his stone.

9

JOAQUÍN HAD MADE TWO DOLLARS THAT DAY BUYING FISH AND TURNING AROUND and selling them off again. Two dollars was not very much, and he considered for the hundredth time whether he should pay less for the fish or whether perhaps he should sell them off again for more, but as he had concluded all the ninety-nine times before, neither option held much appeal. If he paid the fishermen less for their catch, they would stop doing business with him. And if he sold the fish for more, customers would stop buying. No, he had established his prices and now he was stuck. It was entirely possible, he also thought for the hundredth time, that he was a lousy businessman.

Lately, he had been losing customers to a vendor named Li Jie who had opened a stall next to him in the market. From what Joaquín could discern, Li Jie was courteous and he spoke perfect Spanish, but it was hard not to begrudge someone who was taking your customers. Finally, he had worked up the balls to ask one of his former customers, a woman with an unfortunate shadow of a mustache above her lip, what the hell was going on. The woman told him that Li Jie was said to know at least fifty different preparations of fish, and that each time you bought from him, he would tell you a new one. She had already gotten six new recipes, she gushed, each one better than the last, and if the rumor was true she would get forty-four more! Joaquín, who had assumed himself victim of a more devious price-fixing scheme, had been dumbfounded. Recipes! He could not compete with that. Yes, yes, he had lively banter to share, and he had quality fish, but who knew that everyone was so desperate for innovative ways by which to cook them? He comforted himself with the thought that at some point Li Jie's recipe inventory would have to run out, and when it did hopefully his customers would come back.

On top of such ruminations about work, Joaquín walked home through the streets of Panama City with a certain amount of dread. Ever since the rumors had surfaced about a dam being built in Gatún, Valentina's moods had been all over the place. The fear was not only that she and her sister would have to abandon their family home, but that everyone would. That because of the dam, the entire town as they knew it would cease to exist.

Every day as soon as Joaquín stepped into his apartment, he braced himself for the possibility that Valentina had heard something new, some fresh horror over which she was incensed or saddened or both. And not without reason. These were incensing and saddening times. He understood that, he did. But at the end of the workday Joaquín wanted a break, a chance to sit down in silence, soak his feet in a bucket of cool water, close his eyes, and just breathe. He wanted peace. Just for ten minutes, and then he would be ready to listen to all that his wife had to say.

Their apartment was outside the wall of the city, on the second floor, and when Joaquín walked up the stairwell and opened the door, he found Valentina sitting by the window with a tear-streaked face. Gingerly, trying not to further upset her with any sound, Joaquín closed the door.

With her face still toward the window, Valentina said, "It has gotten worse."

Just ten minutes. Was that too much to ask? Apparently yes.

"What is it now?" Joaquín asked instead, kicking off his shoes.

"It's Eliberto el Cid."

"What?"

"Eliberto el Cid."

Joaquín stood still, trying to strategize the next thing out of his mouth. He had no idea what his wife was talking about, but to admit this was to invite a look of disappointment that Valentina reserved, it seemed, only for him. Not even Horacio was a recipient of a look like that. Only him. And he tried in every circumstance to avoid it if he could.

The apartment where they had lived since the day they married was comfortable and cool. The open shutters let in street noise, yes, but also a breeze. There were two bedrooms as well as a front room with slightly uneven wood floors and high ceilings in which twenty years' worth of accumulated things, baskets and books, newspapers and knives, pots and pans, were piled along the walls up to the height of the windowsills. Through the bottom left corner of the window, if one crouched, it was possible to see between a space in the buildings across the street all the way to the square. An apartment with a view, they had laughed when they first rented it. Now, unfortunately, no one was laughing.

Slowly, Joaquín said, "Ah, yes, Eliberto el Cid."

He had taken care to repeat it in exactly the way Valentina had said it, but when she turned from the window, she frowned. Even teary-eyed, she looked beautiful to him. Her black hair, lately threaded with a few strands of gray, was held back with hair pins. She had deep-set dark eyes, and though her frame was diminutive—she was hardly five feet tall—the force of her personality most certainly was not. Which he appreciated. His wife's considerable passion was one of the things he loved most about her.

"Do you even know who that is?" Valentina said.

"Of course I do. It is Eliberto el Cid."

The frown deepened. "But who is that?"

All day long at the fish market people treated him as an authority, and it was fascinating to Joaquín how Valentina, the love of his life, could make him squirm. "Why, you know who he is."

"*I* do."

"An interesting man," Joaquín went on. That seemed safe. The same could be said for most anyone, no?

Fortunately, Valentina nodded. "Apparently, he has had enough," she said.

"Well, yes, everyone has." Joaquín still did not know exactly what they were talking about, but, confident that he was on surer ground, he walked across the room to the table, peeked beneath the cloth that lay covering a bowl, and found, to his delight, flaky empanadas inside. He took one out and bit into it. Seasoned beef. As he had hoped. He stuffed the rest into his mouth.

As Valentina watched him, the frown returned. "Not everyone," she said.

Joaquín hurried to swallow his food. "No, no, not everyone certainly. When I said everyone, I did not mean *everyone*."

"Not my sister, I hope."

That was a foothold. That was something he could grab on to. The shape of the conversation took on more clarity then.

"Your sister! Of course she has not had enough."

"I received a letter from her today."

"Did you?" A letter was not good. A letter was surely the source of new news.

"She said that someone came to the house with a paper for her to sign. And Eliberto, who apparently has had enough of the whole situation already, advised her that she should!"

Joaquín remembered now. It was difficult to keep track of Valentina's childhood acquaintances, but he had heard her mention Eliberto before. He lived a few houses down from Valentina's childhood home, if recollection served.

Joaquín popped another empanada into his mouth and, as he chewed it, asked, "Well, what does the paper even say?"

"I don't know."

"It would be good to know, wouldn't it?" He swallowed. "After all, it could be that Eliberto is right."

And then, there it was: the disappointed look. As if she questioned how on earth she could have married such a man. Joaquín winced. Now he had to redeem himself.

"Or naturally he could be wrong," he tried.

"I think we should go to Gatún," Valentina said.

"What?"

"We should go to Gatún to see for ourselves. As you pointed out, we do not even know what the paper says, and it would be good to know, right?"

In all the years of their marriage, Joaquín had been to Gatún on only a handful of occasions, and each time grudgingly. He had gone back when Valentina had her heart set on spending Christmas there one year; and he had certainly gone for the funerals of both of her parents, who were buried in the local cemetery. He had even gone when the home of the priest, Father Suárez, was destroyed in a storm and Valentina enlisted him to help in the rebuilding effort. But every time Joaquín went, he found himself counting the hours until he could leave. Valentina visited every year without fail, but he frequently managed to wriggle out of the trip for one reason or another, usually having to do with work. There was nothing wrong with the town per se. It was a perfectly fine place with all the usual establishments—a church and a schoolhouse and restaurants and shophouses and so forth—but it was not the city, which was where Joaquín felt he belonged. Not to mention that going to Gatún meant having to see his sister-in-law, Renata, whom, truth be told, he did not care for, not only for the matter of her appearance but for her dull personality, too. This, however, was clearly an important visit, and the disappointed look, it distressed Joaquín to see, was still etched on Valentina's face.

He said, "Of course, my love."

||||||

VALENTINA COULD HEAR Joaquín in the bedroom, changing out of his work clothes. She sat at the window and sighed at the fact that he had not remembered the name of an old neighbor she must have mentioned before. She could never decide whether the problem was that her husband was simply forgetful or whether the problem was that he did not listen to her. Lately, in order to address the latter, if she was speaking and he seemed distracted—sharpening his knife while she spoke, filing his fingernails, snapping open the newspaper

as if he thought he might read while she was talking to him—
she stopped, looked directly at him, and said, "I would like your
undivided attention, my love. I deserve nothing less." The first time
she said it, he had looked at her with bemusement, and she kept
her expression deadly serious until Joaquín dropped the half smile
from his face, crossed his arms over his broad chest, and said, "Go
on." Since then, she had needed to say it only a few more times. He
was getting the idea. If, on the other hand, the problem was truly
forgetfulness, there was nothing she could do about that.

Twenty-four years ago they had met through a mutual friend,
and Valentina at first had not been overly impressed. She did, however, like how he looked—he was burly and strong with a perpetual
grin—and immediately, without the slightest blush, she had a vision
of how deftly he might handle her in bed. Which turned out, by the
time she came around to the rest of him, to be true. He was thrilling
in that regard, and together their performances were so energetic as
to be almost acrobatic. Such vigorous lovemaking was part of what
had kept their marriage afloat.

It was also, thanks to God, what had blessed them with a child.

Valentina was forty-four years old. She had spent the last twenty
years of her life in service to her son, Horacio. Twenty years spent
rising early every morning to cook eggs and dice fruit, buttoning
his shirts, smoothing the hairs that curled behind his ears, wiping
his chin, teaching him manners, clutching his hand as they walked
through the streets, keeping him safe, standing at the stove cooking
lunches and dinners and lunches and dinners, marveling at how
much he could eat, feeling his forehead for fever, cradling him until
he refused to be cradled anymore, scrubbing his clothes, listening
to him laugh, watching him change, watching hair grow in places
where hair had not sprouted before, worrying about him, asking
too many questions, reminding him over and over to clear his plate
from the table and to pick up his things and to get a good night's
sleep, telling him that she loved him even though he made faces and
squirmed out from under those words. For twenty years she had given

Horacio everything—and now what? He had gone off and married. He did not need her anymore. Which was the point of parenthood, Valentina told herself. To raise children who were capable of going off on their own. Although it was a perverse point, as she saw it, since raising children to go off on their own meant that the children inevitably . . . went off on their own.

Without Horacio, there was a discomfiting aimlessness to her days. It was not the same cooking meals for only Joaquín and her to eat. It was not the same strolling through the city by herself. There were other women she knew in the same predicament, and with those women she sometimes had a cafecito and shared a good laugh, but none of it was the same. She had given everything to her son, and he had taken it, and now what did she have left?

Valentina stood up from her seat by the window and smoothed out her skirt. Basta. She had cried enough today. She was not going to start contemplating the emptiness of her life without Horacio and feel sad about that now on top of everything else. Now was not the time for wallowing about such things. And perhaps, she consoled herself, everything happened for a reason. Perhaps no longer being in service to her son gave her time to be in service to something else. For while Horacio may not have needed her anymore, it seemed her town did.

||||||

BY THE TIME the train pulled into the station at Gatún that Saturday afternoon, Valentina had steeled herself for what they might see once they arrived. She had reread all of her sister's letters from the last year, and even though Renata could be laconic and the letters were short on details, Valentina nonetheless used them to piece together an image in her mind of what had happened since the last time she was there.

The town had undergone transformations before. Valentina was old enough to remember when Frenchmen had arrived and built blocky machine shops across the river from the town. The machine shops spewed smoke all day long, and for years everyone in Gatún said that the food they grew tasted different because of it. Anytime her father, who was a banana farmer, picked a brown-spotted banana, he blamed the spots on the smoke.

She was not old enough to remember the period before that when the railroad had arrived, although she had heard stories about it. That was when men hoping to find gold came rushing through Panamá in a wild stampede, trying to get to Upper California as fast as they could. There were apparently three main ways to get from the east coast of the United States to the west. One way was for a person to hitch a horse to a wagon and travel three thousand miles over rugged land, trying to locate trails as they went. The second way was to take a ship from a port in the east, sail down along the side of the Americas, hugging its coast, hook around Cape Horn at the southernmost tip, and then sail back up and westward, to the port at San Francisco. That route was safer, but it took three months, which, for people in an urgent mood, was impossibly long. The third way was through Panamá. A person could depart from New York or New Orleans and sail due south until they ran into the isthmus. From there they would continue on foot and canoes, trekking fifty miles across rivers and jungle and land, and once they reached the other side, they would board a second ship that would take them across the Pacific to California, to the glittering promise of gold. The Panamá route took a mere forty days.

"Complete pandemonium" was how Valentina's father remembered that time. According to him, boats arrived every day, and men too desperate to wait to be brought to the shore jumped overboard and splashed through the water like strange sea creatures, holding their rucksacks up over their heads. On land, they brandished pistols, demanding to be fed. To escape the heat or the rain, they rudely let themselves into people's homes and took naps on the floor. They stole mules from people's farms and used them as transport. They walked into the church and lit their cigars using candles that were meant as offerings to the saints. They spit tobacco juice in the dirt. "They had the madness of men who were starving," her father said. "We had never seen behavior like that before."

By the time Valentina was born, men hungry for gold were still traveling through, though the chaos was not so consuming as it had been at the start. Eventually, the North Americans completed a railroad across their own broad land. With it, people could travel safely across the whole of the United States in only a week. Traffic through the isthmus naturally slowed. For the time being, the North Americans did not need Panamá as the way through.

On the train ride out to Gatún that day, Valentina repeatedly assured herself that a town that had survived all of that could survive anything that was to come, but when she and Joaquín actually stepped foot in Gatún, she was horror-struck by what she saw. It was not the sight of the town itself, which, situated on the western bank of the river, looked largely untouched—the church with its steeple, the rectory next to it, the dentist's office and the post office and the various shops, the houses, the laundry hanging on rope—or even, on the eastern bank, the sight of the six steel-bodied machine shovels and the many tall stacks of wood boards and the encampment of tents and the numerous buildings that had not been there before— none of that did her in. It was the sight of the trees—hundreds of what had once been leafy banana trees on the eastern side of the river where her father and others had collectively farmed. All of those trees had been burned until they were nothing but charred sticks poking up out of the ground.

||||||

RENATA OPENED THE door when they knocked. By day she picked fruit on a nearby farm, but as it was Saturday evening when they arrived, she was home.

"¡Hermana!" Valentina said, and fell upon her sister in an ardent embrace. Renata had barely managed to stammer, "What are you—?" before Valentina said, "We came for a visit," and pushed her way into the house. Reluctantly, Joaquín kissed his stunned sister-in-law on both of her cheeks and followed Valentina in.

The house, one of a dozen or so along the river, looked the same as Joaquín remembered with bamboo-and-clay walls and a pitched thatched roof. Inside, with its packed dirt floor, he was always surprised by how spacious it actually felt. An open room in the center was flanked on each side by a bedroom—one that Valentina and Renata used to share, and the other where their parents had once slept. In fact, the first time Joaquín had been to this house was to meet Valentina's parents. Her father had sat Joaquín down at the table that was still here in this middle room and asked him what his intentions were. Joaquín had responded with the only sensible answer to a question like that: "To marry your daughter, Señor," and Valentina's father, who had been an affable man, smiled and sent Joaquín home that day with his blessing as well as an armful of ripe yellow bananas.

Lamentably, Renata also looked the same as Joaquín remembered, with her broad forehead and downturned eyes and a hairline that was either too far forward or too far back, he could never decide, but it was definitely not where it should be. Truly, how she and Valentina were related was one of the great mysteries of the world.

Renata, still flummoxed by their unexpected arrival, managed to prepare coffee, and the three of them sat. Joaquín presumed that Valentina would right away say why they had come, but instead she started reminiscing about her time in the house.

"Do you remember, hermana, the time we had a leak in this roof?"

"Yes. You can still tell where it was patched." Renata pointed.

"Papá could fix anything," Valentina said, gazing up with reverence.

The coffee was so hot that Joaquín burned his tongue, but he kept sipping it, thinking that if he did, it might spur Valentina to sip hers, too, and the sooner they both finished their coffees, the sooner they could turn to the business at hand—reading the letter, offering their advice—and thus the sooner they could return to the train station and head home. Valentina, however, was so engrossed in her recollections that she hardly sipped the coffee at all.

"Do you remember the smell on Christmas morning when Mamá made her tamales? And the ron ponche that I always tried to sip? Mamá would get so drunk. She would kiss everything in sight! The pots and the pans, the firewood. One time she kissed the goat on the tip of his nose!"

Valentina went on—and after a time Joaquín covertly slid the cup of coffee closer to his wife as a small reminder, a suggestion, that's all.

She did not seem to notice it, though. Joaquín cleared his throat. Nothing. Under the table, he nudged her knee with his, but that only startled her and she knocked the cup of coffee such that it spilled. Valentina jumped up, embarrassed, and Renata rushed to clean what she could. When she said that she would pour a new cup of coffee for Valentina—in effect *starting over*—Joaquín, who could take it no more, spoke up.

"Where is the paper they asked you to sign?"

Renata looked at him as though she had forgotten he was there.

"The paper," Joaquín prodded. "We would like to read it for ourselves."

"The paper about the house?" Renata asked.

The mind of his sister-in-law, Joaquín had long observed, had all the sharpness of a spoon. It could take a few times before something got through to her. "Yes," he said. "That's the one."

Renata walked into the bedroom and returned a few seconds later with a piece of paper, which she handed to him. Valentina peered over his shoulder.

The language was straightforward enough, but what the letter actually said was extreme. In six months' time, the entire town of Gatún would be moved. Every man, woman, and child, every storefront, every farm would have to relocate to the opposite side of the river. Buildings and houses would need to be dismantled by their owners or else they would be destroyed. The Isthmian Canal Commission would cover the costs of transport for those who signed.

Joaquín set the paper down. While they were reading, Renata had poured a second cup of coffee for Valentina and, he noticed, refilled his own. Well, at least they understood the situation now. That was progress. Although what the paper said was not good, not good at all.

"You cannot sign this," Valentina said.

"I didn't."

"But Eliberto told you to?"

"Yes."

"So he did?"

"I assume so." Renata was looking at them wide-eyed and anxious.

Valentina shook her head. "Unbelievable. Gatún has been in this very spot for centuries. Do they know that? And now what? It will be erased? Now, in only six months, they expect us to move everything we have built?"

"Well, not *us*," Joaquín said.

Valentina glared at him.

As gently as he could, he said, "Your sister, yes. But not us. We live in the city, my love."

Joaquín thought that, as usual, he had probably said the wrong thing, so he was somewhat shocked when he saw Valentina's face brighten.

"That's it," she said.

"What's it?"

"We should stay here and fight."

"I didn't say that."

"But you said we're not here."

"True—"

"So perhaps we should be."

Joaquín saw where this was going. "But what does that even mean—fight?"

"I don't know. We will figure it out."

"Well, can't we figure it out in the city?"

"And then what? Come back again? That does not seem very efficient."

"My love," Joaquín said, working a bit more firmness into his voice, "whatever shape this so-called fight takes, I do think we can wage it from the city. In a battle, you have to disperse your troops."

"No, in a battle you have to position your troops where they will have the greatest impact. If we fight from the city, it will not be the same."

"But where will we stay?"

"Here." Valentina circled her arm in the air.

Here? Joaquín thought. In this house? The three of them together? He glanced at Renata, whose mouth had dropped open wide enough that an entire hard-boiled egg could have fit perfectly in the gap.

"Valentina," Joaquín said in an imploring tone.

But Valentina ignored him and looked at her sister and said, "We will stay in Mamá and Papá's bedroom, yes? You will hardly know that we're here."

Joaquín looked at Renata again, hoping she would have the good sense to object, but she was still standing dumbstruck.

Frustrated, Joaquín said, "What about my work?"

"You can take the train there," Valentina replied.

"My love—" Joaquín began.

"It will only be temporary," Valentina said.

"How temporary?"

"Just until we can do something about this."

"But what can we even do?"

"I told you I don't know yet."

Valentina watched her husband drag the palm of his hand down over his face, then again down the back of his neck. She knew he was struggling to keep himself composed. But to her it was easy. Twenty-four years ago, she had chosen him. Now, she needed him to choose her. She needed him to understand that Gatún *was* her. That although she lived in the city, Gatún was the place whose air she had breathed, whose dirt she had walked barefoot upon, whose streets she could follow blindfolded, the place where she had learned how to cook and how to climb and how to argue and how to love, the place that had made her. Without having to say all of that, she hoped he understood.

Finally Joaquín looked at her and said, "All right. *Temporarily.*"

Valentina smiled. "Of course."

10

THE WHITE HOUSE ON THE HILL WAS GRAND. ADA, WHO HAD NEVER STEPPED FOOT in a house so splendid, much less lived in one, could not believe her good fortune every morning when she woke up. To have gotten this job in the first place—caring for Mr. Oswald's wife, who was ill with pneumonia—had itself been a turn of good fortune, and now, she told herself over and over again, it was a job she had to keep. Another one would not come so easily, and it would certainly not pay so well. At the Oswalds' she was earning so much that in only six weeks, if her arithmetic was right, she would have enough for Millicent's surgery. Six short weeks, and then she could go home.

Ada's first impression that Mr. Oswald was someone important was only confirmed by the grandeur of the house. It had thirteen rooms and the largest veranda Ada had ever seen, completely encased by screens. The entry hall was bare but for a grandfather clock embellished with intricate carvings of flowers and leaves. The clock, Mr. Oswald had told her when he first showed her around, had been shipped in a crate from Tennessee and had not run properly since the moment of its unboxing, something about the humidity interfering with its inner gears. The dining room had a gleaming cherrywood table with seating for twelve, and in the center of the table a brass candelabra that held the same number of candlesticks. There was a parlor decorated with beautiful looking glasses in gilded oval frames and a bookcase full of books that, according to Mr. Oswald, had suffered the same fate as the grandfather clock, the humidity attacking them until the pages rippled and the covers mildewed, and even keeping the books behind glass did not help. The kitchen, which Mr. Oswald described as the domain of the cook, had a cast-iron stove and its own icebox. The open shelves of a cupboard were stacked with saucepans and boiling pots and colanders and bowls. On the countertop, there was a measuring scale and a salt box and a machine with a crank handle, the purpose of which Ada could not conceive. A worktable in the center of the room held a knifeboard and a bowl piled with fruit. And off the kitchen, Mr. Oswald had informed her, was the room where she would stay free of charge. To be on the premises was part of the job. Naturally a doctor would come daily to administer medical care, but between his visits Ada was to be available at every hour, was that clear? Ada had said yes, and she had peeked inside. The room was small and windowless, with space for hardly more than the bed, but unlike the boxcar, it had a door that clicked shut, and it was dry, and she was grateful for that.

||||||

MRS. OSWALD WAS quarantined in a bedroom at the end of the hall. Ada started each day by bringing breakfast up to the room, although Mrs. Oswald—just like Millicent—hardly wanted to eat, and Ada carried the untouched meals back down to the kitchen where the cook, Antoinette, frowned as though to leave the food uneaten was a personal affront. Ada might have assured Antoinette that it was not her fault—her cooking, which Ada enjoyed by virtue of living in the house, was delicious, the meat always tender, the stews wonderfully rich—except that Antoinette had been so standoffish to her since the moment they met that Ada refused to give Antoinette the satisfaction of an assurance like that. If Antoinette wanted to be unfriendly toward her, Ada would not go out of her way to be friendly back. For years Cordelia Bennington, a girl Ada and Millicent had gone to school with, had been spiteful toward them, and though Millicent often tried to be conciliatory, even kind, Ada derived more pleasure from getting under Cordelia's skin. One day when Ada had worn a new dress to school, a dress that her mother had made in a print of bright orange and red, Cordelia had said right to her face, "You look ugly to me." Ada had wanted to punch Cordelia straight in the belly or pull the white ribbons out of her hair, but their teacher,

Miss Cook, was nearby, so all Ada said was, "Well, look away then."
All morning Ada had stewed, thinking about what other things
she might have said instead. That same afternoon during class Miss
Cook explained that there were places in the world covered all year
round with ice and snow, a concept that prompted Cordelia Bennington to declare that she would never go somewhere like that.
"No one would ever choose a land of such cold." It was a declaration
so infuriatingly definitive that Ada raised her own hand and, while
staring at Cordelia and her stupid white ribbons, said, "I think it
might be beautiful there. Some people don't know beauty even if it is
staring them right in the face."

For much of the morning until the doctor arrived, Ada went to
fetch washcloths or she propped up the pillow so that Mrs. Oswald
could sit upright or she pulled the sheet higher if Mrs. Oswald
shivered. Ada had never looked after a white woman before, but far
from being demanding, as Ada had assumed she might be, Mrs.
Oswald seldom asked for anything, and she always thanked Ada for
even the smallest deed. She seemed appreciative simply for Ada's
company, and during their first morning together she had not only
asked Ada where she was from, but when Ada told her Barbados,
with genuine interest she had said, "Tell me about it. I have never
been." Ada described the limestone soil and the smell of hibiscus and
the schooners in the harbor that came ashore with cordwood stacked
on their decks and the trams that ran through the city and the taste
of fish cakes, but she did not reveal anything about her mother or
Millicent or their house and the road where they lived, even though
the whole time she spoke she was thinking of those things. She had a
sense that she ought to keep such personal details to herself. She was
there to do a job, after all. Mrs. Oswald smiled weakly and remarked
that it all sounded lovely to her.

At the end of each day, after the bedpan had been rinsed and Mrs.
Oswald was in her nightdress, and the doctor had twice come and
gone, Ada sat in the cane-backed chair long-side the bed, listening
to each of Mrs. Oswald's strenuous breaths as she fell into a fitful

sleep. She couldn't help but think about Millicent, who was so far away. Couldn't help but recognize how she was trying, by the grace of God, to make both Millicent and Mrs. Oswald well.

She had mailed one letter home so far just to say that she had arrived safely and had taken a job. Every day at noon a mail messenger, a slim Black American boy who wore his uniform trousers rolled above his ankles, trudged up the hill to the Oswalds' house to collect any outgoing mail and to deliver the incoming. A week was not long enough that her mother could have sent a reply, but each time the mail messenger arrived, Ada ran down the stairs to meet him. The boy, who had introduced himself as Michael after the third time Ada rushed to the door, always smiled and tipped his blue postal cap, but day after day he brought nothing for her.

||||||

ON THE LAST day of September, at precisely 11:30 a.m., Dr. Pierre Renaud climbed the hill to the Oswald house, as he had been doing twice daily for the past week. Coming to the house was certainly an improvement over the Negro ward. When Pierre had heard that John Oswald needed a physician, he seized the opportunity to fulfill a role more fitting for a man of his pedigree. The house was more stately than any other he had seen in Panama, and when Pierre stood on the veranda that first day, waiting for someone to answer the door, such a sweet and cooling tropical breeze caressed the air that for a moment he was happy to be in Panama just to experience it. Now the feeling from the first time had dissipated, but he was pleased nevertheless to arrive there and have important work to do.

Pierre let himself in and walked upstairs to the bedroom. From the bed, Marian Oswald looked up—she appeared quite wan—and Pierre bid her hello. The nursemaid girl was sitting in the chair, apparently reading from a Bible on her lap. She stopped when she saw him and set the Bible, open, on the bureau. Pierre believed a Bible should be closed when it was at rest, but he did not say a word about it. Nor did he say a word about how light it was in the room that day, though he thought it unusual that the drapes, which ordinarily were closed, had been opened for some reason.

Pierre set his medical bag on the floor and walked to Marian's side of the bed. The nursemaid girl remained in the room.

"How was the night?" Pierre asked Marian.

"It seems I survived it," Marian said.

Pierre smiled. Good humor was an encouraging sign. "As I expected you would."

He checked Marian's pulse and asked her to open her mouth while he scraped her tongue with a wooden stick. He held the stick up to the light to inspect what he had collected before dropping it into a paper bag. Then Pierre took out his stethoscope, a single elegant tube made of wood and brass, and set one end of it on Marian Oswald's chest while he listened at the other end. The first time he had come, he had asked her to say "eeeeee" while he listened, and the way the sound had come through had been the confirmation he needed to diagnose pneumonia. Today he listened for any intensified rattling and crackling, rusty lungs throbbing against the cage of the ribs. There was not much, and that, too, was a good sign.

"What do you hear?" the nursemaid girl asked.

Pierre turned, peering over his shoulder. The girl always hovered about during the exam, asking question after question. *How high is the fever today? Do you see anything new on that stick?* Why could she need to know such things? He needed to know them certainly, but she only needed to know how to fetch ice and change the sheets. And when she was not asking questions, she was saying superfluous things. *She hasn't eaten today, but I did ask Antoinette to prepare some broth. She used the washroom twice during the night.* Useless information. Unless she could tell him the thickness of the pleural lining or the chance of cardiac thrombosis or any other actual medical fact, she should keep her thoughts to herself. He did not care for an outspoken woman. A woman might be moved to share her opinions with a diary, but she should not share them with the rest of the world.

"I hear the lungs," Pierre said.

"But how do they sound this morning?"

Pierre forced a brief smile. "Fine."

Rumor had it that John had put in a request for a trained hospital nurse when, impressed by some act of compassion he witnessed on the street, he hired this other girl instead. Pierre understood that there had been an urgent need, that desperation could make a man do many a strange thing, but in his opinion John would have been much better served had he waited for his request to be fulfilled.

Pierre turned back to Marian. "The systems are steady. You are battling through."

Marian coughed a few times, and the girl rose to grab the bedpan, but Pierre held up his hand. "The coughing should not produce anything now." When the coughing subsided, he saw that he had been right. He stood and leaned down to start packing his bag—he would be back, of course, later that afternoon—when quite unexpectedly John stepped into the room.

It was the first time Pierre had seen John since starting the job a week earlier. He was dressed in a crisp white linen suit, and his stiff brown hair was combed to the side. His round spectacles sat high on his nose. Upon his entrance, Pierre stood.

"John, is that you?" Marian asked from the bed.

"Yes."

"You're here."

She reached her hand out to him, but John remained where he was, just inside the door as though he were scared to venture any farther. Pierre had witnessed such trepidation many times—a fear of being proximate to illness.

"How is she?" John asked.

Pierre said, "There has been no improvement, but neither has there been further deterioration. Nothing significant, I should say. It is the most we can hope for at this point. It will simply take time."

"And her lungs?"

"The same."

"Is there anything more you can do?"

"Not now, no. Keep her here. Let her rest."

In fact, there were other treatments Pierre might have tried, procedures like bloodletting or maggot debridement, but he did not have the stomach for those, and furthermore he doubted their efficacy. He had seen a hundred such cases, and from what he could tell, Marian Oswald's case was much like the rest. There was fluid in her lungs, but not much, and she was otherwise strong, which boded well. Everyone wanted an intervention, but in his experience the natural systems of the body were often the most curative. He would keep an eye on things, of course. If it got worse, he would not hesitate to act. But for now the prescription was simply to rest. In a few weeks' time Marian Oswald would be the picture of health, and when that happened, John Oswald would shake his hand and everyone in the Canal Zone would know of the Frenchman who had been—far from a failure—an unqualified success.

Pierre again leaned down to pack up his bag when the Oswalds' cook, wearing an apron tied around her waist and a piece of fabric tied around her head, arrived at the room with a tray that held a bowl of hot broth. "Good morning," she said. "I have soup for Missus."

"Antoinette?" Marian said.

"Yes, ma'am."

She walked into the room and put the tray on the bureau. She turned and looked at everyone gathered—Ada, Mr. Oswald, Mrs. Oswald, and the doctor—and said, "There a party in here? That why the drapes open today?"

She meant to say something cheerful to offset the gravity that always weighed down the air in that room, but the way the tall doctor grimaced told her she had made a mistake.

"Yes, why are the drapes open?" Mr. Oswald asked, suddenly glancing around the room.

"I had that same question myself," the doctor said.

"You did not open them?" Mr. Oswald asked.

"Certainly not. They were like that when I arrived."

Standing by the head of the bed, Ada spoke up. "Missus Oswald wanted them open," she said.

Antoinette and the doctor and Mr. Oswald all turned to look at her.

"What did you say?" Mr. Oswald asked.

"Missus Oswald wanted the drapes open."

"She did?"

"Yes. And I thought . . . well, that the light might do her good."

"You thought—?" Mr. Oswald said, furrowing his brow. He turned to the doctor. "Is that true? Is the light good for her?"

Pierre said nothing for a moment. He felt embarrassed for John. First the cook with her ill-advised joke and now the nurse-girl who could not even bring herself to say "sir" when she was talking to him. And more than embarrassed, Pierre was flabbergasted to see that John, whom he knew as a powerful man, who *was* a powerful man, did nothing to scold either one. But before Pierre could speak, John continued.

"You said let her rest. I imagine in that case the drapes should remain closed, shouldn't they?"

Antoinette waited, but no one in the room stirred. For eight months she had been at the Oswalds', and all that time, it had been just the three of them. Now, though, this mixed-blood will-o'-the-wisp from Barbados had moved in. Yes, the girl was pretty—Antoinette had noted with resentment the way the girl's dress nipped in at the waist and settled over her hips—but why did she not wear a head tie? Why had she no manners or tact? Going so far as to boast about sleeping in a boxcar the first night she was here—a strange thing to boast about, Antoinette thought. Was that how children in Barbados were raised? Truthfully, she wouldn't mind if the girl returned to that boxcar. Then things could go back to how they had been. The last thing she needed was to be replaced by yet another young flower who believed it was her turn to stand in the light.

All at once Antoinette strode across the room to the window

and yanked the drapes shut. "The dark do help people rest," she declared.

In bed, Mrs. Oswald suddenly coughed so hard that she sat upright, and Ada rubbed her back while both the doctor and Mr. Oswald looked on with alarm.

Marian lay back after the fit of coughing was done. Her throat was raw. Her chest felt brittle. Her whole body ached. That morning, before the rain had begun, Ada had asked her quite innocently whether she wanted the drapes open or closed. "They've been closed since I got here, but I have been meaning to ask." Ada had been standing by the window, ready to open the drapes at her command. The fabric was a thick, plum-and-gold-colored brocade. Marian remembered John closing them when she first relocated to this room. "John prefers them like this," Marian had said to Ada. After a pause, Ada had asked, "But is it what you prefer?" The question had nearly made Marian cry. It was so rare that someone asked for her preference, so rare that she had a say in her own life anymore. Years ago, John had walked into her world and cast a shadow over her. To everyone, he was more important than she was, more intelligent, more interesting. That would always be true. And the knowledge of that, her place in his shadow, had darkened something in her. "No it isn't," she had said, and Ada had opened the drapes. Just like that, light had streamed in.

Now, with Ada and Antoinette and Pierre and John all crowding around her, Marian took a shallow, scraping breath. "Open them, please. I prefer them open," she said.

11

ON THE RARE OCCASION THAT MILLICENT BUNTING ALLOWED HERSELF TO CON-
template death, she imagined it as a cavalry of horses thundering down a long dirt road with her at the end of it, pinned in place, unable to move. They were snorting gray horses with hooves big as church bells. Their manes whipped in the air. Millicent tried to close her mind to the possibility of those horses, but even when she was not gazing down that long dirt road, she could hear the echo of their thunder rumbling all the way down to where she was, and it was then that she worried that death was nearer than she wanted it to be.

If Ada were there, she would have told Millicent that horses were horses, that they were not death, and that Millicent was going to be just fine. The two of them might have laughed about the horses, the way they laughed when someone broke wind in the middle of a church service or when Ada imitated their mother's scolding tone of voice, usually after she had been scolded herself and their mother was safely out of earshot again. Or the way they did the time that a bird relieved itself on Cordelia Bennington's left shoulder and she screamed so loud that a whole flock of bullfinches flew up out of the tree, flapping as they scattered away. Millicent did not think it right to laugh at anyone to their face, but when it came to Cordelia, who acted so high she might as well live in the tops of the trees with those birds, Millicent could not help herself. It was a little bit funny seeing Cordelia brought down to earth. Laughing now would have made Millicent feel better for a time. Or if not better, it would have distracted her at least, and helped her forget how terrible she felt, sick with hardly any improvement for the whole last month.

After Ada left, the first thing Millicent had done was get up out of her bed and climb into Ada's instead. It was a means of feeling closer to Ada when she was so far away. Millicent had dragged over her quilt, pieced and sewn by their mother, who could do anything with a needle and thread, and burrowed herself underneath it. It amazed her, in that small room where their three beds were arranged like a U around three of the walls, how different the view was from here. Millicent's bed was along the back wall of the house, with a window that she only saw out of the corner of her eye. Ada's bed, with its foot toward Millicent's head, faced that same window, and when Millicent lay there, she could see straight out to the blue of the sky. Maybe that explained the difference between them, Millicent thought. With that view of the wide-open sky, who wouldn't think that the world was beckoning?

The horses were louder at night when the sky through the window was dark but for stars. Both her body and her mind were weary then; both came closer to surrender. Those were the worst times. While her mother slept, Millicent lay in the dark, trying to comprehend what it would be like if the cavalry came. What happened to a person as they were taken from one world to the next? Did you feel it? What was that moment of leaving like? What was every moment after that like? And then Millicent cried because she was scared.

During the day, it was different. When her mother fed her dumpling soup and the fever waned and the sky was blue, Millicent felt sporadic surges of strength and she thought that if she could just hold on a little while longer, she might make it yet. The doctor had said a surgery would help, and though the thought of that was nearly as terrifying as everything else, she would do it if that's what it took. She was not ready to die. What had she even done with her life? For seventeen years she had gone to school and finished her chores and eaten her meals and cleaned up after herself. Every responsible thing. She had liked a boy once who liked her back, a dalliance that Millicent had told no one, not even Ada, about. He was a polite boy named Howard, and he had a lisp when he spoke that Millicent found charming, especially because he was self-conscious about it. She had met Howard a few times in a cove by the sea, and Howard and she had sat there in secret and chatted and shyly he had held her hand and once he kissed her full on the mouth and then all up and down her neck in a way that tickled. Then one day Millicent waited for an hour with her arms round her knees, watching the merrywings over the sand, but Howard did not show up, and the next time Millicent saw him he was with someone new. It was something and then in a flash it wasn't, and she was such a coward that she never said anything to him about it. She just let him go. If she were more like Ada, she might have made a fuss. She might have confronted Howard and made certain everyone knew that he was not as polite as he wanted to seem. But she was only herself, and try as she might, she could not manage to be any other way. There were times she longed to be different, but she guessed everyone felt that way at one time or another, and so in wanting to be different, everyone was the same. Anyway, Howard with his dotish lisp was hardly worth thinking about. He was a shiver in the wind. If anything, he reminded Millicent what her mother had told Ada and her a dozen times or more: A woman should have no need for a man. Millicent could sit by the sea and hold her own hand, she supposed. It was why she had two.

|||||

LUCILLE WALKED INTO the room with a cup of bush tea and urged Millicent to drink. Millicent had sipped a number of bush teas in the last three weeks, but none of them seemed to have any lasting effect.

"Come, fresh lime leaf in this one here," her mother said, helping Millicent sit up in bed.

Lucille held the cup to her daughter's lips. Once or twice she had lifted the lid on the tin where the black cake was fermenting, hopeful that if she let a bit of the rum-sweet scent escape, the aroma alone would rouse Millicent from bed. But it hadn't. Not yet. The scent would get stronger with time—the cake would be ready by Christmas—but Lucille did not know how much time they had. She tried not to think about that. That the doctor required £15 for the surgery was every day on her mind. She had gone to the church to ask if there was anything they could do (the reverend had told her they could pray), and she had been sewing till her fingers ached, trying to sell what she made, approaching past clients to see if she could interest them in buying something new, and Mrs. Callender had let her pluck cherries from her lovely trees and take the cherries to market to sell. But £15 all at once was a sum Lucille had never had in her life, and no matter how she tried to get it, so far her efforts had yielded only £2 plus prayers.

"How you feel now?" Lucille asked after Millicent drank the tea.

"The same."

She put a hand to Millicent's forehead. "No fever at least."

Millicent sank back down under the cover of the quilt and said, "Read the letter again."

"I read it ten times already."

"I want to hear it again."

Lucille slid her hand into the patch pocket of her dress and pulled out the small postcard, which she had folded in half. The paper was thick, and the crease down the middle resembled a braid. The letter had been brought by a mail messenger who came up the road shouting, "Bunting! Bunting!" since there were no house numbers to tell him just where to go. The letter had been addressed to only a street and a name. The first time Lucille read it, she had to do so slowly to decipher the words, but she had the whole thing memorized now. From the side of the bed, Lucille recited it.

> After six days on the big ship, I made it to Panama. I am well. I found work already. It is true—work comes down upon you easy as rain. (And there is plenty of rain!) I will send money next time—just as soon as I can. I miss you both terribly.
>
> Ada

Lucille refolded the postcard and tucked it back down in her pocket again. *I am well.* She clung to those words. Each time Millicent begged her to read the letter and she opened it up, she was afraid that sentence would be gone, that she would find she had misremembered it or that somehow it would have disappeared. She was relieved to see it was there again now.

Millicent had memorized the letter, too. She liked to hear her mother read it aloud, but even in between those times, Millicent recited it in her head, trying to picture Ada on the big ship, as she called it, and then in faraway Panama with its plenty of rain. The interesting thing was that Millicent could picture it easily, even though all she knew of Panama was the stories she had heard from the men who had come back after working there already, stories about crocodiles in the swamps, and a ditch they were digging that was deeper than the ocean, and a lake they were making that one day would be as big as Barbados itself. Thirty-two different men from their church alone had gone, and the ones who had returned were welcomed like heroes. After service they stood outside and told tales of what it had been like while people gathered round, eager to hear. Some of them, like Enos Mann, were humble about their adventures, Enos saying only that he had worked hard, day and night he had worked, and that he was grateful just to be a small part of something so big. Others, like Edward Wainwright, were showy, pompasetting about, coming to church in a new three-piece suit and pulling a shiny gold pocket watch out of his vest pocket every few minutes so everyone could see just how gold and shiny it was. He was always flipping the timepiece open, making sure it caught the light of the sun, and announcing the time even though no one had asked. "I see it quarter past nine!" "It now upright six!" A few kind people would sometimes respond, "That it is, Mr. Wainwright," or, "We thank you for the report," while others, like her mother, just rolled their eyes. The pocket watch was accompanied by a new collection of hats, one for every Sunday of the month, each with a feather that annoyed her mother so much that she called him Edward Peacock when he could not hear. Half the men in Barbados, it sometimes seemed, had gone to Panama already or else wanted to go. Millicent had heard of only a few women who were doing the same, and even then she'd heard of none as young as her sister going off on their own. She was incredulous not only that Ada had done it but that she had done it for her.

After listening to her mother read the letter again, Millicent looked out the window across the room. Ada was somewhere out there, probably not even scared.

"What sort of job you think she got?" Millicent asked.

"Knowing your sister, could be anything."

"Not a washerwoman, though."

Her mother chuckled. "No."

"You think she truly misses us?" Millicent asked.

"Of course."

Millicent coughed. "Seems I feel even worse with her gone away."

Maybe it was because of the horses, because she sensed they were near. Maybe it was because Ada was courageous and she wanted to be that way, too. All at once Millicent said out loud something she had wondered for a long time. "Do you think he misses us?"

"Who?"

The ache in Millicent's chest was so deep at that moment that she could not tell whether it was from the illness or something else. She was, these days, always short of breath, but she took the deepest inhalation she could and said, "Our father."

Lucille nearly dropped the empty teacup in her hand. Her shoulders and legs and hips all went loose, and the looseness traveled straight up to her mind. How to answer a question like that? When Millicent was a child, she had asked questions every now and again. What was his name? What was he like? Why did he never come back to see us? The questions were painful, and to answer them, Lucille always believed, would be to let that pain singe the girls, too. So Lucille had always answered each question with as much ambiguity as she could muster. *Rest your mind. We don't need him. We're fine just us three.* At that moment, though, with one daughter across the world and the other, she feared, not long for it, Lucille considered telling the truth. What if Millicent went to the Lord without knowing it? Would she have robbed her daughter of something that was her right to know? But what if delivering that truth is what the Lord was waiting on, the path fully cleared, and as soon as Millicent knew it, He would unhitch Millicent from this world and guide her into the next?

Lucille was not thinking clearly, everything so loose and muddied as it was. Gently, she put a hand to Millicent's forehead again— still only warm—and then leaned down and kissed her there. "I imagine he must," she found it within herself to say, and she left it at that.

Millicent thought she knew, though she never aired her suspicion out loud. She often wondered whether Ada harbored the same intuition, but anytime Millicent tried to shoulder up to the idea, to make some comment or other that grazed what she thought the truth might be, Ada never even flinched. Millicent watched. Confirmation could come through the briefest shared glance. *Do you know? Yes. I've always known. It's true then? Yes.* But Ada never exhibited the smallest expression of recognition, and Millicent did not want to be the one to spoil her sister's ignorance. She herself would have been better off not knowing, she sometimes thought. It was more upsetting to think that her father was so near and yet never came round than to think that he was absent altogether. And what sank Millicent's heart even deeper was that he had cast them out. That is what she believed: Their father did not want them, so he had told them to leave.

The Camby Plantation was not quite three miles from the plot on Aster Lane where they had rebuilt their house. It was a story that her mother, if she was in the right mood, liked to tell. With pride, her mother recounted how she and a few other people had built the house here, how they had worked all night till it was done. The point of the story, as Millicent understood, was to show Millicent and Ada how capable their mother was, to impart the lesson that a determined woman could do such things, build a house from the ground up, and in so doing build her own life. Her mother always skipped over the part about leaving the estate, and if Millicent asked, her mother merely smiled and pointed out something about the house that she liked, as if to prove that what they had now was better than what they had left. And there *was* much to like. The house sat on the side of a long dirt road, raised up off the ground, and Millicent and Ada had grown up playing on the small front porch, where they could sit and look out at the giant tamarind tree and at the grass flecked with sunshine, at the Penningtons' three-legged pot steaming with stew and the stack of cordwood Mrs. Callender kept on her porch.

Nearly a year before Millicent fell ill and Ada left for Panama, Millicent went to the estate one afternoon. She wanted to see the place where they had lived, the place where Ada and she had been born. She wanted to see the man who sired them, for she thought she knew.

She often went for walks by herself, taking her old school tablet with her and finding places to sit outside and draw. She sketched the birds and the trees, and the next time she went out, she erased what she had drawn the time before and drew something new. When she grabbed her tablet and walked away from the house that day, neither her mother nor Ada thought anything of it.

The sky had been radiant with yellow sunshine as Millicent had walked. Holding her writing slate to her chest, she had felt her heart thud at the thought of what she was going to do. What if he was there? What if she saw him? What if he saw her? Would he recognize her? Would he know who she was? She would watch his face, the way she watched Ada's sometimes. Would he tell her by a change in his expression that she really was right, that they shared the same blood? It was that thought in particular that made Millicent's chest tight. What if she was right? What then?

Her heart picked up its pace as she stepped through the tall grass. She usually did everything with purpose and deliberation, but she had no plan beyond walking to the plantation and standing on the grounds hoping to glimpse a man's face, to see if it would give her the answer to all the questions she had.

When she came to the drive leading up to the grounds, she could scarcely breathe. The drive was lined on both sides by mahogany trees, and they nodded to her in the breeze. She thought that was encouragement maybe, and she kept on. As she rounded a bend, past a hedge of hibiscus, the house came into view. It was almost as she had imagined it would be. A two-story house, pale gray with white trim. It had gracious balconies that spanned the width up top and a porch down below. In the far distance she could see the still blades on the stone windmill. What she did not see was another living soul anywhere, and she guessed that somewhere beyond the house was the area where everyone else who worked on the plantation lived, the area where her own house had once been. She thought about walking there just to see, but she was nervous already about having come this far. Standing on this gravel lane was possibly the one courageous thing she had ever done in her life. Millicent turned around, looking back in the direction from which she had come, and allowed herself to feel a moment of pride. She was still looking down the lane curving away from her when, from behind, the gallop of horse hooves came barreling up. She looked back over her shoulder to see a driver, a Black boy, sitting up tall in the front seat of a carriage, holding two leather reins and snapping them against the flanks of the horse to which the carriage was strapped. Millicent caught her breath. Quickly, she stepped behind a large tree. She clutched her tablet tight to her chest. She heard the driver say, "Yeeeuh," to the horse. Millicent peered out past the tree as the carriage neared—and inside it, under a dun-colored collapsible hood, was a man she took to be Henry Camby. He was clean-shaven, with a black hat on his head that cast a shadow over his long, elegant nose. He was alone in the carriage, gazing in the direction where Millicent stood hiding behind the trunk of a mahogany tree. She was seized by the need for him to see her. She stepped out to the side, clear of the tree, into plain view. She squeezed her tablet so hard that her finger joints popped. She watched his expression. He was maybe fifteen feet from her. Millicent watched and waited, but the look on Henry Camby's face, weary and lonely, did not change, and Millicent felt the ache of disappointment in her breast, wondering whether he had seen her at all.

12

HENRY CAMBY WAS SPEEDING ALONG IN A CARRIAGE, LATE FOR AN APPOINTMENT.
He had seen her. He had thought he was seeing a ghost and had
taken pains to keep his face straight. The ghost sightings had happened before. There were spirits on the plantation grounds, a fact
that everyone knew. It was part of the reason Henry tried to treat
people well. If you were not good to people in life, he believed, they
would almost certainly come back to haunt you in death.

Over the course of his forty-some years, Henry Camby had seen
three apparitions. The first was when he was urinating behind a row
of cane that he had estimated was high enough to create a curtain
of sorts as he took care of his business in the southern field. The
spirit, hovering above the ground, was doing a dance in the wind,
swaying out of rhythm with the waving cane stalks, and the out-of-
rhythmness of it was what drew his attention. That spirit had a face
that Henry could almost make out, but as soon as he squinted to see
who it was, the spirit disappeared.

The second sighting occurred in the dining room. A surprising
place, for what had ever happened there that would cause a spirit to
return? *Unless it was hungry*, Henry had thought, and then laughed.
His wife, Gertrude, who was seated at the table with him, had shot
him a quizzical look. "We have company for supper," Henry had
wanted to say, but he had restrained himself. Not for concern that
Gertrude would think he were crazy—he knew with certainty what
he saw: a translucent Negro boy sitting himself down at the table,
unfolding a napkin on his lap, awaiting his meal—but because as a
general rule neither of them talked to the other more than was necessary, a habit that had been their practice for the last few years. Theirs
was a contractual marriage, arranged by two sets of parents who

believed, incorrectly it turned out, that they were suitable for each other. They had not had children together and had little to bind them beyond documents. In any case, the Negro boy only stayed through the first course, which was rabbit stew, before he, too, disappeared.

The third time Henry Camby encountered a ghost on his property was in the boiling house. This ghost was more formed than the other two. It was a woman whose edges and face were clear. Round cheeks and jowls, wiry hair, eyebrows that nearly met in the middle. Henry recognized her. She was a former employee named Roberta, who two months prior to his sighting had been ill. Henry had been regrettably slow in recruiting a doctor to see her. Too slow. The doctor, when he did arrive, assured Henry that the woman's demise was not his fault, but Henry had trouble forgiving himself. He prayed at night over it, fervent remonstrations, but guilt nevertheless clung to his soul. He could not shake it loose. Which is why, he believed, Roberta had come back. He had wronged her in life, so she haunted him in death. That seemed to make perfect sense. The first two, however, remained a mystery, and he took no responsibility for them. The property had been in his family for nearly two centuries. Henry had not taken it over until he had returned from university in London. Anything could have happened before he was in charge. The first two, he believed, had been wronged before his time, a theory that explained their haziness, too.

But then—a fourth? A girl by the road. A girl frighteningly clear in every detail—her oddly handsome sack-brown dress cut high at the neck, the piece of slate that she held to her chest. But there was something else. She looked strikingly like someone Henry had known and had loved. That was the part that scared him the most.

He sat with the fear as the carriage bumped down the road. Henry, driven by a St. Thomas Parish boy named Eli who had been his driver for two weeks by then (the last one having quit), was headed into town to see about procuring a loan from the bank. The year was 1906, and the price for one ton of muscovado sugar, which was the type he produced, was at a near record low. Ever since Henry had come home from England, times had been rough. A punishing drought in 1895 during which nothing would grow. A hurricane three years later that killed over a hundred unfortunate souls. Then three years again after that, in the month of July, a flood that drowned still more. And now Barbados had returned to drought and parched earth. Difficult conditions under which to harvest sugar. But the climate, of course, had always been a concern. The bigger problem now was the rise of beet sugars in Europe, which had led to a declining demand for the type of fine sugar produced here. Other owners Henry knew had been forced to consolidate their estates or subdivide and sell off part of their land. A few had declared bankruptcy. And the effects were not limited to the owners, of course. The consequences of collapse were felt all over the island. It was near impossible to find work. Every day one saw pitiable beggars in the streets. It was no wonder, given the circumstances, that everyone was leaving for Panama. He had heard stories, as everyone had, of men who had gone and returned with enough money to buy themselves a plot of land or a house, the sort of personal transformation that, repeated en masse, could very well transform the whole island. Which was precisely what many estate owners feared. The shifting balance of dependency. Three of Henry's own tenants had gone, but he could hardly blame them. It was difficult nowadays to eke out a livelihood at all.

As they passed the ghost, Henry nearly asked the driver to stop, but he thought better of it. He kept his mouth shut, kept the fear bottled up. He braced his hand on the carriage door. For the full fifteen minutes that it took to get to the bank, Henry held on to the door and the fear.

He went through with the meeting, which was successful from a business standpoint, but the entire time as he spoke and shook hands and signed papers, Henry could not stop thinking about the girl he had seen.

As soon as he was back home that evening, Henry summoned his longtime lawyer, J. R. Robinson, who was one of the only people on earth he felt he could trust, and asked for a favor.

"Would you comb the newspapers and registers, please, to find record of a woman who may have passed on? Lucille Bunting is the name."

For the next few nights, as J.R. searched, Henry had trouble sleeping. He did not want to believe it was true. Could Lucille, the woman he had loved so much it had put every other feeling in his life to shame, really have died? Had the ghost of her really come back to him now? He had always held on to the notion that he might somehow see her again. Even now, sixteen years after she had left the estate, he had thought that might yet prove true. Never once had he supposed that seeing her as a spirit was how it would occur. And why should that be? He had been good to her, had he not? He had been exceedingly fair. He had let Lucille take the house and everything in it—in fact, he had urged her to—because he understood it was a way to protect both her and the girls. He knew very well how wrathful Gertrude could be. The fact that Gertrude, afterwards, burned all the clothes that Lucille had ever sewn for the house servants—tossing them into a terrific bonfire out in the field where everyone on the grounds far and wide could see—only proved his point. He had to let Lucille go. Not because he wanted to but precisely because he didn't.

From the very moment Henry had seen Lucille at the back of the house, he had been struck. That was the only word to describe it— struck. And he had not been able to stop thinking about her since. In the middle of the night, he would creep out of the great house and walk soft-footed over the grass through the dark until he came to the small two-room house 256 steps from his own. He counted the steps each time in his head, both as a measure of distance and as rising anticipation. If anyone were to see him outside, he was prepared to say that he was given to bouts of sleepwalking.

He never knocked on the door. He simply let himself in. That was the arrangement they had. He gently closed the door behind him, and then it was just the two of them, alone. The first time he went to her, he admitted that he had not done anything like this before. It seemed important that she know that. She had looked shocked and said, "You never been with a woman?" He had laughed and said she had misunderstood. *That* he had done, but like this, with a tenant on this property—never. "That how you think of me?" she had asked, and for a moment he worried that he had offended her, but the coy arch of her eyebrows and the upturn of her mouth made it clear she was teasing.

"No, but I do think of you. Often."

"How often?"

"Often enough that it draws me out of bed to come see you."

At that she had frowned, a look of admonishment, as if she were cautioning him. "But these nights—that's all it can be."

He knew she was right. And he understood furthermore that those nights were all she *wanted* it to be. A nocturnal affair, nothing more. When he arrived, she usually walked toward him and unbuttoned his nightshirt without so much as a word. Even when Lucille was with child—his child—they kept their relations confined to the dark. From the house, Henry brought small sacks of ice that he placed upon her swollen feet. He brought slices of sweet bread that no one would miss. He brought packets of sugar, and when he dipped his finger into the rough crystals, Lucille would smilingly lean forward and lick it all off.

When the baby arrived—Millicent, they named her—Henry returned to the house in the nighttime again and again. He had perfected the 256 steps by then. Lucille still unbuttoned his shirt but now Henry lay with the babe against his bare chest. He had had a good life, he always thought, filled with the richest, most wonderful things, but those nights in that small two-room house brought him more happiness than anything that had come before or anything that would come after.

Around the time Lucille became pregnant a second time, things took a turn. Henry would never quite understand why.

One night, Gertrude got up in the middle of the night and found to her surprise that her husband was not there. She usually slept as soundly as a sheep, but the cook had served something for supper that had caused in Gertrude a bout of indigestion, and she woke up in the night to use the washroom. After she did, she lit a candle and carried it with her as she walked through every open room of the house only to discover that Henry was not in any of them. She hissed his name but got no reply. Then she called it louder, not caring whom she woke, but the only person who responded was a maid who poked her head into the hall, and Gertrude, annoyed that the girl should have the nerve to insinuate herself into her marital affairs, sharply ordered the girl back to bed. In her nightgown, Gertrude walked down to the front door and found it unlocked. That was not right. The front door of the house should always be locked overnight. One never knew when an uprising could start, and they should be protected, of course. She turned the doorknob to be sure. She told herself that the door being unlocked might have been nothing more than a simple mistake, but as soon as she told herself that, she knew she was wrong. Henry had left the house. And she knew enough about men to know there was likely only one thing he could be off doing in the middle of the night. She stared out into the darkness and released a great sigh.

In the morning when Henry appeared at the breakfast table Gertrude did not ask him where he had been. She wanted to see whether he might tell her himself. He did not. In silence, Gertrude drank her tea and watched Henry, her husband, butter his toast.

The next night, Gertrude forced herself to stay awake. She lay in bed next to Henry, pretending to be asleep while she waited to see what he would do. Around eleven o'clock, Henry climbed out of bed. Gertrude pretended to stir. She moaned and rolled over. The effect was as she intended. Henry, startled, got back into bed. She had stopped him from leaving. It was as simple as that. She had done it not out of love, per se—Gertrude had never loved Henry, she knew—but out of possessiveness. He was hers. Before God, that was what they had once declared.

Over the next weeks and months, as often as she could—though the lost sleep made her cantankerous—Gertrude pretended to sleep, then pretended to wake to keep Henry where she wanted him. There was the possibility that he went out on nights where she couldn't manage the ruse, the nights where drowsiness took over, but morning after morning Henry never said a word. It was not until several weeks later when Gertrude heard that one of their tenants, a Negro woman who had birthed two girls on their property, was moving off the estate grounds, and furthermore that Henry himself had permitted her to take her house with her when she went, that her husband effectively told Gertrude everything she needed to know.

13

EVERY DAY FRANCISCO DRESSED AND WALKED OUT OF THE HOUSE AND LOOKED down at the ground for footprints in the mud, but there were none. Inside, the bowl of salt was on the windowsill where he had left it the night before. The chairs at the table had not been budged by even an inch. The loose eggs on the counter sat untouched. Numbly, Francisco walked down to the shore, untied his boat, and got in. As he paddled out in the stark morning light, he stared back at the land, at the house, at what he could see of the road, but the boy did not appear.

In the beginning, Francisco paddled back to the shore in the evening with bits of hope in his heart. Maybe Omar would be there when he walked into the house. Maybe he would be seated at the table, rubbing his eyes. Maybe he would be standing at the washtub, cleaning himself. Maybe Francisco would not live the rest of his life alone, having lost the only two people he had ever loved. But each time Francisco stepped hopefully into the house, Omar was nowhere to be found. And after the first several days of disappointment, the feeling Francisco had when he came back to the shore was closer to dread. The thought of walking into the house only to discover that his son was not there—again—made him nauseous. For if the boy was gone, what had happened to him? Had he really, as Francisco had thought from the start, found a new place to live, away from his father? Had the six months of prolonged silence between them finally chased him away? Or was it, as Francisco had tried not to think, something far worse? That last thought in particular set the wave of nausea loose, and multiple times in those days Francisco leaned over the side of the boat and threw up. The idea did occur to him that he could go search for his son, but that brought the same strangling feeling of dread. For if he searched, what might he find? No. It was easier, Francisco had learned, to live in a world of delusion, which was after all not so different from hope, than to stand face-to-face with the truth.

|||||

AFTER ESME HAD disappeared, Francisco had stopped fishing for a few years. He had no choice. He could not take a baby out on the boat all day long, nor could he leave a baby at home. Instead Francisco bought a knock-kneed goat and milked it and poured the milk into a cheesecloth that had been filled with rice and let Omar suck the milk out. He mashed up plantain and papaya and boiled ñame and greens, and fed that to him, too. When the goat died, he butchered it and ate the cooked meat. While Omar was sleeping, Francisco built boats like the one he had made for himself, and with Omar tied to his chest, he dragged the boats to the city and sold them to people. They got by this way.

But as soon as he could, as soon as Omar was old enough to stay home by himself, Francisco started fishing again. He found that out on the water, he felt closer to her. He knelt in the hull of the boat and peered over the sides. With his hand, he ruffled the water, which flashed in the sun. If she was magical—and he believed that she was—then she might come back. "Esme!" he whispered in case she could hear. Sometimes he dove in. He could hardly see more than he had seen from the boat, but the miraculous thing, the thing that made Francisco dive in again and again over the years, was not only desperation and grief but the fact that sometimes when he went under the water, it smelled distinctly of violets.

In 1899, nine years after Esme went from being the most magical creature ever to walk the earth to the most tragic ever to try to walk upon the sea, war broke out. At the time, Panamá was the westernmost department of the Republic of Colombia, and although the war started as a battle between the Liberals and the Conservatives in the Department of Santander farther to the east, it soon spread

like ink, staining every part of the country. Francisco could remember hearing the sonorous boom of gunboats stationed in the Gulf of
Panamá. On the streets of the city he saw children dressed in military uniforms so oversized that even with their belts cinched tight,
they looked like crumpled bags, children who nevertheless had been
enlisted to fight. When Victoriano Lorenzo, a Liberal leader who
had fought valiantly to defend his people's land rights, was executed
in the Plaza de Chiriquí before a firing squad of twelve soldiers, it
was impossible not to be horrified. And yet, somehow, much of life
went on. Francisco fished, and he went to the market, where people
discussed every development of the war—one day the Liberals had
won a victory at La Negra Vieja, the next day the Conservatives had
killed two hundred men, back and forth, an eye for an eye, until
it was hard to tell who had the upper hand. Joaquín, who had begun avidly reviewing the newspaper, stood at his stall and as people
gathered around—Francisco among them—imparted what he had
read. Stories of villages burned in the mountains, a blockade on a
river, a skirmish atop a bridge. For three years, war raged. And then
one day in November 1902, a battleship from the United States arrived, a ship with the strange name *Wisconsin*, which no one could
pronounce. Some people said it was the size of Noah's great ark,
but others said no, it only appeared so big because Panamá was so
small. To Francisco both sides were saying the same thing and they
were furthermore missing the point. The United States had arrived
to meddle in the affairs of Panamá. But upon that ship, a treaty was
reached, and the deadliest war in Francisco's memory finally came
to an end.

After the torment of the war, everyone in the country was exhausted and enraged. Instead of discussing battles and what kinds
of weapons had been shipped over in piano boxes and which bridges
were damaged and how many thousands of men had been killed, the
people in the fish market, who were the only people Francisco saw
all day long, started clamoring about the idea of una separación from

Colombia. The talk was timid at first. Even the word, Francisco felt, was timid. A separation. As if it could all be so polite. But as time passed, the talk grew more intense. His entire life he had heard Panamanians dream that they might become a country that belonged to itself. In the eighty or so years since declaring independence from Spain, Panamanians had tried numerous times to extract themselves from Colombia, hopeful that they might control their own interests without answering to the whims and demands of Bogotá.

The difference between the talk of La Separación this time and every time before was that now Panamanians had someone on their side who could ensure their success—the United States. The United States, Joaquín explained to anyone who would listen, wanted to build a canal. Some of the men in the fish market, those who recalled that twenty years earlier Frenchmen had declared the same thing, laughed. The French effort had lasted nine dismal years, and by the time the French went home, they had made only minor progress. Why, since the time of Christopher Columbus people had wanted to create a canal across the isthmus, and no one yet had gotten it done. What made the North Americans think they could do it now? Audacity, Joaquín told them, and Francisco knew his friend well enough to know that he meant it as praise.

Joaquín summarized what he had read. The United States had attempted to negotiate a treaty with the government in Bogotá in which they had offered to pay $10 million, plus $250,000 every year for one hundred years, if Bogotá gave them the rights and sovereignty over an area of land six miles wide for the length of the canal. Joaquín recited the terms with a certain melodrama. "And do you know what the government said to that offer?" he asked. "They said no!" he sputtered. Francisco listened politely. Joaquín shared the attitude of many Panamanians who believed that the tiny strip of land upon which they lived had been chosen for greatness by God Himself and that a canal across the isthmus would finally bring the region of Panamá the prosperity it deserved. In their view, to have

Bogotá deny them their God-given fate as well as their future wealth was sacrilege. In Francisco's view, he would rather everything simply be left alone.

The Panamanians who favored separation became quite vocal after that. Every time Francisco went to the market, Joaquín spoke of riots and uprisings. Francisco himself saw new ships in the harbor— first one displaying a Colombian flag, and then one flying the flag of the United States, as if in direct response—which made it seem as though something serious were afoot. "The United States will not take no for an answer," Joaquín effused. "Thanks to them, we might get our canal after all." It was not until later that Joaquín and Francisco understood just what the United States had done. They had not simply stood up to the government in Bogotá; they had tacitly offered military support to the separatists in Panamá. For if the separation occurred, then the United States could try anew to negotiate a treaty for the canal—only this time with a country that wanted it anyway. One day in November 1903 people heard that two Colombian generals had been jailed, and they saw the Colombian ship in the harbor retreat, and word spread that the Republic of Panamá had been born.

At the fish market, Joaquín stood up on a crate one afternoon and waved a newspaper in the air. The provisional junta had published something they were calling the Manifesto on Panamanian Independence.

"Listen here!" Joaquín said, and everyone did. "It says, 'The transcendental act that by a spontaneous movement the inhabitants of the Isthmus of Panamá have just executed is the inevitable consequence of a situation which has become graver daily. The Isthmus of Panamá has been governed by the Republic of Colombia with the narrow-mindedness that in past times were applied to their colonies by the European nations—the isthmian people and territory was a source of fiscal resources and nothing more.'"

Francisco watched as people around him nodded.

After several minutes, Joaquín came to a part that said: "The people of the Isthmus, in view of such notorious causes, have decided to recover their sovereignty and begin to form a part of the society of the free and independent nations, in order to work out its own destiny, to insure its future in a stable manner, and discharge the duties which it is called on to do by the situation of its territory and its immense riches." Everyone cheered. "¡Viva el Istmo Libre!" Francisco thought they were fools. With bright eyes, people went around reciting the words. Part of the society of the free and independent nations! Its own destiny! They drank them in, intoxicated. But Francisco believed he understood something that they did not. To be independent and to be sovereign were two different things. Panamá, detaching itself from Colombia, had merely done an about-face and attached itself to the United States instead.

In the years to come, Francisco might have had any number of grievances. He might have complained that the American immigrants who flowed into Panamá brought their strange music and their strange food. He might have complained how few of them tried to learn Spanish or about how they imposed taxes on goods imported into the Canal Zone, even goods from other parts of Panamá. No one had ever heard of such a thing. A tax on goods imported *from* Panamá *to* Panamá was absurdity of the highest degree. He might have complained about all the United States flags that were suddenly strung up everywhere, fluttering in the sea breeze, or about how the cobblestone streets were now being paved, as if their unruliness were in need of being smoothed out, or about how the names of so many of those streets and plazas were being changed from what they had always been, or about how everywhere Francisco looked, there were new stores, new hotels, new restaurants, none of which he could afford. Measure by measure, the world as he knew it was giving way.

But what happened with the tinaja is what put him over the edge.

Francisco and Omar never had visitors on the road where they lived, so it was with considerable alarm that, eighteen months or so after the treaty, Francisco was awoken early one morning by a great ruckus, a profusion of sound that at first he mistook for a plague of locusts, insects that sometimes raided the coast, bleating in a mad chorus and scraping their dry, discarded shells. He sat up in bed. The sun had not yet risen, but it was huddled somewhere just below the horizon and gave off the subtlest glow of light, just enough to allow him to see.

Francisco looked around his bedroom in confusion, trying to remember the last time the locusts had come. They tended to keep to a schedule—every three years, every seven, Francisco did not know what it was, but he knew that right then was not their appointed time. He got out of bed and walked to Omar's room, but the boy was asleep. Seeing that only added to Francisco's confusion. How could Omar sleep through all of this racket? Was the commotion only in Francisco's head? He stuck a finger in each of his ears to clean out any wax in case that would help, but now the noise sounded louder to him than it had before.

Frightened by what he might find, Francisco crept through the house and very slowly opened the front door. What he saw out on the road, beyond the aloe plants in the yard and the snails and the frogs lazing in the dirt, was not a swarm of locusts but a swarm of men. In the darkness of the morning, he could barely make them out. But they were no doubt men, maybe four or five of them, whistling and walking and carrying things—Francisco was not sure what—as if they were in a parade. Francisco watched them march all the way to the end of the road and stop in front of his house. Again he thought: *Is this all in my head? Is this only a dream?*

One of the men from the swarm came forward and, in imperfect Spanish, said, "Hello! We are the fumigation brigade." He walked through the yard toward the front door where Francisco stood peering out in his underwear. It was only when the man was close enough that Francisco could see he was white. He was carrying an aluminum oil can.

Francisco did not know the meaning of "fumigation brigade." It sounded like a military operation, perhaps. He asked, "Are we in another war?"

The man at his door laughed. "Yes. In a manner of speaking. A war against mosquitoes."

That was not what Francisco had expected the man to say, and now, though Francisco was the one standing there in his underwear, he felt pity for the man before him, who had either made an asinine joke or else was so delusional that he thought a war against mosquitoes was one worth fighting, a war that could actually be won. Francisco, who only minutes earlier had been frightened and confused, suddenly felt the dynamic between them reverse and believed that he was on top, looking down upon this poor misguided man.

Francisco came out onto the step and closed the door behind him. He smiled and, simply to humor the man, said, "How can I help?"

The man did not answer but nodded and whistled to the rest of the brigade still standing in the road. They were dark-skinned men, though not Panamanian it seemed, and at once they stormed toward the house, some going in one direction, some going in another, all of them moving with efficiency and purpose, speaking to one another in English, and Francisco watched, at first with amusement and then with increasing concern as one of the men rested a ladder against his roof while another tore long strips of newspaper and began gluing them to the windows while yet another poured some sort of liquid into the aluminum oil can.

"What are you doing?" Francisco shouted to a man on the roof. "There are no mosquitoes up there!"

It was such a bizarre sight, these men in their futile swirl of activity descending upon his small house, that part of him still clung to the idea that it was all some sort of ludicrous dream.

But when the man Francisco had first spoken to set fire to the liquid in the can and said he needed to put it inside the house, Francisco threw himself in front of the door and held his arms out to the side, blocking the man's way.

"I do not know what you are doing here, but I will not let you burn down my house."

"The fire stays in the can," the man said. "It's the smoke that we need. The smoke suffocates any mosquitoes inside."

But that sounded as preposterous as the rest of it. And Omar was inside. Though surely he could not still be sleeping, could he?

"I will not let you in," Francisco said.

The man frowned. The sun was coming up, lightening the day, and Francisco could see more clearly by then. The man, clean-shaven, was holding the smoldering oil can in his hand. In Spanish he said, "Then you will be fined."

"Fined? For what? Not allowing you to set fire to my house? Under whose authority are you here?"

"The Americans'."

Francisco balked. "The North Americans', you mean?"

"I mean the Americans'."

"But that is all of us."

"Who?"

"Those of us from the Americas."

The man pointed to his chest and said slowly in Spanish, over-enunciating each word, "I am an American. They are West Indians. You are a Panamanian."

Francisco, greatly annoyed, jabbed a finger to his own chest and, just as slowly, said, "I was born here, in the Americas. Therefore, I am an American."

The man raised his eyebrows.

Francisco said, "We were Americans long before you were."

There was a pause. And then the man at whom Francisco was staring simply shrugged. "Until a year ago, you were Colombian. Now please step aside."

But Francisco did not. "Are you saying that the United States sent you here? To burn down my house?"

"To get rid of mosquitoes."

"But that cannot be done."

"We are going to try. Now, if you will stand to the side . . ."

Francisco stayed where he was, his body an X in front of the door, naked except for his thin underwear.

The man looked sternly at him. "These are my orders. And if you do not comply, you will be fined or imprisoned."

Francisco understood that another reversal had occurred, that the men in his yard and crawling all over his house saw *him* as a fool, the object of *their* pity, a man whose delusion was that he could stand up to the power of the United States and not be squashed like a pest. And maybe he was.

"No," Francisco said.

The man looked surprised. "Did you understand what I said?"

"I will not let you in."

"What is your name?"

But Francisco stood with his arms and feet wide and said nothing more.

And finally, after releasing a great sigh of frustration, the man walked back out into the yard and put the flaming can on the ground and doused it with another liquid that extinguished the fire and stopped it from smoking. In English, he called the men down from the roof. They hoisted the ladder up on their shoulders and carried it back to the road. As his parting gesture, the white man walked over to the tinaja filled with rainwater Francisco kept by the side of the house. As it was too heavy to lift, he pushed it over onto its side, and Francisco watched in horror as the water he had collected for months gushed out, darkening the dirt. "No open containers," was all the man said. Then the brigade left his property, and Francisco watched them go. As a group, they trekked back up the road toward the house of Doña Ruiz, where possibly they would try to do the same thing. Who knew? All Francisco knew was that they could not come in his home, and if they returned, he would stop them again.

As it was, they did not return because the boundaries for the fumigation efforts were revised such that Francisco's house fell outside the lines. The area of more pressing concern became the city proper. But Francisco did not know that. When no one came back, he regarded it simply as his personal success. He had turned them away. He yanked the strips of newspaper down from the windows and wadded them up, he scrubbed off the glue, and the only thing left behind from the encounter was the bitter feeling Francisco had for the meddlesome Yankees who, like a plague of locusts, had invaded Panamá.

||||||

FRANCISCO FELT THAT same bitter feeling come flooding back when, many months later, Omar told him that he had gotten a job working on the canal. At the very suggestion, Francisco had flown into a fury so that Omar would stop saying things Francisco did not want to hear.

The problem was that it worked. It was effective beyond reason. Not only did Omar stop saying things Francisco did not want to hear, but he stopped saying things altogether, and Francisco, in his rage and disappointment, decided that for one entire day he would do the same. For a full day, he walked past Omar, looked past him, ignored him completely.

He should have ended it there, having gotten his point across, but when Francisco woke up the next day, the outrage still boiled, so he did it again. Maybe two days in a row would change the boy's mind, make him reconsider his mistake. By the third day, Francisco was mostly annoyed that his silent protest was not having the desired effect. He could feel Omar looking at him at times, but the boy did not speak, did not apologize, did not ask for forgiveness, said nothing at all, and Francisco understood that they were both dug in. It was a cockfight in which both of them were pecking at the air, circling each other to see who went down first. Francisco resolved it would not be him. An action born from righteousness quickly transformed into one sustained by pride.

Now, he had said nothing to the boy for nearly six months.

Many days, Francisco woke up in the morning with every intention of saying something to his son. Sometimes he thought he might say, "I am sorry. Let us stop this," and they could move on. Other times he thought the better approach would be to act as if nothing had happened and say something banal, like "Bananas are yellow," and see how Omar would respond. They could have an honest debate about how bananas were sometimes green and sometimes brown, it didn't matter the topic, as long as they were talking about *something*. Still other times Francisco had the idea that he could just say a word, any word under the sun—"Butterfly" or "window" or "spoon"—and that one lone word would be enough to break apart the accumulation of silence. But every time Francisco opened his mouth he could not get even one single word to come out. The original outrage still simmered, but it was not even that. Speaking was so impossible that he would have thought the problem was physical except that when he went to the fish market and talked to any other person, his voice still came out loud and clear. The impasse was only with Omar. Until his son stopped working in the Mouth, Francisco could not open his.

Not speaking to someone was one thing. But not speaking to no one was another thing entirely. The whole time that Omar did not come home, there was no one for Francisco to assiduously ignore. At some point, he started to feel he was coming undone. He stood in the middle of the house and shouted, "¡Hola!" just to hear the sound of his voice, which he had not heard in the house for nearly half a year. He shouted, "The rain is drowning the frogs!" He shouted, "I cannot make sense of this life!" And then he stood alone in the echo and felt worse than before.

When he went to the market, Francisco interacted with Joaquín, but those interactions always involved less speaking than listening. Joaquín liked to vent about whatever happened to be on his mind— the weather, his wife. One day Francisco lumbered up to Joaquín's stall with his catch, and Joaquín was carrying on about Panama hats.

"I ask you, my friend, what is a Panama hat?"

Francisco replied that he did not know.

"Have you seen the straw hats that all the so-called important men wear?"

"No."

Joaquín recoiled a little and gave Francisco an exasperated look. "Don't you ever go out anywhere?"

"I come here."

"Here, yes, fine. But there is a whole other world out *there*." Joaquín pointed behind him toward the city, indeed the whole country, that lay beyond the dock.

Francisco shrugged.

"Well, if you went anywhere, you would see them. They have become ubiquitous on men of a certain station. They are pale, finely woven hats with a black ribbon band."

"You mean Ecuador hats?"

Joaquín clapped his hands. "You do not let me down after all! Yes, Ecuador hats! Do the Yankees not know those hats are made in Ecuador? But now they are calling them Panama hats. And they sell them that way."

"But why?"

Joaquín leaned over that day's heap of fish and sifted them, their silver bodies slipping over one another. "Why do you think?"

"They are using our name."

"They are using every part of us that they please." Joaquín plucked one fish up by the tail. "It is like this fish. Someone can use the scales for jewelry and the eyes for bait and the flesh for a meal and the bones for a soup, and when they are done, there will be nothing left." He tossed the fish to the side.

Francisco stared at the space that was left in the air. He remembered during the time of La Separación how optimistic and hopeful Joaquín had been. "I call it La Boca," Francisco said.

"Call what?"

"The canal."

"You call it the Mouth?"

"Yes. It is eating us."

Solemnly, Joaquín nodded. "That is right, my friend. We are the fish."

||||||

AFTER ABOUT A week, desperation took hold and Francisco walked up the road to the house of Doña Ruiz. It was a Sunday, the day of rest, and Francisco found her lying in repose in a hammock stretched between two cedar trees. Her eyes were closed, and her hands were folded over her chest as though she were dead.

Francisco walked up next to the hammock and stood there, looking down. Doña Ruiz was wearing a colorfully embroidered bata, and her feet were bare.

Without opening her eyes, she said, "Why are you here?"

Francisco blinked, then he snorted in a mocking way. "Aren't you supposed to know?"

He saw Doña Ruiz grin. "Ah—he speaks."

Chastened, Francisco closed his mouth. Doña Ruiz opened her eyes and stared up at him. Francisco, afraid of her gaze, looked away.

"Five months and twenty-two days, by my count," Doña Ruiz said. "That is a long time for a man to behave like a stone."

Francisco had not come to be reprimanded. "Do you know where he is?"

"I know where he is not."

"Where?"

"Here."

Francisco had an urge to spit on the old bat. Why had he thought she would help him? Just because she had once predicted that he would marry Esme? Anyone could have predicted that. Anyone could have taken one look at the two of them and said the same thing. That was not even a prediction. That was eyesight and common sense. A long time ago he had vowed to himself to steer clear of Doña Ruiz, and he should have upheld his vow. Not here. Of course the boy was not here. Francisco had cautioned him, too, not to go near this old cow. He should have listened to his own advice.

"Have you looked for him?" she asked.

"No."

"No? Well what do you think? That if something is lost it will come to find you? Open your eyes, Francisco Aquino. Your mouth is one thing, but you need to open your eyes." Then it was she who laughed in a mocking way, a sound that wounded him and repulsed him.

Francisco stumbled back and still she laughed, and had Francisco not been so eager to escape her presence, he would have pointed out that until a minute ago, she was the one who had her eyes closed.

||||||

THROUGH THE BRANCHES of the trees that hovered high above her head, Doña Ruiz looked up at the sky from her hammock. Fifteen years ago, she had been given the hammock by a poor soul from Portobelo who had no money to pay for his palm reading, and lying in it on Sundays had been her tradition ever since. Ordinarily, Doña Ruiz would have had little sympathy for someone who had sought out her services knowing that they had not a single silver coin in their pocket, but in her youth Doña Ruiz had been to Portobelo, and the town had made a lasting impression on her. Many Panamanians undertook an annual pilgrimage to the ancient town to worship at the feet of the Black Jesus that was housed in its church, and Doña Ruiz's mother had insisted the whole family take part. It did not end up being the journey her mother had envisioned. Customarily, people walked most of the way and then fell to their knees and crawled to the church for the final mile or so, but Doña Ruiz's mother, in her extreme piety, wanted the family to crawl for the full three days. Doña Ruiz's brothers, Armando and Ismael, kept poking and swatting each other as they crawled, and they wrestled and roughhoused so much that the family kept having to stop so that Doña Ruiz's mother could scold them and pry them apart. After a time, her father stood up and announced that he would walk the rest of the way. His knees were bloody, he groused. Her mother had snarled, "That is the point." But her father had merely shrugged and walked upright beside them until her mother finally relented and sent the men home. It took young Doña Ruiz and her mother another two days to arrive, and by the end their knees were indeed bloodied almost down to the bone. When they got to the church, it was ringed with so many worshippers scrabbling beneath the blaze of the sun that no one could get close enough to actually see El Cristo Negro. "What bullshit is this?" her mother said. Before long, a spirit of revolt spread through the crowd. There was talk of storming the church, of tearing down the wooden walls so El Cristo Negro would be revealed. There was shoving and squirming. And then, amid the agitation, a dark shadow passed over the crowd, as if day had plunged into night, and everyone stopped and looked about in confusion. When Doña Ruiz looked up, she saw in the darkened sky the figure of a man, which was really a cloud, but which in her mind she took for El Cristo Negro, as if he had departed the church and revealed himself to those with the daring to look up. To this day, lying in the hammock, she always made sure she did.

Doña Ruiz was older now, though, and getting out of the hammock was not as easy as it used to be. Because of that, she stayed in it for hours sometimes. She napped and let her mind wander and she plotted how she would get out, rolling her body one way then the other to gain some momentum, hooking a leg over the side.

On the day that Francisco came to her, she had been lying there already for two hours, enjoying the breeze before the rain that would surely come.

Francisco was a hot wind, and when he had blown up beside her, she could tell he was there without opening her eyes. Doña Ruiz had known Francisco for quite some time. She had already lived on this road when he arrived to build his small house, and though he was never friendly and they rarely spoke, he had walked up and down the road so many times, passing her house each time, that she had had ample opportunity to watch him and read his energy even from afar. In the early years, he was determined, bringing in the supplies and materials to erect his house, and from her front patio sometimes, Doña Ruiz could hear the echo of the hammer knocking sticks of wood into place as he worked. Then there was the period of sublime happiness, the sort of happiness that only comes from falling in love, and it was not long before Doña Ruiz saw Francisco walk down the road with a woman at his side, a brooding raven-haired woman named Esme. Doña Ruiz predicted their matrimony before Francisco himself realized it would occur. From experience she had learned that when a man is stupefied with joy as Francisco was in those days, there are only two possible outcomes—marriage or heartbreak. As it happened, Francisco would get both. The period of happiness ended a year and a half after it began and was followed by a period of intense and smothering grief. Esme disappeared. Doña Ruiz never saw her again. The next thing she saw was Francisco walking down the road with an infant strapped to his chest and the weight of all the rest of the world saddled onto his back. In time, Doña Ruiz watched the baby grow into a boy and then into a young man. He had a very different temperament from his father. He was shy and quiet but open to things, pliable, flexible, eager to learn. At one point she'd had a mule that took her to the city, but the mule had died, and when it had become harder for her to walk to the city herself, she had asked Omar to run errands for her, an arrangement that lasted for some years. He was always polite; he always did as she asked. Doña Ruiz never saw Omar and Francisco together, but because they were all the other had, she imagined they must have been close. The day Francisco came to her, she had not seen him in quite a while. She was surprised to find that in all that time his energy was as yet unchanged. He was as sorrowful now as she had observed him to be in the days of his grief, and she pitied him because it was clear to her that for seventeen years, he had been trapped in that sorrow. Lying there in the hammock, she asked the gods to lift it from him.

14

OMAR FOUND THE MEN IN HIS GANG AT A PLACE FARTHER SOUTH FROM WHERE THEY usually stood, next to a massive heap of red-and-pink clay that, to his recollection, had not existed the last time he was there. It was raining, and they were all—Clement and Prince and Joseph and Berisford—standing in front of the clay, holding their picks down at their side, waiting for the morning whistle to blow. Omar made his way toward them through the mud.

"Look who here!" Berisford said, smiling widely when he saw Omar walk up.

Prince waved. Solemnly, Joseph nodded hello and tipped his hat. Clement, standing with his arms crossed over his chest, merely shifted his gaze sideways at Omar without so much as turning his head.

Berisford clapped Omar on the shoulder and said, "Happy to see you, brother. I fearful you resting in peace."

Omar smiled. "I was resting in the hospital."

Berisford looked shocked.

"I had malaria," Omar said.

"Malaria? Even with all the quinine you drink?"

Clement said, "This again?"

"What? Prove my point that the quinine don't work."

Clement looked at Omar. "Answer me this. What you have in the hospital make you well?"

"Quinine," Omar said.

Clement smirked at Berisford. "Prove *my* point."

Berisford turned so that only Omar could see him and dramatically rolled his eyes. Omar smiled again. It felt good to be back, to return to the things that had become familiar to him—the steady click of railcar wheels, the feel of the pick in his hands, even Berisford and Clement's bickering. He may have been digging in a new spot, but otherwise not much had changed, and he found some comfort in that.

Berisford gestured to the heap of clay. "You hear about the slide?" he asked Omar.

Berisford explained that one night while they were all off sleeping, part of the mountain wall had come undone and crashed down. It had buried two steam shovels and plenty of track. "We here fighting the earth," he said, shaking his head.

Prince stuck his neck out. "And the earth fighting back!"

When the whistle finally blew, Omar raised his pick and sank its point into the gargantuan mountain of clay. All down the line, one by one, every man cranked his arms and started to dig. The feeling of that movement was familiar to Omar, too, and between it and the way Berisford had welcomed him back, he felt the tug of belonging—however slight—that he had been seeking when he first came here.

Yesterday, after two weeks in the hospital, Omar had been discharged and had walked all the way home. It was the middle of the afternoon, and when he got to the house his father's boat was not at the shore. Omar had gone inside and taken off his boots and clothes and hat and washed them and laid them all out to dry. In his underclothes, he had walked to the kitchen and eaten a few soda crackers from the tin that his father kept on a shelf. Then he had ambled through the house, trailing his fingertips over the things he had missed—the square kitchen table, the bowl filled with salt, his father's rusty machete, the pebbles buried in the clay of the walls. He was the only one there, but the house did not feel empty to him. Through the windows, he could hear the birds singing their songs, he could smell the saltwater air of the ocean. His father never talked about his mother, but Omar knew that she had taken care of him in this house, that she had fed him and walked with him upon the earthen floors, and sometimes Omar imagined that her footprints lingered beneath the surface and that her breath was still in the air. He felt closest to her when he was at home, where he knew she had been. He walked into his father's bedroom and sat on the bed. His father's comb was on the windowsill. Omar leaned forward and picked it up. He ran a finger over its tines and smiled when it made a sound.

He had hoped that when he walked through the front door, his father might be there, waiting for him, but of course his father had been out at sea. What had his father thought while he had been gone? Surely he had been worried, no? Unless his father somehow believed that Omar had stayed away of his own will, that he had chosen not to come home. In which case his father was probably upset, but his father was already upset, so that would be no different from how it had been before. But if his father had been worried, then when he walked through the door later that night and saw Omar again for the first time in weeks, he would be elated, wouldn't he? Omar imagined the moment, how his father, after an instant of shock, would succumb to his elation and without even thinking would say something to him. Just like that, the Reign of Silence would end.

Dusk had fallen by the time his father walked into the house. Omar was sitting at the table, and at the moment his father stepped through the front door and saw him, he stopped. Omar, who all afternoon had been holding on to his hopeful dream, the dream in which his father, overjoyed at seeing his son, would pull him into his arms, ask him where he had been, what had happened to him, say ¡Gracias a Dios!, say My son has returned!, say something, anything, even hello, sat at the table and stared across the room at his father who was staring at him. For the span of one agonizing minute it all seemed so possible, but while Omar waited, at some point he saw his father tighten his jaw and lift his chin, and with that, all possibility came to an end. His father had walked through the room and past Omar without saying a word.

||||||

"**I HOPE YOU** came ready to work today, boys!"

Omar glanced over his shoulder to see Miller marching up behind them in his black rubber boots. Miller was one thing Omar had not missed.

Berisford stood tall and yelled. "We always ready, sir!"

"What's that?" Miller said.

Berisford cleared his throat. "We always ready, sir," he repeated, less loudly this time.

Miller sauntered up until he was close enough that if he had held his arm out straight, the tip of his fingers would have touched Berisford's chest.

"You being smart?"

"No, sir."

"No," Miller said. "No chance of that."

Omar glanced at Berisford's face, but it was stony and still. Rainwater dripped off the brim of his hat.

Miller stayed where he was but looked sideways down the line as he shouted, "Another day in the wet, but you have to push through! The first hurdle to clear is to dig out from the slide. Once you do that, there is still the matter of the one million cubic yards to be dug."

They had not met the goal last month, but Miller swore to himself that this month not even a slide would get in their way. By hell or high water, this division would be at the top of the rankings, and that sparkling number—one million—would be printed for everyone to behold. After that, he felt sure, people would see him as more than just another man turning the wheel.

"And if you can't do the job," he went on, "I'll replace you with someone who can."

"Yes, sir!"

Miller snapped his gaze back to the man directly in front of him, the one always wearing the same red handkerchief. "Why are you saying 'yes, sir' so cheerfully? You think that's a bluff? There's a thousand like you who'd be happy for this job."

At that, Miller saw the man's face twitch, and he knew he had gotten to him. In matters of gambling, which Miller enjoyed, a twitch like that was what they called a tell.

Miller grinned. He took several steps back and looked out at the massive mountain of rock and clay. "Dig like hell, boys!"

|||||

ONCE UPON A time, in what seemed like another life, Miller had been a gambling man. He didn't typically have enough money for alcohol, which was where the gambling came in. If he played his cards right or made a smart bet, he could win enough for a whiskey or two. A whole bottle, if fortune was on his side. But then the whiskey made him more likely to place another wager—it loosened his mind and his rational self—and if he won big, he rewarded himself with yet another drink, and if he lost big, he consoled himself with the same, provided he had money to spare. He didn't always, and that was a problem. But the two were linked in his mind—whiskey and wagering. In the end, it was the wagering that got him. And actually it wasn't the wagering but the man with whom he had wagered. That's who Miller blamed. A Negro whom Miller discovered one evening sitting at the bar at Jensen's Saloon out near Boise, Idaho. For every night of the three weeks Miller had been in Boise he had gone there after work to kick up his boots and let off some steam. Occasionally, he could persuade one of the other men to buy him a drink, but more often than not Miller had to play a few hands of poker before he acquired enough money for the sweet stuff. What little Miller earned on the railroad he sent back to his poor mother in South Carolina, who was the only woman he felt any affection toward. He'd had relations with other women, more than a few, but affection was not part of the equation those times.

The Negro who had been seated at the bar that night had his shirtsleeves rolled up to his elbows and his bare forearms resting on the lacquered bar top like he belonged there. He also had a drink in one hand when Miller did not, and that seemed unfair.

Miller walked over and asked the bartender, "Why you serving him?"

"He come in," the bartender replied.

"You serve everyone who comes in?"

"We do if they have money."

"He had money?" Miller asked sourly.

"He did."

The bartender was lanky and wore a bow tie, which Miller had not cared about before but which struck him as suspect now. What sort of bartender wore a bow tie these days?

"Well, you ask where he got it?"

"Why would I do that?"

"Never know with them kind. Probably thieved it if he has any at all."

"You thieve it?" the bartender asked.

"I did not," the Negro answered. He had a low voice.

"You see," the bartender said.

"Why you believe him?" Miller asked.

"Got no reason not to."

Miller eyed the Negro, who was hunched over, sipping his drink. Miller licked his lips at the sight of that whiskey. It just did not seem right.

"How much money you got?" Miller asked.

"Excuse me?"

"How much money you got?"

The Negro's eyelids were heavy. If he was that drunk it meant he must have had a bundle to spend, and it might mean he had more. How he acquired it Miller still did not know, but now his only thought was how to get that money for himself.

"I got what I got," the Negro finally said.

"Ten dollars? Fifteen? Twenty? Twenty-five?"

Impassively, the Negro took another sip of his whiskey.

"Goddamn. Fifty? You got fifty dollars to your name?" Miller shook his head. How could that be? The world had turned plumb upside-down if this man had fifty dollars to his name and Miller at that very moment had none.

"Tell you what," Miller said. "I'll make you a bet. I'll bet your fifty dollars that you can't stand up upon that rail for five seconds straight."

Miller pointed to the wooden handrail that ran all around the edge of a second-story walkway that looked down over the saloon, like a balcony of sorts.

The Negro rolled his head back on his neck and smiled. "You give me fifty if I can stand up on that rail?"

"For five full seconds, no less. And if you can't, you give me your fifty instead."

"You have fifty?"

"Of course I do."

The Negro worked his jaw like he was pondering it, then he stood and climbed the staircase to the second floor, a bit more steady than Miller would have thought he would be. When he got to the top nearly everyone in the saloon was watching from down below. He hoisted himself up on the rail, one foot and then two. He let go of his hands and straightened up, and then he was standing, like a king lording over them all. Miller held his breath while the bartender started to count out loud. "One, two . . ." Everyone joined in. "Three." The Negro swayed. Miller clenched his jaw. "Four." Then the man toppled. Some people gasped. Miller let out the breath he was holding and grinned. Fifty dollars to him. That would buy drinks for close to a year. The cracking sound that came next seemed to run up the walls and puncture the air. People crowded up around the man, and Miller leaned forward, trying to see. Someone screamed. "He busted open his head!" The grin dropped off Miller's face. "He's bleeding a river!" There were shouts for a medic and for rags and for giving the man space. Miller looked all around. The bartender said, "You landed yourself in some real trouble now." He pointed at Miller. "It was his idea!" the bartender yelled, and enough folks turned that Miller took a step back. When he glimpsed two men pushing toward him through the crowd, Miller bolted away. The one good thing—maybe the only good thing—about being sober while everyone else was not was that he had his wits about him and could run. He ran as fast as he could for a long, long, long time.

He had never told anybody about that evening, though it did haunt him sometimes. It came back to him in dreams that felt, by their very occurrence, that they were damning him, but in the light of day, he told himself he had done nothing wrong, that if a man was fool enough to climb up on a two-story railing when he was three sheets to the wind, well, that was his own fault. What happened after, Miller was unaccountable for.

||||||

AFTER AN HOUR of digging, Omar was drained. He had started the day feeling strong, but the malaria had taken something out of him, and by midmorning his pace had slowed. He only hoped Miller would not notice.

Prince whistled a song that the other men knew, and they sang as they worked. *Nattie oh, Nattie O gone to Colón.* Berisford encouraged Omar to join in, but Omar shook his head and said that he just liked listening. "Come on now," Berisford goaded. Omar had heard the song dozens of times, enough that he knew the words, and to make Berisford happy he opened his mouth and sang a few. Berisford yelped with glee, which made Omar blush and laugh. Clement frowned and told them to keep their heads down and work if they knew what was good for them.

The noise in the Cut was the same as ever—constant and shrill—so when a train whistle blew, none of the men so much as flinched. It was not until Miller barked at the men to stop what they were doing that they glanced all around, unsure what was going on. By the looks on their faces, the other men were just as confused as he was.

"Hold your picks! Line up!" Miller yelled, signaling them back. "And smile so he can see how goddamn happy you are."

Omar and the others took several steps back as the train whistle bleated again. When the men were all shoulder to shoulder, Berisford untied his handkerchief and mopped his whole face. Whatever was happening, Omar was relieved to have a moment to rest. Certain men kept craning their necks to peer down the track, but Omar could tell by the sound that the train coming toward them was chugging slowly. Only when it was close enough did he see that it was not a typical train but a black motorcar draped with bunting that had the same stars and stripes as the flag of the United States.

"It the colonel?" Berisford asked.

Omar said, "No, the motorcar of the colonel is yellow."

Joseph said, "That Oswald, I believe."

"We supposed to do something?" Berisford said.

"Like what?" Prince asked.

"Wave hello?"

"Be still," Clement growled.

Together, standing at attention, the men watched as the motorcar inched by, letting off thick gray smoke. As it passed, Omar saw through the window a man staring out, saw his white hat and the glint of his spectacles and the expression on his face, which was cheerless and grim. He had heard the name Oswald, but he had never seen him before. As Omar stood in the mud with his pick in his hand, a strange feeling came over him. In the midst of the work, the men had all stopped what they were doing and stood to the side. It was just that, nothing more. They stood to the side. Here, in the country where Omar had been born and had lived every day of his life, a man had arrived, and Omar stood to the side.

|||||

WHEN THE LUNCH whistle sounded, all of the men climbed up out of the Cut and walked to one of the thatched-roof kitchens where, for the cost of 27¢ a day deducted from their paychecks, their meals were supplied. The kitchens were furnished with neither tables nor chairs, so the men ate outside on the ground, sometimes leaning up against trees, which gave cover from both the sun and the rain.

"Rice and beans," Berisford said, nodding toward his plate when Omar walked outside and sat down next to him. "All the time rice and beans. How them expect a man to live on so much rice and beans?" Berisford was sitting cross-legged beneath a large banyan tree. He had taken off his hat and placed it next to him on the soggy ground.

Prince, who was sitting there, too, stopped shoveling food into his mouth long enough to say, "Careful. They arrest you if they hear you complaining too loud."

"Arrest me?"

Prince nodded. "Plenty rules here. Rule against where a man stand, rule against how long he standing there for. Soon they going to outlaw a man standing at all!" He laughed.

Omar took a bite of the food. It was bland, and the rice was too hard, but at least it was warm.

Clement was with them, lying on his back with one arm slung over his eyes. Joseph usually ate elsewhere before going to a midday church service.

Miserably, Berisford stirred the beans on his plate. "There better food in the penitentiary at least?"

"You know what the Yankees eating in them hotels?" Prince asked.

"What?"

"Plum pudding and tomato soup and mashed potatoes, too."

Berisford clutched his stomach and moaned with envy.

"Spaniards and them getting wine. They eating as kings!"

"And here we eating like paupers!" Berisford said.

From the ground Clement said, "Be glad you eating at all."

Omar hunched over his plate and shooed away the flies that came near. Lunch was the only meal he ate with the men, and though he sat with them and they let him, he never talked much. He was grateful for their chatter, though, especially since his meals at home were so quiet now.

Omar listened as Berisford and Prince began talking about the camps where they lived, how the cots sagged, how there was but one long shelf upon which everyone stored his things, how men were packed in tighter, Prince said, than fleas on a dog. But the worst, Berisford said, was the watchman who came round every night at nine o'clock sharp to make sure they were sleeping, as if they were children.

Berisford turned to Omar. "You live in the camps?"

"No," Omar said.

Prince and Berisford stared at him, as though they were waiting for him to say more.

Prince chuckled. "Like he being charged by the syllable."

Omar felt his cheeks warm.

Kindly, Berisford asked him where he did live.

"With my father. Outside of the city."

"The city of Panama?"

"Yes."

"And every day you come here?"

"Yes."

"For what reason?"

Before Omar could answer, Prince said, "Same reason as all you! Money, of course."

Berisford told them that when he had enough money, he was going back to Barbados to buy a house and get married.

"You have a sweetheart?" Prince asked.

Berisford nodded. "Naomy her name, and she all in my head."

"That mean she not real?" Clement asked. His arm still covered his eyes, but Omar saw him grin.

"Course she real. Look." From under his belt, Berisford pulled out the black-and-white photograph that he carried with him so that anytime he wanted, he could open it and see Naomy's face gazing back up at him. The two of them had known each other since they were young. They used to go out picking gooseberries together, and with her teeth Naomy always peeled the skin off the berries and chewed it up separate from the part underneath. Berisford liked watching her do it, that careful act of unwrapping, and when he asked her once why she didn't just eat the gooseberries whole, she replied that some things were worth taking your time. That turned out to be true. It took a long time, years and years of being no more than friends, before Berisford mustered the nerve to tell her how he felt about her, but to his surprise, Naomy had smiled bashfully and confessed that she felt the same. They had been sitting outside, and Berisford had said, "I should like to kiss you if I may," and softly Naomy said that he may, and when they both pulled away, with his eyes still closed, Berisford murmured, "I should like to kiss you forever," and with a smile that even his closed eyes could detect, Naomy said, "You may." They were both twenty years old, ready to marry, but Berisford had wanted to earn money first to give them a comfortable life. Naomy had put up a fuss about him leaving, had begged him not to go, but he had promised that when he returned from Panama, they would have each other and more.

Berisford unfolded the photograph and handed it to Prince, who made a sound of approval before passing it to Omar, who said, "She is very pretty."

Without sitting up to look at the photograph, Clement said, "Man, keep your pretty. Me gal beautiful. Beautiful as the day long."

"Oh?" Berisford said. "Then what happen at night?" He screwed up his face so that it was crooked and ugly with his tongue stuck out and his nostrils flared.

Prince laughed so hard that finally Clement sat up. Berisford contorted his face even more, and Prince fell over in hysterics. Omar tried and failed to hold back his own laughter.

Clement waited for the three of them to compose themselves, then calmly he said, "At night? Hooooboy. She *wild* at night."

Clement winked, and Prince howled. Victorious, Clement lay back down on the ground.

15

VALENTINA STOOD OUTSIDE THE FRONT DOOR OF IRINA PRIETO'S HOUSE AND PATTED her hairpins to make sure they were secure. She was wearing the same dress she had worn when they arrived in Gatún the day before—she hadn't anticipated needing a change of clothes—and on top of that, without her usual cremes, her hair was a mess. Renata, apparently, did not even own a comb somehow. Yet despite her dishevelment, Valentina had forced herself to leave the house. The first thing she needed to do, she determined, was to talk to the neighbors, to find out who among them had received the same paper and who had signed it already.

She rapped her knuckles against Irina's door.

"Valentina! Is it you?" Irina gasped when she opened it. Irina was ninety years old, and impossibly her hair was still a light shade of brown, though she did look frail in her housedress. A gray cat slunk around her ankles. "You remember Simón," Irina said.

Valentina reached down to stroke the cat, but he whimpered and ducked away.

"Bah, ignore him," Irina said. "He is more temperamental than me. But why are you here? Do you want to come in? For a coffee? Or a sweet? I have a few of those caramels that you used to like."

Valentina smiled. She did like the caramel candies that Irina had always kept in a jar, but no, she was there for a different reason today.

"Irina, did you receive a notification about being required to move because of the plans for building a dam here?"

Irina's face clouded. "Ah, yes."

"Did you sign it?"

"Heavens no!"

Valentina smiled again. "Good. I just came to make sure."

Irina scooped the cat up into her arms. "Tell her, Simón. I may be old, but I am not senile yet."

At the next house, Salvador Bustos, too, invited Valentina inside, but Valentina got right to the point and was pleased when, like Irina, Salvador scoffed. "Why would I sign it? No. Absolutely not."

At the house of Xiomara Vargas, Valentina also found Josefina Santí. Since being widowed, Xiomara and Josefina had become the best of friends, and when they insisted Valentina come in, not taking no for an answer, she saw that the two of them were embroidering a tablecloth. "I started at one end and Josefina at the other," Xiomara said, "and the idea was to meet in the middle, but you can see how much farther I have gotten than her."

Josefina laughed as she pulled the needle through. "Yes, and you can also see whose stitches are neater."

Valentina quickly complimented the work of each before inquiring about the notification.

"You mean the eviction notice?" Xiomara said.

"I threw it in the garbage," Josefina said without looking up.

"Claro, where it belongs." Xiomara nodded. She looked at Valentina. "Why are you asking?"

"I just wanted to check. Renata received one, and she has not signed it, but I hear that other people"—she did not want to name names—"have."

"Other people are imbeciles," Josefina said.

Xiomara nodded again, but she looked at Valentina nervously. "Is it a lot of people? You can tell us."

"I don't know. That's what I'm trying to find out."

"So what if it is?" Josefina said. "Those who sign it will go and those who don't will stay, no?"

Xiomara glanced at Valentina again. "Is that how it works? I can't remember what the notice said."

Valentina chewed the inside of her cheek. There were too many questions, and going door-to-door like this was not the most efficient way to get to the bottom of them. "Perhaps we should have a town meeting," she suggested. Both Xiomara and Josefina said they would attend.

At each house after that, besides asking about the eviction notice, as she started to call it, Valentina also mentioned the meeting. The majority of people she visited had not signed the paper yet, thank God, although a handful confessed that they had—some because they felt that they had no choice and some because they viewed the relocation as, truthfully, not that bad. The latter rationale left Valentina stunned. Both rationales broke her heart.

At the end of the day, Valentina circled back to Irina and Salvador to invite them to the church, too. Irina said, "Wonderful. A church is the perfect place for us to figure out how to give them hell."

⁂

THE INTERIOR OF the Catholic church in Gatún was traditional in design, with fifteen rows of wooden pews to either side of a center aisle and a modest altar in front of an equally modest wooden crucifix depicting Jesus nailed to the cross in his crown of thorns. Two lancet windows were on each of the walls.

Into this space, in addition to herself, Renata, and Joaquín, fewer than a dozen people had amassed, a number that to Valentina was slightly disappointing. She had hoped there would be twice as many.

Standing at the front of the church, Valentina waited to see if any more people would file in. The residents who were there, however, were growing restless—Dante Bustamientos had already gone outside once to smoke—and when Father Suárez, who was sitting in the first pew next to Renata and Joaquín and who had granted Valentina use of the church, gently motioned that perhaps it was time to begin, Valentina cleared her throat.

"Friends," she said. It had seemed like sacrilege to stand on the altar, so she was standing in front of it instead, level with everyone else. "Friends, bienvenidos."

She waited for people to quiet. She had never addressed a crowd before, yet she was not nearly as nervous as she had thought she might be.

"It brings me great joy to be here with you all, but the reason for our gathering brings me enormous concern." She had come up with those words earlier this morning and had been waiting to say them out loud. "You all received the paper saying that by April the entire town of Gatún will be forced to move to the eastern bank of the river so that here, where we are at this very moment, a dam can be built for the canal."

Several people nodded.

"Well, I for one do not think that is right."

"Neither do I!" Salvador Bustos shouted.

"Nor me either," said someone else, but Valentina did not catch who it was.

"Bueno. We are here, then, to discuss our options."

Alfredo Ríos, the local barber who was seated in the third pew, said, "Options? We don't have options, do we? We all know the dam will be built. The work will not stop just because we happen to be in the way."

Irina said, "But couldn't the dam be built somewhere else? Why does it have to be here?"

"That's a good question," Valentina said. "Does anyone have a pencil with them?" In her pocket she had Renata's eviction notice, which she had folded into quarters and brought with her in case she needed to reference it during the meeting. Now she pulled it out and smoothed it open on her thigh, and when Father Suárez handed her a pencil, she wrote the question down.

Hilda Sáez said, "One option we have is to pray."

Alfredo said, "Prayer is not going to help us right now."

Calmly, Hilda responded, "Prayer helps everyone always."

Alfredo rolled his eyes, and Father Suárez momentarily stood and turned toward the crowd. "We should continue to pray," he said, smiling, "for in prayer we communicate our true selves with God, but of course that should not stop us from doing other things as well."

"Like what?" Alfredo asked when Father Suárez sat down.

"I agree with Alfredo," Dante said. "There are no options for us. For the dam to exist, the town cannot. It is as simple as that."

"If that's what you believe, then why are you here?" Raúl Saavedra shouted to him.

"Because I was *invited*, Raúl," Dante said.

"Not by me," Raúl muttered.

Again, Father Suárez stood up and turned. "Gentlemen, please."

Dante and Raúl had a long-standing antagonism, something to do with a fence, but Valentina did not want to get into that now, and she was grateful when Father Suárez looked at her and said, "Go on."

"Thank you," she said, and looked out again over the small crowd. "According to the notice we have six months until the relocation begins. That gives us six months to fight. Even if today we do not know what to do, even if some of us believe we are without options, six months gives us time to think of some, no?"

Everyone was quiet. Valentina had hoped for some agreement, but when she looked to Salvador, who had been the first to say that he, too, did not want to go, he said nothing. Josefina, she noticed, was silently sewing the tablecloth she had brought. Dante could not stop bouncing his knee up and down.

"We cannot just surrender!" Valentina said.

Alfredo scoffed. "I would rather surrender than be crushed beneath rock."

"Who is being crushed?" Esmeralda asked.

"You, if you stay."

Esmeralda gasped, and Father Suárez stood for a third time and said, "Let us all remember to speak with the love of the Lord in our hearts."

Valentina felt the meeting getting away from her. Alfredo's fatalism had infected the air, and aside from Irina's question and Hilda's invocation for prayer, no one had yet produced any ideas as to what they could do. Including her. She glanced at Joaquín, but he merely sat there with his beatific grin, a grin that was usually endearing but that at the moment was extremely irksome. How could he be grinning at a time such as this? Was he even listening? She had the urge to shout her line about requiring his undivided attention, but as she was standing in front of so many people, she did not. She looked at Renata instead, hoping that she might chime in, but Renata was staring at Valentina as though she were watching a theater production instead of attending a meeting she might participate in herself. Valentina loved her sister, but there were times—and this was one of them—when she would have appreciated Renata showing some fire, some verve, for God's sake! But since they were children, that had not been her way. Renata instead went along with the current, a trait that could often be useful, except that in this instance going along with the current would mean ending up on the other side of the river.

Valentina took a deep breath and peered at the faces before her. What could they do? What could any of them realistically do? But there had to be something, no? She was about to ask whether anyone other than Alfredo had something to say when, in the fourth pew from the rear, Justo de Andrade, who must have been seventy years old by now, gripped the seat in front of him and stood. It took several seconds of effort before he was up on his feet, by which time everyone had turned around to watch.

"It is a matter of respect," Justo said.

Justo had a tree farm with orange trees and lime trees, caimito and calabash. Every year at Christmas, he welcomed the children of Gatún to the farm to pick as many oranges as they could carry, no bags or buckets allowed. It was a tradition that Valentina had loved when she was a girl.

In a slow, measured tone, Justo went on. "Gatún is an important place. It has been important for centuries." From the crowd came a smattering of assent. Salvador briefly clapped. "Sadly it seems the North Americans do not understand that. To them, we know nothing and have nothing—nothing worth knowing or having, as far as they are concerned. I have heard them say that the work they are planning will bring things like progress and civilization and modernity to this place—I am sure you have heard those words as well—as if the tools we have already created, the buildings we have already constructed, the land we have already cultivated, the society we have already organized is not, somehow, progress or civilization or modernity, but outside of those things. As if we are nothing more than primitive people with a few primitive huts that can be so easily moved. We—all of us in this church—know that is untrue, and even if they do not, I ask at the very least that they respect us, respect us as we for so long have respected them."

For a moment there was absolute silence. A stunned vibration coursed through the air. Justo nodded, as though he had said his piece, and lowered himself back into the pew.

"Thank you," Valentina finally said, near tears.

"Justo for president!" Raúl shouted, and a few people laughed.

"I'm sorry," Alfredo said once everyone had turned around again, "but they are not going to give us respect just because we ask them to."

"Well, they certainly won't if we don't ask," Irina said.

"Forgive me," Xiomara said, "but respect aside, what makes them think they have the right to force us out of our homes?"

Alfredo said, "Because our own government gave them that right."

"Is that true?"

Máximo Pérez, who was an attorney, said, "Yes. According to the terms of the original treaty."

"But why would our government have done such a thing?"

"Because the United States paid them ten million dollars!" Alfredo said.

"But no one paid us," Xiomara pointed out.

"Well, perhaps they should," Salvador said. "Either they pay us fairly or we refuse to go."

"Now there's an idea," Dante said.

Xiomara said, "Forgive me again, but I still do not understand. Our government gave them the right to do what exactly? Build a canal?"

Máximo said, "And to use any land necessary for the purpose of the canal, yes."

"And that is Gatún?"

"Yes."

"But don't we also have rights?"

Josefina, who was sitting next to Xiomara and through everything had been sewing, said, "Perhaps we should ask that as well."

"Ask who?" Salvador said.

"Our government. Or the National Assembly. Or whoever is in charge."

"We could write them a letter!" Valentina said, holding up the paper and pencil she still had in her hands.

"A letter?" Alfredo frowned.

"We all received letters, no? So we will reply with one of our own."

"A letter of resistance," Salvador said.

"Yes, we can ask all of our questions and list our concerns."

"And then what?" Alfredo asked.

Valentina thought for a moment. "And then my husband can deliver the letter to the government offices when he goes to the city for work." She turned toward Joaquín, who looked at her startled, like a schoolboy caught not paying attention in class. "Won't you?" she said.

It was possible he did not even know what he was agreeing to, but Joaquín, bless him, said, "Of course, my love."

||||||

FROM GATÚN, THE train took nearly two hours to reach Panama City, and quickly they had become the best two hours of Joaquín's life. Actually, that was not true. The two hours home, *after* a day of work was done, were the best, but the two hours there were a close second. Two peaceful hours in which he had to do nothing but sit and rest.

He would have liked to actually sleep on the train, but despite the early hour, he had found that since staying in Gatún, he was never tired enough for that. Renata had made a bed of straw and grass on the floor of the unused bedroom, a bed that had appeared lumpy and uncomfortable, but after sleeping on it the first night, Joaquín had woken up more rested than he had been in years, perhaps because of the bed, or perhaps because of how much quieter it was in Gatún compared to the city, or perhaps because of how much cooler the air was on the floor of the house than on the second story of the apartment building, even with its breeze. The important thing was that in Gatún he was sleeping like a rock. The salubrious effects of their environment must have extended to Valentina as well, for even she had not woken him up with her dreams.

Notably, he was also eating better than he had in some number of years. The news that Valentina and he were staying in Gatún had motivated neighbor after neighbor to come to the house, their arms laden with sugared breads and bowls of arroz con pollo and platters heaped with tender tamales. On top of that, Renata, it turned out, was an excellent cook. In recent years, now that Horacio was gone, Valentina had not put the same effort into cooking as she once had. Joaquín had thought at first that something had happened to his tongue to cause the meals that had once tasted flavorful to be so unflavorful now, but when he bit into a banana or a pineapple or slurped the pulpy juice of a coconut, those all tasted the same as they ever had. Perhaps Valentina was skipping steps in the recipes or neglecting to add salt, but the bottom line was that she now cooked with less care than she used to, and the food—and his belly—suffered for it. Not so in Gatún. In Gatún his belly was as full as the sea.

In reality, the only negative aspect of staying in Gatún was that Valentina would not stand for any frisky behavior due to the fact that they were sleeping in what used to be her parents' bedroom. It was not entirely clear to Joaquín why that should stop them, but when he tried anything, Valentina tsked and said, "Not here." His wife, after all this time, still drove him wild, and he would have liked to do something about it. The most Valentina would allow was a kiss, but the kisses, far from satisfying his desire, only strengthened it. He resorted to taking care of his needs in the dark after she dozed off. Come to think of it, perhaps that was another reason he had been sleeping so well.

In Panama City, Joaquín stepped off the train and began walking in the direction of the Presidential Palace. It had taken over an hour for the residents at the meeting yesterday to write a letter to the government officials in Panamá. There had been vociferous debate over what to include. Joaquín had tried to stay out of it for the most part. But in the end they had come up with a letter comprised of several fundamental questions: Why had the government done this to them? Was there nowhere else the dam could reasonably go? Did anyone, either the Panamanian government or the United States government, care about the misery they were inflicting upon the people of Gatún, people who were being forced to sacrifice everything they had worked for and built? Did they not deserve more respect? And what would happen to them if they went? Were they not entitled to fair compensation for all that they were being obligated to give up? Would they be entitled to future protection if they acquiesced? Could anyone guarantee that after this they would be left in peace?

All logical questions, Joaquín thought, and now it was up to him to make sure that their questions reached someone.

Joaquín had never been to the Presidential Palace before, and it was refreshing to see different buildings and plazas as he made his way there. He smiled at the bougainvillea blooming on the balconies, and when a woman leaned over the railing to shake out a towel that rained dust down over his head, he even smiled at that. He knew the general direction—south from the passenger terminal, then east to the bay—and as the streets were more or less laid out in a grid, it was easy to keep track of where he was. Except that after walking for ten minutes, Joaquín had the feeling that somehow, at some juncture, he had taken a wrong turn. He walked up to the nearest street sign, which said in Spanish, "West 13th Street." For a moment, that only made him more confused. "West 13th Street" was not a street name that was familiar to him. He stood on the corner and turned around and around. It was not until he saw the cattle warehouse in the distance that everything became clear. This was Slaughterhouse Street. Or it had been Slaughterhouse Street until someone had apparently renamed it. Joaquín looked at the street sign again. Truthfully, he had always found Slaughterhouse Street to be a disgusting name and of course West 13th Street did not sound disgusting in the least, so arguably the new name was an improvement. But West 13th Street! Joaquín shook his head.

There had been a time during La Separación when he had been hopeful about the fate of Panamá. It had seemed that at last, freed from the tentacles of Bogotá, Panamanians would be allowed to manage their own destiny. They would be allowed to take advantage of their geographic good fortune and reap the rewards. And yes, he had understood that it was not quite as simple as that, nothing was simple of course, but he had believed that in time, everything would work out. But now with the letter in his pocket and the new street sign before him, Joaquín felt his hope drain away. He cringed, remembering himself standing atop a crate in the fish market, sermonizing to the crowds. He squinted again at the sign. West 13th Street! No Panamanian would have given this street that name. It was so . . . bland. Scrubbed spotlessly clean. Disconnected entirely from the history of what this area had for so long been, which, yes, yes, was poor and smelled to high heaven, but that is what it was. That was the truth. There on the street corner Joaquín made an agonized sound—something between a moan and a roar. Then he took a deep breath and turned.

Eventually, Joaquín found his way to the Presidential Palace, a beautiful mansion facing the bay. It was surrounded by security forces who would not allow him to enter, so the best he could manage was to give the letter to a guard who said he would deliver it, even though Joaquín did not really believe that he would.

||||||

THAT EVENING, WHEN Joaquín walked into the house in Gatún, he found Valentina on her hands and knees, her face inches from a newspaper that was spread open on the dirt floor.

"What are you doing?" he asked.

She did not move. Her rear end up in the air like it was gave him a shiver of pleasure.

"I'm reading the newspaper," Valentina said.

"But why are you down on the floor, my love?"

"Because the table is covered."

The table was indeed covered with dishes and utensils and bowls, which Joaquín assumed had been left behind by Renata, who he noticed now was nowhere to be found.

"Where is your sister?" Joaquín asked.

"She had an errand in town."

"Oh?" Joaquín grinned. It had been a dispiriting day, but perhaps now, if they had the house to themselves . . .

Before he could get any further with such a thought, Valentina said, "Did you deliver the letter?"

"I did," he said slowly.

"What does that mean?"

"I took the letter to the Presidential Palace, but I was not permitted inside."

Finally, Valentina sat back on her heels and looked up at him. "Okay. So?"

"So I gave the letter to a guard who promised he would deliver it."

"Promised?"

"Said."

"Deliver it to whom?"

"The president, I suppose."

Valentina sighed. Joaquín knew that she had hoped he would have something more encouraging to report. He himself had hoped the same.

"Perhaps we should think of something else," Valentina said.

Joaquín looked at his poor wife down on the floor, newspapers scattered about. He suspected she was trying to glean any new details about the dam. It was a shame because if she were in a different mood, he would gladly get down on the floor with her. He would not object to certain activities down on the floor. And then Joaquín had an idea. He would not have called himself a visionary. If anything, Valentina was more that than he. But the sight of her sitting before him now inspired a thought.

"We should sit," he said.

"What?"

"In front of the house."

Valentina pushed out her lips as if what he was saying did not make any sense.

"To protect it. Or at least to show that we are willing to protect it." Joaquín's voice rose. He believed he was onto something. "Imagine if everyone in the town did the same. Imagine every resident sitting in one long line in front of the houses along the river here. It would be like a wall. Like a barricade! Like a demonstration of solidarity that cannot be ignored!"

Valentina cocked her head slightly. Joaquín could see she was coming around to the idea.

"And we could chant," she said.

"Yes, yes, we should absolutely chant."

"And hold flags in the air."

"Flags are very symbolic."

"And perhaps get even more people involved. People from other towns."

"The more the merrier."

"We would welcome anyone who believes in the cause."

"And who wouldn't believe!"

She gestured at the newspapers arrayed around her. "Maybe the newspaper will even write about it."

"They should."

Valentina struck the fist of one hand into the open palm of the other. "We are not a people to whom things can be done."

"No."

"We are a people who can do things!"

"Yes," Joaquín said excitedly. He loved it when his wife got animated like this. "That could be the chant!"

"No, that is a terrible chant."

"Of course. We will think of some other chant."

Valentina, his beautiful wife, looked up at him with a determination that might have been forged out of steel. "So we know what we will do. We will sit and we will not be moved."

16

THE DAYS MARCHED AHEAD INTO OCTOBER. ADA HAD BEEN WORKING UNDER THE Oswalds' roof for nearly two weeks, and in that time she had mailed home a second letter along with most of the money—the equivalent of nearly £5—she had been paid so far. A letter could take a week or more to arrive, but Ada was hopeful that her first note at least had reached her mother by now and that her mother had written a reply. Every day when Michael knocked on the front door, Ada flew down the stairs to meet him and took the envelopes he handed her and flipped through them, looking for her name on the front of just one.

Michael, who was fifteen years old, had a soft spot for Ada. Of all the stops on his route, he most looked forward to walking up the hill to the Oswalds' house, where he knew the girl with the high round cheeks and the lavender eyes would come to the door when he knocked. It used to be the cook who answered, a brusque older woman who had hardly even smiled at him when he arrived. To Michael, it had been a welcome change when the girl started coming to the door instead. She had an easy smile, and she was eager to see what he was delivering that day, and though Michael knew—because he sorted through the envelopes himself before he got to the house—that he was bringing nothing for her, it still pained him to see how the girl's expression tumbled from the high point of some mountain to the valley down below when she saw that same fact for herself. He wanted to tell her, Maybe tomorrow. Maybe tomorrow whatever she was waiting for would come, but every next tomorrow brought the same nothing as the yesterday before.

Despite visits from the doctor and despite Ada's constant attention and care, Mrs. Oswald's condition kept getting steadily worse. The fits of coughing came more frequently now. Her skin had a purplish flush. She slept on and off throughout the day, weakened by the disease.

When Mrs. Oswald was awake, however, she spoke to Ada much the way she had since the start—as though grateful just to have someone to speak to at all. She recounted the months she had spent in Panama thus far, the beautiful views from the veranda, the tedium of the dinners she'd had to attend.

"John wanted to come," she said one afternoon. "It was important to him. They all believe it is the most important work of their lives."

Ada watched Mrs. Oswald arduously draw in a breath. She lay on her back in the bed, the sheet folded down at her waist. Her face was damp with sweat. She looked up at Ada and said, "Did you go to school?"

"Yes."

"What did you study?"

"Reading and writing and some arithmetic."

Mrs. Oswald smiled feebly. "That's good. It's important to learn such things. It's important for a woman to use her own mind. I studied the science of plants before I met John."

"There's schooling for that?"

"Yes, I have a degree in botany."

Ada said, "My mother knows about plants."

Mrs. Oswald smiled again. "I imagine your mother knows many things that I have yet to learn."

Ada nodded. "She's always trying to teach us—my sister and me." It was the first time Ada had mentioned either her mother or her sister to Mrs. Oswald.

Mrs. Oswald coughed. "I do hate being confined to this bed," she said. "If I had the strength for it, perhaps you and I might go for a walk. You could tell me what your mother has taught you. And we could look at the flowers. The flowers here are wonderful. Ixora, Passiflora, heliconia . . ."

Marian stopped, recalling their first days here. She had been so desperate for fresh air that during a break in the rain, she had begged John to join her on a walk. They had followed a footpath toward the next town, and Marian had spied the most remarkable, creamy white orchid, growing tall amid the brush. She had stepped off the path and started walking toward it when John said, "Don't, Marian!" She had looked back over her shoulder at him. "I just want to see it," she'd said, and John had replied, "Yes, but you don't know what else might be in there, too." She might have argued—he needn't be fearful of *everything*—had she not recognized the stern expression on his face, and with great reluctance she had forced herself to walk back over to where he stood rooted to the path.

Marian looked up at Ada sitting by her bedside. "You should take that walk yourself," she said. "I'm afraid I won't be able to join you in this state." She cleared her throat, felt the ever-present pain in her chest. "But if you go," Marian said, "promise me that you will take whatever path you please."

She saw Ada nod, even though Marian imagined she was not making much sense.

The day after she and John had taken that walk, John had come home with a potted pink orchid, which he placed on the floor at her feet as she sat on the veranda again. "Now you may see it," he said. It was a different variety, not nearly as stunning as the orchid she had spotted in the brush, but it was the only time he had ever given her a flower, and she thanked him for it. It was always curious to her, though, how a flower like that could look better to John in a pot than it did growing free.

||||||

THAT DAY WHILE Mrs. Oswald slept, Ada went out to the hill. It was the first time she had stepped away from the house, and it felt good to have the sun on her back. The talk of plants had made Ada think about how her mother always made a batch of bush tea when one of them was unwell, and she hurried over the hill, plucking stems from the ground, until she had enough to make a strong brew.

Quickly, she took what she gathered back to the kitchen, filled a pot with fresh water, and set it to boil. The water had just started to rumble when Antoinette came in carrying several paper-wrapped packages. She frowned at Ada. "Why you in here?"

"I am making bush tea."

Without setting the packages down, Antoinette walked to the stove and peered into the bubbling pot herself. "With what?"

"Some plants I found on the hill."

"Outside?"

"There's an inside hill?" Ada said.

Antoinette glared. She set the packages down and shooed Ada away from the stove, flicking her wrists back and forth, saying that she could well finish brewing the tea herself, Ada was not the only one who knew about tea, a bush tea from Antigua was superior to a bush tea from Barbados any day of the week, so go on now, get out of my kitchen and back to where you belong.

|||||

IN THE DAYS that followed, Ada hardly left Mrs. Oswald's side. She sat, waiting to be needed, praying that the next hour was when Mrs. Oswald's condition would improve, that her breathing would sound less like a husk scraping against the ground. She could not help but think that if Mrs. Oswald improved, it would be a sign that across the ocean, Millicent might be improving, too.

When Mrs. Oswald was awake but too weak to talk, Ada occasionally read passages from the Bible out loud. Yesterday, she had read from Matthew in the New Testament, but she had only gotten as far as Jesus healing fevers with a single touch, and today she thought Mrs. Oswald might want to hear what else he would do. She had just started to reach for the Bible on the bureau when Mrs. Oswald, who aside from her raspy breathing had been quiet for the past twenty minutes or so, said suddenly, "We lived in the mountains."

Ada returned her hand to her lap. Mrs. Oswald's oak-colored hair was limp with sweat.

"The mountains?" Ada said.

"The Great Smoky Mountains. In Tennessee, where both John and I are from. They were beautiful." Mrs. Oswald took a few labored breaths. "All morning I've been thinking about them." Quietly, she started to cry.

"Shhhh," Ada whispered.

"We had a baby," Mrs. Oswald went on. "Never born, but we had one. We buried her in those mountains."

Ada grabbed a cloth from the bedside table and pressed it to Mrs. Oswald's hot cheek to stanch the tears that seeped from the corners of her eyes. She did not know what to say. She only stopped when Mrs. Oswald turned her face away.

It was raining again. Marian struggled, through the tears that filled her eyes, to see out the window on the wall to her left. She was confined to this room but at least she could see out, and what she saw were the tops of smoky blue-gray mountains even though those mountains were hundreds of miles away. Those were the mountains where she had walked over ground matted with golden pine needles and stroked her hand along the bark of the trees, mountains that soothed her, that somehow let her think and breathe better than any other place in the world. And they were the mountains where, next to a yellow birch tree, she and John had buried the baby's remains, or what there had been of remains—the blood-soaked cloths she had asked the doctor to leave behind, that blood being all that was left of the baby, she thought. The burial had happened only at Marian's insistence, and by herself she had put the stiffened, claret-colored cloths in a box that she held on her lap during the carriage ride up to the place where the land started to slope. The carriage driver walked behind them with a shovel, and when John told him to, he dug. It took less than a minute to dig a hole that small. John was the one who placed the box inside because Marian could not bear it, and Marian remembered looking up the side of the mountain as far as she could see and back down again at the top of the box nestled in the earth, and she nodded and with the nose of the shovel the carriage driver pushed the dirt he had loosed over the box. It made a quiet thumping sound when it fell. When the box was entirely covered, John and the driver returned to the carriage. Marian had not been able to bring herself to leave. She had stood there trembling, staring at the dirt that covered the box that now held all that was left of the baby she had once held within her. "Come, Marian," John had called from the carriage. He and the driver were waiting for her. She had crouched and pressed her hand flat on the dirt so that it left an impression. Then she stood and walked away, too. Her life was in those mountains, and just that morning she had realized that she might never go there again.

|||||

MR. OSWALD WAS at work and Antoinette was out picking limes on the day that Mrs. Oswald had the worst fit of coughing Ada had yet seen. Even when the coughing petered out, Mrs. Oswald shivered with fever and twisted the sheet, and Ada hurried to gather cloth sacks of ice and lay them on Mrs. Oswald's head and on the crooks of her elbows and against the soles of her feet. The doctor was due any minute, thank goodness, and Ada held the ice sacks in place while she whispered, "It's all right," over and over again. But by the time the ice had melted and the water wept through the fabric, the doctor still had not arrived, and Ada ran to the icebox again, tying new sacks, wondering where he could be. He was never late, and she could not imagine that the Lord would let him be so today of all days. The second time she returned to the room, Mrs. Oswald was quiet but for her strenuous breathing. She was still on her side. Ada lay a hand on her forehead. She was burning. Ada placed the sack down and glanced at the door. Where was the doctor? She could not wait any longer. To Mrs. Oswald she said, "I'm stepping out to fetch you fever pills, but I'll hurry back and the doctor will be here any minute, I hope." As soon as she saw Mrs. Oswald nod, Ada ran down to the kitchen, sifted through a drawer in the cupboard until she found a commissary booklet, then rushed out of the house without even bothering to straighten her dress.

|||||

PIERRE HAD BEEN sitting on the train to Empire, thinking about what he would eat for supper that night, when quite suddenly the train had come to a standstill. He and his fellow passengers looked around at one another. Someone shouted out, "Why are we stopped?" There was general confusion and murmuring—some men stood up to peer out the windows and one man actually stepped out of the train car. After a moment, he came back on to say, "There is a cow on the track!" The man started to laugh. Pierre, however, did not think it funny. A delay meant he would be late to the Oswalds'. It was the sort of thing that might well keep John Oswald from recommending Pierre for some future post. And most annoying was that any tardiness in this case would not be his fault.

In his seat, Pierre sighed. More passengers were looking out now, and some had gotten off the train entirely, eager to see what Pierre imagined was a fat stubborn cow standing on the railroad track. Where had a cow even come from? Had it been out for a stroll in the jungle and lost its way? Though it was a humorous thought, Pierre would not permit himself to laugh, as he was still, mostly, annoyed. They had been stopped for what seemed like an extraordinarily long time, given the issue at hand. How long could it take to shove a cow off a track? Pierre's brief amusement turned back to anxiety. He needed to go, for heaven's sake. He had somewhere to be.

By the time, fifteen long minutes later, the cow was coaxed off the track and the train started again, most everyone on board was exasperated and impatient to move on. Pierre was so wound up that he thought he might burst. As soon as he got off at Empire, he charged up the hill. He let himself into the house and rushed up to the room. When he walked in, he was relieved to see that Marian Oswald was sleeping in bed. But when he looked around the room, he realized she was alone. Quietly, Pierre placed his bag on the chair. The drapes were open, of course, but he took the opportunity to draw them closed and light the lamp on the table instead. He guessed the girl was probably in another part of the house. He tried to enjoy the relative peace. There were no sounds in the room besides Marian Oswald's hoarse breaths. No one peering over his shoulder, no one asking questions that were not her concern. In a day when Pierre had already suffered one annoyance, the fact that he could work uninterrupted, on his own terms, was a pleasant surprise.

The last of the adrenaline that had built up from the train and the rushing up the hill flowed out of him as he stood there. Carefully, Pierre pressed his fingers to the inside of Marian Oswald's wrist. Her pulse was weak. He removed the cloth from her forehead and felt it for fever. It was quite high, upwards of 103 if he guessed just from touch. The girl would need to draw an ice bath. And where was the girl anyway? It seemed odd that she had not returned to the room by now.

Pierre looked down at Marian Oswald and felt distinctly less confident about her prognosis than he had at the start, though that was not something he would admit out loud. He reached into his pocket and rubbed his stone. However, aside from the raspy breathing, she was sleeping tranquilly and maybe that was what she needed more than anything he could offer just then. Not wanting to disturb her rest, Pierre picked up his bag from the chair and walked out of the room.

On his way out, as he passed through the entry, he ran into the cook, who was stepping through the front door with an enormous basket of limes.

"Doctor," she said when she saw him.

Pierre did not think she had seen him arrive, which meant that she did not know he had been late, which was good.

"Excusez-moi. I just completed my exam," he said, and the cook nodded. "But the girl was not there. Do you know where she is?"

The cook said no, she did not, and as there was nothing more for him to do at the house until he returned later that afternoon, Pierre opened the door and walked out. He thought, as he started back down the hill, that the girl's absence was one more thing he would have to report to John.

||||||

THE COMMISSARY IN Empire, like all the canal commissaries, was divided in two. One half was for employees who were paid in gold and the other half was for employees who were paid in silver.

Ada was well aware that day which door she was supposed to go in—she was what people called colored, but that was not white enough—but because she was shopping for the Oswalds, she decided to walk through the gold entrance instead.

The cashier, a young woman with the longest blond hair Ada had ever seen, glanced up at her when she walked in. "May I help you?" she asked, and her voice when she said it was perfectly kind.

Ada mustered her nerve. "Do you stock fever pills?"

The cashier smiled. "We have small jars against the back wall."

Quickly, Ada walked to the back and scanned the shelves. There were glass jars and vials, various powders, dried herbs. She looked and she looked but saw no fever pills.

Another woman, a petite white woman carrying a small patent leather purse in her hands, came and stood next to her. Out of the corner of her eye, Ada glanced at her, but the woman said nothing, and Ada returned her gaze to the jars on the shelves. The electric fans that hung from the ceiling turned in lazy circles overhead, pushing around the hot air.

Then, quietly, leaning forward as she spoke, the woman next to her said, "I believe you may be confused." Her tone was sympathetic, as though she were truly concerned. "This is the gold commissary."

Ada clenched her jaw while she went on running her eyes over the jars. Fever pills. Fever pills. Where could they be?

"Next door is silver," the woman continued.

Fever pills. They had to be here somewhere.

"Did you hear me?" the woman whispered. "This shop is only for gold."

Ada stopped and looked at her. The woman was not much older than twenty if Ada had to guess. She was pretty, with a sweep of freckles across the tops of her cheeks. Sugar dusting, Ada's mother might have said.

The woman waited. There were other shoppers in the store, but none near them at the moment. The fans kept turning.

Now the woman, this slight, freckled woman, pointed to the floor in front of her and said, "Gold." Then she pointed to the left, her finger jabbing the air. "Silver." When she dropped her arm back down to clutch her purse, she said, "Do you understand?"

Ada fought a feeling that was spiraling up inside her, a bilious thing. Of course she understood. There was not a soul on the isthmus who did not understand. And yet here was this woman, telling Ada her place, and saying it in a way like she honestly thought Ada was confused, or else like she was witless, to which Ada took even greater offense. Of all the ways a person had ever described her, witless was not one.

Ada seethed, but she did not move. She kept her hands at her sides as a kind of heat vibrated through the tops of her ears.

The woman sucked a quick breath through her pretty petal-colored lips. "Excuse me," she called to the blond-haired cashier at the other side of the store.

In the middle of a transaction, the cashier looked up, and the young freckled woman nudged her elbow in Ada's direction as if to say, *This one. This one doesn't belong here, you see.* Maybe she expected camaraderie from the cashier, but the cashier merely glanced at both the woman and Ada and promptly returned her attention to the customer she was ringing up.

The freckled woman sighed, evidently with frustration, and now, loud enough that every shopper in the store could hear, she said, "This commissary is for Gold Roll."

Everyone in the store—the cashier and the customer at the counter, two more women from the next aisle, as well as one woman in a lace-trimmed bonnet who walked all the way around a corner to see what the commotion was about—stared.

The heat in Ada's ears let loose all through her, tingling under her cheeks and down into her fingertips, spreading through her chest. But there was some perverse pleasure in it, too, letting the woman get so incensed when the whole time Ada knew what she needed to say to put the thing to rest. She had it locked inside her like a secret, and there was something sweet about that. She might have let the woman carry on, too, might have let her wrap herself ever tighter in her thorny nest of vexation only to make her look like more of a fool when Ada said what she was about to say, except that Mrs. Oswald was at the house, burning with fever, and Ada did not have time for delay.

"I'm the Oswalds' nurse-girl."

The woman, who seemed at first stunned that Ada had spoken at all, stopped and stared at Ada with her pretty mouth hanging open, her cheeks turning so pink it looked as though they'd been plucked.

"What's that?" she managed to ask.

"Mrs. Oswald is sick."

"Oh. Oh, yes. I . . . I did hear about—"

"I'm buying her fever pills. They're only sold here, on the gold side."

That last part may or may not have been true, but it made the woman squirm with discomfort. Ada kept staring in her eyes, and what she saw there was shame. Shame, and anger at being shamed. Well, good. Even though the heat still pulsed beneath Ada's skin. Even though the triumph, small as it was, was not enough to make the whole encounter worth it.

When the woman took a step back and then scurried away to another part of the store, though she offered no apology, Ada felt the thrill of that very small triumph. She looked again at the shelves. On the second shelf from the bottom, she found something called Sappington's Anti-Fever Pills. She took the jar to the counter, tore a ticket from the commissary booklet, and used it to pay. "Send Mrs. Oswald my best," the blond cashier said, and Ada nodded.

Outside the store, the sun was bright and there was a hum in the air that all of a sudden Ada felt the urge to match. "It must be now the kingdom coming," she sang as she walked down the commissary steps, carrying the jar of pills in her hand. She felt good, and at that moment she did not care who heard. "And the year oh jubilo."

17

OMAR RECOGNIZED THE VOICE. HE WAS STROLLING ALONG THE STREET AFTER lunch with his hands in his pockets when he heard it and looked up.

He saw a young woman in a brown-and-yellow patchwork dress walking down the commissary steps. The town was busiest at this time of day, but even amid the noise, he could hear her singing. He was stopped now on the same side of the road where she was, and he lifted the brim of his hat to get a better look. She was holding something in one of her hands. Could it really be her? Through the general din, the horse hooves and rolling wooden carts, he listened as the young woman continued to sing. *And the year oh jubilo.* Yes, it was her. There was no question in his mind.

When she got to the bottom of the steps, the young woman turned left, away from where Omar was standing. She walked briskly between and around other people on the street. Omar trailed behind her, some distance away. A mule cart stopped in front of her once and Omar watched as she hurried around its back end.

He followed her for a full block, her dress swaying as she strode, before he felt foolish enough that he realized he would have to do something else if he wanted to talk to her.

Before he could think about it, he jogged down the street, shielding himself behind passersby and idling carriages, until he estimated that he was far enough out ahead, then he stopped, turned, and walked as casually as he could so that it appeared he just happened to be walking her way. He shoved his hands back into his pockets and tried not to trip over his own two feet.

The young woman stopped when she saw him. She had just passed a pole to which a horse was tied, and right there, she stopped. Squeezing his hands in his pockets, Omar kept walking toward her.

He did not break stride. Although the instant he got to where she was standing, he realized he did not know what to say.

She spoke first. "It's you."

She remembered him, then.

Omar took off his hat and held it to his chest. "Buenas," he said, and immediately cringed. He had meant to speak English, but he was so nervous he had spoken Spanish instead. He blinked a few times to calm himself down. He was not made for moments like this.

"The man from the street."

"Yes," Omar said.

She stared at him with genuine shock. "I didn't know . . . I hoped . . . Well, I did wonder but . . ."

"I am fine now."

Just behind her, the horse lowered its neck and nudged its nose in the mud.

"Because of you," Omar added.

The young woman shrugged. "I just did what they all ought to have done."

She was extremely pretty. Her skin was lighter than his, her cheeks high and round. Her eyes appeared gray in the light of the sun. He had never seen anyone with eyes like that before, and suddenly Omar found himself wanting to know everything about her, all her secrets and sorrows.

"What is your name?" he asked.

"Ada Bunting."

"My name is Omar."

She cocked her head slightly and said, "But how did you know it was me? Your eyes were closed the whole time I was with you."

"I remembered your voice. You sang to me."

She grinned. "Don't let my mother hear you saying that."

Omar glanced around. "Your mother is here?"

The grin disappeared. "No. My mother is back in Barbados. My sister, too. It's just me who came here."

"To work?"

At that, as though she had been reminded of something, Ada startled and raised the jar in her hand. "I have to be getting back!" She started hurrying past him.

"Where?"

She spun around. "To the Oswald house, where I work!" Then she ran.

Omar stood in the street, his hat still in his hand, and watched her go, mud spraying the back of her dress as she went.

18

ADA HAD JUST RUN PAST THE TRAIN STATION AT THE BOTTOM OF THE HILL WHEN the clouds unleashed a sudden downpour. Up and down the hillside, people scrambled into their houses, but Ada kept her head down and charged ahead, watching her skirt drag in the mud. By the time she got to the top, she was dripping wet. Under the cover of the veranda, she stomped her feet once and snapped the skirt of her dress, and when she looked up, she saw Antoinette standing at the threshold of the open front door.

"I got medicine from the commissary," Ada said, holding up the jar.

Antoinette shook her head.

"Her fever came down?"

Again, Antoinette shook her head. "Just now . . ."

She spoke so quietly that amid the thrashing rain, Ada could not quite hear. "What?"

"Just now . . ."

Ada saw Antoinette's lip trembling, and she knew. "Just now?" Ada whispered.

Antoinette nodded and turned back into the house.

||||||

WHEN MICHAEL ARRIVED, he found the girl standing on the veranda with a look of pure shock on her face. She was holding a jar of pills in her hand, and vaguely he wondered what they were for. Before he could find out, however, before he could even say hello, the girl, as soon as she saw him, said, "Go fetch Mr. Oswald and send him here to the house. Tell him hurry. Go as quick as you can."

Michael, who would have done anything the girl asked him

to do, darted back into the rain with his mailbag heavy across his shoulder. He ran down the hill to a district office and asked where Mr. Oswald might be found. "It's an emergency," he said, and when an engineer there suggested maybe the field hospital, where John Oswald was known to keep an office, Michael ran there and asked the first doctor he saw, and the doctor said he had not seen him today but maybe the field hospital in Culebra, where he often went, and Michael ran the one mile to Culebra and asked a young medic there, and the medic said Mr. Oswald had gone down in the Cut earlier that morning but he had not seen him since, and in all Michael ran to five different locations—the mail delivery would be late for many people that day—until at last he found Mr. Oswald sitting alone in one of the hotel restaurants eating a pork chop smothered in gravy with a side of green beans. Breathless, Michael announced that there was an emergency at the house. "Go back," he panted, and John Oswald did.

||||||

ANTOINETTE PACED IN circles, wringing her hands and thinking to herself. *Lord, Lord, Lord, such terrible things down here on this earth. Lord have mercy, what has happened this day? And why did it have to happen when she had been here by herself?* She did not want to be blamed. Antoinette ran over it in her mind like a finger over a fish, trying to feel for the bones. The girl should not have left. That was to start. Even the doctor said he had not seen her, which meant she must have been away for quite a long time. And where had she gone? That whole time at the commissary? Couldn't be. How long could it take a person to run to the commissary and buy a bottle of pills and run back again? How long on those fresh young legs? However long it should have taken, it took longer than that. Far too long. Lord only knew what the girl had been off doing all that time when she was supposed to be here. And it wasn't the first time she had left. There was that day she went out gathering herbs to make her pitiful bush tea. In addition to pacing and wringing her hands, Antoinette nodded as well.

It was true that the terrible thing had happened when she was here by herself, but she was sure not to blame, and if Mr. Oswald came to question her, she had her defense.

||||||

AS ANTOINETTE PACED down below, Ada stood in the bedroom upstairs, staring at Mrs. Oswald. Tentatively, she took a step closer and hovered her hand beneath Mrs. Oswald's nose. No breath. She had never seen a deceased body this close before, and in one strange way she was relieved by how ordinary it looked. The person in front of her was still Mrs. Oswald. That had not changed. And if there was another life beyond this one, as Ada had been taught to believe, she would still be Mrs. Oswald there, too. Ada burst into tears. The image of Millicent lying in bed rushed to her mind. Millicent huddled under the quilt, breathing low. She tried to see Millicent getting out of that bed and smoothing the quilt and folding it back as Ada had seen her do so many times, as their mother expected them both to do even though between the two of them Millicent was the only one who obeyed, but Ada's mind would not budge and all she could see was Millicent in bed, the same place Mrs. Oswald was, the only place Ada had ever known her to be, and now she had come to her end, and Ada stood there and cried.

After a time, she heard the front door downstairs open and close. Ada wiped the tears off her face and lifted her head. Mr. Oswald was here. She took a deep breath to collect herself. Across the room, the drapes were closed—probably Antoinette's doing—and before Ada left the room she walked around the foot of the bed and dragged them open again. It was still raining outside, but Mrs. Oswald would have wanted them open.

||||||

MR. OSWALD SUMMONED the doctor, who returned to the house at once. That was perhaps the saddest part of all, Ada would think later, for calling the doctor betrayed a level of hope. As if maybe, just maybe, there was something yet to be done. But when the tall doctor arrived and walked into the room where the three of them—Mr. Oswald and Antoinette and Ada—had gathered, he removed not a single tool from his flat-bottomed bag. All he did was lay one hand on her chest and two fingers of the other against the side of her neck. Then he removed both his hands and turned to them and nodded. Ada again burst into tears and excused herself from the room.

She was still standing in the hallway, sniffling, when the doctor came out of the bedroom. He stopped when he saw her and shifted his bag. "You returned, I see."

He was at least a head taller than she was, and Ada raised her eyes up to meet his.

"You were not at the house when I came earlier," he went on.

"I went to the commissary—"

The doctor appeared surprised. "The commissary?"

"To get medicine for her fever, yes."

"Ah, but the medicine is my job. Your job was to stay here, was it not?"

"Yes, but—"

"And at the critical moment, you left."

Ada stared at the doctor, dumbfounded. She wanted to point out that he himself had been late, and that if he had been here on time she would not have needed to leave, to find fever pills on her own, but at that moment Mr. Oswald stepped into the hall and very quietly closed the bedroom door. He turned to face the two of them standing in the dim hallway, but pointedly, Ada noticed, he did not look at her. He looked only at the doctor and said, "Pierre, a word with you, please."

|||||

LATER, THE CORONER came to confirm and record the death, raising the sheet over Mrs. Oswald's face and leaving her body in the bed. He would be back the next day, he told Mr. Oswald, to prepare it for burial.

Two men from the newspapers arrived, not only *The Canal Record*, but the *Star & Herald*, too, and Antoinette brought them both glasses of limeade as they sat in the parlor with Mr. Oswald, who answered their questions while the newspapermen took notes. Both papers ran a full obituary that identified Marian Oswald as the wife of Mr. John Oswald and told that they had been married for eleven years with no children between them. Neither of the obituaries said anything about Marian's degree in botany or about the work she had done before she met John, although the *Star & Herald* did run a photograph of her along with the announcement.

The coroner returned the next day with the death certificate. He was a no-nonsense gentleman with a thick black mustache and equally thick black eyebrows that were so unkempt that they hung over his eyes like awnings. In two years in Panama, he had attended a death nearly every other day. Typically, he was enlisted to the hospital, and it was rare that he had business at an individual home. He would never say so, but he thought that John Oswald, brilliant as he was rumored to be, had been wrong to keep his ailing wife at the house rather than send her off to receive better care. He was also wrong to have hired Pierre Renaud as the attending physician. Renaud was fine in character, but the coroner knew him to have an ego that at times interfered with his practice.

Unfortunately, what was done was done. The coroner rolled up his sleeves and asked for a bucket of hot water and rags. He carried everything into the bedroom and commenced the work of cleaning the body, the way he had so many times before.

19

ADA TRIED TO KEEP BUSY. THERE WAS LITTLE TO OCCUPY HER NOW, AND SHE expected that Mr. Oswald would let her go soon. She would have to find work somewhere else, but until that happened, she saw no reason not to make herself useful here. She soaked linens and scrubbed bedpans and put the Bible away. She wet a rag with vinegar and cleaned the looking glasses in the parlor. She wiped the walls, which were papered, even though in many places the paper had peeled and curled at the seams. Worry seeped into her mind at certain moments, remembering what the doctor had said to her in the hall, wondering whether Mr. Oswald had overheard. But if Mr. Oswald asked her about it, she told herself again and again, she would simply explain. She had gone to get fever pills. She had been trying to help. What she did not know is whether that would be reason enough to keep him from being angry with her.

By Saturday, after three days of cleaning, Ada was out of things to do. To escape the feeling of grief that had settled all through the house, she went outside, where the air was fresher and a hot wind tousled the trees. It was just past the noon hour, and in her boots and her patchwork dress, Ada wandered down the hillside, this time in search of flowers that she could take to Mrs. Oswald's funeral the next day. She found plenty of starlike white ones growing among patches of groundcover, but those were not good for picking, and she passed them by. Small yellow flowers were everywhere, but they were also too tiny for picking, their stems less than one finger tall. Behind an outhouse, Ada spotted a cluster of striking coral-colored blooms, and she uprooted them and held them as she kept on.

She was more than halfway down the hill, her eyes trained on the ground, when out of the clear air she heard someone calling her name. She looked up and saw Omar several feet away.

He walked closer and took off his hat. "I thought that was you," he said. With his free hand, he pointed. "Now I recognize the dress."

Ada tugged once on the skirt to make sure it hung full. "My mother made this dress," she said. "Her specialty is making dresses that stand out. She can't seem to make them any other way." She smiled. "What are you doing up here?"

"It is my lunch."

"Well, aren't you supposed to be eating it, then?"

"I ate already. But every day after lunch I take a walk."

"And you walked here?"

He nodded. "You told me where you work. I hoped to see you."

Before she had ever stepped foot on the isthmus, she had heard that Panamanians were resentful of outsiders like her. But she didn't get even the faintest hint of a feeling like that from Omar.

"You are busy, though?" Omar asked.

"I was gathering flowers." Ada held up what she had picked so far.

"Ah, pluma de gallo."

"What?"

"That is the name of the flower. In English it is 'the feather of a rooster,' I think."

The thought that Mrs. Oswald would have known the name of the flower, or would have liked to have known it, made tears well in Ada's eyes, and she reached up to wipe them away.

"I upset you?" Omar asked with alarm.

Ada shook her head. "These flowers—they're for a funeral tomorrow. Mrs. Oswald . . ." She could not say the rest.

Omar's face dropped. "I am sorry," he said. "I did not know."

Ada nodded, and suddenly she was crying more than she would have liked. Omar pulled a handkerchief from his back pocket and gave it to her. She wiped her face with the threadbare square of cotton, and when she passed it back, after gulping a bit of air, said, "My sister is sick, too. And after what happened to Mrs. Oswald, I can't stop thinking . . ." She bit her full bottom lip to keep from crying again.

"That is why you came to Panamá?" Omar asked. "For your sister?"

Ada told him about the doctor who had visited the house, about his opinion that Millicent needed surgery, about the £15, which was a sum of money that was hard to come by, about leaving without telling anyone, about traveling over on the big ship by herself.

Omar looked at her with a sort of gaping astonishment. "You are brave."

"Am I? My mother prefers to say I'm impetuous. She'd rather I didn't do half the things I do."

Omar nodded, then said, "My father is also that way. He does not understand the things that I do."

"Like what?"

"He is angry that I work in the canal."

"Could be he's just worried about you."

"I think he does not understand. He is a fisherman, so he is always by himself. But when I come to work, I can see people. The men in my gang say hello to me when I arrive and wish me well when I leave. They let me eat lunch with them, and they talk to me and we laugh. I have never had anything like that before."

"Well, you tell your father all that?"

"My father does not want to hear anything that I say. We are not speaking to each other now."

Ada tried to imagine her mother and her not speaking to each other, but it was impossible. Her mother could get angry, of course, usually whenever Ada behaved of her own accord, outside the bounds of good sense, as her mother would say, but even amid the anger, Ada knew—she never doubted—how profoundly her mother loved her. Ada had fallen into a bramble of nicker nuts once and come back to the house dripping with blood, and her mother had frowned and asked what had happened, how could it have happened, Ada was supposed to have been doing her chores, chores that had nothing to do with nicker nuts, of that she was sure, but even as her mother said all of that, she set Ada on the chair—pressing a towel to every perforation until the blood dried to beads and dabbing aloe onto every cut—and when she finished both her ministrations and her lecturing, she cupped a hand round Ada's head and kissed her at the temple and sighed.

Glumly, as though talk of his father had pained him, Omar put his hat back on and said, "My break is ending. I should go."

He looked terribly sad, and Ada did not know what to say. "Thank you for telling me the name of the flowers."

He nodded. "I am sorry to hear about Mrs. Oswald," he said.

They both had their sadness.

Omar started backing away. Before he was too far, Ada said, "If your father won't talk to you, you can come talk to me anytime."

At that, as he walked down the hill, Omar smiled, as Ada was hoping he would.

||||||

ADA CARRIED THE flowers back to the house. In the kitchen, Antoinette gave her a sidelong look as Ada filled a glass with water and set the stems inside. Antoinette was standing at the worktable, using a dish towel to fan a huge pink ham that, from the look and the smell, had just come out of the oven.

"What are you doing?" Ada said, placing the flowers by the window to save them for the next day.

Antoinette sucked her teeth. "What it look like?"

"Cooling a ham."

"Well, your eyes no deceive you."

"But where did it come from?"

Antoinette said, "Ham come from a pig."

With all the faux innocence she could muster, Ada said, "True? And here I been thinking it comes from a toad."

Antoinette frowned. "You don't have something else to do?"

"I picked those flowers for the burying."

"Mmmhmm."

"But I can help if you need. I know how to cook some things."

Antoinette scoffed. "Me don't need help with the food."

Ada walked closer to the ham on the counter and leaned down to sniff. It smelled like suckling pig, and her mouth watered at the thought.

With her hip, Antoinette bumped Ada aside. She threw the dish towel over her shoulder, cut two thick slices of the warm ham, and laid them on a plate. "You want to help," she said, "deliver this to Mister Oswald for me."

Ada stared at the plate. She had hardly seen Mr. Oswald these past two days. If the newspapermen or the chaplain weren't at the house, he shut himself up in his study, and that was more than all right with her. Somewhere mixed in with his grief, she did worry he was angry with her, so she would rather keep clear of him if she could.

"Go on," Antoinette said, thrusting the plate forward.

But Ada shook her head. "I hear you don't need help with the food," she said.

20

ON THE THURSDAY BEFORE THE DEMONSTRATION, VALENTINA RODE THE SOUTHBOUND train all the way to the city. She was off to do an errand that, yes, she could have asked Joaquín to do for her, but the last time she had entrusted him with a similar task—delivering the letter to the Presidential Palace—it had not gone so well. Better on this occasion, she thought, just to do it herself.

It had been over a week since she and Joaquín had come to Gatún. Every morning when Valentina woke now, she was seized by the sort of vigor and purpose she had not felt in years. At her insistence, everyone had gathered again to plan a demonstration, and together they had decided on a date (Monday, October 14), a time (10:00 a.m.), and a place (in front of her childhood home). When Alfredo asked just what they thought a demonstration would accomplish, Valentina explained that they would sit side by side, creating a sort of barricade, although the real goal was to attract enough attention that someone from the zone government or the Panamanian government or even the Land Commission would come. "And then what?" Alfredo had asked. "And then we can talk," Valentina said. "We can voice our concerns as we did in the letter, but this time to their faces, which will have greater effect." Reina Moscoso, the town baker, had agreed to bring food. Flor Castillo had said she had a full barrel of water, already boiled, that she could distribute to people in cans and bottles. Raúl volunteered to bring noisemakers to "enhance the atmosphere," as he said. And Máximo, who knew some of the former municipal officers, had promised he would tell them of the plan. They had no real authority now that municipalities had been eliminated by the U.S.-run zone government, but perhaps there was still something they could do.

Aside from the meeting, while Renata and Joaquín were at work, Valentina had made it a point to visit every shop and business in town, inviting the owners to the demonstration the following week. She stopped people on the street, trying to drum up support.

Once, she had even crossed the river to see with her own eyes the place where the North Americans were proposing the entire town of Gatún should be moved, and the sheer logistics of what would be required—taking apart nearly one hundred homes as well as the school and the church, herding everyone's cattle and goats and pigs over the river, replanting farms and remaking roads—seemed insane to her. Valentina had walked out past the steam shovels and the labor tents already present and had stood by herself on a patch of open land, gazing back across the river where she could see her town—for now. If Gatún disappeared, only to be replaced by an enormous earthen dam, the cruelest thing, Valentina realized as she stood there, might not be the disappearance itself, but the fact that from this opposite shore, the people of Gatún would be able to see the place where they used to live and be confronted with its burial day after day.

The only good that had come from that crossing had been when she had spotted a man sitting on a wooden box in front of his tent. He was reading a newspaper she had never heard of before, something called *The Canal Record* it appeared when she tried inconspicuously to see. Later, when she had mentioned it to Joaquín, he had said, yes, yes—in the city he sometimes saw Americans reading that. "Perfect," she had said. And though he had looked at her, puzzled, Valentina had not felt the need to explain. She should have guessed that the Americans had their own newspaper. They had their own everything, but for once, that might work to the advantage of the people of Gatún. The Americans were exactly the audience they needed to reach.

||||||

THE CITY, WHEN she arrived, was more boisterous than Valentina remembered. So much noise, so many people, such sticky restlessness in the air! She had moved here only because of Joaquín. But after these ten days away, it was suffocating to be plunged into it again.

She walked all the way to the editorial offices of the newspaper. There, outside the door, Valentina smoothed her hair and took a deep breath. Then she twisted the knob. The door swung open so easily that she stumbled inside, and she found herself suddenly in a room full of desks, each occupied by someone who, upon her clumsy entrance, stopped what they were doing and looked up. Valentina used her heel to nudge the door closed behind her. She flashed her winningest smile.

A man at the desk nearest her said something, or he asked something—it was impossible to know which. Unfazed, and with all eyes still trained on her, Valentina said, "¿Alguien habla español?"

The people at the desks—both men and women—looked at each other in confusion, some of them shrugging, some of them shaking their heads. Outwardly, Valentina kept the smile on her face, but inwardly she frowned. Could it be that not one of them had learned Spanish by now?

"¿Español?" Valentina tried again.

Finally, from a desk in the rear, a man in a dark suit stood and motioned for her to come back. As gracefully as she could, Valentina walked between the desks as everyone watched her. Thankfully, when she got to the back, the sound of clattering typewriters resumed.

The man, who had a prominent cleft in his chin, remained standing and in passable Spanish asked her why she was there.

"I am from the town of Gatún, where, as I am sure you know, there are plans to build a dam for the canal. The dam means, however, that our town will be forced to move, which, as you might imagine, will cause the residents there considerable pain. So we, the people of Gatún, have organized a demonstration to take place on Monday at ten o'clock in the morning to voice our objection."

The man was staring at her. Valentina was not certain how much he understood. From the desk to the left, a young girl—her long blond hair was so fine that she probably needed no cremes—was also staring, clearly eavesdropping. She had her fingers on the typewriter keys before her, but she was not moving them.

To the man, Valentina said, "It is our hope that the newspaper will write a story about it."

The man nodded. "Gracias."

Valentina waited. What did that mean? Was he going to write an article about it or not?

"It is very important," she said.

"Sí. Gracias."

Again—what did that mean? Did "sí" mean that yes, he agreed it was important?

"Monday," she said again. "At ten o'clock in the morning. In Gatún." She wanted to make sure he had caught the relevant details at least.

"Gracias."

At the third "gracias" Valentina felt herself deflate. She was doing no better, it seemed, than Joaquín. Although she was inside at least, so perhaps that was progress, even of the smallest sort. But just as she thought that, the man extended his arm as though he were directing her out.

"Señora," he said with all the pretense of civility.

She could see what he was doing. Rudely trying to push her out while pretending to be polite. Well, she had said what she had come there to say, no? And obviously it was not in her interest to anger him if she wanted him to write the article, so Valentina smiled widely again, hoping to appear friendly and reasonable. Without delay, she turned and, with her head held high, walked out the way she had come in, though if the man had been a true gentleman, she thought, he would have been courteous enough to see her to the door.

||||||

SITTING AT HER desk, her fingers resting lightly atop the typewriter keys, Molly watched the woman walk out. It was only her second day on the job. Earlier that same week Molly had heard the sad news that Marian Oswald, whom Molly had always found more sincere and less frivolous than many of the women she usually interacted with, had passed away. It had jolted her. Life was short. What was she doing spending hers inside a commissary, sorting payment coupons and stacking fruit? All while her camera was gathering dust. She had asked her father if he might pull some strings to get her a job at *The Canal Record* instead. They did not run photographs from what she knew, but a job there—any job—could be the first step to a career. And maybe, Molly thought, if she took photographs that were important enough, the paper would use them. She could be a pioneer, just like Jessie Tarbox Beals.

For the time being, however, she was an assistant doing the menial work of typing up more senior reporters' field notes. But that day a petite woman had come in, telling Mr. Atchison, the editor who worked at the desk next to Molly's, about a demonstration in the town of Gatún, and Molly, who had taken the time to learn a fair bit of Spanish, had listened to every word the woman had said.

||||||

VALENTINA STOPPED AT her apartment in the city before getting back on the train. She walked up to the second floor and let herself in. Everything was as they had left it—cluttered, overstuffed. Much like the city itself. She raised the window to let in some air.

In the bedroom, she opened the door of the old wooden armoire where she kept her clothes. It smelled musty, having been unopened for weeks, and she hoped it had not become infested with moths. Valentina owned only a few dresses, and of those, she prized one above the rest—her pollera. She lifted it out of the armoire and held it up. It was the traditional style, with a long, full skirt and an off-the-shoulder blouse, both of which were adorned with hand embroidery and tiers of lace. She had not worn it in years, but when she stripped off the dress she had been wearing for weeks and pulled on the pollera instead, she was pleased to see it still fit.

Valentina walked back out to the front window and closed it again so that she could catch her reflection in the thick glass. She smiled at the image she saw. Yes, if nothing else, a dress like this would draw attention all right.

21

LUCILLE'S HANDS TREMBLED. EVER SINCE THE MORNING SHE HAD WOKEN UP TO discover that Ada was gone, they had been shaking while she sewed, and now the stitches she made were as uneven as teeth. Just the other day it had taken her a full ten minutes to slip the thread through the eye of her needle because one hand would not hold the needle steady and the other could not follow as the eye bobbed up and down. The trembling would not matter so much if she weren't trying to make a dress so elaborate, so fine, that she could sell it for enough to help pay for the doctor to return to the house and perform the surgery he had talked about. The hospital, which the doctor had also talked about, was to her little more than a morgue. She would never send Millicent there. She had heard far too many horror stories about butchers' aprons and large open wards where sick people huddled and patients went unfed. No, she would earn the money for the surgery the same way she did everything: by herself. She still had some time.

All night, Lucille sat by the hearth, guiding the needle, piecing together squares of bold blue and bright yellow with accents of black, pulling taut ruffles, forming gathers. She had made hundreds of dresses in the past, but this, she kept telling herself, was more important than any of them. Her mind wandered into worry as she sewed. One of her girls gone and the other seeming as though she was preparing to leave in a different way. The thought that she could well lose them both terrified her. Millicent and Ada were all she had in the world. They were her two bright stars in every dark sky. Her reasons for being. Once upon a time she had walked off the Camby grounds, the place where her parents and grandparents all lay in the earth. She had left her whole life behind, and Millicent and Ada were the reason why. Lucille herself could have handled Madam Camby's suspicions, the way she ranged at the edge of the fields at times with her mouth pulled tight and her eyes narrowed, surveying every woman she saw, wondering who among them was causing her husband to leave their bed so many nights. Let that vile woman do what she wanted, say the worst things, spew all her hate. But to let the girls be subjected to that—no. So she had marched out into the world with the girls in her arms and rebuilt a whole new life where one had not existed before.

Hour after hour Lucille pricked the fabric with the tip of the needle and pulled the thread through. It was up to her to keep everything in her world stitched together, she thought. But amid her worry and exhaustion and the low light of the lantern, her hands trembled and her eyesight sometimes blurred with tears, and often the stitches would not come out straight. Even after she ripped the thread out and started again, sewing the sleeve to the bodice, then the bodice to the waistband, she could not get it right. Nerves had the best of her. She set everything down on her lap, took a deep breath, and listened for her mother's voice, but as usual it did not come. It was up to her. Lucille lifted the garment from her lap, squeezed the needle between her fingertips, and tried again.

||||||

IN THE MORNING, Lucille walked out the front door of the house with the dress over her arm. It was not as expertly crafted as she would have liked, but it was finished at least. Quietly, she closed the door behind her. She hated to leave Millicent alone in the house, and she hesitated with her hand on the knob, but there were certain things that needed to be done. Millicent was sleeping. Lucille would not be long.

When she started down the steps, she saw the figure of a man walking up Aster Lane. By his limp, she recognized it was Willoughby. She was in no mood for Willoughby Dalton that day.

Lucille kept walking and when she neared Willoughby, he

smiled at her and tipped his silly hat and said, "Good morning." Then he opened his hand. "For you," he said.

Lucille stopped to see. On Willoughby's palm was a small bell, about the size of an ackee.

"I picked it up from the street," he explained, "but it was missing its tongue. Couldn't make no sound. I fitted it with a new piece so that now it can sing. Try it."

Lucille picked up the small bell and shook it. It made a dull, tinny sound. He brought her such worthless things. The least he could have done was bring her something with enough value that she might be able to sell it, but no.

Lucille felt a thickness in her throat all of sudden. She had no interest in letting Willoughby see her cry. So without bothering to thank him as she always did and without even bothering to say goodbye, Lucille slipped the bell in her pocket and, clutching the dress hung over her arm, hurried past Willoughby, on up the lane toward town.

||||||

WILLOUGHBY STOOD IN the lane and watched Lucille go. He was disappointed that the bell had not worked better, but that failing did not diminish the happiness he always felt upon seeing her again. He knew what he wanted, and he would keep trying for it, pleasantly, calmly, with a patience that most people he knew did not possess. He just had to wait, he believed, and one day, by the grace of God, the things he wished for would come true.

He had no reason to think it. Willoughby had wished for his own horse to ride when he was a boy, a big horse with a glossy black coat, but a horse had never materialized and Willoughby had spent every day of his life getting places on his feet instead, so much walking that one of his good legs had worn out and gone crooked at the knee, so now he limped on the remaining good leg, which dragged the exhausted leg behind.

Willoughby had wished for a mother and father who loved him, and he had received only half of that equation. He'd had a mother who had loved him in the fiercest way imaginable until the moment of her death, and a father who had merely been fierce. His father whipped him and was in general unkind, and whether he loved his own son, Willoughby never could tell. For years and years, he had waited for his father to say that he did, but those particular words never passed his father's lips.

Willoughby had waited to discover what his life was to be made of, whether there was any talent he had or a gift the good Lord might have bestowed upon him, a signal for what he should do with his days. But that never came, either, and Willoughby had spent the years since he was about twelve trying one thing and then another, waiting until something felt right. After carving furniture, stretching leather, hammering horseshoes, staking fences, and portering luggage for travelers at the wharf, he had not yet found the gift the good Lord might have given him, but if he kept waiting, he told himself, one day he would surely know what it was.

At some point, what Willoughby had begun wishing for was to be around Lucille Bunting, whom he knew from church. He did not know her well—although that was part of the wish. He wanted to be around her to know her better because what he did know was lovely. Besides, she did not have a man, and he thought that meant she might have room for him. With his tired leg and his rootlessness regarding work, though, Willoughby worried that he had little to offer her. He had tried to make up for that by bringing her things. A bunch of flowers, a pencil, a transparent dragonfly wing, a small clay bowl, breadfruit, a pair of black leather boots. Lucille took everything he brought, so Willoughby kept coming back bringing more. He always tried, when he came, to say a few words to her, too. Sometimes she allowed it and sometimes she did not, and he could not determine what swayed her from one visit to the next. He only knew he was grateful when they exchanged pleasantries. But of all the things he had offered her and she had taken, what he really wanted was to offer himself. Take me, Willoughby wanted to say. But of course he did not. He was patient. He waited, hoping and believing that it would happen one day.

|||||

THE MARKET WAS sparse, filled with only a dozen or so vendors and even fewer people wandering about. Years ago when Lucille used to sell clothing here, the market had been bustling with activity. When people had money to spend, Lucille had no trouble selling enough of her clothing each week to get by. Enough to purchase more fabric to make more garments for the week to come, and after that enough to pay for the girls' schooling and for food. But with so little work to be found, so few people had money to spend that even to stand there in the market had not made sense. Lucille had started doing what other women did—knocking on people's doors—and though at first people answered and at least listened to what Lucille had to say, more recently all the doors remained closed.

That day when Lucille arrived at the market with the dress, it had been with hope that things might be better than she remembered. Her heart sank when she saw they were not. A smattering of other women sat in the market, most of them seated behind trays of fruit or potatoes or greens, one next to an assortment of pottery lined up on the ground. A few people walked through, but none of them were stopping to buy. Outside, a man trundled past, rolling a syrup spider. Everyone, it seemed, had fallen on hard times. Still, Lucille walked to her old spot and held the dress up by the shoulders, calling out to any soul who came near: "For sale a dress! A beautiful dress!"

People turned. Some people smiled. Most people walked on. It used to be that there were regulars who sought out her clothes. Now she saw no one she knew, no one who knew her. Now she was just any woman standing in the market hawking a product that no one wanted to buy.

After forty minutes or so, a woman did stop and look admiringly at the dress. Encouraged, Lucille held the garment high. "You won't find another like it anywhere, look."

The woman nodded as she inspected it. Pinching the dress by the shoulders, Lucille spun it round so that the woman could see the row of cloth-covered buttons she had meticulously made herself with matching fabric so that they blended perfectly and did not interrupt the line of the dress. The woman nodded again, and that seemed a good sign. She touched the skirt with its copious gathers and stroked the fabric, and that seemed promising, too. Lucille watched as the woman lifted the skirt and ran her hand all the way down to the hem, which she flipped up. At that, Lucille cringed. Every jagged, irregular stitch was visible now, every knot, every pucker. The woman leaned closer to look.

"See the bright colors," Lucille said, trying to shift the woman's focus elsewhere.

The woman said nothing. She dropped the hem.

"The gathers all made by my own hand," Lucille tried.

The woman looked at Lucille and sorrowfully shook her head. "Pretty dress on the outside, but—"

"My daughter sick," Lucille blurted.

The woman dropped her shoulders as if pity alone might make her reconsider.

"She needs a surgery. I . . . It's a fine dress. I . . ."

"Cuh-dear," the woman said softly, to Lucille's surprise. She put an arm around Lucille's shoulders as Lucille started to cry.

Lucille lay her head on the woman's breast. The dress hung down over her arms. She cried for a good minute while the woman held her and whispered, "Shhhhh, shhhhh." Then Lucille wiped her face and lifted her head, and the woman smiled at her. "There now," she said.

Lucille sniffled once and took a deep breath.

The woman reached into her purse and produced a coin that she held out. "I pray for you and your daughter."

In another time, Lucille never would have accepted a handout from a stranger. But neither could she have imagined a time when she would stand out in public, crying on a stranger's breast, and with her pride already in ruins, she raised her hand and let the woman press the coin into her palm.

"God be with you," the woman said as she did.

After she walked away, Lucille looked down at the coin. It was a fisherman's penny, worth 1¼ pence. Lucille slipped it into her pocket and held the dress up again, shouting more desperately than before.

"For sale a dress! A true beautiful dress!"

After some minutes a man poked his head around the dress to have a look at Lucille behind it.

He grinned. "Beautiful dress *and* beautiful woman, I see."

Lucille glimpsed only his face from around the side of the dress, which she was holding up between them like a curtain. She clenched her teeth before she replied. "Beautiful dress here for sale. Made brand new. Perfect for any occasion you can think."

"The occasion I thinking of, you not wearing no dress."

"Go on away," Lucille said.

"Other things I might pay for." The man puckered his lips in case she had not known what he meant.

Without breaking her gaze, Lucille stamped her bare foot down on his. The man jumped back and yelped. "You mash my foot!"

"Go on away, I tell you now."

"Eh, you a wutless woman!" the man yelled as he walked off, shaking out the pain in his foot. "No one wish to buy such a dress in these times!"

Unfortunately, he was right. After standing in the market for longer than she would like and failing to attract any legitimate interest, Lucille reluctantly folded the dress back into a square and took a deep breath. She had labored over the dress, but if she could not sell it—well, then she could not. She would just have to find another way.

With the dress in her arms, Lucille left the market and walked south across the bridge to the almshouse on Beckles Road. She had resisted the idea of approaching the parish vestry for assistance, hoping to earn her own money somehow without having to ask for it like a beggar. But after that morning, when even the boldest dress she had ever sewn attracted no one but a critical woman and a boorish man, she took a few more steps down into the valley of desperation.

||||||

THE VESTRYMAN HAD just poured his morning cup of black tea and had been about to sit down to drink it when he heard a knock at the door. He was an older white gentleman with overgrown white whiskers down to his jaw. He left the tea where it was and went to the door. When he opened it, he was greeted by a petite Negro woman with some item of clothing tucked up under one arm.

"Yes?" he said.

"My name is Lucille Bunting."

The vestryman had lived in Bridgetown all of his days, and he took special pride in knowing the ins and outs of everyone's lives. He had never seen Lucille Bunting before, but he had heard even before she arrived at his door that one of the Bunting girls was ill. It was a bit of information that he had dismissed as soon as it had come to him, for he knew, too, that the girls had been fathered by Henry Camby, which meant that they had access to money and therefore did not need what the almshouse had to give.

"Yes, and how may I be of assistance?" the vestryman asked. Although he already knew most things, he made a habit of pretending otherwise.

"I come to ask for aid, sir."

"On what grounds?"

"Medical aid, sir. For my daughter who ill."

"Ill with what?"

"Fluid in her lungs, sir."

The two of them were still standing at the door. The vestryman told Lucille to step inside. He closed the door behind them, and when he walked back across the room he glanced at his tea, which sat steaming on its tray. When he turned to face her again, he struggled to remember the last thing she had said, and after some effort he cleared his throat and said, "Fluid, you say?"

"That's what the doctor say. Some weeks back he come examine her and say she has fluid left over in her lungs."

"Left over? From what?"

"Pneumonia, sir."

"She has pneumonia?"

"Not anymore, sir."

"So she is no longer ill."

"She did recover from the worst of it, yes, but there fluid left over now, and she needs surgery to remove it, sir."

The light in the vestryman's office was dim, but it was enough to see how pretty the woman standing in front of him was. Probably even prettier some twenty years ago or however long it had been since Henry Camby had been with her. Certainly he could understand how she had caused Henry, whose family the vestryman had known for decades, to succumb to weakness. Then again, Henry had a reputation for weakness sometimes. Other planters thought he was far too lenient with his workers, far too kind, and truly the only reason he was accorded respect was because of his family name. But that was neither here nor there. The matter before him—quite literally before him—was this woman asking for aid.

"Many other people are ill," the vestryman said. "And many with worse than a . . . leftover fluid. We cannot distribute aid for everyone, I'm afraid. We must reserve our funds for the neediest cases. God's earth is bountiful, but our resources are not."

"Please, sir," Lucille said.

"You do have other means."

"I'm sorry, sir?"

He had to be careful not to bring up Henry's name, more for Henry's sake than for hers, since the vestryman assumed that Henry would not want the matter discussed. It was a bone that had been buried a long time ago, and the vestryman imagined Henry would not care to dig it up now. Besides, his wretched wife would have Henry's head if the truth were ever confirmed. Maybe both of his heads. The vestryman chuckled at his own joke and then, realizing he had made a noise that Lucille could hear, gathered himself and said, "You do own your own home, is that not right?"

"My home, sir?"

"That is but one idea."

"To sell my home?"

"It is something you might consider."

Lucille looked at him with horror, as though he had suggested she quarter an elephant and serve it for supper. The vestryman knew of course that Henry had given her that house, so he could concede that perhaps it had sentimental value to her, but the monetary value was what mattered right now. Selling the house struck him as a perfectly reasonable solution, although reasonableness and women did not always go hand in hand.

The vestryman glanced over his shoulder at the tea and was dismayed to see that the steam was gone. Was there anything worse than a lukewarm cup of tea? "Well, now . . ." He moved to usher her out.

"Sir?"

"I have offered you the only thing I can—my advice."

"But, sir—" Lucille begged.

"Now if you will excuse me—"

"Please, sir. I have never come . . . I have never asked before. I have been on my own—"

He started toward the door himself, crowding Lucille back until she had no choice but to make her way toward it as well. "I do believe you can find a way," he said before closing the door, and he hoped that Lucille Bunting knew what he meant.

||||||

LUCILLE WALKED HOME with the dress in her arms and a growing hopelessness in her throat. What was she going to do? Selling the house was not something she wanted to think about. She had taken a few steps down into the valley of desperation, but she was not yet at the base. Even her children did not understand what it meant to her to own that house, how miraculous it was to own anything at all. Lucille's grandmother had owned nothing, not even herself. Lucille's mother had owned nothing except for herself. And now Lucille owned herself and also a house. She did not want to contemplate letting it go. There was another option of course, one she had also not wanted to consider. If she could not sell the dress and would not sell the house and the vestryman had turned her away and the Lord was so fickle that He had not yet answered her prayers, then perhaps this is what it had come to. When Lucille had left the first time, sixteen years ago, it had taken all the courage and hope that she had. Returning there now would take more of the same. But if Ada could sail across the ocean for Millicent, Lucille told herself, then surely she could do this.

Not even a year after she had left the estate with the girls, a courier had arrived at their house one morning. Lucille had been out in the yard and she had seen the young man dismount his horse and walk toward the house. He had been carrying a silk pouch, and when he had come closer he said, as Lucille knew he would, "I come from Master Camby, ma'am. He ask me to bring you this." He held the pouch aloft. Lucille had wiped the sweat from her forehead and stared at the bag dangling there in the air. "Don't you want it?" the young man asked. He had a lazy eye that looked like it wanted to roll away out of his head. Lucille had reached up and grabbed the pouch. "Gift for Millicent Bunting, he say. On the occasion of her birthday." It was cinched by a drawstring, and it had taken Lucille a good few seconds to loosen the knot. When she finally looked inside, she saw three gold crowns. Quickly, she had pulled taut the drawstring and tried to give the pouch back, but the courier, holding his hands up in the air, had said, "I supposed to give it to you, not take it back." He started walking away. It was not the money that bothered her exactly; it was the intrusion into their lives. She had wanted, she had tried, to make a clean break. She did not appreciate that Henry had let the blood seep past the bone. She had kept the coins, and though there was a bank in town that served the free-colored population, she did not want to rely on the bank with something as precious as money, so she tucked the pouch up high on a shelf behind a tin canister and refused to touch it again. She wanted to prove to herself that she did not need his money. She was fine on her own. She did not need anything from him anymore. It had been surprisingly easy to let Henry go when she left the estate. By that point, his love was not something she wanted. She had wanted it once, had enjoyed his love on the nights they spent together, had even believed a few times that she could love him back, but by the time she left, that feeling had disappeared, and curiously and mercifully it had never returned. The coins displeased Lucille enough that she had sent word to Henry that he was not to contact them again. Ada's birthday would be in a few months and Lucille did not want another gift showing up at their door. *Leave us be*, Lucille had written—nothing more, nothing less—and posted it to the estate. That was the last communication she had had with Henry, and on Ada's birthday, when nothing arrived, Lucille was relieved.

Two weeks ago, Lucille had remembered those coins. She had slid the canister forward and reached behind it only to find that the pouch was gone. She had taken everything off the shelf, looking for it. Her first thought was that they had been robbed, but no burglar would come and take one single pouch and leave everything else that they had in the house, even though that everything else was not much. Her second thought was that Ada had taken the pouch, and if that was true, then Lucille was glad. At least Ada had traveled with some money in her pocket. At least Lucille had raised the child, however impetuous she was, to have some common sense. Now, though, as Lucille walked back from town, she found herself wishing she still had that money. It was not enough, not even close, but it would have helped.

22

HENRY CAMBY WAS STANDING AT HIS BEDROOM WINDOW ON THE SECOND FLOOR OF the house, looking down over his estate, when he saw her walk up the lane. His heart nearly stopped, but he knew with certainty it was her. A year ago when someone resembling Lucille had shown up on his estate, standing in the daylight next to a mahogany tree, he had tremulously believed that it might be her ghost. He had asked his closest friend, who also happened to be his lawyer, to search the newspapers and the registers, and in the end J.R. had reported that Lucille Bunting was alive. That was a finding that had brought Henry immense relief. But it meant that there was only one other explanation then for who the girl on his property had been.

Now, it was the first Sunday in October. Holding his breath, Henry stood and watched. Lucille's body was softer and rounder than it used to be, but he recognized the way that she moved, and she walked up the lane with just as much determination as she had walked down it sixteen years earlier. He had stood at this very same window then and watched her go. When she came near enough, he rose on his toes and turned his face down to catch every glimpse of her before she stepped up and under the roof of the veranda. The venetian blinds were raised, and he leaned his forehead against the glass, listening for her knock and wondering what he would do when it came.

||||||

GERTRUDE HAD JUST come in from the garden out back, where she had been sitting in the shade sipping a glass of lemonade. The lemonade had been sour since Henry had instructed Sarah the cook to use sugar sparingly if at all. Which was idiocy. What was the point of owning a sugar plantation if they could not have some of the sugar for themselves?

Gertrude had sat in the garden asking herself this and letting her frustrations well up. Upon finishing the lemonade, she had put the cool, wet glass against her cheek. The lilies were still in bloom, and they were supposed to be pretty, but their necks drooped dumbly toward the soil, and Gertrude had found herself frustrated with them, too. With the flowers, with the entire garden, with the lemonade, with her life. And why could a butterfly not simply fly in a straight line? When a small one flew by, she swatted at it with her foot and wished she had stomped it instead. Showoff. Flitting about. She had lowered the glass to her lap, curious how hard she would need to squeeze to make it shatter. Henry was in the bedroom doing Lord knows what. It was where he went on Sundays, his only day off, and though he claimed he needed time to recuperate from the week, she guessed it was merely that he wanted to be away from her. If the shattered glass drew blood, would it make him come down?

Gertrude had stayed in the garden, contemplating this, until sweat beaded along her hairline. Angrily, she wiped it off, but when it returned, she stood and went inside, wondering if she needed to bathe for a second time that day, which was an excess, yes, but was the only way she knew to effectively deal with the endless bother of sweat. She had just walked back into the house with the empty lemonade glass in her hand when she heard a knock at the door. Had she not been so full of her frustrations, she would have called one of the servants to come answer it, but as she was in no mood to talk to any of them, Gertrude answered it herself.

A Black woman was standing on the veranda, a Black woman who looked vaguely familiar. In the next second, Gertrude's memory came into focus. She nearly fell over in shock when she realized who the woman was.

The woman appeared unnerved herself, and neither of them spoke for a moment until finally Gertrude, in a tone that revealed her distemper, said, "Why are you here?"

"Madam," the woman said. She nodded slightly, but even through the nod, she looked Gertrude right in the eye.

Gertrude clenched her jaw, but she managed to say, "We have not seen you in quite some time."

The woman nodded again.

Gertrude had not known the woman's name while she was in their employ. It was possible she had heard it once or twice, but if so it was an arrow sailing across her attention, there one instant and gone the next. But after the woman had taken her house apart and left, a momentous event on the Camby estate, everyone whispering about it and standing around to watch, Gertrude—having gathered at last who her husband had been going to night after night—went to their lawyer, J. R. Robinson, and asked him the woman's name. The fact that J.R. resisted telling her was additional confirmation. Gertrude had said to him, "I am but asking for her name, J.R." J.R. had always been exceedingly loyal to Henry, which Gertrude appreciated, but at that moment his loyalty was getting in her way. J.R. stammered something incomprehensible. Calmly, Gertrude had said, "I will wring your thick neck if you do not tell me now." Finally, J.R. had told her. "Lucille Bunting." For many years Gertrude held on to that name.

This woman standing on the veranda now was doubtlessly her. She looked older, but she was still attractive, Gertrude saw, and suddenly all of her rumbling, petty frustrations turned into fury.

"Well, what is it?" Gertrude snapped.

"I am looking for Master Camby, ma'am."

Gertrude snorted. "Yes, as I recall, you were always doing that."

She wanted to shame her, but impressively the woman did not flinch.

"I need to speak with him, ma'am."

"He is not here."

"No?"

Unhurriedly, Gertrude worked her tongue side to side behind her clenched teeth. Then she spit in the woman's face.

"Leave," Gertrude hissed. "Leave, and don't you ever come back."

She watched the woman wipe her face, and she waited to see whether she would do or say anything else in return, but after a second, the woman simply turned around and walked down the front steps and started down the gravel lane. Before the woman was even out of her sight, Gertrude, hot with rage, flung the drinking glass she was still holding down on the floor and watched it burst into shards. Sarah the cook came running at the sound, but Henry did not.

||||||

HENRY STOOD PERFECTLY still in the bedroom, forehead against glass, but he did not hear her knock. He heard nothing at all, not even the tick of the clock on the bureau, which over the years had kept him awake many a night. The clock was an heirloom passed down along Gertrude's side of the family, and she would not let it go. She wanted it right where it was—she claimed the ticking soothed her, although Henry suspected it was just that she knew it bothered him—and Henry had long ago given up the cause of moving it to a different room. He might have fought back—about the clock, about many things, really—but confrontation was not in his nature. That afternoon, with his heart pounding and the blood rushing up to his ears, he heard nothing for a long minute or more. Then, with his head on the glass, he saw Lucille walk away. Henry widened his eyes and, for the second time in his life, watched her go.

He remained at the window, wondering why she had come. Was it for him? After all these years? He had always dreamed she might return. In the beginning, every few weeks or so, Henry had a dream in which she was standing at the back door of the house, where she had been the day he first laid eyes upon her, dreams in which he was weightlessly happy, but as soon as he woke, he grew despondent again. It was a terrible fate to know that nothing in one's actual life would equal the world of one's dreams.

Henry sighed under the weight of what his life had become—all that he had and did not want, and all that he wanted but did not have. For it wasn't only Lucille he had waited for. After deducing who the girl by the mahogany tree had been, a part of him always hoped that Millicent, too, would return.

Some mornings Henry woke, and there was a kind of charge in the air, and he thought, *Today she will come. Today is the day I will see her again.* And on those days, even if Henry had no business off the property, no reason to go into town, he would order his driver to hitch the carriage and take him down the long gravel lane where he had seen her that once. "Slow," Henry instructed the driver, and the horses would trot as though they were out merely to enjoy the sun on their backs. From his seat, Henry would stare out the carriage for any sign of a girl. When they passed the same mahogany tree, he paid particular attention, but of course he knew she could be anywhere a second time. When his driver let slip that Gertrude had approached him, demanding to know the meaning of these strange carriage rides on the lane, Henry stopped making them. Now he only looked when he had legitimate business that took him out anyway. Or he looked from his window on Sundays like this.

Letting them go was one of the hardest things Henry had ever done. The right thing, though, Henry reminded himself again and again. Something in the air anyway was put to rest once they were gone. Gertrude, who had at that time been suffering from strange bouts of insomnia, tossing and turning almost every night, was suddenly still as a bone, sleeping straight through the night for the first time in months.

It had not been difficult to find out where they had settled, of course. J.R. was useful for such information. Nine months after they left, when the first of the girls' birthdays rolled around, Henry slipped three gold crowns into a small silk pouch and arranged for a courier to deliver it to the house. He had thought that it was something he might do every year for each of their birthdays, but not long after he sent it, he received a letter in reply that said, *Leave us be.* That was all. He had turned the paper over, hoping for more, but he could find only that. It was another small break to his heart. He knew Lucille was the one who had written the words. *Leave us be.* And so Henry had obliged.

||||||

HENRY MOVED THROUGH the rest of the day agitated. He stayed in the bedroom until it seemed that the bedroom would suffocate him; then he went out in the sun and walked the grounds. A total of 256 steps. He counted them and came to where a new house had at some point been built. He sighed and turned and walked away.

It was hot as he wandered through the fields. The land was barren, stripped of cane stalks. In the distance the great stone windmill was still. He walked in circles, not knowing what to do with himself, and by dusk Henry had found his way out to the lane and felt that was the right place to be since it was where he had seen Millicent a year earlier and it was where he had seen Lucille that day. He paced up and down it until J.R. found him in the twilight and said, "Henry, stop."

Henry, lost in thought, did not hear him at first.

"Henry!" J.R. called, louder. He had been riding his horse up to the estate when he came upon Henry walking in the humid, buggy air. He dismounted his mare and held her by the reins and called to his old friend again. "Henry!" They were far enough from the house that no one would hear them.

Finally Henry turned.

Leading his horse, J.R. walked closer. He had imagined this was the sort of conversation that would happen inside, in the study, over a glass of brandy or at least a cup of tea. But he supposed now was as good a time as any.

"I thought you might want to know . . . ," J.R. began. As he came closer, he saw how awful Henry looked, and he hesitated before continuing.

"What is it?" Henry asked.

"Are you okay?"

"Fine. Perfectly fine."

J.R. nodded slowly.

Henry said, "What is it I should know?"

J.R. measured the moment. It was perhaps not the right time to say it, after all, but it was his duty, he always felt, to help Henry however he could—and in any case it needed to be said. "The girl is ill."

"What girl?"

J.R. paused before saying, "Your girl, Henry."

The light was dim, night settling in. J.R. saw Henry open his mouth and close it again. The horse made a noise, and J.R. reached up to stroke its flank.

Standing on the lane, Henry looked at his friend, his loyal friend who had kept Henry's secret all of these years. A decade from then when Henry died at the age of fifty-five from influenza, J.R. would be rewarded for that loyalty. In his will Henry would leave certain assets and savings to Gertrude, but he would bequeath the whole of the estate to J.R., trusting that he would do with it what he felt was right.

"Is it serious?" Henry asked now.

"Yes."

"Ill with what?"

"Pneumonia, it seems, that has not yet resolved."

"For how long?"

"It has gone on for some time."

"But you're only telling me now?"

"I only learned it myself. The vestryman told me something about a surgery she requires. He thought you might want to know."

"The vestryman?"

"I never breathed a word to him, Henry. He merely suspects."

Henry nodded and looked off down the lane. *Ill*, he thought. So that's why Lucille had come. It was not about him. He stood in the dusk, nursing his private pain.

"I thought you should know," he heard J.R. say, "in case you felt moved to do something about it."

"Felt moved" struck Henry as an interesting phrase, and if J.R. was not such a good friend, he might have taken offense. Of course he felt moved. But feeling moved and being *able* to move were two different things. What could he do? What was he honestly expected to do? He sighed. Lucille herself had told him once, in writing, to leave them alone. Although the fact that she had come now said something else. But even if he were to offer something—money, a room at the hospital—somehow Gertrude was bound to find out. Henry was certain of that. Gertrude had begun mistrusting him a long time ago, interrogating not only his driver but the house servants, too, about his comings and goings, inspecting the financial ledgers that Henry kept on the shelf, asking about him in town. Henry had learned to be careful. If she caught even a whiff of anything he might do in this case, she would hunt it down until she found where it led. And what then? Would she confront Lucille? Make both of their lives thereafter a living hell?

Henry sighed again. J.R. was waiting for him to respond, but it seemed to Henry that there was nothing to say. His hands were tied, and it was late, and all he wanted was to return to the house and rest.

23

OMAR BATHED AND DRESSED IN THE FINEST CLOTHES HE OWNED—BLACK TROUSERS
and a white cotton shirt—and around his neck he tied a flat black
ribbon into a bow. His father glanced up at him as he walked toward
the front door. As much as Omar wished he would, his father did
not ask why Omar was dressed as he was or where he was going. His
father simply looked at him and took another bite of his boiled egg.

Outside, as Omar walked down the dirt road, he wondered in
despair when the Reign of Silence would finally end. He could have
been the one to speak, he guessed, but no matter what he said, it
would be pointless, no? His father would not listen to him. Besides,
why should he be the one to say something? He had not done
anything wrong. His father was being unreasonable. Of the two of
them, his father should obviously be the one to come around first.
But would he? He had said nothing even after Omar had been gone
for weeks, and by now Omar felt so discouraged about the situation
between them that he did not know what to do.

Near the end of the road, Omar passed Doña Ruiz lying in her
hammock. He lifted his hat in greeting and called out, "Buenas,
Señora," with the thought that perhaps he could ask her for advice.
But from the hammock, Doña Ruiz raised one hand to wave and
replied, "Vaya con Dios," which he took to mean, *Keep walking. Do
not bother me*, so with his hands in his pockets, Omar did just that.

He was sweating by the time he got to the city. In the newspaper,
Omar had read that the funeral was to take place at La Catedral
Basílica Santa María la Antigua, and as he headed that way he tugged
at his shirt buttons, trying to air himself out. It was no use. Sweat
trickled down his back. The benefit of bathing that morning had
already been undone. Although at least, he told himself, his attire

was more presentable than his muddy work clothes, which is what he had been wearing every time he had seen Ada so far. In the days since learning that she worked at the Oswalds', he had started taking his after-lunch walks on the hill, back and forth along the base, up partway and back down, hoping to see her. Finally yesterday he had discovered her picking flowers, and together they had stood in the sun. He had told her about his father—she was the only person he had told—and she had not judged either one of them, had not said either of them was wrong. She had simply listened. And then she had told him he could talk to her anytime—which now was exactly what he wanted to do.

Omar had never stepped foot inside a church before. His father, who was not a believer, had never taken him to a Mass. "The sea is my church," his father liked to say. Or it is what his father used to say back when his father had said anything. When Omar walked into the cathedral, he found a cavernous space packed with people piled into pews and crowded into the side aisles. Omar stood at the back, awed by the rows of stone columns, the arches that soared overhead, the altar that gleamed as though made of gold. He looked for Ada, but nowhere amid the mourners did he see her.

It was not until an hour later, when the Mass was over and four uniformed Marines carried the casket down the center aisle and out into the sun, that he finally laid eyes on her. Mr. Oswald, wearing a black three-piece suit and a high silk hat, walked behind the Marines, and behind him, another dozen or so men in suits, and several paces behind them—Ada. She was carrying the pluma de gallo and wearing the same patchwork dress. Omar stood as still as he could, hoping he might catch her eye, but she simply walked out of the church and by the time he walked out, too, there were so many people crowded out front that he could not see where she had gone.

The plaza was lined with guayacán trees not yet in bloom, and from the buildings surrounding it, children clung to wrought-iron balconies, women leaned out of windows and made the sign of the cross, shopkeepers stood in their doorways and watched. Omar had never seen anything like it before. So much attention paid to one person's death.

By the time the procession began a few minutes later—as soon as the Marines slid the casket into the rear of the carriage and Mr. Oswald, his face even more sullen than the day Omar had seen him in the Cut, climbed up into the front seat next to the driver, who snapped the reins at the horses to urge them ahead—Omar still had not glimpsed Ada again. Those carrying on toward the cemetery had formed a single line snaking through the cobblestone streets, and Omar fell in at the back. After leaning out to one side a few times, finally he saw Ada up near the front. He wanted to make his way closer to her, but at the moment there was no possibility of doing that without drawing attention to himself.

||||||

THIS WAS THE sixth funeral he had been to in his life, Pierre noted as he walked with the procession through the cemetery gates. Several months earlier he had gone to a funeral for a parakeet named Sunshine. The wife of one of the doctors here in Panama had taken the bird in as a pet. Pierre had attended an elaborate supper at their house where Sunshine had greeted each guest at the door, cawing, "Come in! Hello! Come in!" Not long after that evening, Sunshine flew into a pot of boiling milk and died. Pierre had then attended an elaborate funeral in which the doctor's wife placed Sunshine in the dirt beneath a hibiscus tree while her husband earnestly read a lengthy tribute he had prepared. At least thirty people had gathered for that event, which was quite a lot for a bird, but it paled in comparison to the number who today had lined the streets and crowded into the church.

The procession made its way over the green grass dotted with rows of small white crosses until the carriage at the fore halted atop a gently sloping hill. Pierre stood under the blaze of the sun, watching people file in behind him. As he waited, a man wearing an onyx pin in his cravat stepped over to him.

"You were the doctor?" the man asked.

"I am a doctor, yes."

"You were her doctor, though?"

Pierre nodded.

"Tell me," the man said, "was it really so bad?"

Pierre tightened his jaw. He thought he detected some skepticism in the question, as if Marian Oswald ought to have been saved and Pierre ought to have been the one to save her. Once, some years after Pierre had begun practicing medicine, a panicked mother brought in her infant who was boiling with fever and covered with a frightful rash. Pierre's partner had rushed to take the child from her arms and, upon examination, diagnosed the child with scarlet fever. But, the mother protested, she had seen scarlet fever before and it had looked nothing like this. Pierre had listened as the two argued back and forth. When it was clear they were getting nowhere, Pierre walked around the curtain partition and asked if he might examine the baby himself. Upon observing the small, bright red spots all over the child's body, Pierre had said, "It is scarlatinal rubella." It was a new diagnosis, one Pierre had read about in a medical journal. "Scarlatinal rubella?" his partner had asked. "You're familiar with it?" Displeased that his partner was calling into question his expertise, Pierre said firmly, "It is scarlatinal rubella. I am certain of it." Seared into his memory was the look of relief that washed over the widow's face. Confidence and authority were what mattered in the end. Even when the sediment of doubt lay underneath, one had to project certainty.

"In fact it was," Pierre said now to the man on the hill. "It was among the worst cases I have ever encountered. A typical progression would be in the range of five to eight days. It is highly unusual to see pneumonia last beyond eleven days, as this did. If for no other reason than that, I would classify it as extreme."

"So is there a different kind of pneumonia here?" the man asked. "A tropical type new to us?"

Again, Pierre bristled at the implication that perhaps he did not know what he was doing, that he was not versed in the full spectrum of pneumatic possibility.

"I can tell you that no matter the type, every case of pneumonia is serious. And I will tell you, too, that I did everything I could have possibly done for her, and there is not a physician in all creation who could have done more." It was what he would choose from then on to believe. What had happened was in no way his fault.

The man nodded. "George," he called to another of the gentlemen standing nearby. "Come meet the good doctor." One by one, the men walked over to shake Pierre's hand and say a word of condolence or thanks. Several of them Pierre recognized, and he was pleased to be in their company, even under the circumstances. Even when the conversation turned to baseball, a sport about which Pierre knew very little. There was a popular American league that had been formed in the zone, and the man with the onyx pin asked whether any of them had seen the home run that Lucky Brewster had hit to give Culebra their win over Empire.

A man with a rather large nose said, "I'm afraid I didn't go to that game."

"Didn't go? Land sakes, Richard! What kind of patriot are you?"

"The kind who works during the day," he replied, and all the men laughed.

"Don't tell me I'm the only one down here enjoying myself on Uncle Sam's dime!" the man with the onyx pin said.

"If you would enjoy yourself less, Hugh, we might finish sooner."

"Who wants to finish? We have hotels and clubhouses and good food and tropical breezes at night. We're in paradise here."

In a low voice, another man said, "We're at a funeral, Hugh."

That shifted the mood and the men stood around then with nothing to say. Pierre rubbed his stone.

"Do you know who that is?" one of the men finally said, breaking the silence, and all of them turned to watch an olive-skinned boy, alone by the looks of it, walking up the hill, rounding out the tail end of the processional march.

Pierre thought the boy looked familiar somehow. He squinted and stared, but he could not make the connection, and he decided it was nothing after all. Hired help, perhaps. Who could say? There were thousands of boys who looked like him here, and certainly he could not be expected to tell one from the next.

|||||

AS OMAR WALKED up the grassy incline, he arrived just in time to see the Marines remove the casket from the carriage and place it on the ground. Sweat prickled his back. He walked to the edge of the crowd and respectfully took off his hat. Ada was at the front, still clutching the pluma de gallo, and though he wanted to stand next to her, he was uncertain whether he should. What was he doing? He did not know how to have friends. In his solitary life with his father, he'd had almost no practice at it. Perhaps if his mother had been alive, it would have been different. Perhaps she would have taught him about things that for a hundred years his father would not teach him about. Perhaps his mother would have taken him out, visited people, thrown parties. Perhaps within the walls of the house there might have been more music or laughter or conversation—more life.

|||||

THE CHAPLAIN, A short man from Pennsylvania, walked forward to deliver a prayer. He had gotten wind that Marian Oswald had a typical female fondness for flowers, so he made a point to recite Bible verses such as, "The flowers appear on the earth; the time of the singing of birds is come, and the voice of the turtle-dove is heard in our land," which was from Song of Solomon, and "The grass withereth, the flower fadeth; but the word of our God shall stand forever," which was from the prophet Isaiah. He delivered myriad burial sermons each year, each one the same as the last, the words so familiar he could recite them in his sleep. He did not usually make the effort to include anything personal in those sermons, but given the importance of this one, he had.

"Behold, I tell you a mystery: We all shall not sleep, but we shall all be changed, in a moment, in the twinkling of an eye, at the last trump: for the trumpet shall sound, and the dead shall be raised incorruptible, and we shall be changed."

Someone in the crowd began to cry.

The chaplain thundered, "For this corruptible must put on incorruption, and this mortal must put on immortality."

He thought that even if John Oswald had not noticed the parts about the flowers, the fact that he had brought at least one person to tears meant he had done his job.

Antoinette stood in the glow of the sun and silently thanked God for letting the light shine through today. He was an almighty God, capable of doing anything He pleased, and as if to prove it, that very week He had taken Mrs. Oswald up to His side. One had to believe He had a plan, for if not, it would be hard to make sense of all this. She did wonder if God's plan included Ada leaving the house now that there was no reason for her to stay, no reason anymore for her to be strutting about, eliciting stares from everyone from the coroner to the mail boy, living free of charge in a room that no one had ever thought to offer Antoinette, refusing to so much as deliver a plate when she'd been asked. It had been days since Mr. Oswald had inquired whether Ada had indeed left the house on the afternoon Mrs. Oswald passed, and Antoinette had of course told him yes. And yet somehow Mr. Oswald had not sent the girl on her way. Antoinette had faith in God's plans, but Mr. Oswald's plans were a different matter. It could be Mr. Oswald had too much on his mind, and dismissing the girl was just one more thing that he intended to do. Well, if that was the case, maybe she could assist in speeding things along. All the better if Mr. Oswald believed that Antoinette, ever dutiful, had only been trying to help.

Pierre put up a hand to shield his eyes from the sun. It was the brightest day he could remember, not a drop of rain to be found. Too bright, perhaps. Pierre blinked. There was nothing for him here, he suddenly thought. Not the rain or the sun or the lowliest hospital ward or a revered role as a personal physician—none of it made him happy, and he blamed that not on himself but on Panama. All at once, he felt he should leave. Ten years later, Dr. Pierre Renaud, at age forty-eight, would find himself assailed by a similar feeling. He would by then be back in France, one of hundreds of civilian physicians swept up in the Great War. On that mild morning as Pierre rode with the ambulance unit, he would reach for his stone and find a hole in his pocket instead. Pierre would have an idea, a fanciful idea, that the stone had somehow traveled back to the Indrois and nestled itself among the other stones lining the bank, returning to the spot where Pierre had found it one cool day. The idea made him think it was time for him to go back to where he came from, too—to the Val de Loire, where the air smelled of roses and bread. Two hours after having that thought, Pierre Renaud would be dead. He would be shot by an incoming round of artillery while kneeling on the battlefield, wrapping another man's wounds. It would not be the way he imagined it, but he would go home.

Ada stood in the cemetery, trying her best not to listen to anything the chaplain said. She did not want to think about buryings, wanted no part of them, not this one or any other. She feared that even by being at one, she was in some way taunting God, and she thought that at least if she did not listen, if she did not know how a burying was supposed to transpire, then He would not think she was ready for another. She wanted Him to know she was not. She stood holding the flowers she had picked the day before, and as the chaplain spoke, she stared at the tips of her boots poking out from beneath the skirt of her dress. Since the moment she had first stepped off the train at Empire almost three weeks ago, those poor boots had never been truly clean. She had scraped them and wiped them, but the mud in Panama was everywhere, it seemed.

When the chaplain finished, Ada watched Mr. Oswald walk up to the casket and bow his head. After a minute, he stepped away. One by one, other people did the same. Silently, Ada walked up to the casket and laid the flowers on top of it, letting go of them at last. When she turned to walk back to the spot where she had been, she saw Omar at the outskirts of the crowd. The shock of seeing him stopped her for the duration of exactly five heartbeats, long enough to see him nod as they caught each other's eye.

||||||

OMAR REMAINED WHERE he was even after the casket had been lowered and Mr. Oswald climbed back into the carriage and rode off. The sound of low conversation filled the air as people began to disperse. Ada walked over to him.

"What are you doing here?" she asked.

He told her the truth. "I came to see you."

She smiled. "Same as before."

"You said I could come talk to you anytime."

"Something happen with your father?"

"No," Omar said, embarrassed that he did not have anything in particular to say. He had simply wanted to see her again, to talk about anything under the sun. But swept up by that thought, it seemed he had chosen the wrong moment, the completely wrong day. "I am sorry again about Mrs. Oswald," he said.

Ada cast her gaze down and squeezed one hand in the other.

"It is not what will happen to your sister," he said quickly, trying to dispel the clouds that he knew had settled upon her thoughts.

She looked back up. "I've been waiting for a letter, but I have yet to hear anything. I did send money, so maybe they used it. I don't know. I just hate being so far from them now. Sometimes I wonder whether I did the wrong thing coming here."

"You are trying to help."

"But what if it isn't enough?"

He felt a kinship with her, both of them carrying around their own private heartache over someone they loved. He smiled. "You saved me on the street, Ada," he said. "If anyone can save your sister, I believe it is you."

24

JOHN OPENED HIS EYES AT THE SOUND OF A KNOCK.

He was limp on the floor of his study. How he had gotten there, he could not recall. He remembered coming home after the funeral, the way the sorrow of the day had seized him as he was riding to the house in the carriage that was by then empty in the back. He could hear the carriage sway and creak with its emptiness, and John told the driver once to slow down so that the ride would smooth out. The driver pulled on the reins to ease the horses into a trot. After that, the creaking abated, but the slower pace meant that John spent more time with the emptiness, and that was almost worse.

The improbable sun had dried some of the mud, and the horses had less trouble getting back up the hill at the end of the day than they'd had earlier that morning getting down. John was eager to step off the carriage, to get away from its lonesome emptiness, but as soon as he turned to face the house, he realized it, too, was filled with the same, and the sorrow that had seized him during the carriage ride tightened its grip. Emptiness was everywhere now, and it would be everywhere for a very long time.

He had gone straight to his study and closed the door. There he opened a bottle of whiskey and poured himself a glass. Usually he abstained from alcohol. He had a low opinion of men who consumed enough to get drunk, men who stumbled out of brothels and saloons walking at an angle, unable to keep themselves upright. But after Marian's passing, he had found himself craving alcohol's anesthetizing effect, telling himself that even respectable men had a drink now and then. Somehow, "now and then" had turned into five steady days.

John groaned and rolled over onto his back. He must have fallen asleep at some point. He had started off in his desk chair—he did remember that—but he must have slumped down to the floor for he was still in his suit, and his spectacles were bent. When he took them off, he saw that the left arm was askew, the hinge at the temple having twisted. He tried to twist it back. No use. He sighed and held the spectacles loosely in one hand. His head pounded, and everything he could see from the floor—the edge of his desk, the top casing of the window, the plain painted ceiling—appeared blurry now, so despite the knock at the door, he closed his eyes again and lay still.

Perhaps he was to blame, he thought. After all, it was he who had wanted to come to Panama, and because she was good, Marian had agreed. Instinctively, she had understood what it would mean for his career. And perhaps she had known that it was more than that, too. Panama gave him the opportunity to leave Tennessee, to become something more than his family name. When he and Marian had moved from Knoxville to the mountains, he had hoped it would accomplish as much, but moving had merely stretched the cord. He wanted to sever it and never mend it again.

He had never truly felt like one of them. The youngest of three boys and, as far back as he could remember, perpetually the odd one out. His two older brothers, Thomas and James, were always conspiring with each other, compelled by pursuits—fishing, hiking, shooting rifles at trees—that held no interest for him. When they were old enough, his brothers took over different parts of the family business, and before long they had demure wives and rosy-cheeked children, and all was exactly as it should be, exactly as life for the Oswald boys was supposed to go. Except that he wanted none of it. Not the work, not the wife. In college, he had been introduced to the emerging field of tropical medicine, and it had captivated his mind. It aimed to make healthful parts of the earth that had not been healthful before, locales that had been inhospitable to men like him because of disease. What could be more important? Finding new places where Americans could safely venture and live. The West had been settled, the limits of the land reached. They required a new frontier. It could only be realized, however, if they could vanquish tropical disease. And that, John soon learned, meant understanding the mosquito, that unsuspecting insect, light as a filament, that scientists had begun to posit was the actual vector of transmission for some of the most devastating diseases yet known to man. The mosquito theory was the future of medicine. It could be, John saw, the key to the very future of mankind. To his father, however, it was a laughable pursuit. Medicine was one thing, but dedicating one's life to studying mosquitoes? No. No son of his.

After college, John resigned himself to a role at the family's lumber company, a nominal role that let him keep his distance from the office most days while doing enough to satisfy his father. With work settled, his mother took up the cause of finding him a wife. She arranged picnics and outings with young women she knew, daughters of friends, newcomers to town. Excruciating, all of it, and not a woman he found interesting in the least. Not one he could talk to, not one who thought at all like he did: dispassionately, empirically, interested in the rigors of science, in the discoveries that were then at man's fingertips. But at some point John understood that his mother was not going to relent until he was wed. Aggravated, he had marched into the lumber company one day with the intention of asking out the first woman he saw, to show his mother that he had taken the matter into his own hands and therefore that she could give up the cause. In the room where all the stenographers sat, he had walked over to a young woman typing at her desk, not the most attractive among them but pretty enough, and he had said, "If you are free, may I take you out tonight?" Straightforward, without embellishment. He had felt all eyes in the room on him, all the other stenographers who had perhaps, he realized then, wanted him to ask them the same thing. A dreadful moment. He had never before asked anyone for a date, and for a brief second he experienced the horror of the possibility that she might say no. There, in front of everyone. Thankfully, she said yes.

He had been unprepared for two things: the capaciousness of Marian's mind and how good she was. He learned, during that first evening they spent together, that she had gone to college—only a woman's college, but still, she was educated, and even more important, she could think. She *wanted* to think. She was curious, especially, about the natural world. She could refer to plants using their Latinate names, could explain root systems and habitats in scientific terms. On the eve of their wedding, he had given her a leather-bound edition of *On the Origin of Species* meant to communicate things he did not know how to say—that he valued her mind, that he was astonished to have found her, that he would be eternally grateful he had. There was not a woman on earth with whom he had dreamed he would ever be able to talk about his work. With ease, she grasped the essence of it, the complexity of the problems, the challenges ahead. She did not laugh when he told her about the mosquito theory. She said, "My God, John, what if it's true?" She did not complain about the hours he spent in the laboratory, peering at water and dirt samples through a microscope, monitoring larvae, poring over records of breeding habits and life spans and flying radii, studying the effects of elevation and air temperature and rainfall, mapping epidemiological patterns, dissecting infected mosquitoes, marveling at the fact that what was contained in their bodies had the capacity to so radically alter the human world, trying to understand, trying to *see*. Marian understood the significance of what he was doing—the fact that it was not just scientific inquiry but pivotal to the future of civilization—which he supposed was the reason why, as they had stood together on that cool late-autumn evening in Tennessee, she had agreed to come. Or perhaps it was the other reason: simply because she was good.

If only they had known what would be in store. That first day when they had stepped off the ship onto the dock, some native pranksters had run up to them and dangled long strings in the air, and when John had demanded to know just what they were doing, one of them in very good English had said, "Measurements for the undertaker, sir." The boy had laughed. Just a joke. But perhaps he should have known then.

He had warned her to stay in the house, hadn't he? He had told her dozens of times. Mosquitoes were rampant in the wet. Although it was not even a damn mosquito in the end, but another pernicious effect of the rain: pneumonia. Of all things. An illness she could have contracted anywhere on this earth. No number of screens would have saved her from that.

The knock sounded again. Slowly, John rose to his feet and put his spectacles on, but when he remembered that they were bent, he laid them on the desktop. It was still raining outside. He poured some whiskey and threw it back in one gulp before he said, "Who is it?"

The cook answered. For the past number of days she had been bringing him food even though he had not asked her to. Confounding, that was. He thought she should have understood without him saying so that food was not foremost in his mind. And yet she had come with roast beef and sweetmeats and stew and once even with a fresh mango pie. Of the pie, he had taken several bites before he set the fork down.

The cook opened the door and stepped into the study. Without his glasses, everything was hazy, but nonetheless he could tell that she had no food in her hands. Even more confounding.

"Yes? What is it?" he said.

"Sir, I did want you to know—it seems the girl left."

At those words, something struck in his mind, but it had all the clarity of a bell underwater. John rubbed his eyes. He recalled that the cook had brought him ham once, too. Of that he had not had even a nibble. Had that been yesterday? Or the day before? Time was no longer a solid thing.

"You hear me, sir?"

"What's that?"

"The girl, sir. Ada."

There had been a bat in the house when they first arrived. John did not know why he thought of that now. After the very long journey, he and Marian had opened the door to this house to be met with a flying creature that tore through the air. John, terrified, had not known what to do. He had taken off his boot and thrown it at the thing. He missed, but he picked up the boot and threw it again while the bat, with its accordion-fold wings, darted around making small squeaking sounds.

"Ada?" John repeated. His head felt too heavy for his neck to support, and he would have liked to lie back down on the floor.

"Yes, sir," the cook said.

He had tried multiple times with the boot, fine calfskin and suede, until Marian, who had not once screamed at the bat, screamed at him: "Don't hurt it, please!" He had said, "But we need to get rid of it, Marian! Do you want it to live here with us?" She did not, but maybe, she suggested, there was a humane way. "We could make a great deal of noise, perhaps?" And she had started stomping her feet right there in the parlor. She stomped and yelped at the bat, which was then clinging for dear life to the top of a window frame. John had thought the stomping absurd, but when the bat stirred, craning its neck and flexing its wings, he began stomping, too. What a sight the two of them must have been, standing in an otherwise empty house, rattling the floor and whooping at a bat. But then it had flown away, hadn't it? Out the open door. Darkness unleashed, or something like that.

Through the haze, John looked at the cook again. He felt unsteady on his feet. He reached behind him and picked his spectacles up off the desk and put them on. They did not rest squarely on his ears, but even so they improved the view. His head throbbed. For a second he thought he could actually hear it from the inside out, and then he realized it was only the sound of the rain.

"What's that you say?" John asked. He could not remember now.

The cook repeated that it seemed the girl had left. All of her things were gone from her room.

"Left?" Again, the bell struck, but John could not tell what it meant.

He tried to conjure an image of the girl. Very pretty, a man visiting the house had commented once. Was it true? Was she pretty? Was he supposed to have been attracted to her? He had not even managed to want his wife. He had tried. He had come as close as he could, close enough that what he felt—a genuine caring, a reliance on her, a gratitude for her support, a sometimes affection—could pass for wanting. The fact that it fell short of the actual feeling was not Marian's fault, it was his. He had never wanted any woman. He was not capable of a feeling like that. And why not? What was so wrong with him? Something was. Something he had tried to bury under layers and layers of his heavy soul, something he had pushed down to a place far enough away that he could almost forget it was there. Almost. But not quite. Even far away and deep below, he felt it niggle sometimes. A tiny black seed that wanted to grow. He could cut off its light and deprive it of air, but the dark seed remained. He had not deserved Marian. The thought had occurred to him every day of their marriage. He wanted her to be happy, but long ago he had realized his inadequacy in this, how ill-equipped he was to make anyone truly happy, perhaps. She deserved someone better than he was. But he never said that out loud lest he introduce an idea that, upon hearing, she would recognize as the truth. He did not deserve her and yet he did not want her to leave. He needed her, it turned out. As a companion and partner. And because without her, the whole house of cards would collapse. He knew she never confessed to anyone how infrequently they lay together in bed, how infrequently they had been with each other, only a handful of times, encounters so ungratifying and strange that John cringed when he thought of them now, and then those times when they tried in vain to have a child, something he had wanted to give her if for no other reason than that she might have someone to love her the way she deserved. But he had not been able to give her even that. Fifteen successive months of trying to conceive, and in the end the doctor who had come to the house had said simply, "There was nothing that could have been done." He meant it as consolation, but it was a terrible phrase, a way to make impotence out of rage, a way to deaden a feeling that one felt nonetheless. It had been enough to make him want to slap the doctor, but of course he had done no such thing. Stiffly, he had shaken the doctor's hand instead and watched the doctor leave, watched him climb back into the carriage and ride off into the cruelly bright day.

And then, suddenly, it came back to him. The bell cleared the water. Something Pierre had told him. The girl had left. At the critical moment. That was the phrase he suddenly remembered the doctor had used. He had overheard Pierre say it in the hallway, and when the two men spoke in private, he said it again. *She left at the critical moment, John.* If anyone were to blame . . . It was all coming back to him now. Pierre had urged him to report it—such a lapse warranted punishment, he maintained—but John had first wanted to confront her himself. He had intended to do that but kept putting it off. After the funeral, he had told himself. He could only handle so much at one time. Whatever the story, he would deal with the girl after the funeral was through. Although the story did seem clear enough. Even the cook had confirmed that the girl had left the house—the one thing she was not supposed to do. And because she had done it, the only person he had cared about in the world, the only person who had truly cared about *him* perhaps, was gone. He was alone. Or maybe it was just that the veil had been raised. Maybe he had been alone every day of his life—born into a family that had never loved him, married to a woman he could not love—and he would remain alone for every day to come. That was how it would be. There was no way out of it without courage, and courage was just another one of the many qualities he lacked. What was so wrong with him? And why? When he had broken his ribs, Marian had asked him with great tenderness, Does it hurt? And he had wanted to scream, Yes!

Something hurt. But not in the way she had meant. Why could he not retrain his thoughts and be a different sort of man, free of the darkness in the pit of his soul? Let the seed wither. Let the bat fly away. Why could he not root it out once and for all?

John reached behind him and, with a quavering hand, picked up the tumbler and raised it to his lips. He wanted a sip of whiskey, but the glass was empty. He fumbled for the bottle but found that it was empty, too. Emptiness and sorrow. That was his lot.

"Well, why did she leave?" he finally asked.

"Sir?" the cook said.

"The girl!" he erupted. "Why did she leave?"

Through his crooked spectacles, John watched the cook shrug. "Lord only know what got into her head."

25

IT WAS PAYDAY IN THE CUT.

Tucked inside the waistband of his trousers was a small pouch Omar used to hold his coins once he got them. The men were paid every two weeks, and so far with the money he had earned, Omar had purchased new boots to replace the first pair after the soles split apart, but the rest of it he simply stashed in a small box at home, saving it for something, he supposed, though he did not yet know what.

The pouch rubbed his hip, and Omar stopped to adjust it. The heat in the Cut that day was punishing, over one hundred degrees without benefit of the breeze, and between the heat and the drizzling rain, the whole gorge steamed. Omar wiped a sleeve across his forehead and took a deep breath, inhaling smoke and the heavy, hot air. All around, drenched men shoveled while chains of dump cars clattered on the tracks. There was always more dirt before them, more of the earth to be pried open and moved.

Omar swung his pick. He felt fully recovered from the malaria now, malaria that his father still did not even know about. That, Omar thought, was another mountain before him. There was always more silence, it went on and on, and he could not understand when or how it would come to an end.

"Big day," Berisford said, breaking Omar out of his thoughts.

"What?" Omar said.

"Payday today." Berisford grinned. "Soon I have enough money go back home, buy a house, marry my gal."

Clement said, "You mean the gal in your head?"

Berisford just ignored Clement and sang, "Big day coming! Big day here!"

||||||

MILLER PACED THROUGH the rain, smoking his second cigar of the morning. They were Havana cigars, which cost 7¢ each, though that seemed a small price to pay for the pleasure they gave him. The cigars were the only thing that got him through the days here sometimes.

It was mid-October, and the men were still working to dig out from the ruinous slide that had bedeviled them recently. There was so little, Miller observed, that was within his control, and the slides, it seemed, were just one more thing. Not even the engineers were able to predict when they would come or why. Something about an "angle of repose" that had yet to be reached, from what he had heard.

Miller removed his cigar and paced as he yelled. "This is the day of reckoning, boys! You'll work straight through lunch if you have to, but you *will* get it done! And"—Miller stopped and looked out— "if you're still standing by the end of it, we have a treat for you."

"Ice cream?" Berisford said to Omar, and grinned.

Miller, thinking he had heard something, glanced over and frowned, but he wanted to finish what he had been saying. "It's payday, boys!"

A cheer rose up like Miller knew it would. Money was the great motivator. That was true every place in the world.

He saw that the man with the red handkerchief was the one who had interrupted him. Miller threw down the stub of his cigar before grinding it out. Then, through the rain, Miller walked over to him. "You say something just now?"

"No, sir," Berisford said.

Miller sighed loudly through his nose. He was tired of it, the same round and round. Was he a circus ringleader or a man? He raised his arm high in the air like a ringleader might and pictured a pride of lions gathering in a formation of some sort—a pyramid maybe or ten high on a ball. Miller had never been to a circus, but one had come through South Carolina when he was a boy, and talk of it had captured his imagination. He sighed again, a sort of grumbling snort. He was supposed to have been something by now. The world, it seemed, had promised him that. But the world, changing quicker than he could keep up, had reduced him to this.

Then Miller had an idea. From his pocket he pulled out the man's chit, a slip of paper that Miller was responsible for giving each of the men if they were to be paid. The men were supposed to present the chit to the pay clerk in order to collect their wages.

"I'll make you a bet," Miller said, holding the chit in the air, not caring if it got wet. "You—on your own—dig four cars of spoil today, then I'll give you this. You dig anything less, I'll burn it instead."

He wished his cigar was still lit so he could demonstrate, but he had tossed it out and his third cigar—he allotted himself three a day—was in his other pocket, where he was saving it for an afternoon pick-me-up.

"That my chit, sir?" the man asked.

Miller looked at it. "If you're 360412, then it is."

"Sir, I earn my money these weeks."

"Not yet you didn't. You dig four full cars of spoil today, and then you earn it. You don't . . ." Miller wiggled his fingers to represent flames.

"Sir, I work hard all these weeks."

"That remains to be seen."

"Please, sir."

"We have a saying down South. You know what it is?"

"No, sir."

"The saying is, Don't count your chickens before they hatch. Well, you best not count your chickens because I got the eggs." Miller closed his fist around the wet chit and grinned.

"Four cars, sir?"

"No less."

"I alone?"

"You're the only one whose chit I got in my hand." It was an inspired idea, Miller thought. A wonder he had not come up with it sooner. "Go on. Time's a-wasting," he said, and he watched until the man started to swing.

||||||

"BACHRA RIFFRAFF," BERISFORD grumbled after Miller walked off. "Why he picking on me all the time?"

"You can do it," Omar said.

"But what reason I got to do it? These weeks I work the same as everyone, no?"

Clement looked Berisford in the eye. "Because Miller have your chit, that's why."

Berisford slumped his shoulders and cast his gaze down the line in the rain. "Four cars make a long day for me."

"Always long days for us," Prince said. "Long days, short life."

"I will help you," Omar offered.

But Berisford's cheerfulness from earlier had disappeared. Sulking, he said, "I do four cars, seem I should get more than a paycheck. Four cars, I should get a prize, too."

"No prize but the glory," Joseph said.

Clement shook his head. "Not even that. We do the work, but the glory for them."

||||||

BERISFORD PLANTED HIMSELF in the mud and churned his arms through the air. He swung and he swung, and the pile of spoil grew behind him, and every so often the neck of the steam shovel bent down to the ground and scooped some of it up and dropped the heavy clay and the mud on the bed of the dump car directly in line with where Berisford stood. Omar, working beside him, occasionally tossed the clumps that he picked over to Berisford's pile instead, to help his friend meet his goal. If Berisford noticed the gesture, he did not say. He was focused on the task at hand. He just grunted and heaved.

Miller sauntered by every now and again with one hand tucked under the bib of his overalls. Omar saw him look down at Berisford and nod and walk on.

Near eleven o'clock, the hour when on any other day the men

should have stopped for lunch, Miller walked up to Berisford and said, "So what do we have?"

Omar watched. He saw Clement and Prince and Joseph all glance up, but Berisford did not. His wet shirt was pasted to his back as he hunched, his trousers matted with mud. He kept swinging his arms.

Standing in front of Berisford, Miller said, "Looks to me like you're coming close to finishing your first car."

Without breaking pace, Berisford said, "This my second, sir."

"Is that right?"

"I fill another one before this and it already go on away."

"Well, how am I to know about that?"

"I telling you, sir."

"This is the first one I see."

"Ask Mac up there." Berisford jerked his head in the direction of the steam shovel operator, who was sitting in his cab nearby.

Miller glanced up. How would this pick-and-shovel man know the operator's name while Miller did not? That did not seem right. If anyone should be friendly with a steam shovel man, it should be him.

"You don't know any Mac," Miller said.

"He been there the whole time. He can tell you, sir, if you ask."

Miller crossed his arms. "I don't need to know whatever anyone has to tell me when I can see it with my very own eyes."

Berisford, still swinging his pick, still rotating his arm back-down-and-up, said, "It my second car, sir."

Miller was tired. The days down here lately filled him with displeasure. He wanted to go back to the United States, back to the South, where things still made a certain amount of sense. He was tired of wandering. All of a sudden, he just wanted to rest. Put his feet up. Drink a sweet pink lemonade somewhere in a reasonable sun. Get away from this heat and this mud and this goddamn rain. See his mother again, see how she was getting on.

Miller looked at the man. "I say this is your first."

Omar opened his mouth to say something, to stand up for his friend, but that small movement somehow caught Miller's eye, and Miller glared at Omar and said, "You have a problem now, too?"

His face burning, Omar closed his mouth and swallowed his words. Embarrassed, he struck his pick at the ground.

Next to him, Berisford was still swinging, too.

"That's the way!" Miller said.

Berisford yanked the pick back again and again. Up and back, down and pull. His arm like the turn of a railcar wheel. Up and back, down and pull.

For nearly a full half hour, well after the lunch whistle blew, Miller stood with his legs spread wide, watching Berisford work. And for that full half hour, Berisford swung without pause. He shifted his feet every so often and grunted louder as the work went on, but unbelievably, there was not a single break in his rhythm. Furiously, over and over he heaved his pick at the ground.

Omar worked a little faster, too—all of them did, since Miller was standing right there—but however fast Omar worked, he could not match Berisford's speed. It did not matter anyway. Miller was not looking at him anymore or at anyone else. He had eyes only for Berisford now. Miller stood and he watched. He barked out an order or two. And when Miller finally got bored, when he sighed and straightened the soaking wet hat on his head and mounted the berm and strolled off, Berisford brought his pick down once more and then left the thing there, the tip of it wedged in the mud. He was breathing hard, snorting air and blowing it out again through his lips. Berisford bent over with his hands on his knees. He panted for a minute, then threw up.

"Berisford," Omar said.

As Berisford wiped his mouth with his red handkerchief, a look passed between Clement and Omar.

"Ease up," Clement said. He had been in Panama for two years, doing various jobs, and he had seen more than one man keel over from pure exhaustion before.

Berisford panted. He was spattered with mud, glistening with rainwater.

"Berisford," Omar said again.

But Berisford was not in a listening mood. He wiped his mouth again, this time with his wet shirtsleeve, and stood up straight. Vomit sat in a puddle at his feet. He grabbed his pick still wedged in the mud and pulled it free. He set the handle back over his shoulder and, without a word, he swung again.

||||||

THE RAIN KEPT falling and falling, and in his mind Berisford was playing a game with it, seeing who could hold steady for longer—the rain or him. "Keep falling," he said, and as he was in a kind of delirium, he did not know whether he said it in his mind or out loud into the air. So long as the rain did not stop, he told himself, neither would he. He thought of Naomy and how proud she would be of the way he was keeping up. Of course, knowing Naomy, there was a chance, too, that she would say he was a fool for thinking he could outwit the rain. That was probably what she *would* say, but that was not what he wanted to hear, so he chose to believe that Naomy would be proud. He chose to believe that if she saw him at this moment, she would smile to see him working harder than God. He wanted that pay chit. He needed the money that he would get once he turned the chit in. Twenty dollars in Panamanian silver would be one more brick in the life he was trying to build—for himself, for Naomy, for the babies that one day they would have if they were so blessed. All of it started here. Dig the land in Panama, buy some land back home. If he could earn enough money, it would set them up right. He was not after a fortune like some men seemed to be. He just wanted enough to set them up right. They could have a wedding at last, and what a happy day that would be. In his mind, he saw Naomy in a long white gown and even a veil, and he would peel that veil back at some point during the ceremony the same way she peeled skin off of gooseberries, slow, taking her time, and her face underneath would be far, far sweeter than any berry in all of creation. Everything that he wanted was just on the other side of some digging and some rain. But the rain did not stop, and after a time—he had no idea how long—Berisford, as he kept digging, shouted up at the sky, "You not playing fair!" It would not relent. He had put himself up against a formidable foe. Still, he would beat it, he thought, for all that he wanted was on the other side.

Hour by hour he swung his arm. Up and back, up and back. And hour by hour, the sky kept sending the rain. It just would not quit. Berisford glanced up again at the sky and saw the underside of all those millions of drops falling down, no end in sight, and he had a new thought: Just a short break. That's what he needed. So short that no one would notice, not even the rain, and then he would be right back to it, ready to take down the foe, ready to win, ready to get over to all that awaited him on the other side. Berisford stumbled and suctioned his feet through the mud. He was so worn out that it was difficult to move. The rain's fault, he thought, meaning both his exhaustion and the endless plains of mud. He was angry at the rain now, and he wanted to get out of it, just to take a short break. He kept lurching from side to side, trying to move, but the mud kept holding him back. He fell to his knees. He folded forward and put his hands in the mud and felt himself sink. *Maybe I can crawl to the other side*, he thought.

||||||

TO THE MEN who saw it, Berisford crumpled like a stalk of wheat under the thrashing of rain. Out of the corner of their eyes as they swung their own picks, Clement had watched, and Prince had watched, and Omar had watched, too, as Berisford swung and swung and swung again. He had shouted out once, something about not playing fair, a comment that Omar had assumed was directed at Miller even though Miller was not near enough to hear it. Miller had walked up the rise, and every other pick-and-shovel man had walked off for lunch. It was just their gang toiling down in the Cut. Berisford most of all. He had swung until at some point Omar saw him let go of his pick and stagger toward the railroad tracks behind them like he was struggling to walk. "Are you okay?" Omar had called. But Berisford either had not heard him or did not have the energy to respond. He had sunk to his knees, then collapsed.

"Berisford!" Omar cried. Holding his pick, he ran over and rolled Berisford onto his back. Berisford's eyes were closed and his body was slack. The rain fell upon him. "Berisford!" Omar screamed again.

Clement rushed over, too.

Omar said, "He fainted, I think."

"He breathing?"

"I do not know."

Clement held his hand under Berisford's nose. He put an ear to Berisford's chest. Then he frowned and lifted Berisford's wrist. He lowered it, slowly, and looked Omar in the eye.

"We can take him to the field hospital," Omar said.

Clement shook his head.

"We can. It is not far."

"Too late now."

"Too late?" Omar sputtered.

Clement merely looked at him like there was nothing more to say.

"But—"

"Best thing we can do is start digging before Miller come back."

Omar stared at Clement with incomprehension.

"We have to dig a grave," Clement said.

"Here?"

"Better here than who know where else they put him."

Omar was too stunned to move. He looked at Berisford lying still on the ground. It did not seem possible. He had just been digging. He had just been working with them. Hesitantly, Omar put his hand on Berisford's chest, waiting to feel a heartbeat, but there was not one.

Clement grabbed Omar's arm and pulled him up. "We got to hurry. Come on."

Clement motioned Prince and Joseph over, and together, without any discussion, the four of them dug. Omar blinked back tears. As fast as they could, they sank their picks and shovels into the ground, and when the hole was deep enough, they carried Berisford over and laid him down. They gave him back to the earth so that he could rest.

IIIIII

WORDLESSLY, THE MEN trudged back to the line, but Omar, with a queasiness in his gut, could not bring himself to move. He just stood next to the freshly turned earth with his pick in his hand. The mountains towered around him. The rain fell lightly and prickled the ground. In the distance Omar saw Miller hike up higher onto a plateau. He was gazing out northward as though enjoying the view. At some point, he stopped and struck a match to light his cigar. Omar squinted, watching Miller cup his hand over the flame. Such painstaking care to keep that one flicker alive.

All at once, Omar dropped his pick. His boots squelched in the mud as he charged past the men. He did not stop until he had climbed all the way up to where Miller was standing, looking off to one side, smoking his loathsome cigar.

Miller turned, startled. He pulled the cigar from his mouth. "What are you doing up here?"

Omar was trembling as he said, "Someone died."

"Well, people die every day."

"Because of you."

Miller experienced a wriggle of worry he had not felt for some years. "Me? I sure as hell didn't kill anyone."

Omar was shaking, but his voice did not waver. "You did."

"That so? When?"

"Just now."

Miller scoffed. "I don't know how that can be when I've been standing up here."

"You did," Omar said again.

Miller took another puff of his cigar. There wasn't time for these antics. There was work to be done. He ashed his cigar and looked the boy in the eye. He was the lone Panamanian in the whole division, never trouble till now.

"No," Miller said slowly. "But since you seem confused about what I did and did not do, let me explain it to you. I came to this country and helped you make something of it, see? No one in their right mind wanted to set foot here before, and if they did it was only to make their way through. But now everyone wants to be here. And why do you think that is? Because of something you did? No. You people had this place to yourselves for hundreds of years and you managed to make it a swamp. But we got rid of yellow fever and built bridges and towns. We paved your streets and gave you water that runs through pipes underground. That's civilization, see? We brought Panama out of the jungle and into the God-fearing light. *That's* what we did. We gave you a gift." Miller leaned forward. "You're supposed to say thank you when somebody gives you a gift."

Omar tightened his lips. His chin quivered in rage.

"Say thank you now."

"No."

Miller took a step closer. "What's that?"

"No."

There was only a fleeting second of satisfaction before Omar felt the blow—Miller's fist to the hinge of his jaw. Omar stumbled back.

Miller said, "It will behoove you in this life to be grateful. Now try it again. Say thank you."

Omar tasted blood in his mouth.

"Say it."

But Omar refused. He turned around, his jaw throbbing.

"There you go," Miller said. "Back to work now."

With tears again in his eyes, Omar walked toward the terrace of stairs that led up the mountainside. Miller yelled after him, but Omar did not look back. One step at a time, he climbed out of the Cut.

26

ON A MONDAY MORNING IN MID-OCTOBER, DOÑA RUIZ SAT AT HER TABLE EATING A corn cake and drinking her cup of cold black tea. She had woken up that morning determined to get to the bottom of a mystery that had plagued her for weeks—the mystery of Francisco Aquino and his son.

Throughout Omar's absence, Doña Ruiz had kept count of each day that he had not come home. Periodically, she had gazed up at the heavens for a sign, but there had been no murky shadows, no black birds, no shattering flashes of lightning, nothing whatsoever to indicate that the boy was anything other than fine. Because Doña Ruiz knew that anything was possible, it was possible of course that the signs could be wrong, but as they had never been wrong before, she chose to believe them. Eventually, she had told herself, Omar would return. She had not told Francisco of her belief the day he had come to her with all his worry and hot air in tow. She had not mentioned the signs in the sky, nor had she assured him his boy would be fine, but she had given Francisco advice meant to set him straight. Open not only your mouth but your eyes. What she had meant was that regardless of when Omar returned, Francisco needed to find his son, really find him. It was not a physical imperative but a spiritual one, as so many things are.

And then, one evening as Doña Ruiz was tending to some peppers that she had growing in her yard, Omar did return. The heavens had predicted he would, but still she was so surprised that the only thing that kept her from thinking it was a ghost was the soft sound of his footsteps on the muddied dirt road. Ghosts, in her experience, did not make the sound of footsteps. She had glanced up, shocked and then enormously relieved at seeing him, and she had watched him trudge down the road in the same manner as always, though from the way his clothes hung, he appeared to have lost weight in the two weeks since she had last seen him.

The very next morning Doña Ruiz had heard the squelch of those footsteps again, and she had peered out her window to see the boy walking in the opposite direction, toward the city again. The sequence repeated. He came home at night, he left in the morning, and all that was as it had been until yesterday, when Doña Ruiz, lying in her hammock, had heard the footsteps again and had opened one eye to see Omar, dressed not in his work clothes but in his Sunday best, walking up the long dirt road. This was new. Francisco and Omar did not go to church—Doña Ruiz knew that and held it against them—and not once in her life had she ever seen one of them walking up the road on a Sunday, dressed for the gods. Not once in her life had she ever seen one of them walking up the road toward the city on a Sunday at all. And yet it had happened. The boy had called out to greet her, and she had called back a blessing, and on he went. Mystified, Doña Ruiz had thought about it all day, and by the time the boy had returned in the late afternoon, she was thinking about it still. She had half expected Francisco to approach her again, as he had the Sunday before, but though she had stayed outside all day long, enjoying the rare sunshine and the absence of rain, he had not, which was puzzling. What to make of it all? All the coming and going, and the fine starched clothes, and the fourteen-day absence, and now the Sunday sojourn? Something was amiss, and she wanted to know what it was.

So today after breakfast, Doña Ruiz threw her shawl around her shoulders and put on her straw hat. For the first time in her existence, she walked all the way down the muddy road, along which the butterflies darted in the tall, tangled grass and the lemon trees grew in such abundance that they fragranced the air. She walked until she came to the spot where the road ended at the edge of the bay. It was raining again, but even in the rain, the view was dazzling. Past large boulders and blanket-sized patches of sand, the broad graceful ocean opened ever outward, dimpled by raindrops, kissed by the sky. The smell of the salt water and the rain and the mud and the lemon trees was a heady mixture. Doña Ruiz paused for a moment to take it in. She took a deep breath, wondering why she had never come here before and grateful for the reminder that, truly, wonder was everywhere. There was more wonder in the world than any one person would ever know.

Doña Ruiz then turned to her left to face the small thatched-roof house that Francisco had built. She straightened her wet shawl and strode up to the door.

No one answered when she knocked.

"Francisco Aquino," she said. No one came.

But she had seen the boat tied up at the rocks. She knew he was home.

"Francisco! This is Doña Ruiz," she called through the door. There was only the sound of the birds and the rain.

She pushed the door and felt it give. She nudged it wider. When she peeked through the opening, she saw Francisco sitting on a chair across the room, his eyes closed, his head bowed, his hands in his lap.

"Francisco," she hissed.

When he did not move, she had the thought that he might be asleep. But as Doña Ruiz stepped into the house and started to walk toward him, he opened his eyes and said, "What do you want?"

Doña Ruiz gasped and then dropped her shoulders and said, "Why are you sitting there like that?"

"Why are you here?"

"Why didn't you answer when I knocked on the door?"

"Why were you knocking on my door?"

"Why didn't you answer when I called your name?"

"Why were you calling my name?"

Doña Ruiz sighed. "One of us has to answer the other's questions and not just keep asking more."

Francisco shrugged. He still had his head bowed. The room was dim, and the air within it was suffused with unmistakable sorrow. Doña Ruiz sniffed. It was an old, stale sorrow, one that had lingered for a very long time. Is this how they lived? Doña Ruiz thought to herself. Suffocated by sorrow?

"What is wrong with you?" Doña Ruiz asked.

Sitting in the chair, Francisco stared at his hands. They were weathered and wrinkled from a lifetime of work out on the ocean, coarsened by nets, calloused by paddles, dried by the salt air. That morning, he had gotten up like always to fish. He had dressed and walked down to the water and untied the boat and rowed out with his net. It was more force of habit than anything else. But as soon as he had rowed out far enough and was sitting in solitude on the water, he had been overcome by an uneasy feeling. It was the culmination of an unease that had started almost immediately after Omar had returned home from his mysterious fourteen-day disappearance and that had been steadily growing ever since. Francisco had lived with the feeling for a week, but that morning as he had bobbed atop the waves, it was more powerful than ever. It turned his stomach and muddled his mind to the point that he could not even concentrate on the job at hand. He had tied the fishing net with such an imprecise knot that it came undone, slipped off the side of the boat, and sank down like a spiderweb melting into the sea. Without thinking, Francisco had leaned out to grab for the sinking net, and before he knew it, he had fallen in, too. He was so stunned that he sank like a rock until he remembered to swim. When he surfaced at last, the net was gone and the boat was several feet away. He swam toward it, pulling his arms through the water as his chest tightened. When he got to the boat, he heaved himself up and slumped to the floor. He was gasping for air, blinking with water still in his eyes. He spit a few times and blew his nose on his sleeve. It had been a long time since he had been in the water. He used to dive in of his own volition, looking for her, but eventually, as the scent of violets had diminished, he had settled for merely peering over the side of the boat each day instead. Falling in that day sent his heart racing. He was old, so much older now than he used to be. Time had passed. It was passing still. Yes, he was old, and now he was also scared. He was not in the mood for fishing that day. Francisco blew his nose one more time, and then, uncharacteristically, he had cut short his workday before catching even a single fish and rowed back to the shore.

Now, staring at his old, battered hands, Francisco wanted to cry. What had he done? How had it all come to this? That night when Omar had come home, Francisco had walked through the front door, and at the first sight of his son he had been overwhelmed by the most intense gratitude and relief and happiness and awe, a riot of emotion the scale of which Francisco had not experienced for a very long time. And yet the riot, as explosive as it was, was something that Francisco kept inside. Somehow, despite everything, he carried on in the same manner that he had for the nearly six months previous and did not utter a word. He should have done it right away, at the very moment he saw Omar sitting at the table. Omar, who had been wearing only his underclothes, had looked up at him, and the two of them had locked eyes. Right then, Francisco should have opened his mouth and let escape even one syllable of what was thrumming inside him. There had been a brief opportunity, an opening, and he should have taken advantage of it, he knew, but he had faltered and every second that elapsed thereafter had compacted his failure until after a minute, the whole thing was hardened again. Some irrevocable threshold had been crossed. A minute into their strained reunion, Francisco and Omar were back in the same place they had been—saying nothing at all.

Oh, but what agony it had been, not to talk to each other after that! Not talking before, when all Francisco felt was his own stubborn, righteous anger, had been easier. Every time Francisco had seen Omar come home in his work clothes, every time Francisco had seen the boots the boy had purchased, boots that by their very presence seemed to rebuke Francisco's entire way of life, his life as a fisherman in which one would never, ever need boots—every time

Francisco saw those things, his anger was renewed. But now that Omar had returned, something had shifted. The anger had weakened, and crowding around it were all of the other emotions that Francisco had felt upon seeing Omar again—the gratitude, the relief, the happiness, the awe. Even with time, those feelings had not disappeared. They had stayed locked inside him, so that now when Francisco looked at Omar, he saw not only the work clothes and the boots but also his *son*, whom he missed.

The day that Omar had returned, Francisco had gotten up in the middle of the night and walked to the boy's room just to see him again. To assure himself that yes—Omar really was here. In the dark, Francisco had stood barefoot in the doorway and peered into the room. He could hear Omar breathing, a miraculous sound. Francisco pictured his son—his long nose and dark eyes, the half-moon shape of his ears. He resembled his mother. As Francisco stood there, all the feelings from earlier swirled up through his chest. And there was something else. Love. He felt such love for the boy. He always felt it, though he never knew how to express it. It was a love encased in pain—he could not look at Omar without thinking of Esme—but it was love nonetheless, and it existed for the very same reason: because Omar reminded Francisco of Esme. Something surged in his throat. Francisco parted his lips and pushed his tongue against the back of his teeth. He wanted to say something, even there in the dark, even though Omar would not hear him if he did. He stood with his mouth open until his lips turned dry. Then he swallowed the lump in his throat and walked back to his room.

Between that moment and this morning when he had fallen off the boat, guilt and regret had also crowded in alongside every other emotion Francisco felt. And such a mass of emotions had led to a sense of crushing unease. It was too much to handle. Something, Francisco had been thinking as he sat in the chair, had to change. That morning on the boat had reminded him of what he, more than anyone, should have known: One never knew how much time one had left with the people one loved. Yes, something had to change soon. He had to find a way to talk to his son.

Doña Ruiz, who had come to the house to get to the bottom of things, realized as she looked at Francisco slumped in the chair that she knew the answer to her own question. She knew what was wrong. And she knew there was only one way to make it right.

"Go," she said.

Francisco did not budge.

"Did you hear what I said? I said go."

He scoffed. "Did the stars tell you that?"

"No, they did not."

"Some other black magic?"

"Not everything is magic! This is simple, you ass. You need to go."

"Go where?"

In Doña Ruiz's experience, there were only so many times a person could be told. People, especially the hardheaded variety like Francisco Aquino, sometimes needed a shove.

Doña Ruiz pulled Francisco up by the arm and turned him to face the open door. She gave him a push from behind.

"Go to your son," she said.

||||||

FOR THE FIRST time in his life, Francisco boarded the train. The railroad that spanned Panamá had been built, from what Francisco understood, because the United States needed a way to transport its mail from the east coast of that massive country to the newly conquered west. At least, that is how it began. The rest—how suddenly Panamá was overrun with people looking for a shortcut to gold, how the railroad company scrambled to finish the track so that they could profit from whisking foreigners through—was known by everyone who lived here.

In the city, Francisco had seen the locomotives, of course, those hulking steel snakes with their cyclops eyes, rudely bellowing smoke. They looked like monsters to him. Monsters that belonged to the Yankees, no less. And now, incredibly, he had stepped inside the belly of one.

Francisco, who was wearing his fishing clothes and sandals and hat, all of which were damp, stood in the aisle of the train car and looked around with great suspicion at the open windows and the wooden seats and the people sitting in them. None of the people in this car were white, but many of them were speaking English, it seemed, and he wondered if they in turn were looking at him, if he appeared as out of place to them as he felt. His palms started to sweat. Why had he listened to Doña Ruiz anyway? What did she know? Barging in and pushing him out the front door of his very own house—what kind of behavior was that? And why was he so spineless that he had not fought back? Instead, he had walked all the way to the train station in the city as if under a spell. At the ticket window Francisco had slid a coin across the counter and said to the man behind the counter, "Emperador." It was the only thing Francisco knew with any specificity about where Omar worked. The employee at the ticket window was an American man who had looked at Francisco, confused. "Emperador," Francisco repeated. The man wrinkled his forehead, and said, "Empire?" It did sound similar, but Francisco was not at all certain they were referring to the same place. The stop that he needed was called Emperador, and he said it a third time. The man at the window responded a second time: "Empire?" Francisco, at a loss, had stood there not knowing what more he could say, and finally the man shrugged, took the coin, and handed Francisco a ticket.

Francisco wiped his sweaty palms on his pants and returned to the thought that this was all Doña Ruiz's fault. She and her dark arts had led him astray. Standing in the center aisle of the train car, Francisco crossed his arms over his chest, secure in the certitude of his blame. Around him, more passengers climbed aboard and sat down on the hard wooden seats. He would not sit, he decided, as a matter of pride. But a minute later when the locomotive lurched away from the station, Francisco stumbled and nearly fell onto his rear end. A man reading a newspaper looked up sympathetically and scooted in toward the window, motioning to Francisco that he was welcome to sit. But with the same furious pride that had prevented him from sitting down at the start, Francisco merely held the seatback to steady himself and stood in the aisle for the rest of the ride.

||||||

WHEN THE TRAIN pulled into the station at Emperador, Francisco was so happy to get off that he almost forgot where he was arriving. The other passengers streamed away in every direction, and from the platform, Francisco watched them until he was the only one left. The rain that had fallen all morning long had stopped.

Several of the passengers walked across the train tracks toward the open end of a broad, paved street. From where he stood, if he craned his neck, Francisco could see that the street was the start of a town that was much bigger than he had expected. Emperador, he knew, had long been a railroad town, but what he saw now was more like a carnival. People were everywhere, all sorts of people in all different shapes and sizes and colors and clothes, in addition to carriages and mules and many tall wooden poles with thick, black wires draped in between. The buildings, on streets that seemed to stretch on forever, were two and three stories high with balconies and awnings and U.S. flags. ¡Dios! When had they built all of this? And where was Emperador? Surely this was not it. He could not imagine the old town had looked like this. But where had it gone? Had the United States really swallowed it whole?

A newfound dismay filled Francisco as he stepped down off the train platform into the mud. Even from here, he could hear the horrific noises from La Boca, which told him it was not far away. His palms started sweating again as he walked.

Had he turned right and crossed the railroad tracks, Francisco would have seen that, in fact, the original town of Emperador remained. Every new building and residence that the Americans had built was on the opposite side of the tracks in a space they had claimed as their own. But Francisco turned left, and with each step he took beneath the midday sun, he wondered if he should not turn around. He told himself that if he turned around now and got back on the train, no one would even know he had come. He could just talk to Omar tonight. As Francisco considered that scenario, however—Omar arriving home and immediately going around back to strip off his work clothes, Omar walking with soft footsteps through the house, coming into the kitchen for something to eat, the two of them making room for the other to pass, Omar taking his food back to his room and Francisco watching him go—he knew it would not work. He no longer believed in such things, but lately he had found himself wondering whether Doña Ruiz had put some implacable curse upon the house that would not allow him to speak. Why she would do such a thing was unfathomable. And after this morning, it seemed improbable as well. But the fact remained: He could not speak in the house. His only hope then was to try in some other place. Unfortunately, this was the only place Francisco knew Omar could be.

||||||

THE EDGE OF Emperador backed up to the edge of a cliff, which is where, before long, Francisco found himself. Without even looking down, from the smoke and the noise, he knew he had come to the worksite, and when he finally gathered the nerve to lower his gaze, what he saw made him gasp. The Mouth yawned. Down its sides, the earth had been stripped and carved bare. There were layers of dirt and clay and rock in shades of every color, it seemed: black, yellow, blue, brown, orange, pink, and red. They flamed in the sun like a vast open wound, one that was not meant to heal. But even more bewildering than what had been done to the land—what had been done to his country—was how many hundreds of men were participating in it. It might have been thousands from what Francisco could see. All down the sides of the mountains, upon plateau after plateau of dirt, there were men and machines, machines and men, moving as though they were one and the same, shoveling and digging and lifting and doing who knows what. And unlike the passenger train he had just ridden upon, down in the valley Francisco saw work trains, endless tangles of black locomotives towing long caravans of open-topped boxlike containers filled with nothing but dirt. On multiple railroad tracks the trains wove in and out and around and back again in a loop that seemed to have no beginning and no discernible end. And amazingly, alongside them were still more men, gangs of them lined up and shoveling, all while the train whistles blew and rocks crashed down and thick, black odorous smoke billowed up. He tried to take everything in. What he saw as he stared across that vast chasm was not simply a canal, but a great divide that would sever Panamá in two. All at once every emotion that Francisco had felt for the past four years, since the time of La Separación, came swirling together into one great knot, and what the knot amounted to was not anger, as he would have expected, but sorrow. Seeing his country like this was one more extraordinary sorrow on top of all the rest.

Francisco started to cry.

It was the first time he had cried since the disappearance of Esme, and the sensation of tears on his face was unfamiliar. He reached up and quickly wiped them away. The thought of someone seeing him here had been bad enough, but the thought of someone see-ing him here *crying* was worse. The tears, though, had a mind of their own, and they kept falling for several minutes during which Francisco wiped them again and again until the palms of both of his hands were wet. But when he looked at his hands, those old, battered hands, he remembered why he was here. Omar. And at the thought of his son, Francisco became resolute. He threw back his shoulders and straightened his spine. He wiped his hands on his pants. He had come this far. He imagined himself descending into the Mouth not as a traitor or a martyr or a sacrificial lamb but as a father whose love was infinitely greater than his sorrow or fear. He would find

Omar and say something to him. Never mind that he did not know what that would be; the point was that it would be something, yes? Yes. He could do that.

Not far to his right was a long staircase set into the mountainside. Francisco walked over to it and, with as much courage as he could muster, started down one step at a time. His legs shook due both to age and to nerves, but miraculously, step after step, he did not fall. And when he finally reached the bottom and looked up, he was once again taken aback. He, Francisco Aquino, was in the Mouth now.

He took another deep breath and turned left for no reason at all. There was so much noise echoing between the walls of the mountains that it was hard to think straight. Clattering and rumbling and crashing and clanking. Relentless vibration rattled the air. Were they digging it out or merely shaking the earth till the whole thing came undone? Tentatively, Francisco started walking through what seemed certain hell.

Francisco was wearing a pair of leather sandals that crossed in an X over his feet—sandals that he had cut and hammered himself, the only shoes that he owned—but as he stepped over the rocks, those sandals, which seemed perfectly natural everywhere else, looked ridiculous here. Suddenly he understood why Omar had purchased boots shortly after taking this job. Francisco had scoffed at the time, but he could not deny what an improvement boots would have been in conditions such as these.

Everywhere Francisco looked as he walked, there was something to see. Slabs of broken black rock. Piles of crushed, powdered stone. Machines as enormous as trees. Locomotive wheels nearly as tall as his house. Processions of men carrying crates atop their heads. Men leaning out of signal towers, yelling to more men below. Almost all of them dressed in the same blue shirts and khaki trousers that he was used to seeing Omar wear. And the odor! Good God, the pungent odor of smoke was atrocious! Was this really where Omar came every day? Francisco found it hard to believe. Omar, after all, was the boy who used to spend his days catching butterflies, a fact that

Francisco knew only because once, when Omar had held a butterfly for too long and it had died in his hands, he had been so distraught that he had sat with it enclosed in his hands all day long, waiting for his father to return home and asking tremulously what they should do. Francisco would have chuckled had Omar not appeared so distressed, and in the end they had buried the butterfly in the backyard next to a banana tree. Omar was the boy who lined up seashells on the sand, the arrangements of which Francisco saw when he pulled the boat back up to the shore at the end of the day. He was the boy whom Francisco could hear sometimes whispering to himself in the dark at night, even though Francisco did not know what he said. He thought perhaps Omar was praying, and he did not have the heart to tell his son what he had come to believe after Esme died, which was that clearly there was no God worth praying to. No one was listening to them. No God would have let his mother leave like she had. When she had disappeared, everything that Francisco believed about God, mystery, and faith had disappeared, too. For him those things had ceased to exist. They all died with her. But Francisco had never said any of that, because Omar was also the boy who was too sensitive to hear the truth—that his mother had taken her own life. Instead, Francisco had said simply that she had died. From illness, he said when Omar had asked how, and that was, after all, a certain form of the truth. But was the boy Francisco remembered really the same boy who worked down here in this loud, smoke-ridden, perilous place? It occurred to Francisco just then that perhaps he did not know his son, that the Omar he still thought of as a boy had somehow, without Francisco even realizing it, turned into a man. Then, colliding with that first thought, he swiftly felt the force of another: Perhaps he had *never* known his son. He knew things about him, yes, but what did he know about what Omar truly thought, what he held in his heart, how he saw the world? They had never had conversations like that. Even before the months of silence between them, how often had Francisco ever really spoken to him? As he walked through the mud and the noise and the stench, Francisco finally understood. If there was indeed a curse on the house, he had put it there himself.

Francisco felt sweat collect under the collar of his shirt. He watched machines whose necks jutted out at an angle dip down to gobble up the piles of broken rock that waited below. Once the rock was in its grasp, the neck reared back up, and the entire body of the beast turned. Then the neck opened its jaws and the rock crashed down onto the bed of a train car that had only three sides. This happened again and again. "Look out!" people called, and Francisco quickly learned to hurry off to the side, to leave room for a passing train or an explosion of rock. He wove around piles of spoil and ducked under swinging machines, looking every direction at once, for there was so much activity and noise and commotion that he had to be vigilant, to watch where he was going and what was coming for him from all sides. He looked up once to make sure that the mountains had not closed in around him and that he could still see the sky, but looking up only made him feel even more overwhelmed. It was an experience similar to how he felt out on the ocean sometimes, but the feeling on the ocean was a kind of surrender to the grandeur of the world. Here it was different. Here, he kept thinking, instead of surrendering to nature, they were foolishly attempting to make nature surrender to them. Francisco was still looking up, about to walk on, when, amid the acrid odor of smoke, he smelled violets. He froze. It made absolutely no sense. There were no flowers down here. Of course there were not. But the smell, a delicate, powdery smell just like he remembered, was unmistakable. Francisco closed his eyes and took a deep breath. *¡Dios!* he thought. And for the second time that day, for the second time that very hour, he cried.

For so long Francisco had thought that when he had lost Esme, he had also lost his faith—his faith in mysterious, magical, unexplainable things. Such things had not even seemed *possible* to him anymore, as though in the wake of her death, Francisco's imagination itself had withered and, devoid of imagination, his entire world had shrunk to the point that he could not see beyond what was right in front of his face. He was aware, having experienced it before, that there was another dimension to life, but, frustrated that he could no longer access it, he had eschewed it altogether, rejected its powers, and derided it in order to make himself feel that he had lost nothing at all. He had convinced himself that it was enough to live in the rational world, which is what most people did. There was nothing wrong with that. Yes, it might have been smaller and less wondrous, but what did he need with wonder? He had had something wonderful once and it had only broken his heart.

When Francisco opened his eyes and looked down the length of the valley in which he stood, the wide rocky chasm between the peaks of the mountains, he saw what he had not seen before, what he had not even been able to imagine before: an ocean filling the space where he stood. Now when he looked up, he saw not the sky, but the underside of a massive ship, its brown wooden hull perfectly visible to him in every detail. In one way it was frightening to see it, for Francisco understood what it meant—the canal would be completed, they would find a way through—but more than being frightened, Francisco was awed to find that his imagination had returned. He was almost afraid to move lest his resurrected imagination be tied somehow to this exact spot. But when someone yelled and all the men nearby went scrambling away, he ran away, too, as a small blast ignited and scattered pebbles and smoke through the air. Nervously, Francisco gazed up again. He saw, high over his head, the hull of a different ship, long and lean and gray, floating on the surface of water that did not yet exist. He did not like the canal. He had never liked it, and for as long as he lived, he told himself, he would not change his opinion about that. But the sight of that ship in that moment brought him tremendous relief.

With new vigor, Francisco walked on.

"Omar!" he called out. It was the first time in six months he had said his son's name. "Omar!" he kept calling, thrilled by the sound of it, but if anyone heard him, no one looked up.

Eventually, he found himself walking between a railroad track and a line of men. The men were swinging pickaxes at the mountain face before them, and Francisco peered at each one, looking for Omar's slender frame and his straw hat banded with rope. He watched the men chip off flakes of the mountain again and again, a process almost as effective, Francisco thought, as using a toothpick to carve out a tree.

"Omar!" Francisco yelled.

A voice yelled back. "You! You there! Who are you?"

The words were foreign, spoken in a language Francisco did not understand, but he understood that the man was speaking to him. He was a robust white man, wearing overalls and tall rubber boots, and from up on a rocky ledge he was pointing at Francisco, jabbing his finger in the air. A few men within earshot stopped digging and turned to look at Francisco. Francisco shouted, "Omar?" The men, all of them young and dark-skinned and speckled with mud, stared at him blankly. "Omar Aquino? Él es mi hijo," Francisco tried again. It was a doomed interaction from the start. The men who had turned shrugged their shoulders or else shook their heads. One of the men, a man with sideburns that stretched all the way down to his jaw, looked at Francisco for longer than the rest, but when the white man in overalls started shouting again, all of the men on the line turned back to their work. Francisco sensed the futility, but he tried one last time. "Omar Aquino? Estoy buscando a mi hijo."

None of the men on the line understood what Francisco had said. They heard "Omar," but none of them knew Omar's name. If Clement or Prince or Joseph had not followed Omar's lead and climbed up out of the Cut earlier after seeing what Miller had done, they would have known. Before the end of that day, each of them would find work doing other things on the line. Clement would secure a job as a brakeman making 16¢ an hour instead of just 10¢. Joseph would work for a few weeks building a bridge before he would leave to go home. And Prince would whistle as he unpacked dynamite in Bas Obispo, which he would do for a year until a premature explosion killed him and twenty-five other men, and he would whistle no more. If Berisford had been there, he, too, would have known, but Berisford was dead. The men had buried him earlier that day. And when the white man started stomping down from the rise, waving his arms wildly through the air, Francisco hurried away.

Francisco wandered through the Mouth, walking up and down the line, past men pulling up railroad ties, past men mounted on top of drills like giant grasshoppers, past control towers and dirt cars, over railroad track and rocks, until he had seen everyone he thought he could see, sometimes seeing the same man more than once. He called Omar's name, but no one who answered was of any help. His son was nowhere to be found. Francisco did not know what to do. He had come all this way. His head pounded from the noise; his eyes watered from the smoke. He was tired and muddy and sopping with sweat. When the work whistle blew at the end of the day, a swarm of men, none of whom it seemed were his son, dropped their tools and clambered out of the Cut. Bedraggled and defeated, Francisco climbed out, too.

27

RENATA, VALENTINA, AND JOAQUÍN SAT CROSS-LEGGED, ALL IN A ROW, IN FRONT OF the house, facing the pitifully denuded riverbank. Valentina, wearing her pollera, held up a small Panamanian flag that she had sewn herself. She had also braided her hair and wound it up like a crown in an attempt to portray a certain stately air.

It was 10:00 a.m. and the three of them had been sitting for maybe fifteen minutes, staring out at the mighty river, waiting for other people to arrive.

"Where is everyone?" Valentina asked. Not a soul was walking toward them along the riverbank. Not a soul was walking anywhere, from what she could see. Even the town center, visible in the distance, was disconcertingly empty.

Joaquín said, "They are running on Panamanian time."

Ignoring him, Valentina asked Renata, "Did you remind people?"

Renata nodded. "I knocked on thirty doors yesterday."

"And you?" Valentina asked Joaquín.

"Me? I must have knocked on a hundred."

"There are only ninety houses in town."

"Is that so? Then I must have knocked on thirty as well, just like both of you."

Two weeks of living in Gatún had changed Joaquín's feelings toward the town. He found life out here to be pleasant, carried along by a hum that was softer, less jagged than that of the city. People waved to him on the street as he passed. There was a particular pig on the property of Chucho Martínez, a pig with a large patch of brown on its back that Joaquín swore recognized him now, for every time Joaquín neared the fence, it ran up, pushed its snout through, and snorted at him. Justo de Andrade, who had a fruit stand by the train station, had twice tossed Joaquín a free orange in the morning and, like a parent, exhorted Joaquín to eat. When Joaquín had gone door to door yesterday, so many people stood outside and had conversations with him that he felt like one of their actual neighbors. Even Renata had become somewhat tolerable to him. He found her no more attractive and no less dull, but at least she was an excellent cook.

Valentina looked at Joaquín. "Did you tell your clients? Everyone at the market?"

"Of course, my love. I told them, 'The future of Panamá hangs in the balance!'"

"Well, why aren't they here?"

"Perhaps they are on their way."

Valentina expelled a vigorous sigh. She snapped the flag that she was holding up over her head and shouted once, "We will not be moved!"

But there was no one to hear them, just the rushing river and the birds in the sky.

Valentina lowered the flag and looked at Joaquín again. "We should think of a better chant than that."

"I agree."

"Well, what do you suggest?"

Joaquín squirmed. The mud had made his rear end wet, and he was loath to admit that he had no suggestion. He said, "But it is not just up to me." Joaquín leaned forward. "Ideas, Renata?"

"What?"

"Do you have ideas for a chant?"

"A chant? I thought we were sitting to show that we are willing to do what it takes to save this town." With her customary blankness she looked at Joaquín. "Isn't that why we are here?"

Valentina nodded. "That's not bad."

Joaquín said, "What's not bad? 'We are willing to do what it takes to save this town'? That is not a good chant. No offense, Renata. But we might as well stick with 'We will not be moved.'"

"No, the other part," Valentina said. "'We are here.'" She raised a fist and tried it. "We are here!" She looked at Joaquín and smiled. "You see?"

"Ah, yes," Joaquín said.

Valentina raised the flag again and together the three of them shouted in unison, "We are here! We are here!"

|||||

FINALLY, AT A quarter past ten, a few people arrived. First, Salvador and then Xiomara and Josefina together. Enthusiastically, Valentina waved them over, and as Joaquín had come to expect each time people saw one another here, whether it had been a year or a day, the greetings were joyous—much turning of faces, much patting of cheeks, much chitchat—and it would have been no use reminding anyone that this was not a party but a protest, for they were who they were, demonstrations of love being more important than demonstrations of pain.

By the time the three of them took a seat, one after the other to the left of Joaquín, more residents had arrived. Esmeralda, Irina, Máximo. Justo hobbled over carrying a wooden crate on which he sat, explaining that he was too old anymore for sitting on the ground. "Even if I make it down, I will never make it back up."

Irina, who was older than Justo and already on the ground, laughed and said, "Thank you, Justo, for making me feel so young!"

Reina Moscoso showed up with food, as she had promised she would. "I am sorry I wasn't here earlier," she said, lugging an enormous basket at her side. "It took a long time to make sixty loaves of bread!"

"But they smell delicious," Máximo said.

Reina put the basket down. "Here," she said, handing Máximo the first small loaf. "Que Dios te bendiga."

"Muchas gracias," he said, and Reina handed a loaf to everyone.

Hilda Saéz showed up with a basket of her own, and from it she took out crosses she had fashioned from long blades of grass, placing one cross in front of everyone who was already there.

Raúl came with castanets and a dried goat bladder that he was going to use as a drum. "I also brought firecrackers loud enough to shake heaven," he said.

Hilda frowned.

Elbert Clabber and Solomon Whyte, both of whom lived in Gatún by way of Jamaica, walked over to the growing crowd, and Valentina, who knew them as hardworking farmers who had tilled the earth here for decades, smiled and said, "Sit down, both of you. Have some bread."

By the time the church bell rang at eleven, neighbors from all over Gatún were sitting side by side in the mud. Carolina and Alonso Rey arrived with their four children, and Alonso unfurled a kite into the air and let each of the children hold it at times. With delight, everyone watched it dip and soar overhead. For a few minutes, people sang the lyrics to a popular song. Raúl shot a firecracker into the air.

All this time Valentina had been periodically glancing in the direction of the train station to see if a reporter might arrive, but she had not seen one yet.

"Remind me what the man at the newspaper told you," she said to Joaquín.

"You already know."

"But tell me again."

Joaquín frowned. After Valentina had divulged her efforts at *The Canal Record*, he had suggested that perhaps *La Estrella*, being a Panamanian newspaper, might be more sympathetic to their cause. But when he had gone to their offices, the reporter with whom Joaquín had spoken had been dismissive, saying that it was hardly news that some Panamanians were upset, some Panamanians were always upset, and suggesting that Joaquín come back if something actually happened that was worthy to report. Joaquín had told him, "But we are trying to prevent something from happening." To which the reporter had replied, "I understand. But the problem for you is that 'something happening' is what constitutes news."

With reluctance, Joaquín cleared his throat. "He said that something has to happen before they will write a story about it."

Valentina narrowed her eyes. Joaquín did not particularly want to get into it again, so he was relieved when at that moment he heard a noise and looked back over his shoulder to see a man emerging from the house two doors down. Joaquín elbowed both Valentina and Renata. "Is that . . . ?" he asked.

"Eliberto," Valentina murmured.

The man who had emerged, far from appearing villainous, as Joaquín would have expected, was merely someone with a gray mustache and moppish gray hair and his shirtsleeves rolled up. Valentina, Joaquín knew, had been avoiding Eliberto these weeks, but neither she nor Renata nor Joaquín could keep their eyes off him now as he took a few steps forward and stopped. He put his hands on his hips, surveying the crowd. Raúl was thumping his drum, and the Rey children were fighting over who got to hold the string of the kite, and Reina was guarding her basket of bread from the flies, and most of the others—about twenty-five people in all—were sitting down chatting with whoever was nearby. There was every possibility, Joaquín thought, that Eliberto would say that they were making too much noise, or complain that people were sitting too near his house, or otherwise voice his opposition in some way. But after a minute, Eliberto took a few more steps forward and squeezed himself in between Irina and Máximo, who looked at him with a mixture of irritation and surprise, and sat.

"A miracle of God," Valentina whispered.

She needed a miracle of a different order, however, and as it was coming up on the time when the next passenger train was due to arrive, she peered at the station again. She watched for several minutes when, down the bank to her right, a man wearing ivory pants strode up.

"Who is that?" She pointed.

Joaquín looked up and saw Li Jie walking toward them. Of all people. When Joaquín had informed his customers at the market that he would not be there today, encouraging them to take part in the demonstration with him, he had done so with the fear that each of those customers would flock to Li Jie's stall in his absence, and that some of them might never come back. But what could he do? Some things were bigger than fish, which was the very argument Horacio, of course, had made to him once. Perhaps the boy had some brains in his head after all. But Joaquín had not told Li Jie about the demonstration, which meant he must have gotten wind of it somehow. And what's more, Joaquín realized, Li Jie must have closed his stall for the day to be here as well.

Joaquín jumped up and waved. As soon as Li Jie got to him, Joaquín gave him a hug. The two stood goofily smiling at each other, exchanging greetings, until Valentina tugged on Joaquín's pant leg and told him to sit back down. He did, and Li Jie nodded slightly before he walked to the end of the line and sat, too.

"Who was that?" Valentina asked.

Someone I believed was my enemy, Joaquín wanted to say. Instead he simply answered, "A friend."

After a time people started arriving whom they did not recognize, people from outside of Gatún. A man poled downriver from the town of Chagres, saying he had seen the kite in the sky, and he tied up his bungo and sat down with them, too. Another man, shirtless, galloped up on horseback holding a flag of the republic as he rode. He dismounted with a flourish and then planted himself in front of the crowd and swished the flag back and forth in great arcs a few times like a conquistador until someone shouted at him to stop showing off and sit down, for God's sake. A couple even came from Limón, saying that they feared a similar threat in their town, not from the dam but from the lake that the dam would create, which would flood the place where they lived. They had come to see a model of how they, too, might resist.

"But how did you hear about it?" Valentina asked.

"People are talking," they answered.

Valentina grinned at Renata and Joaquín. "It is working," she said.

28

ADA HUDDLED IN THE CORNER OF THE BOXCAR WITH HER ARMS WRAPPED ROUND
her knees. It was light outside, and she could hear rain. She would
have liked to go outside and let the rain stream over her, to scoop
up some mud and scrub it on her elbows and knees and the back
of her neck, working the grit of it over her skin, and then let it all
wash away, to get everything off her. Doing that might make her feel
better, she thought, but she was too scared at the moment to step
outside lest anyone see her. She wanted only the trees to know where
she was.

Last night after the funeral Antoinette had knocked on Ada's
door. When Ada had opened it, Antoinette had said she was about
to depart for the evening, but before she went, she thought Ada
should know that Mr. Oswald had come recently to question her.
He had asked her whether Ada really had left the house that fate-
ful day, and of course, Antoinette said, she did have to tell him the
truth. She had paused, as though waiting to see what Ada would
say, but when Ada said nothing, she went on. "Me wonder what
he might see fit to do now. Send you back to Barbados? Call in
the police?" Even accounting for the fact that Antoinette disliked
her enough to say anything, the very words had made Ada's heart
pound. She had made herself be still, though, had kept her face as
impassive as a stone, determined not to reveal the panic rising high
in her chest, until with a pitying look Antoinette shrugged and bid
her good night.

Her heart had not stopped pounding since. She drew her knees
up tighter to her chest. Coming back to the boxcar had been the only
thing she could think to do, but how long could she stay hidden here?
She cursed herself for having mentioned the boxcar to Antoinette

once. How long before Antoinette told Mr. Oswald about it and he sent someone looking for her?

Water dripped through the ceiling, but only a little and not near where Ada sat. She watched it and listened to the clatter of raindrops outside upon the trees. At home during hurricane season when the wind howled and the trees lashed, Ada used to scramble into Millicent's bed, and Millicent would snap her quilt up in the air and let it drape over them both. "This is our storm house," Millicent said. "So as long as we're in it, nothing bad can come to us." Ada used to believe her. It was nothing but a blanket and a story, but those two things together felt as sturdy as steel. She could have gotten her quilt out of her sack and draped it over herself now, Ada thought, but she didn't. It would not be the same, not only because Millicent was not there to tell her that nothing could happen to them but also because that didn't seem true anymore.

||||||

WITH THE MAILBAG at his hip, Michael ducked under low-hanging branches and pushed back the feather of ferns as he walked. The leaves blotted out the light, but he had never been one to be scared of the dark, and there was a sense of calm in the dimness at least. He had heard people describe the jungle as wild, as though wild was something bad, but now that he was here he thought the jungle seemed more peaceful and more welcoming than the rest of the so-called tamed world out there.

He crept through tendrils and reeds, thick trees and thin. He saw a few darting lizards and, once, an orange frog about the size of a quarter dollar sitting still upon a doily of olive-green moss. He knew about doilies because the boardinghouse where he had stayed for eight weeks before coming to Panama had a pretty white cotton doily on the bureau by the front door. That bureau also had two brass candlesticks and a small ticking clock, and once, on his way out, he had stopped to touch the bulbous curves of one of the candlesticks, imagining what it would be like to own a thing like that, imagining a day when maybe he would have enough money to buy it for himself, when from across the room the stern white woman who ran the boardinghouse, the woman who had given him a room only because he paid double and who kept an eagle eye on him nonetheless, snapped at him and said, "That ain't for you." He had snatched his hand away as quick as if he had touched something hot and then turned to see the woman standing in the far doorway with her arms crossed over her chest. "I wasn't—" Michael had started to say. "That ain't for you," she repeated. Had she merely told him to keep his hands to himself, he would not have been so bothered. But it was the assault on all he had been imagining, the assault on his future, that stung. He was fifteen years old, without any known kin in the world. Orphaned when he was young, treated poorly at times, cheated and scammed growing up on the streets. He had been alive long enough to know that what the boardinghouse lady said applied to a great many things—at least for a boy like him. He already knew it deep down, but in that moment, like a shadowy vision suddenly snapped into focus, the boardinghouse lady put words to the feeling and solidified it. For him, there would always be limits in the land of the free. That was the day he made up his mind to leave, to see what else the world had in store. His job at that time was as a newspaperboy, and he had seen many a headline in the newspapers about a place called Panama where the Americans were building a mighty canal. Selling newspapers had put enough money in his pocket that he could purchase a one-way pass on a ship, and he figured he would earn enough while he was there that he could purchase a return pass if things did not work out. He had nothing to lose. He had set out thinking he was venturing off to a whole new place, but what he found in the Canal Zone was not much different from what was in the small town in Virginia he had left. Of course the climate was different and the landscape, too, but apart from those things what he found was a sort of miniature reproduction of the United States, like they had come there to put on a play. There were post offices and barbershops and ice-cream socials and Friday-night dances. And limits.

The same sort of limits. Here they called it different—gold and silver instead of white and black—but it worked just the same. Along with everything else, the attitude of his country had been imported down here, and he wondered sometimes if he would ever escape it, and he feared he would not.

In his four or so months on this land, Michael had not ventured into the jungle before, but he was on a mission that day to find the girl who used to reside at the Oswalds' house and who, the cook had informed him, had left. "Off in a rush," the cook had said, and when he had asked where, she had shrugged and muttered something about a boxcar out in the bush for all that she knew. She had closed the door before he could even say thank you.

Around him everything was ablossom, every sprig and leaf unfurled, flowers bright and bursting. There were buzzing nests in the trees and twittering birds and so many long, hanging vines that he had to push them aside to walk through. But nowhere in that rich world did he see a boxcar. And he had not passed one yet as far as he knew. He had thought he was heading north, but now he was not so sure. He took another few steps forward and then turned what he believed was due west with the idea that he would walk awhile in that direction. He started counting his steps to keep track of where he was and so that later he would have some idea how to get back out. After a while, when west yielded nothing but more trees and ferns and mud puddles, he turned north again and walked that way for a time. He wondered if he should leave, but nothing good ever came from giving up, and when he stepped into a patch where columns of sunlight streamed between the thick leaves overhead, lighting everything copper and gold, that was enough for him to go on.

He had gone every direction he could think of when at last he saw it—an old boxcar. It was rickety and rusted, veiled by ferns, strangled by vines, and its back end was sunk in the mud, as though the jungle were slowly devouring it.

Michael stayed where he was and clutched the handle of his bag.

He was suddenly afraid to call out. There was every chance that this boxcar was occupied by someone else, someone who might not take kindly to seeing him there. He knew how the world worked. But he had come to find her. Michael took a deep breath.

"Ada Bunting?" he said.

29

IT HAD BEEN A GOOD MANY WEEKS SINCE MILLICENT BUNTING HAD FELT THE SUN ON her toes. That day, though, she got up out of bed—her own bed— and walked out the front door and took a seat in the rocking chair where her mother usually sat. Her mother was in the garden behind the house, tending the crops. Millicent rested for a time. It had taken considerable energy even to walk out to the porch, and the longer she sat the more she recovered some of what she had lost. When she felt she could, Millicent stood up and slowly walked down off the porch. She was still in her nightclothes—an ivory, loose-fitting gown—but if any neighbors were watching, she did not care. She stopped at the foot of the steps, where the heat of the sun reached not only her toes but also the crown of her head, and dropped to her knees. With some effort she turned, lowered herself down on her back, stretched her arms out to each side, her palms upon the dirt, which was pebbly and rough, and closed her eyes. A breeze whispered through the air. The birds sang in the trees. It was a beautiful world. Tears seeped from the corners of her eyes and dripped down to the dirt as she thought how she had almost left it, but thank God she had not.

|||||

THE DAY BEFORE, early in the morning, a low buggy had thundered up to the house. When Millicent heard the horse hooves, when she heard them rumble as they came down the lane, she thought the end had finally come. That specter of horse hooves had been taunting her all along, but now the sound was real. She was certain of that as she lay in Ada's bed, and she curled her fingers around the bound edge of her quilt and pulled it up over her mouth and her nose and felt her heart race. She did not cover her eyes because part of her, the minuscule part of her that was occasionally brave, felt compelled to look.

Under the quilt, Millicent waited. The horse hooves had stopped. But through the open window she could hear the horses snorting. There was no doubt they were there. Then she heard a man's deep voice. Millicent squeezed her fingers tighter around the quilt. Murmuring. She could not make out the words. The door opened and closed. Footsteps. They were coming toward her.

||||||

HE WAS A Black British doctor, handsome, with a sonorous voice. He introduced himself as Dr. Jenkins. He took off his hat, set it on the foot of the bed, placed his bag on the floor, then looked down at Millicent and said, "I hear you have been feeling unwell."

From under the quilt, Millicent did not answer or move. Her mother was standing next to the doctor.

"May I?" he asked, and reached to fold the quilt down. He smiled as he uncovered her face. "I would like to start with an examination so that I may see for myself. I can make an assessment from there. Do you agree?"

Millicent looked at her mother, who looked back at her and nodded. "Yes."

Leonard Jenkins, forty-six years old, Cambridge-educated, had met J. R. Robinson many years earlier when both of them had been living in London. They had encountered each other by chance. Each of them had been pleased, so far across the pond, to have found a fellow countryman with whom they could talk about home, and they had, during their London days, gotten together periodically over pints of Burton ale and done just that. Later, once they were both back in Barbados, they had run into each other from time to time. When Leonard's wife had died, J.R. had sent his condolences. Still, they did not regularly spend time with each other these days, so it was with some surprise that last evening after the sun had gone down, Leonard, who had been enjoying a pipe, heard a knock at his door and opened it to see his old friend. Leonard had greeted him warmly and asked him inside, though he understood that J.R. was not there simply to spend time with him in friendship. People did not come round knocking on a doctor's door on a Sunday evening for that. Sitting together in the parlor, Leonard had listened as J.R. told him about a young girl who needed medical care. J.R. said he did not know the extent, only that pneumonia was involved, and he had reason to believe that the situation was urgent. Leonard held his clay pipe by the shank and considered whether to ask exactly who the girl was. J.R. had many clients on whose behalf such a request might be made, but there was only one Leonard knew of with whom J.R. was enough of a friend that he would come late on a Sunday evening seeking Leonard's help. He told J.R. he had patients to see the next morning, and he did not know if their appointments could be rearranged. J.R. said he would pay any price Leonard would name as long as Leonard was discreet. Under no circumstances could he say who had sent him, and it was preferable that he simply say nothing at all. "It will have to be early," Leonard said. "The earlier the better," J.R. had replied.

Leonard folded the quilt down to the girl's waist and, amid the distinctive scent of black cake in the air, lowered his ear to her chest. As her mother looked on, he gently pressed his fingertips to various spots along her ribs and her back. Her breathing was labored. He could hear the dull, percussive sound of fluid on the left side. He asked her to speak and detected evidence of egophony, again on the left. Yet the heartbeat was strong.

"Can you perform the surgery?" the girl's mother asked.

"Surgery?" Leonard said.

"Isn't that the reason you come?" She looked at him with the sort of heartbreaking hope he was used to seeing after so many years in this field.

"She does not need a surgery," Leonard said.

"But we had another doctor, and that's what he say."

"I imagine the last doctor was concerned about pneumothorax, but your daughter has pleural effusion, which is far less severe. It means that although she does indeed require intervention, it is not a surgery per se but rather a simple aspiration."

"What?"

Leonard's wife, when she had been alive, had sometimes laughingly accused him of speaking in a language people could not understand. He tried again. "A needle will be inserted through the back of the rib cage to drain what fluid there is."

"But before . . ."

In his mind, Leonard questioned how thorough the previous examination had truly been, but he did not want to cast aspersions on another physician, so instead he allowed himself to say, "The potential for pneumothorax was a logical concern, but I find no evidence that it has come to fruition. We need only drain her lung."

"You sure?"

He looked directly at the woman. "I would stake my life on it."

Millicent, listening in bed, felt hope rise in her heart.

"When?" her mother asked softly.

"I can do it now. It takes only ten minutes or so."

"Now?"

"I have with me everything that I need."

Millicent watched her mother. Her eyes were wide, and she started blinking fast as if she were holding back tears. But she said nothing. So even as the doctor was still looking at her mother, from the bed Millicent herself said, "Yes."

||||||

LUCILLE FELT ALMOST dizzy with disbelief as she helped Millicent out of the bed and walked her to the kitchen, where the doctor was setting up. Not even half an hour earlier she had been sitting on the porch, sunk in desperation, convinced that the only option left was to sell the house. The house and the land. Her piece of the world. She had been studying the wood floorboards, wondering how much she might get for the wood. How much for each window sash and nail and joist? How much for the solid front door? Were the stones that held the porch worth anything? They were worth plenty to her—adding the porch had been a mark of her success—but would someone else pay well for them? At the sound of horses, she had looked up to see a buggy bumping down Aster Lane all the way to her house. A man had climbed out of the buggy and she had sat still as he walked up to the porch, carrying a black leather bag, and even when he came to the foot of the steps and said, "Lucille Bunting?" she answered yes but did not stand. Lucille had the terrible thought that he was a messenger coming to tell her that something had happened to Ada in Panama. She tightened her fingers round the arms of her chair.

The man had tipped his hat. "Dr. Leonard Jenkins," he said.

That was such a shock—not at all what she was expecting—that she had to ask him to say it again. He repeated his name and asked if she had a daughter who required medical care, and when Lucille, overcome, whispered that she did, he said, "I am here to offer that."

"You come from the vestry?" she asked.

"No. I have a practice in town. I do travel for calls such as these."

Slowly, Lucille nodded. If the vestry had not sent him . . .

"How much?" she asked hesitantly.

"There will be no charge."

It would take some time from that day, but Lucille would save every pence and shilling she could. She would stash it all in a glass jar, and on the day she finally accumulated what she guessed was enough, she would take the jar to the Camby estate—the final time she would ever go there—and set it by the front door. She would not be beholden to him. That was important to her. She wanted to walk through the world without owing anyone, especially Henry, a thing.

||||||

THE DOCTOR HAD Millicent sit upright, leaning over the kitchen table. He tapped his finger over her ribs, counting aloud as he went. He said, "Sit still now." Then the needle slid in with a sharp bolt of pain. Millicent winced but tried not to move. "Good," the doctor said. "Hold your breath now." Her mother was sitting across from her, holding her hands, and Millicent had her eyes closed. She could hear small sounds: breathing, the doctor placing something down and picking something else up. "You're doing well," he repeated now and again. After a time, he said, "Hum for me, please."

Millicent did not know what to hum until she heard her mother start—and what her mother hummed was not even a song, but a note. A single note that she held, rolling out through the air steady and strong. It was the only time outside of church that Millicent had heard her mother make a sound approaching music at all. Millicent took a breath and matched the note, and suddenly, she felt a new burst of pain.

"It is out," the doctor said.

Millicent opened her eyes. She could feel the doctor affixing a bandage, securing the wound. His hands were gentle as he worked. Across the table, her mother was still holding her hands, looking into her eyes. "Is it done?" she asked.

"It is done," the doctor replied. "And I have every faith she will be just fine."

Millicent watched her mother again blink back tears. She squeezed Millicent's fingers and whispered, "The Lord will take care."

Her mother helped Millicent back to the bed while the doctor packed up his things, and after her mother tucked the quilt around Millicent's shoulders and kissed her on the forehead and went to see the good doctor out, Millicent lay there by herself. She felt a peace come over her, a peace that she had been trying to find a year ago and that now, she believed, had come to find her. Her mother would never say how she had the means to pay for the second doctor, and Millicent would never ask. She thought she knew. From the bed, she listened to the clomp of the horse hooves as the buggy started off down the lane and wondered why she had ever imagined that the sound of horse hooves was something to fear. Maybe it was something she had read once in a book.

IIIII

WILLOUGHBY'S LIMPING LEG was tired, but he pulled it along, telling himself, *Just a few more steps now*, even when it wasn't, and then telling himself that again. Little by little was the only way he knew to get through this life.

In one hand he had a copper kettle that had once belonged to the church. Years of use had worn it out, and the church had recently purchased a new one. Without shame, Willoughby had asked whether he might have the old one, and he had spent the past few evenings working out the dents and resoldering the leaky spout, and then, when he had repaired as much as he could, polishing it with a rough cloth and buffing it with a fine one. Now it was a handsome, shining kettle, one that anyone would be happy to own, though there was only one person Willoughby wanted to give it to.

The day was mild and wrapped in good feeling. Willoughby knocked on the door. He expected Lucille to answer it as she always did if she was home or not in the garden out back, but when it opened, he was greeted by the sight of Millicent instead. Willoughby's mouth dropped. It was the first time he had seen Millicent in over a month, and in all that time she had been unwell. He knew how much it worried Lucille. She shushed him sometimes when he came to the door, telling him Millicent was sleeping and that she should not be disturbed. He himself had brought a few things over the weeks that he thought might improve her condition, though he had no idea what the condition was. He only knew that it was serious and that Lucille fretted, and he took care not to ask more beyond that. Some folks at church said that Lucille's other daughter, Ada, had even gone to Panama to earn money for the cause, and though it was true that Willoughby had not seen Ada for as long as he had not seen Millicent, he had never asked Lucille directly to confirm it. He did try to be respectful in that regard. Now, though, Millicent was before him, up on her feet, and Willoughby could hardly believe his own eyes.

"Good afternoon, Mr. Willoughby," she said, and smiled.

"Millicent," Willoughby stammered.

She looked thin—too thin, she had fallen away—but time and good cooking would remedy that.

From inside the house, Lucille called out, "Who there?"

"It's me—Willoughby," he said from the porch.

Lucille walked up next to Millicent and smiled at him, too. In as many weeks as Millicent had been unwell, Willoughby had not seen a smile on Lucille's face even once. It was a wonder to witness it now.

Lucille set her hand on Millicent's arm and said, "You see the good news."

"A blessing."

Millicent blushed and murmured that she had something she needed to do. She slipped back into the house, but even when she was gone, the smile stayed fixed on Lucille's face.

In the surprise of seeing Millicent, Willoughby had almost forgotten why he had come, but now he held up the teakettle and offered it to Lucille just as he had offered everything he could think of for the past year.

"What's that?" Lucille asked.

"I bring you a kettle."

"A kettle?"

"A nice, reliable kettle."

"What reason you think I need that?"

"I figure everyone can use a kettle, no?"

She was still smiling at him. "Reliable, you say?"

"I tell you in truth, it is old. I salvage it from the church, but I fix it up, and I believe it can serve you for many years still."

"It looks fine."

He was surprised to hear her say that. "See here. It's made of copper that brings water up to a boil faster than most."

"For true?"

"Yes."

"Well, I could use that."

"You could?"

She nodded. "Seems to take me too long to get things warmed up."

And something about the way she said it made Willoughby wonder whether she was talking about the kettle anymore. He swallowed a little lump that formed in his throat and said, "I imagine this should help," and handed the kettle to her.

Standing in the doorway, he watched as she ran her hand over the side, mostly smooth but still with dents he had not been able to get out. "Thank you," she said.

"You quite welcome." Willoughby shuffled back a step. He knew how it went. Now was the time when he was supposed to walk back down the porch steps and be on his way.

But instead of goodbye, Lucille said, "I do thank you, but you know what else I would like?"

Willoughby tried to think. In all the time he had been coming to her, Lucille had never asked for anything. "What?"

"Some company."

"Company?"

"I can make us some tea," Lucille said, nodding at the kettle. "If you want to come in."

Willoughby nearly laughed, and in the next second he thought he might cry. If he wanted? It was all he wanted. He nodded.

"Good," Lucille said.

She stepped inside the house, past the threshold of the front door that Willoughby had knocked on and walked away from so many times before. He followed her in.

30

OMAR STOOD ON THE TRAIN PLATFORM HIGH ABOVE THE CUT. HIS MOUTH TASTED OF blood, and he was still shaking, the same feeling of disgust charging up through him even now—what had happened to Berisford, the things Miller had said.

He clenched his hands in his pockets and licked his split, swollen lip. There was a roiling in his belly, as if something inside him were punching, trying to get out. Restlessly, he walked to the edge of the platform, peered down the tracks, walked back again. Once he got home, he could clean himself up, wash the taste of blood from his mouth.

From the platform, if he had wanted to, he could have seen the Cut, but he kept his eyes elsewhere and continued to pace as more and more people congregated on the platform, waiting for the southbound train. It was not until two Panamanian men walked onto the platform that Omar stopped—and what caught his attention was not only hearing them speak Spanish but hearing them say something about a protest.

"The residents in Gatún have decided to give the North Americans a piece of their mind," one man said.

"Haven't we given the North Americans too much already?" the other man asked, laughing.

"Exactly the point!"

Omar stared at them and had the sudden irrational thought that he should go to Gatún. He had no idea what was happening there beyond what the men had said, but the events of that morning had unlocked something in him, something fitful and pulsing, and things he would not have dreamed of doing only the day before suddenly struck him as exactly the things he had to do now.

||||||

VALENTINA HAD HER concerns. By noon, she counted at least fifty people who had gathered along the riverbank, and while it was wonderful, even miraculous, to have more than fifty people, all of whom had converged in this one spot for, presumably, this one purpose, the problem was that not one of them, from what she could tell, was a government official or a newspaper reporter or anyone from the Land Commission who could actually get anything done. Not to mention that after two hours, many people were not even sitting anymore. Reina kept walking around making sure everyone had sufficient quantities of bread and water. The young daughter of Isabel Velásquez, a girl Valentina had not seen since she was an infant, was playing the flute as she stalked down the line, pointing her toe with each step. Alonso and Carolina's children were continuously up and back down, reeling in the kite and spooling it out again. And the man who had arrived with a flag and a horse regularly got back up, mostly to check on his horse, it seemed, who was tied to a boulder along the river's edge.

"What should we do?" Valentina finally asked Joaquín.

"What do you mean? We are sitting. That was the plan."

Valentina glanced at Renata, who simply nodded.

"And we are chanting," Joaquín went on. "Remember the chant?"

"Yes, of course I remember the chant," Valentina said. "But who is listening to us?"

"Why, all of these people here." Joaquín gestured down the line.

Valentina sighed. Her husband was such a good man, but he could be so naive.

"These people here are already on our side, but who else—who else anywhere out *there*—will actually hear us, my love?"

||||||

MOLLY FIDDLED WITH her camera on the train to Gatún. The camera had come as a premium with her subscription to *The Youth's Com-*

panion, a magazine she used to receive, and she cleaned the brass lens with a small chamois cloth, wiped the dust from the bellows and the mahogany frame.

Before coming here, Molly had seen photographs of Panama, but all the photographs showed one of two things: either the canal or the jungle. Not once had she seen an image of an actual town. Which struck her as curious. So when a woman had come into the newspaper office saying that her town was going to disappear before long, Molly had the thought that she should take a photograph of it before it did. A photograph, she believed, was its own sort of preservation, a way to ensure that any particular moment or scene or person or town would, at least in one manner, continue to exist.

|||||

OMAR SAT ON the ground amid a group of people who were all, more or less, facing the riverbank in Gatún. A row of houses was behind them. Overhead, the clouds had rolled back to let the sunlight pour through. He had been sitting there for long enough that he had been able to piece together what the protest was about. The entire town was being forced to move. That in itself was heartbreaking enough, but what made it worse to Omar was the realization that he was partly to blame for their pain. He had worked on the canal all these months. He had been digging the dirt that would be transported here to make the huge Gatún Dam. Perhaps it was not the same exact dirt, but the fact that it could be, that he could have had a hand in their misery, was enough to make him feel responsible. And it was one more reason he wanted to help them now if he could.

|||||

VALENTINA LOOKED DOWN the line of people who had assembled with them, thinking again about what the reporter at *La Estrella* had told Joaquín—something had to happen before they would write a story about it. Well, something was assuredly happening, was it not? And yet no one from any newspaper was here.

"Bueno," Valentina muttered. "We will write our own story, then."

Both Joaquín and Renata turned to look at her. "What?" her sister asked.

Valentina fingered the flag in her lap. Sitting like this had been Joaquín's idea, and though it had been perfectly logical, it seemed to her now that they could not just sit.

"We need to get up," Valentina said.

"Did I miss something?" Joaquín asked.

"If they will not come to us, then we need to go to them."

"What are you talking about?" Joaquín said.

"We should take the train to the city."

"Who?"

"All of us. And then we should march to the Presidential Palace and carry on our protest." Joaquín and Renata looked at her as if she were crazy. "Trust me," she said.

Valentina stood up. To her right was Renata, and to her left was Joaquín as well as fifty or so other people, at whom she shouted, "¡Oye!" Salvador and Xiomara and Josefina, who were nearest, glanced up, but Isabel's daughter was still playing her flute and the horse tied to the boulder was snorting and people were talking, of course, and most people farther down could not hear her over all that noise. Valentina cupped her hands around her mouth and shouted again, and that time more people glanced up—Máximo waved as if she were simply saying hello—but it was not until the sound of a whistle tore through the air that everyone, every person sitting and every person who was supposed to be sitting, suddenly stopped what they were doing and looked up.

Valentina turned toward the sound and saw that the police had arrived.

"Shit," she heard Joaquín say.

"Good," Valentina murmured, and, still standing, calmly raised her small hand-stitched flag and held it up over her head.

Joaquín yanked on her skirt. "Do you want to be arrested?"

"I want to be noticed," she said.

In fact, only one police officer had arrived, and Valentina was disappointed not to see an entire army marching toward them in that moment—one lone police officer, a white man wearing a khaki uniform and a peaked hat, advancing, blowing his whistle, holding up his left hand with his fingers spread wide. Where he had come from, Valentina did not know, but even if he was only one person, at least someone was paying attention to them.

The officer strode down the line, along the edge of the river-bank, inspecting the crowd. Somewhere near the midway point, he stopped and shouted something that Valentina did not understand.

Joaquín tugged on her dress again and hissed, "I really think you should sit down."

"No."

Besides Valentina, anyone who had been standing when the whistle first pierced the air had promptly dropped back onto the ground. Now, all along the line, everyone waited to see what would happen next. For a few seconds, the rushing river was the only sound to be heard.

Then Valentina shouted, "We are here!"

The officer snapped his head and fixed his gaze on her.

"Oh my God," Joaquín said.

"We are here and we will not be moved!" she yelled.

The officer sharply blew his whistle and from where he stood yelled something back, but he was speaking in English and Valentina had no earthly idea what he had said.

"Please," Joaquín begged her.

But Valentina kept shouting, and the police officer shouted back, and it occurred to Valentina that just as she could not understand him, he could not understand her. The two of them were shouting things to the other in languages that neither of them could understand. The absurdity of it made her laugh. Out of nowhere, a laugh as big and round as the moon swelled in her and burst forth.

"What are you laughing at?" Joaquín asked from the ground.

It wasn't funny, of course. It wasn't funny at all, but Valentina could not get herself to stop laughing, which only infuriated the police officer, it seemed, since he no doubt believed she was laughing at him. He blasted his whistle several times in a row while Valentina tried without success to compose herself. He walked toward her, but the nearer he came, still shouting out things she could not comprehend, the harder she laughed. For what else was there to do in the face of imminent doom but fight, cry, or laugh? And she had already tried the first two.

||||||

"STOP!" OMAR SHOUTED from where he sat.

The officer, however, seemed not to have heard him. He was still moving toward the woman in the pollera who, for reasons Omar could not comprehend, was laughing.

Quickly, Omar stood up. He could feel the stares of the people to either side of him. In the distance, out of the corner of his eye, he saw a girl crouched down, taking photographs, her blond hair almost white in the sun.

"Stop!" Omar shouted again when he was up on his feet.

The officer whipped around. He set his hand on the end of the baton that hung from his waist.

Omar swallowed hard. "Please," he called out in English. "No one here is doing anything wrong. This is their home. They are trying to save it, that is all."

The officer paused, and for a second Omar believed it might be possible to reason with him. But then, at the other end of the line, the woman shouted in Spanish again, "We are here!" and the officer pulled out his baton and started making his way toward her again.

The officer, whose name was Thomas Rowland, had wandered into Gatún that day not because of any reported disturbance but as a matter of course on his usual rounds. His job, more than anything, was to be a presence, and in his few months on the isthmus, he had done little more than walk about in his uniform, projecting authority. Even when he did not feel particularly authoritative, the uniform alone, he'd found, made folks straighten up and act right. He was unaccustomed to people reacting otherwise, and he was certainly unaccustomed to being laughed at. He would feel better, he told himself, if he could just get the woman to sit down at least. As Thomas walked closer, however, the people directly to either side of the woman stood and began shouting, too. Then, as if someone had given a signal that he missed, suddenly every single person who was still sitting down rose up to their feet, and Thomas found himself face-to-face with a mob chanting something he did not understand.

"We are here!" Omar shouted with everyone else. Their voices were not quite in unison. By the time the chant started at one end of the line and the sound carried down to the other end, the first part of the line had begun chanting again and the words overlapped in the air, but even so, they kept on. The officer, who had been walking toward them at first, reversed course and stepped back. He was holding his baton out in front of himself, as if warding them off, and even though no one did anything other than stand still and chant, the officer kept inching back. He was going to leave, Omar thought with some astonishment. What they were doing was going to work. Then, on the muddy riverbank, the officer slipped and tumbled into the rushing water below.

Immediately, the chanting stopped. People froze in confusion. A split second passed before everyone started running to the edge of the river. By the time Omar got there, so many voices were yelling and so much mayhem abounded that he did not know what was happening until he saw the officer some feet downriver, clinging to an old, protruding tree root to prevent being swept away by the current.

Joaquín ran down even with the officer, squared his feet in the mud, and reached out his hand. The officer, holding fast to the tree root, merely looked up at him. Joaquín stretched his hand farther, wiggling his fingers for emphasis. "¡Ven, hombre!" Then he slipped and went down on one knee, coming perilously close to the water himself. As he recovered, the man with the bungo darted up and held out his pole to the officer, telling him to grab on. By then, everyone was crowded at the edge of the riverbank, shouting instructions to everyone else. On the other side of Joaquín, Valentina knelt down and screamed at the officer to take hold of the pole or her husband's hand, for God's sake! When—finally—the officer made a grab for the pole, the man with the bungo along with three other people tugged as hard as they could. Joaquín reached down to seize the officer's elbow and yanked him up onto land.

Everyone watched as, on his hands and knees, the officer panted. He had lost his hat in the river and he was dripping wet, but otherwise he seemed fine. Everyone waited to see whether he would thank them or arrest them or something else. After a moment, however, the officer merely scrambled up to his feet and, without so much as a word, ran off.

On the riverbank, people patted one another's arms and shook hands and embraced. Salvador and Máximo congratulated the man with the bungo pole. The man with the flag stood on the boulder where his horse was still tied and whipped the flag back and forth through the air, shouting, "¡Viva el Istmo!" and a few people shouted back, "¡Viva Gatún!"

Joaquín sat back on his heels in shock. They had done something, yes? Arguably, they had turned back only one man, and whether they had accomplished that feat or whether it had been accomplished with assistance from Mother Nature was debatable, yes—but still, it was a start. He turned toward Valentina, who was kneeling beside him, and met her eyes. She seemed to know just what he was thinking, his beautiful wife, for she smiled. Joaquín laughed and enveloped her in an embrace, and then, carried away by his jubilation, he stood up and hugged Renata, too.

Valentina listened as everyone around her rejoiced. They had not achieved what she had hoped. Speaking up only mattered if there was someone to hear it, and in the future they would have to find a way to actually get a government official of some sort *somewhere* to listen to them. But for now, for this afternoon, she would content herself with the knowledge that they had taken a first step. There would still be time, she thought, to save themselves.

||||||

MOLLY TOOK FIVE photographs that day. After the images had been developed, she slid them into a brown paper envelope and took them to Mr. Atchison in the hopes that he might run them in the newspaper. Mr. Atchison shuffled quickly through the photographs and handed them back. "Not right for the *Record*," he said. When Molly tried to object, to point out that they had the opportunity to break the story—no other newspaper she knew of was reporting on the unrest in Gatún—Mr. Atchison shook his head. "We don't cover local disputes." He suggested she return to her desk and stick to the work she had been hired to do.

31

ADA STOOD ON THE WOODEN BOARDS OF THE STATION PLATFORM IN EMPIRE WITH
her sack in her arms. It was filled with the same things she had arrived with nearly a month earlier, although this time, unlike the last,
between the little she had saved for herself and the single crown coin
still in her possession, she had just enough money for her passage on
the big ship.

She also had, safe in her pocket, the letter that Michael had delivered to her. She had been huddled in the boxcar when a voice
called her name, but because she had been trying to stay hidden, she
had not answered at first. The voice had called her again, and eventually a face had come up to the opening and peered inside. Michael,
the mail messenger, had smiled when he saw her and had pulled an
envelope out of his sack. "I spent most of the morning looking for
you. I know you have been waiting for this."

Shocked, Ada had stayed where she was. "Mr. Oswald didn't
send you?" she had asked hesitantly.

"Mr. Oswald? No. I didn't speak to Mr. Oswald, miss. Only the
cook. When I went to the house, she told me you'd gone. She nearly
shut the door in my face, but I did manage to ask her where you'd
gone to, and she muttered something about a boxcar out here in the
bush."

"The cook?"

"Yes, miss. I never spoke to Mr. Oswald, I swear."

Of course, Ada thought. She imagined Antoinette smugly saying that Ada was gone. Antoinette had never liked her, and Ada
could never—would never—understand why. She might have cared
to figure it out, to march back to the house and confront Antoinette
herself, except that any thought of such pettiness was erased by the

sight of the envelope Michael was still holding forth. Slowly, Ada had crawled forward to take it from him. Her mother's writing-hand on the front made tears well in her eyes.

"Are you okay?" Michael had asked, and Ada had nodded even though in truth the answer depended on what the letter inside the envelope said.

Years on, Michael would return to Virginia, where he was from, and in a place called Canton Hills he would start a parcel delivery service that he would operate for forty-five years before handing it down to his son. It would be an enterprise successful enough that it would allow him to purchase a house, which he would fill with all manner of personal effects, including a phonograph and an icebox and a set of brass candlesticks. But on that day he had merely handed Ada the envelope, then cleared his throat, and Ada had watched him trek back out of the jungle with the mailbag on his hip.

Now, Ada peered down the track. For forty minutes she had been waiting, with her sack at her feet, for the train that would take her to Colón. She reached into her dress pocket, pulled out the letter, and read it again.

My dearest Ada,

I have been trying to write this for some time, not knowing what to say and being poor at lettering as I am. Your Departure came as a shock, though I know how you are. I know you have always been rootless, not a Tree but a Leaf, taken up by the wind. My thoughts have been of worry, so I was Happy to receive your letter. I was Happy to know you are well, suffering no injury. That leads me to tell you the news. By good fortune and the will of the Lord a Doctor came to the house to accomplish the procedure for Millicent. The Doctor believes she will go on to be well. You can come back to us now. We will be wishing to see you as soon as you are able. Come home. A Leaf can grow again on the Tree.

I send this with all Love from your mother

Ada tucked the letter away and curled her fingers till her nails dug into her palms, so happy she thought she might burst. She had been scared, so scared this whole time, that she would not earn enough money, that time would run out, that Millicent would not make it through. But Millicent was okay. A doctor had come to the house. Ada hardly cared that the money she'd earned had made no difference. The £5 she had sent was probably only now reaching them. But truly she did not care. She only cared that Millicent was well.

||||||

OMAR GAZED OUT the window as the train kinked and chugged. After the officer had run off, the protest had taken on the feel of a festival— people setting off firecrackers and singing—and although Omar had been as exhilarated as everyone else, it had been a long day, and he had been ready at last to go home.

The train made its usual stops, and Omar stared out at every-thing passing by—towns and telegraph poles, palm trees and hills. When the train neared Empire, he felt himself tense. Even from within the train car, he could hear the hammering drills, could smell the bitter smoke. The work never stopped. It would not stop until the canal reached the oceans, and the Culebra Cut, the nine-mile stretch where he had spent the last six months of his life, would be only one part of a larger cut that spanned Panamá. He had al-ways known that, of course, but now it seemed different to him—less promise than pain—and he knew he would not go there again.

Omar averted his gaze. Through the windows along the other side of the train car he saw, just barely through the glass, a flash of bright yellow and brown. Or that is what he thought he saw. He stood, peering around and between the newly boarded passengers who were walking down the aisle, but he could not locate the colors again. He knew only one person they could belong to, though. The train whistle blew. Quickly, without thinking about it, Omar sidestepped out from his seat, squeezed past everyone in the aisle, and got off the train.

||||||

ADA DID NOT know where he had come from. She had been looking up behind her, toward the Oswalds' house, praying that neither Mr. Oswald nor Antoinette could see her down here, and when she turned back, she saw Omar crossing the platform toward her. His clothes were rumpled and muddied, and when he came closer and took off his hat, she noticed the cut on his lip.

She gasped. "What happened to you?"

Omar raised his hand to his mouth, gingerly touching the wound. "Nothing," he said.

"Doesn't look like nothing. Don't tell me you went and got yourself in a fight?"

She had been joking, but he answered, "Something like that."

Ada frowned. "Did you?"

"I am okay," he said.

She studied the cut again. It was fresh, but it would heal before long. Some ice would help with the swelling. She sighed. "Well, you will be in time."

Omar pointed to her sack. "You are going somewhere?"

Ada's face broke into a smile. "Yes, I got word. My sister is well."

"How wonderful!" Omar said, with genuine warmth. But then he furrowed his eyebrows. "That means you are going home?"

She nodded. "There's a ship leaving tonight."

"Tonight?"

"Provided I don't miss it. I been waiting here for some time for the train to Colón."

Several other people were standing out on the platform with them, and Ada took that as a good sign—the more people who were waiting, the sooner the train was probably due to arrive. On the far side of the tracks, Ada could hear the thundering sounds she had come to associate with the canal.

"What about you?" she asked. "You coming up from work just now?"

"No," Omar said. "I was coming from Gatún, on the other end of the zone."

"What were you doing out there?"

"The Americans want to move the town. They want to build a dam across the river instead—for the canal."

"You helping build the dam, or—?"

"No. There was a protest. I was joining the people of Gatún."

Ada grinned. "You were joining the people of Panama."

"Yes."

"That explains what happened to you, then?"

Omar touched his lip again. "No, this was different."

She laughed. "You saying you been in *two* fights today?"

Sheepishly, he smiled, which only made her laugh more.

Not for the first time, Ada thought how much she enjoyed talking to him. At home, she relied so much on the company of her mother and sister, the three of them wound together in their own cocoon, that she never quite made space for anyone else. Omar had shown her how nice it could be, talking and laughing with someone new. He came across as mild most of the time, but there was a rumbling beneath the surface that she recognized.

Briefly, Ada glanced down the tracks again. No doubt the train would arrive before long—she was counting on it—but now she found herself hoping that it would be an extra few minutes before it did.

||||||

EVEN IF DOÑA Ruiz herself had predicted it, Omar would not have believed almost anything about this day. In a matter of hours, so much had happened that he could hardly make sense of it all. And now Ada, standing before him, was leaving Panamá to go home.

He watched her peer down the track, eager for the train. He was happy for her, of course. He knew how worried she had been. He only wished it did not mean that she had to leave.

Omar picked his fingernail lightly against the crisscrossed straw fibers of his hat. He knew what he wanted to say. He wanted to ask her to stay in Panamá longer—even just one day more. There was so much here she probably had not seen yet. He could show her the web-footed geckos that scampered up the walls of his house and the crabs that pinced over the rocks in the bay. He could take her to the fish market or to other places in the city she might not have seen—to Avenida Central, to the plazas, to the squares where women sat behind folding tables with lottery tickets laid out like the scales of a fish, to the carnicerías and panaderías and farmacias, the cafeterías and cafés, to the teatro and the Casa del Cabildo and the seawall along Las Bovedas. Or he could show her the old city, the original city, Panamá La Vieja, and walk with her among the mossy ruins and stand in the cathedral tower that had no roof and stare up at the stars. He could show her how in Panamá it was possible to watch the sun rise over the Pacific and set over the Atlantic all in one day. He could show her places he had only heard about, could see them for the first time with her, the old cannons at Portobelo and the crashing waves at Pedasí, the highlands and the lowlands, the lush green mountains of Boquete and the beautiful dark jungle of Darién. He could show her the mangrove swamps whose roots had spread through the silt for thousands of years, the toucans and shimmering quetzals in the trees, the howler monkeys who moaned every morning at dawn, the glass frogs whose heart and tiny bones you could see through its skin, the silk moths and butterflies that alit on the leaves. He could buy her a bowl of sancocho or an empanada or a boiled tamale. They could sit outside listening to a tamborito in the indigo-orange light at dusk. It did not matter to him what they did. He just wanted to keep being around her, and for the simplest reason: All his life he had been lonely, but when he was with her he felt less alone.

||||||

THEY BOTH STARTLED at the blast of the train whistle. Ada reached down and lifted her sack. "I guess that means it's time," Ada said, smiling wide.

"Ada," Omar said.

"Yes?"

There was a crack in the atmosphere now, just big enough that he could have said what he wanted to say. But her smile, and the pure happiness he knew she was feeling at the thought of going home, made him swallow his words. Instead he said, "I wanted to thank you again. For that day on the street."

The sound of the train engine grew louder as the locomotive neared. He was aware that around him people were shuffling toward the front of the platform, lining up. Ada stood in front of him wearing that same patchwork dress. The sunlight caught in her eyes.

"Well, I thank you, too," she said, "for being my friend."

Behind them, the train slowed to a stop. With a lump in his throat, Omar watched Ada adjust the sack in her arms.

"My mother and sister are waiting for me," she said.

"Como uña y carne," Omar managed to say.

"What does that mean?"

"It means you are very close, like the fingernail and the flesh."

"Yes," Ada said, and her smile as she walked by him and climbed up onto the train was somehow even brighter than it had been before.

Omar stood on the platform, watching the train chug away. Slowly, he put his hat back on and tried to untangle the particular feeling he had then. There was a hollow space in his chest because he would not see her again, and at the same time, in that very same space, a quiet joy because she had called him a friend.

||||||

ONE WEEK LATER, the ship eased into the port at Carlisle Bay. Ada deboarded and, with a smile so big that it made her cheeks hurt,

she walked through the green, past the fountain and the House of
Commons and the savings bank, all of it more beautiful than she
remembered, then up High Street, then left onto Magazine Lane.
When she smelled a fish cake, she stopped just long enough to buy
one from a woman on the street. She was so hungry after the trip
that she could not resist. She popped the entire thing in her mouth,
and it was so perfectly crispy and salty that it brought tears to her
eyes.

When she got to Aster Lane, Ada paused and peered down
the length of it. She took a deep breath of the familiar sweet air.
Then, with her sack bouncing in her arms, she ran. Past the houses
and plots she had known all her life, past the Wimple house, the
Pennington house, the Callender house with its fat cherry tree,
on and on till she got to her own. She stopped and stared. What
a wonderful house it seemed to her now, with its slatted shutters
and porch. But it was more than that. Ada had always believed that
her mother, in rebuilding the house only three miles from where it
had once been, had kept her world piteously small, but maybe what
mattered, Ada thought as she gazed at it now, was not how big or
how small her mother's world was, but that her mother had managed to keep it at all. It must have been no trifling thing to carve
out a space of her own, to protect it and hold within it the people
she loved.

She was panting by the time she ran up the steps of the porch
and set her hand on the knob of the front door. Slowly, she pushed it
open and peeked inside. At the sound of the creaking door, she saw
both her mother and Millicent look up. They were sitting together at
the hearth, sewing. Millicent jumped to her feet first and ran to hug
Ada tight, holding her for so long that Ada thought Millicent might
never let go. From over Millicent's shoulder, Ada saw her mother
stand up as she blinked back tears. She said, "Thank the Lord you
come back." She walked closer and circled her arms around them
both, and as the three of them stood in the light of the house, it was
exactly where Ada wanted to be.

||||||

IN PANAMA CITY, Omar got off the train and walked through the streets, out, out, out until he came to the long road that traced a path to the bay. The sky was speckled with stars, tiny wobbles of light.

He trudged down the road, past the house of Doña Ruiz, past the trees and the ferns. At the mouth of the bay, he walked up to his own house and opened the door. His father, who was sitting at the table, glanced up.

At the sight of his son, Francisco's mouth dropped open. He had looked for so long. Hours, it had been. An entire afternoon during which he had trekked up and down, to and fro, with his feet and his sandals sunk in the mud, a futile afternoon that had left him more disconsolate than he had been at the start—and now? No matter that Omar coming home was entirely expected, that he regularly walked through the front door at this hour. To Francisco, seeing his son standing before him only confirmed what he had felt earlier, a belief that mystery and faith were again part of his life. After so much searching, perhaps he had found all the things that he thought he had lost.

Francisco blinked once. He blinked twice. From his open mouth, he said, "Hello."

32

1913

SIX YEARS LATER, THE SPINE OF THE MOUNTAINS WAS SEVERED AT LAST. AT THE base of the Culebra Cut, steam shovel 222 and steam shovel 230, digging toward each other from opposite directions, met in the depths. The path had been cleared.

In September, John Oswald stood on the lock wall and watched as a tugboat festooned with flags approached from Colón. He was surrounded by thousands of onlookers, all of whom had come to witness the first vessel ever to pass through any set of the locks. Despite the reports in the papers, no one around him that day was talking about the growing possibility of war in Europe. They were focused solely on the canal. A photographer hung from a cableway over the middle of the channel, waiting for the little boat to chug through. There was not a cloud in the sky. As he stood, John considered the report he had left behind on his desk. Malaria had declined in the zone, but he had not managed to eradicate it. "Not yet," Marian would have said. The belief that he might is why he stayed. Maybe it was still possible. Every scientist was only one essential discovery away, after all. John watched as water (as well as a number of frogs) bubbled up through holes in the floor of the first lock chamber. It took a long time to fill. But when the water level in the chamber was the same as the water level of the sea, the steel lock gates—massive double doors that had been manufactured in Pittsburgh, John had heard—slowly cranked open. The tugboat inched through. Once the boat was in the chamber, those same gates closed behind it, penning it in. More water was added, raising the boat up to the level of the subsequent chamber. Again, the gates at the fore opened, the boat slid through, the gates at the rear closed, water surged in, the boat rose. The procedure was repeated once more—a perfect staircase of water—until, in the third chamber, the water level matched the level of the new lake. When the final gates opened and released the small boat, the crowd broke out in cheers. John did not. It was a tremendous achievement. Miraculous to see it operate exactly as the engineers intended it should, but even on the sunniest days, John existed in a cloud of gloom, and the most he could summon was a smile, which no one saw.

As the tugboat navigated the locks, Lucille fed a piece of fabric through her sewing machine, an oak-topped treadle model with a cast-iron foot pedal that she had purchased in part using the money Ada had earned in Panama. Whereas it used to take her a week to sew a single dress, the machine allowed her to finish a garment, sometimes even two, in a day, and those garments, still in her signature bold fabrications, were so impeccably stitched, so cleanly finished, that people were keen to buy them. Millicent sat next to her at the hearth, sewing buttons by hand, as Lucille had taught her. Lucille glanced up to take stock of Millicent's progress. Ada had no interest in sewing, a fact that Lucille had come to accept. Ada was and always would be an own-way child. Millicent, though, had a knack, and had become a wonderful seamstress in her own right. With the buttons that day she was using a decorative stitch that not even Lucille would have thought to add.

That same afternoon, Ada stepped off Dr. Leonard Jenkins's buggy where it had come to a stop on Sweetham Road. She dusted off her dress and followed Dr. Jenkins into the house of a woman who had called him about her awful stomach pains. She watched as he gently pressed the woman's abdomen through her blouse. After so many years as his apprentice, Ada knew just what he was feeling for. When the woman yelped, Ada said, "The appendix?"

Dr. Jenkins smiled at her. "Precisely."

"Is it inflammation or an obstruction?" Ada asked.

"Good question. How can we tell?"

"Whether a fever is present."

"And is it?"

Ada stepped forward and put her hand to the woman's forehead. "Yes."

Later at supper, Ada would tell her mother and sister how she had successfully diagnosed the woman. At no point that evening would anyone mention the milestone in Panama, because although reports of it ran in *The Barbados Advocate*, none of them had read about it.

At the end of his shift, Clement took the train to Gatún, where the tugboat, looking like a toy upon the vast water, was gliding out through the final lock chamber. When the cheer rose up from the crowd, Clement lightly pumped his fist and cheered with them. He felt a complicated pride. It was thrilling to see with his own eyes that the canal truly worked. He felt the urge to tell the spectators around him that he had been part of making it happen, but he did not. When the cheering died down, Clement stepped away from the crowd. He wondered what would become of him now that the project was nearing its end. He had risen to the rank of lead switchman, but, hampered by various injuries and expenses he had not foreseen, he had never made the kind of fortune he'd hoped for, and he was embarrassed to go back to Jamaica, where everyone could see that. As the day darkened, Clement walked back to the train, jingling the coins in his pocket. He did have enough to treat himself to a celebratory meal at Café Antoinette, at least. It was a modest establishment but a lively one, always packed with people from Jamaica and Antigua and Barbados, people like him who had come to Panama and stayed. The woman who owned it made the best callaloo in town.

In the soft light of dusk, Francisco paddled home from the market, where Joaquín had paid him for twenty-two good fish and had lamented the day. "So they have done it?" Joaquín had said. "The first boat went through?" He had refused to say the name of the tugboat, though both Francisco and Joaquín knew very well what it was called: *Gatún*.

Six months after the initial protest, the entire town of Gatún had been moved to the opposite bank of the river. Now, Joaquín was consumed by a rumor that the town was going to be moved once again, this time to an area completely outside the zone. "Do you know," he had asked Francisco that day, "how Valentina says they want to use that land after everyone is expelled? For cattle grazing. Cattle, my friend! Apparently they like the cows more than they like us." Francisco, as usual, had patiently listened, then bid his friend farewell.

The warm air blanketed Francisco as he rowed. At some point he caught a whiff of violets, which came to him every now and again. "Hello, Esme," he said. As Francisco pulled through the water, he told her everything that had happened since the last time they had talked. His knees had started popping when he got out of bed in the morning. Yesterday, his right shoulder had been sore. Omar was well, and there was a girl from Santa Ana that lately he had mentioned quite a bit. "So that could be something," he said. Francisco chattered for as long as he smelled the violets because he knew that Esme was with him. She had returned to him that day in the Cut and had not left him since.

On the floor of the boat, along with Francisco's reel and net, were two white fish that he would cook for dinner that night. With the money Omar had earned from working in the canal, he had bought himself books, a mountain of books that he studied all day and all night, having enrolled in a program that was training him to become a schoolteacher one day. Every night the two of them ate together while Omar told Francisco the things he had learned— that the earth was 2.2 billion years old, that butterflies used their feet to taste, that the earliest poems were carved into clay—all the things he hoped to pass along to his students and in the meantime passed along to Francisco. They talked and debated and disagreed and laughed. It was always Francisco's favorite part of the day, with the world at his back, to paddle across the bay toward the shore and go home.

ACKNOWLEDGMENTS

I am grateful beyond measure to Sara Birmingham, Helen Atsma, Sonya Cheuse, Miriam Parker, Meghan Deans, TJ Calhoun, Nina Leopold, and everyone at Ecco for believing in this book—and in me—from the start. To my inimitable agent and friend, Julie Barer—I cannot thank you enough.

I spent years researching this novel and consulted far too many sources to mention here, but a special thanks belongs to the people who read various excerpts and drafts of this book: Melva Lowe de Goodin, Velma Newton, Caren Blackmore, Kirkaldy Myers, Dionne McClean, Tita Ramírez, Frances de Pontes Peebles, and Nicole Cunningham. Thank you to Mike Oetting and Martha Kennedy, my research librarian heroes. To Yanina Maffla—thank you for always being willing to help me at a moment's notice. Thank you to Carys O' Neill, Jack Neely, Beatrice Murphy, Bridget Kallas, Sheau Hui Ching, Rolando Cochez Lara, and my parents for fielding my many questions. In particular, thank you to my father for cold-calling people on my behalf, making introductions, and sending me a million links to articles, websites, maps, and videos along the way.

My unending thanks to my husband and children, who keep me buoyed even when the water is rough. And, as always, a mountain of gratitude to all of my family, both near and far.